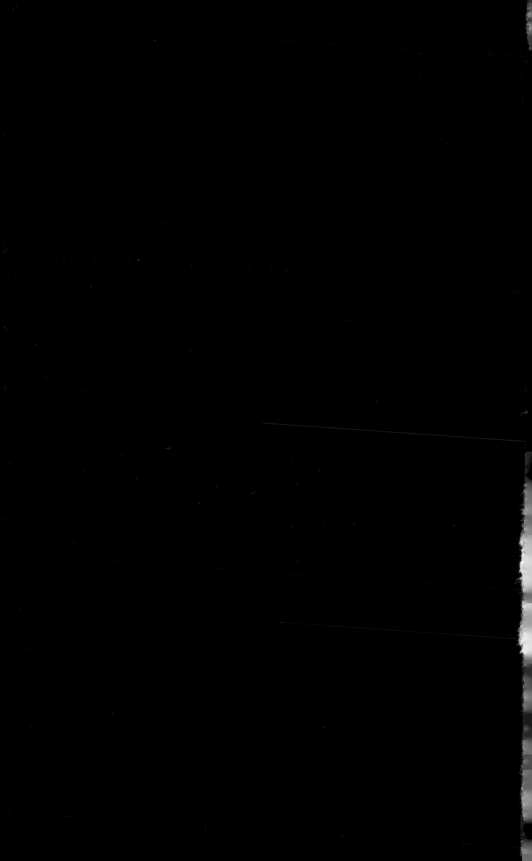

The Dead
Student

Also by John Katzenbach

Red 1-2-3

What Comes Next

In the Heat of the Summer

First Born

The Traveler

Day of Reckoning

Just Cause

The Shadow Man

State of Mind

Hart's War

The Analyst

The Madman's Tale

The Wrong Man

The Dead Student

John Katzenbach

The Mysterious Press
an imprint of Grove/Atlantic, Inc.
New York

Published simultaneously in Canada
Printed in the United States of America

FIRST EDITION

ISBN 978-0-8021-2337-4
eISBN 978-0-8021-9162-5

The Mysterious Press
an imprint of Grove Atlantic
154 West 14th Street
New York, NY 10011

Distributed by Publishers Group West

groveatlantic.com

15 16 17 18   10 9 8 7 6 5 4 3 2 1

"And if you wrong us, do we not revenge? If we are like you in the rest, we will resemble you in that."

WM. SHAKESPEARE, The Merchant of Venice

PART ONE

Conversations Between Dead Men

This is what Moth came to understand:

Addiction and murder have things in common.
In each, someone will want you to confess:
I'm a killer.
Or:
I'm an addict.
In each, at some point you're supposed to give in to a higher power:
For your typical murderer, it's the law. Cops, judges, maybe a prison cell. For run- of-the-mill addicts, it's God or Jesus or Buddha or just about anything conceivably stronger than the drugs or the drink. But just give in to it. It's the only way out. Assuming you want out.

He never thought either confession or concession was part of his emotional makeup. He did know that addiction was. He was unsure about killing, but he was determined that before too long he would find out.

1

Timothy Warner found his uncle's body because he woke up that morning with an intense and frighteningly familiar craving, an emptiness within that buzzed deeply and repeatedly like a loud off-key chord on an electric guitar. At first he hoped that it was left over from a dream of happily knocking back shots of iced vodka with impunity. But then he reminded himself that this was his ninety-ninth day without a drink, and he realized that if he wanted to see the hundredth he would have to work hard to get through the day sober. So as soon as his feet hit the cold floor by his bed, before he glanced out the window to check the weather, or stretched his arms above his head to try to force some life into tired muscles, he reached for his iPhone and tapped the application that kept a running count of his sobriety. Yesterday's ninety-eight clicked to ninety-nine.

He stared at the number for a moment. He no longer felt heady satisfaction or even a twinge of success. That enthusiasm had fled. Now he understood that the daily marker was just another reminder that he was always at risk. *Fail. Give in. Let slip. Slide a little.*

And he would be dead.

Maybe not right away, but sooner or later. He sometimes thought that sobriety was like standing unsteadily on the edge of a tall cliff, dizzily staring down into some vast Grand Canyon while being buffeted unceasingly in the midst of a gale. A gust would topple him off, and he would tumble headlong into space.

He knew this, as much as any person can know anything.

Across the room was a cheap, black-framed, three-quarter-length mirror propped up against the wall of his small apartment, next to the expensive bicycle that he used to get to his classes—his car and driver's license having been taken away during his last failure. Dressed only in his baggy underwear, he stood and looked at his body.

He did not really like what he saw.

Where once he'd been attractively wiry, now he was cadaverously thin, all ribs and muscles with a single poorly executed drunken-night tattoo of a sad clown's face up on his left shoulder. He had thick jet-black hair that he wore long and unkempt. He had dark eyebrows and an engaging, slightly cockeyed smile that made him seem friendlier than he actually thought he was. He did not know whether he was handsome, although the girl he thought was truly beautiful had told him once that he was. He had the long, thin arms and legs of a runner. He had been a second-string wide receiver on his high school football team and a straight-A student, the go-to guy for help on any upcoming chemistry lab or perilously overdue English essay. One of the biggest players on the team, a hulking lineman, stole four letters from the middle of his name, explaining that *Tim* or *Timmy* just didn't suit *Moth's* frequently driven look. It stuck, and Timothy Warner didn't mind it all that much, because he believed moths had odd virtues and took chances flying dangerously close to open flames in their obsession with seeking light. So *Moth* it was, and he rarely used his full first name save for formal occasions, family gatherings, or AA meetings, when he would introduce himself saying, "Hello, my name is Timothy, and I'm an alcoholic."

He did not think his remote parents or his deeply estranged older brother and sister still remembered his high school nickname. The only person who used it regularly, and affectionately, was his uncle, whom he hurriedly dialed as he stared at his reflection. Moth knew he had to protect himself from himself and calling his uncle was pretty much the first step at self-preservation.

As expected, he got the answering machine: "This is Doctor Warner. I'm with a patient now. Please leave a message and I will get back to you promptly."

"Uncle Ed, it's Moth. Really had *the big crave* this morning. Need to go to a meeting. Can you join me at Redeemer One for the six p.m. tonight? I'll see you there and maybe we can talk after. I think I can make it through the day okay." He didn't know about this last flimsy promise.

Nor would his uncle.

Maybe, Moth thought, *I should go to the lunch meeting over at the university's student activities center or the mid-morning meeting in the back room at the Salvation Army store just six blocks away. Maybe I should just crawl back into bed, pull the covers over my head, and hide until the 6 p.m. meeting.*

He preferred the early evening sessions at the First Redemption Church, which he and his uncle called Redeemer One for brevity and to give the church an exotic spaceship name. He was a regular there, as were many lawyers, doctors, and other professionals who chose to confess their cravings in the church's comfortable, wood-paneled meeting room and overstuffed fake leather couches instead of the low-slung basement rooms, with their stiff metal folding chairs and harsh overhead lights, of most meeting places. A wealthy benefactor of the church had lost a brother to alcoholism, and it was his funding that kept the seats comfortable and the coffee fresh. Redeemer One had a sense of exclusivity. Moth was the youngest participant by far.

The ex-drunks and onetime addicts who went to Redeemer One all came from the distant worlds Moth had been told over and over he was

destined to join. At least, being a doctor or a lawyer or a successful businessman was what others who probably didn't know him all that well
thought he should become.

Not a drunk doctor, addicted lawyer, or strung-out businessman.

His hand shook a little and he thought, *No one tells their kid they're
gonna grow up to be a drunk or a junkie. Not in the good old USA. Land of
opportunity. Here we say you've got a chance to grow up and be president. But
a lot more people end up as drunks.*

This was an easy conclusion.

He smiled wanly as he added, *Probably the one or two kids that actually
do get told they're gonna grow up into drunks are so motivated to avoid that
fate that they become president.*

He left his iPhone on the counter in the bathroom so he could hear it
ring and hurried into the steaming-hot shower. Thick shampoo and blistering water, he hoped, could scrub away caked layers of anxiety.

He had half dried off when the phone buzzed.

"Uncle Ed?"

"Hey Moth-boy, I just got your message. Trouble?"

"Trouble."

"Big trouble?"

"Not yet. Just the *want*, you know. It kinda shook me up."

"Did something specific happen, you know, that triggered . . ."

His uncle, Moth knew, was always interested in the underlying *why*
because that would help him decide the overarching *what.*

"No. I don't know. Nothing. But this morning there it was as soon as
I opened my eyes. It was like waking up and finding some ghost seated on
the edge of the bed watching me."

"That's scary," his uncle said. "But not exactly an unfamiliar ghost."
Uncle Ed paused, a psychiatrist's delay, measuring words like a fine car-
penter calculates lengths. "You think waiting until six tonight makes
sense? What about an earlier meeting?"

"I have classes almost all day. I should be able—"

"That's if you go to the classes."

Moth stayed quiet. This was obvious.

"That's if," his uncle continued, "you don't walk out of your apartment, take a sharp left, and run directly to that big discount liquor store on LeJeune Road. You know, the one with the big blinking goddamn red neon sign that every drunk in Dade County knows about. And it's got *free parking*." These last words were tinged with contempt and sarcasm.

Again, Moth said nothing. He wondered: *Was that what I was going to do?* There might have been a *yes* lurking somewhere within him that he hadn't quite heard yet but that was getting ready to shout at him. His uncle knew all the inner conversations before they even happened.

"You think you can turn right, start pedaling that bike nice and fast, and head toward school? You think you can get through each class—what do you have this morning?"

"Advanced seminar on current applications of Jeffersonian principles. It's what the great man said and did two hundred and fifty years ago that still means something today. That's followed by a required two-hour statistics lecture after lunch."

His uncle paused again, and Moth imagined him grinning. "Well, Jefferson is always pretty damn interesting. Slaves and sex. Wildly clever inventions and incredible architecture. But that advanced statistics class, well, *boring.* How did you ever end up in that? What has that got to do with a doctorate in American History? It would drive *anyone* to drink."

This was a frequently shared joke, and Moth managed a small laugh. "Word," he said, the historian in him enjoying the irony of employing teenage-speak already in disuse and discarded.

"So, how about a compromise?" his uncle said. "We'll meet at Redeemer One at six, like you said. But you go to the lunch meeting over at the campus center. That's at noon. You call me as you walk in. You don't even have to get up and say a damn thing unless you feel like it—you just have to be there. And you call me when you walk out. Then you call me again when you walk into the statistics class. And when you walk out. And each time figure on holding that phone up so I can hear that professor, droning on in the background. That's what I want to hear. Nice, safe, boring lecture stuff. Not glasses clinking."

Moth knew his uncle was a veteran alcoholic, well versed in the myriad excuses, explanations, and evasions of everything except another drink. *His* personal tally of days sober was now well into the thousands. Maybe nearly seven thousand, a number that Moth believed he would find truly impossible to attain. He was more than a sponsor. He was Virgil to Moth's drunken Dante. Moth knew his uncle Ed had saved his life and had done so more than once.

"Okay," Moth said. "So, we meet at six?"

"Yeah. Save me a comfy seat, because I might be delayed a couple of minutes. I got an emergency appointment request for late this afternoon."

"Someone like me?" Moth asked.

"Moth, boy. There ain't nobody like you," his uncle replied, slipping into a fake Southern drawl. "Nah. More likely some sad-eyed suburban housewife depressive whose meds are running low and is panicking bigtime because her regular therapist is on vacation. All I am is a glorified, overeducated prescription pad waiting to be signed. See you tonight. And call. All those times. You know I'll be waiting."

"I'll call. Thanks, Uncle Ed."

"No big deal."

But of course, it was.

Moth made the specified phone calls, each time safely bantering about nothing important for a few moments with his uncle. Moth had not thought he would say anything at the noontime meeting, but near the end of the session, at the urging of the young theology professor who ran the gathering, he had risen and shared his fears over his morning desires. Almost all the heads had nodded in recognition.

When he exited from the meeting, he took his Trek 20-speed mountain bike to the university's playing fields. The high-tech rubberized quarter-mile track that encircled a football practice field was empty and despite a warning sign that told students to keep off unless under supervision, he lifted the bike over a turnstile gate, and after a quick look right and left to make sure he was alone, started riding in circles.

He picked up his pace quickly, energized by the clicking of the gears beneath him, the torque as he leaned dangerously into each turn, the steady accumulation of speed mixed with the high cloudless azure sky of a typical Miami winter's afternoon. As he pumped his legs and felt muscles tightening with energy, he could sense *the crave* being pushed aside and buried within him. Four laps rapidly became twenty. Sweat started to burn his eyes. He could hear his breath coming harder with the exertion. He felt like a boxer whose roundhouse right has staggered his opponent. *Keep throwing punches*, he told himself. Victory was within sight.

When he finished the twenty-eighth lap, he pulled the bike to a sudden stop, tires squealing against the red synthetic track surface. Chances were good a campus security officer would swing by any second—he'd already pushed that envelope.

What would he do, yell at me? Moth thought. *Give me a citation for trying to stay sober?*

Moth lifted the bike back over the gate. Then he leisurely retraced his route to the wrought-iron stand adjacent to the science building where he could lock up the Trek and head to statistics. He passed a security guard in a small white SUV and gave a cheery wave to the driver, who didn't wave back. Moth knew he would probably start to stink as the sweat dried after he entered the air-conditioned classroom, but he didn't care.

Miraculously, he thought, it was turning into a small, but optimistic day.

A hundred now seemed not only attainable, but probable.

Moth waited outside a bit, right until a minute shy of six, before going inside Redeemer One and heading to the meeting lounge. There were already twenty or so men and women seated in a loose circle, all of whom greeted Moth with a nod or a small wave. A thin haze of cigarette smoke hung in the room—*an acceptable addiction for drunks*, Moth thought. He looked at the others. Doctor, lawyer, engineer, professor. *Tinker, tailor, soldier, spy*. And then himself: *graduate student*. There was a dark oaken table at the back of the room with a coffee urn and ceramic mugs. There was also a small shiny metal tub filled with ice and a selection of diet soft drinks and bottled water.

Moth found a spot and set his tattered student backpack down beside him. The regulars would easily have guessed that he was saving a space for his uncle—who had, after all, been the person who introduced Moth to Redeemer One and its high-class collection of addicts.

It was not until perhaps fifteen minutes into the meeting that Moth began to fidget nervously when there was no sign of his uncle. Something felt misshapen, a note out of tune. While Uncle Ed would sometimes be a few minutes late, if he said he was coming, he always showed up. Moth kept turning his head away from the speaker toward the door, expecting his uncle to make an apologetic entrance at any moment.

The speaker was talking hesitantly about OxyContin and the warm sensation that it gave him. Moth tried to pay attention. He thought that was a most commonplace description, and differed little whether the speaker was sharing something about morphine-based pharmaceuticals, home-brewed methamphetamine, or store-bought cheap gin. The plummeting, welcoming warmth that permeated head and body seemed to wrap up an addict's soul. It had been true for him during his few years of addiction, and he suspected his uncle, during his decades, had felt the same.

Warmth, Moth thought. *How crazy is it to live in Miami, where it is always hot, and need some other heat?*

Moth tried to focus on the man talking. He was an engineer—a likeable guy, a middle-aged, slightly dumpy, bald-headed man of tolerances and stresses, employed by one of the larger construction firms in the city. The realist in Moth wondered just how many condo buildings and office skyscrapers might have been constructed down on Brickell Avenue by a man who cared more for the numbers of pills he could obtain each day than the numbers on architectural plans.

He turned to the door when he heard it open, but it was a woman—an assistant state attorney, probably a dozen years older than he was. Dark-haired, intense, she wore a trim blue business suit and carried a leather portfolio case instead of a designer pocketbook and even at the end of the workday, she looked carefully put together. She was a relative newcomer to Redeemer One. She had attended only a few meetings and said little on each occasion, so she remained largely a mystery to the regulars. Recently divorced. Major crimes. Drug of choice: cocaine. *"Hello, I'm Susan and I'm an addict."* She mumbled her apologies to no one and everyone and slid quietly into a chair in the back.

When it was his turn to share, Moth stammered and declined.

The meeting ended without a sign of his uncle.

Moth walked out with the others. In the church parking lot he shared a few perfunctory hugs and exchanged some phone numbers, as was customary following a meeting. The engineer asked him where his uncle was, and Moth told him that Ed had planned to come, but must have gotten hung up with a patient emergency. The engineer, plus a heart surgeon and a philosophy professor who'd been listening in, had all nodded in the special way that recovering addicts have, as if acknowledging that the scenario Moth described was most likely true, but just maybe it wasn't. Each told him to call if he needed to talk.

None of the people at the meeting were so rude as to point out that his earlier exercise on the track had resulted in a stale, ripe odor about him. Since he was the youngest regular at Redeemer One, they all cut Moth some slack, probably because he reminded them of themselves—just twenty years or more earlier. And everyone at the meeting was familiar with the foul scents of nausea, waste, and despair that accompanied their addictions, so they had developed tolerances for rank odors that went far beyond the norm.

Moth stood around, shuffling his feet. He watched the others disappear. It was still warm: a humid, thick blanket that made it seem like the evening had wrapped itself around him, cloaking him in tightening shadow. He could feel himself sweating again.

He was unsure when he made the decision to go to his uncle's office.

He just looked up and found himself on his bicycle, pedaling fiercely in that direction.

Cars sliced through the night around him. He had a single flashing red safety light attached to the rear wheel frame, though he doubted that it would do much good. Miami drivers have loose relationships with the rules of the roadway, and sometimes yielding to a person on a bicycle seemed either like a terrible loss of face or a task so difficult it was beyond anyone's innate ability. He was accustomed to being cut off and nearly sideswiped every hundred yards and secretly enjoyed the ever-present, car-crushing danger.

His uncle's office was in a small building ten blocks away from the high-end shops on Miracle Mile in Coral Gables, which was only a mile or two from the university campus. After the shopping district, the road became a four-lane too-fast boulevard, with frequent stoplights, east and west to frustrate the Mercedes-Benz and BMW drivers hurrying home after work. The road was divided by a wide center swath of stately palms and twisted banyan trees. The palms seemed puritan in their upright rigor, while the ancient mangroves were Gordian knots and devilishly misshapen, gnarled with age. Each direction seemed almost encased, tunnels formed by haphazard sweeping branches. Auto headlights carved out arcs of light through the spaces between the trunks.

Moth pedaled quickly, dodging cars, sometimes ignoring red lights if he thought he could zip safely through the intersection. More than one driver honked at him, sometimes for no reason other than the fact that he was there and using up space that they believed they both needed and deserved for their oversized SUV.

He was breathing hard, his pulse throbbing, when he arrived at the office building. Moth chained his bike to a tree in front. It was a dull, redbrick building, four squat stories with an old, slightly decrepit feel to it, especially in a city devoted to modern, young, and hip. There were wide windows in the back of the office that overlooked a few side streets and the rear parking lot and a single tall palm tree and not much else. It was,

Moth had always thought, a very unprepossessing place for a man so successful in his practice.

He walked around the back and saw his uncle's silver Porsche convertible parked in its designated slot.

Moth did not know what to think. *Patient? Emergency?*

He hesitated before going up to the small suite. He told himself that he could simply wait by the Porsche and sooner or later his uncle would emerge.

Something important must have come up. That appointment he said was going to make him late at Redeemer One. Something far more serious than a new prescription for Zoloft. Maybe mania. Hallucinations. Loss of control. Death threats. Hospital. Something. He wanted to believe the story he'd told a few minutes earlier to his fellow Redeemer One regulars.

Moth took the elevator up to the top floor. It creaked and jerked a bit on the fourth-floor landing. The building was silent. He guessed that none of the dozen other therapists in the building were working late. Few of them used secretaries—their clientele knew when to arrive and when to leave.

His uncle's top-floor office had a small, barely comfortable waiting room with out-of-date magazines in a rack. In an adjacent larger room, Uncle Ed had space for a desk, a chair, and an analyst's couch, which he used much less frequently than he had a dozen years earlier.

Moth quietly entered his uncle's office and reached for the familiar small buzzer just by the door. There was a friendly handwritten sign taped above the buzzer for patients: *Ring twice nice and loud to let me know you have arrived, and take a seat.*

That was what Moth intended to do. But his finger hesitated over the ringer when he saw the door to his uncle's office ajar.

He moved to the door.

"Uncle Ed?" he said out loud.

Then he pushed the door open.

* * *

This is what Moth managed:

He stopped himself from screaming.

He tried to touch the body, but the blood and greasy viscous brain matter from a gaping head wound splattered over the desk and staining his uncle's white shirt and colorful tie made him pull his hand back. Nor did he touch the small semiautomatic pistol dropped to the floor next to the outstretched right hand. His uncle's fingers seemed frozen into a claw.

He knew his uncle was dead, but he couldn't say the word *dead* to himself.

He called 911. Shakily.

He listened to his high-pitched voice asking for help and giving his uncle's office address, each word sounding like it was some stranger speaking.

He looked around, trying to imprint everything in his memory, until all that he absorbed exhausted him. Nothing he saw explained anything to him.

He slumped to the floor, waiting.

He furiously held back tears when he gave the policemen who arrived within a few minutes a statement. Then he gave a second statement an hour later, repeating everything he had already said, to first-names-only Susan, the assistant state attorney in the blue suit whom he had seen at Redeemer One that evening. She did not mention that as she passed him her business card.

He waited until the medical examiner's half-hearse, half-ambulance arrived and he watched as two white-suited technicians loaded his uncle's body into a black vinyl body bag, which they placed on a stretcher. This was routine for them, and they handled the body with a practiced nonchalance. He caught a single glance at the red-tinged hole in his uncle's temple before the body was zipped away. He knew he was not likely to ever forget this.

He replied *"I don't know"* when a tired-sounding police detective asked him, *"Why would your uncle kill himself?"* And he had added, *"He was happy. He was okay. His problems were all behind him. Like way behind him."*

He had abruptly asked his own question of the detectives: *"What do you mean he killed himself? He wouldn't do that. Absolutely no way."* Despite his insistence, the detective seemed unmoved, and didn't reply. Moth had looked around wildly, knowing something was telling him he was right.

He turned down the assistant state attorney's offer of a ride home. He stood outside in the waiting room while crime scene analysts perfunctorily processed the office. This took several hours. He spent that time trying to make his mind go blank.

And then, when the last flashing light from all the police cruisers clicked off, he descended into a maelstrom of helplessness and without thinking about what he was doing, or perhaps thinking it was the only thing remaining he could do, Moth went hunting for a drink.

2

You're a killer.

No I'm not.

Yes you are. You killed him. Or her. But you did it. No one else. You, all alone, all by yourself. Killer. Murderer.

I didn't. I didn't. I couldn't. Not really.

Yes you could. And you did. Killer.

One week after her abortion, Andy Candy lay in the fetal position, curled up in pink frills and pastel throw pillows on her bed in the small room in the modest home where she had grown up. *Candy* wasn't her actual name, but a playground rhyme used since her birth by her once-doting, now-dead father. His name had been Andrew, and she was supposed to be a boy and named after him. *Andrea* had been the best at-the-hospital compromise her folks could arrive at when presented with a girl baby, but *Andy Candy* it had been ever since, a constant reminder of her father and the cancer that had stolen him prematurely, a weight that Andy Candy carried permanently.

Her last name was Martine, pronounced with a slightly frenchified tone to it, a family acknowledgment of ancestors who had come to the USA nearly 150 years earlier. Once Andy Candy had dreams of traveling to Paris as an *homage* to her ancestry and to see the Eiffel Tower and eat flaky croissants and sweet pastries and maybe have an affair with an older man in a sort of New Wave romance. This was just one of many pleasant fantasies about what she would do as soon as she graduated from the university equipped with her shiny new English Literature degree. There was even a colorful travel poster on the wall of her bedroom showing a quite stunning hand-holding couple walking next to the Seine in October. The poster underscored the simplistic *Paris Is for Lovers* travel agency vision of the city that Andy Candy believed absolutely had to be true. In reality, she did not speak French, indeed no one she knew spoke French, and other than a high school trip to Montreal for a theater presentation of *Waiting for Godot* she had never been anywhere special. She had never even heard the language spoken out loud by anyone other than a teacher.

But, in any tongue, Andy Candy was now in pain, in tears, in utter despair, and she continued to argue with herself, one second a hand-wringing supplicant, forlornly pleading for forgiveness, the next haranguing herself, like something more than a housewife kitchen scold, more even than a zealous prosecutor: a cold-blooded, dark-hooded, and relentless inquisitor.

I had no choice. None. Really. What could I do?

Everyone has a choice, killer. Many choices. It was wrong and you know it.

No it wasn't. I had no alternative. I did the right thing. I'm sorry sorry sorry, but it was the right thing.

That's so easy, murderer. Just so-o-o-o easy. Who was it the right thing for?

For everyone.

Really? Everyone? Are you sure? What a lie. Liar. Killer. Liar-killer.

Andy Candy hugged a worn toy teddy bear. She pulled a handmade quilt decorated with red hearts and yellow flowers over her head, as if she could shut away the fury of the argument. She could feel two parts warring within her, one whiny and apologetic, the other insistent. She wished she could be a child again. She shivered, sobbed, and thought that by hugging a stuffed toy animal she could somehow shed years, travel backward to a time when things were much easier. It was as if she wanted to hide in her past so that her future couldn't see her and hunt her down.

Andy Candy buried her head into the toy's fake fur, and she sobbed, trying to muffle her voice so she couldn't be heard. Then, gasping slightly, she held the stuffed animal over one ear and cupped her hand over the other, as if trying to block the sound of the argument.

It wasn't my fault. I was the victim. Forgive me. Please.
Never.

Andy Candy's mother fingered a crucifix hanging around her neck, then touched middle C on the piano keyboard. She held her fingers out over the ivories in much the same way that Adrien Brody did in her favorite movie, *The Pianist*, and without making a sound, shut her eyes and played a nocturne from Chopin. She did not actually have to hear the notes to listen to the music. Her hands rolled above the array of glistening keys like whitecaps upon the ocean.

At the same time, she knew that her daughter was sobbing uncontrollably in the back bedroom. She could not actually hear these sounds either, but just like the Chopin, the notes were crystal clear. She sighed deeply and rested her hands in her lap, as if a recital had finished and she was awaiting applause. The Chopin faded, replaced by the concert of sadness she knew was playing in the back of the house.

Shrugging briefly, she spun about on the bench. Her next student wasn't due for at least a half hour, so she knew she had time to go to her daughter's side and try to comfort her. But she had attempted this many times already over the last week, and all her hugs and back rubs and hair stroking and softly spoken words had merely ended in more tears. She had given up on being rational: *"Date rape isn't your fault . . . "* And sensitive: *"You can't punish yourself . . ."* And finally, practical: *"Look, Andy, you can't hide here. You've got to start pulling yourself together and facing life. Bringing an unwanted child into this world is a sin . . ."*

She didn't know if she believed this last statement.

She looked over to the frayed living room couch, where a half-pug, half-poodle, a goofy-looking golden-colored mutt, and a sad-eyed greyhound were all assembled, eagerly watching her. The three dogs had that *What's next? How about a walk?* look about them. When she made eye contact, three tails of different shapes and sizes started wagging.

"No walk," she said. "Later."

The dogs—all rescue dogs adopted before his death by her husband, a softhearted veterinarian—continued to wag, even though she knew they just might understand the reason for the delay. *Dogs are like that,* she thought. *They know when you're happy. They know when you're sad.*

It had been some time since anyone would have used the word *happy* to describe the house.

"Andrea," Andy Candy's mother said out loud, in a tired tone that reflected nothing but futility. "I'm coming." She said this, but she didn't budge from the piano bench.

The phone rang.

She thought she should not answer it, although why she could not have said. Instead, she reached out for the receiver and at the same moment looked over at the three dogs and pointed down the hallway to where she knew her daughter was suffering. "Andy Candy's room. Right now. Try to cheer her up."

The three dogs, displaying an obedience that spoke to her late husband's ability to train animals, jumped from the couch and scrambled down the hallway enthusiastically. She knew if the door was shut, they'd bark and the pug-poodle hybrid would get up on his hind legs and start to paw frantically in *Let me in* insistence. If it was ajar, the mutt, the biggest of the three, would shoulder the door aside and they would all make a beeline for her bed. *Good idea,* she thought. *Maybe they can make her feel better.*

Andy Candy's mother spoke into the phone. "Hello?"

"Mrs. Martine?"

"Yes. Speaking."

The voice on the other end seemed strangely familiar, although a little uncertain and perhaps shaky.

"This is Timothy Warner . . ."

A surge of memory and a little pleasure. "Moth! Why, Moth, what a surprise . . ."

A hesitation. "I'm, umm, trying to reach Andrea, and I wondered if you could give me her number at school."

A brief silence filled the air when Andy Candy's mother didn't instantly reply. She made a mental note that Moth, who wore his own nickname proudly, had often used her daughter's actual name in past years. Not always, but frequently he had employed the formal *Andrea,* which had elevated his status in the eyes of Andy Candy's mother.

"I heard about Doctor Martine," he added cautiously. "I sent a card. I should have called, but . . ."

She knew he wanted to say something about colon cancer death, but there was nothing really to say. "Yes. We got it. It was very thoughtful of you. He always liked you, Moth. Thank you. But why are you calling now? Moth, we haven't heard from you in years!"

"Yes. Four, I think. Maybe a little less."

Four of course went back to shortly before the day her husband died. "But why now?" she repeated. She wasn't sure whether she needed to be protective of her daughter. Andy Candy was twenty-two years old, and most people would have considered her a grown-up. But the young woman sobbing away in the back room seemed significantly closer to a baby this day. The Moth she had known a few years back wasn't much of a threat, but four years is a long time, and she didn't know what he had become. People change, she thought, and she'd been surprised by the out-of-the-blue voice on the other end of the line. Would a call from her daughter's first real boyfriend help her or hurt her right about now?

"I just wanted . . ." He stopped. He sighed, resigned. "If you don't want to give me her number, that's okay . . ."

"She's home."

A second brief silence.

"I thought she'd be finishing up the semester. Doesn't she graduate in June?"

"She's had a setback or two." Andy Candy's mother thought this was a neutral enough description to describe a sudden, unplanned pregnancy.

"So have I," Moth said. "That's sort of why I wanted to speak with her."

Andy Candy's mother paused. She was listening to an equation in her head. More than something mathematical, it was a musical score to accompany runaway emotions. Moth had once played major chords in her daughter's life, and she wasn't at all sure that this was the right time to replay them. On the other hand, Andy Candy might be legitimately furious when she discovered that her once-upon-a-time boyfriend had called and her mother had blocked the conversation out of some misguided sense of protection. She did not know exactly how to respond and so she came up with a mother-safe compromise. "Tell you what, Moth. I'll go ask her if she will speak with you. If the answer is *no*, well . . ."

"I'd understand. It wasn't like we split on the best of terms anyway, all those years ago. But thank you. I appreciate it."

"Okay. Hold on."

If I promise to never ever ever kill anything or anyone again, will you leave me alone? Please.

Don't make a promise you can't keep, killer.

The dogs were suddenly crowding Andy Candy just as they had been ordered. They tried to get to her face under the covers, nosing aside pillows and blankets, eager to lick away her tears, irrepressible in their dog-enthusiasm. The Inquisitor within her seemed to lurk back into some inner shadow as she was besieged by snuffling, odorous, pawing demands for attention. She cracked a small smile and stifled a final sob; it was hard to be miserable with affectionate dogs nudging against her, but at the same time it was hard *not* to be miserable.

She didn't hear her mother at the door until she spoke. "Andy?"

Instant, automatic reply: "Leave me alone."

"There's a phone call for you."

Bitter, expected answer: "I don't want to talk to anyone."

"I know," her mother replied gently. Hesitation. Then: "It's Moth. Of all people to call now . . ."

Andy Candy inhaled sharply. In milliseconds she was flooded with memories, good, happy ones vying against sad, tortured ones.

"He's on the phone, waiting," her mother repeated unnecessarily.

"Does he know . . ." she started, but she stopped because she knew the answer to her question: *Of course not.*

This was one of those moments, Andy Candy instantly understood, where if she said *No* or *Get his number, I'll call him back* or *Tell him to call me sometime later,* whatever reason he had that made him call her right then would evaporate and be lost forever. She was uncertain what to do. The rush of her past captured her like a strong current pulling her away from the safety of the beach. She remembered laughter, love, excitement, adventure, some pain and some pleasure, then anger and a different kind of heartsick depression when they'd split up. *My first high school love,* she thought. *My only real love. It leaves a deep mark.*

A large part of her said: *Tell her to tell him, "Thanks but no thanks. I have more than enough pain in my life right now, if you please." Tell her to say I just want to be left alone. No other explanation is necessary. Then just hang up.* But she did not say this, or any of the thoughts that reverberated around within her.

"I'll take it," she said, surprising herself, pushing herself up, scattering dogs to the floor, and reaching for the phone.

She lifted the receiver to her ear, then stopped and stared fiercely at her mother, who immediately retreated back down the hallway and out of earshot. Andy Candy took a deep breath, wondered for an instant whether she could speak without letting her voice crack, and finally whispered softly, "Moth?"

"Hi, Andy," he said.

Two words, spoken as if from miles and years away, but both distance and time collapsing in an instant, racing together explosively, almost as if he were suddenly standing in the room beside her, stroking her cheek. She raised her free hand reflexively, as if she could actually feel his against her flesh.

"It's been a long time," she said.

"I know. But I've been thinking about you a lot," Moth replied. "Lately, I guess, even more. So, how have you been?"

"Not so good," she replied.

He paused. "Me neither."

"Why have you called?" she asked. It surprised Andy Candy to be so brusque. She thought it wasn't like her to be direct and forceful, although she understood she might be completely wrong about that. And just hearing her onetime boyfriend's voice filled her with so many mingled feelings she wasn't sure how to respond; but she was alert to the idea that one of these feelings was pleasure.

"I have a problem," he said. His voice was slow and deliberate, which also wasn't exactly like she remembered Moth, who was more impulsive and filled with devil-may-care energy. She was trying to detect who he'd become since she last saw him. "No," he contradicted himself. "I have more than a couple of problems. Little ones and big ones. And I didn't know where else to turn. I don't have a lot of people I trust anymore, and I thought of you."

She did not know if this was a compliment. "I'm listening," she said. She thought this was inadequate. She needed to say something stronger to get him to continue. Moth was like that. A little nudge, and he would open up wide. "Why don't you start with—"

"My uncle," he said quickly, interrupting her. Then he repeated himself: "My uncle." These two words seemed accented with some despair and weighted with some ferocity that resonated. "I trusted him, but he died."

25

"I'm sorry to hear that," Andy Candy said. "He was the psychiatrist, right?"

"Yes. You remember."

"I only met him once or twice. He wasn't at all like anyone else in your family. I liked him. He was funny. That's what I remember. How did he . . . ?" She didn't have to finish the question.

"It wasn't like how your dad passed away. He didn't get sick. No hospitals and priests. My uncle shot himself. Or that's what everyone thinks. Like my whole tight-ass family and the damn cops."

Andy Candy said nothing.

"I don't think he killed himself."

"You don't?"

"No."

"Then how . . ."

"Only one other possibility: I think he was murdered."

She was silent for a moment.

"Why do you think that?"

"He wouldn't kill himself. That wasn't him. He'd overcome so many problems, something new—if there was something—wouldn't faze him. And he wouldn't have left me all alone. Not now, no way. So, if he didn't do it, someone else had to."

This wasn't really an explanation, Andy Candy realized. It was more a conclusion based on the flimsiest of ideas.

"It's up to me to find the person who killed him." Moth's voice had grown rigid, cold, and tough, barely recognizable. "No one else will look. Just me."

She paused again. The conversation wasn't at all what she'd expected, though she didn't know what she had expected in the first place.

"Why, how . . ." she started, not really expecting answers.

"And when I find him, I have to kill him. Whoever he is," Moth said. Unexpected ferocity. *Not call the cops or even just do something about it, something vague and indistinct and actually appropriate.* Andy Candy was shocked, astonished, instantly scared. But she didn't hang up.

"I need your help," Moth said.

Help could mean many things. But Andy Candy rocked back on her bed, as if she'd been pushed hard and slammed down. She wasn't sure she could breathe.

Killer.

Don't make a promise you can't keep.

3

He picked a place to meet that seemed benign.

Or, at the minimum, wouldn't evoke something from their past or say something about what he anticipated for their future—if there was any to be had. He rode a bus and fingered a picture he had: Andy at seventeen. Happy, looking up from a burger and fries. But this memory was crowded aside.

"Hello. My name is Timothy. I'm an alcoholic. I have three days sober."

"Hi Timothy!" from the gathering at Redeemer One. He thought the entire group appeared subdued but genuinely glad he was back amidst them. When he had sidled awkwardly into the room at the start of the meeting, more than one of the regulars had risen from their chairs and eagerly embraced him, and several had wrapped him in condolences that he knew were sincere. He was sure that they all knew about his uncle's death and could easily imagine what it had pushed him into. When called upon to testify, for the first time he had the odd thought that perhaps he meant more to all of them than they did to him, but he did not know exactly why.

"Three whole damn days," he repeated, before sitting down.

* * *

Moth put his ninety hours of recent sobriety into a mental calendar:

Day One: *He woke up at dawn collapsed on the red-dirt infield of a Little League diamond. He had no recollection of where he'd spent the greater part of the night. His wallet was gone, as was one of his shoes. The stench of vomit overcame everything else. He was unsure where he found the strength to un-evenly stagger the twenty-seven blocks back to his apartment, once he'd figured out where he was. He limped the last blocks on a sole torn raw by the sidewalks. Once inside, he stripped off his clothes like a snake shedding a worthless skin and cleaned up—hot shower, comb, and toothbrush. He tossed everything he'd been wearing into the trash and realized that it was two weeks since his uncle died and he had not been home in all that time. He was mildly grateful for the blackout that prevented him from realizing what other baseball diamonds he'd slept on.*

He told himself to climb back onto the wagon, but spent the entire day in his darkened apartment hiding, physically sick, stomach twisted, day sweats turning to night sweats, afraid to go outside. It was as if some sultry, seductive siren was awaiting him, right past his front door, and she would lure him into a trip to the liquor store or a nearby bar. Like Odysseus from antiquity and legend, he tried to rope himself to a mast.

Day Two: *At the end of a day spent raw and shaking on the floor by his bed, he finally answered a succession of calls from his parents. They were angry and disappointed, and probably concerned, as well, although that was harder to discern. They had left messages and it was clear they knew why he'd disappeared. And they knew where he'd disappeared to. Not specifically. They didn't need to know the exact addresses of the dives that welcomed him. And he'd learned that he'd missed his uncle's funeral. This detail had pitched him into an hour-long sobbing jag.*

He was a little surprised, when they'd finished talking, that he hadn't gone out for a drink. His hands had quivered, but he was encouraged by even that small show of addiction-defiance. He had repeated to himself a mantra: Do what Uncle Ed would do, do what Uncle Ed would do. That night, he shivered under a thin blanket, although the apartment was stifling hot and the air moist and humid.

Day Three: *In the morning, as his pounding headache and uncontrollable shakes started to diminish, he'd called Susan the assistant state attorney who had given him her card. She didn't sound surprised to hear from him, nor did she think it unusual that he'd waited so long to call.*

"It's a closed case, or nearly closed, Timothy," she had gently informed him. "We're just waiting on a final toxicology report. I'm sorry to have to say this, but it's designated a suicide." She did not say why this detail made her sorry, nor did he ask. He had weakly responded, "I still don't believe it. May I read the file before you put it away?" She had answered, "Do you really think that will help you?" It was clear that her use of the word help *had nothing to do with his uncle's death. "Yes," he said, with no certainty. He made an appointment to come to her office later in the week.*

After hanging up, he'd returned to his bed, stared at the ceiling for over an hour, and decided two things: return to Redeemer One that night because that would be what his uncle wanted for him; call Andy Candy because when he tried to come up with the name of anyone in the entire world who might listen to him and not think he was a half-grief-crazed drunken fool running his mouth irrationally, she was the only remaining candidate.

Matheson Hammock Park was an easy bus ride for Moth. He sat in the back row with the window cracked open just an inch or two so he could pick up the scent of hydrangeas and azaleas carried on the slippery midday heat, without compromising the steady cool wheeze of the bus's air-conditioning. There were only a couple of other folks on the bus. Moth saw a young black woman—he guessed Jamaican—wearing a white nurse's outfit. She had a dog-eared paperback *Spanish Language Made Easy* study book in her hands. Moth could see her lips moving as she practiced the language that was nearly essential to working in Miami.

At his feet, Moth had a plastic bag with a large *media noche* sandwich for them to share, some bottled water, and a fizzy lemonade drink that he recalled Andy Candy had liked on their other picnic-type excursions to South Beach or Bill Baggs State Park on Key Biscayne. He could not remember ever taking her to Matheson Hammock, which was, in no small way, why he had chosen that location. No shared history in this park. No memory of lips grazing, or the silky sensation of young bodies touching in warm water.

Love dreams were best forgot, he thought.

He did not know whether Andy Candy would actually show up. She had said she would, and she was probably the most honest person he knew, now that his uncle was dead. But the realist in him—a very small part, he inwardly conceded—had doubts. He knew he had been cryptic and obtuse and probably a little scary on the phone, with his sudden talk of murder.

"I wouldn't come meet me," he whispered to himself above the sound of the bus engine's slowing for his stop. He rose and pushed himself into the bright early afternoon sun.

He stuck to a wide path that paralleled the entrance drive into the park. More than one jogger cruised past him beneath the cypress trees that shaded the route. He ignored the coral rock building, where a young woman sold tickets and maps and which had a large "Florida's Disappearing Habitat" sign out front, with pictures of how squeezed for territory all the native animals were. He paused near a stand of palm trees that edged up against Biscayne Bay, where a young Latin American couple were going through a wedding rehearsal. The priest was smiling, trying to relax everyone by making jokes, which neither mother seemed to find even remotely funny.

Moth waited at the end of the parking lot on a bench that had a single palm that shaded it. He could hear high-pitched laughter from the tip of the park, where a wide, shallow man-made lagoon created a special place for small children to play. The nearby beach seemed to glow silver in the strong sunlight.

He was going to pull out his cell phone, check the time, but stopped himself. If Andy Candy was late, he didn't want to know it. He thought, *There's always a risk in counting on someone else. Maybe they don't come. Maybe they die.*

Closing his eyes for a moment against the glare, he counted heartbeats, as if he could take the pulse of his emotions. When he opened his eyes, he saw a small red sedan come into the lot and pull into a space near the back. Like many cars in Miami, it had tinted glass, but he caught a glimpse of blond hair and knew it was Andy Candy.

Before she was out of the car, he was on his feet. He waved, and she waved back.

Faded jeans on her long legs and a light pastel-blue T-shirt. Her hair was pulled back in an informal ponytail, the way she typically put it when going jogging or swimming. When she spotted Moth, she slipped off her dark sunglasses. Moth's eyes took her in, trying to see similarities and changes all at once. With each step she took closing the distance between them, he could feel a surge of some runaway feeling gathering within him.

Andy Candy almost stopped in her tracks. Moth seemed thin to her, as if his already-lithe body had somehow been shaved away by the years since high school. His tangled hair was longer than she remembered it and his clothes seemed to hang reluctantly from his body. She had not known what she would say; she was unsure whether she should kiss him, give him a small hug, maybe just shake his hand, or perhaps do nothing. She didn't want to hesitate, nor did she want to seem eager.

She steadily crossed the parking lot. *Not fast. Not slow,* she told herself.

He stepped forward, out of the palm's shade. *Wave. Smile. Act normal, whatever that is,* he told himself.

They met halfway.

He started to lift his arms to embrace her.

She leaned forward, but held her hands out in front of her.

The awkwardness resulted in a semi-touch. Their arms went to each other's elbows. They kept a little distance between them.

"Hello, Moth," she said.

"Hi, Andrea."

She smiled. "Long time."

He nodded. "I should have . . ." he started, but stopped.

She shook her head. "You know, I didn't think I'd ever see you again. I thought you'd just go your way and I'd go mine, and that was it."

"We had some memories together," he said.

She shrugged a little. "Teenage memories. And that's all, I figured."

"More than teenage," he said. "Some were pretty adult." He smiled.

"Yes. I remember those, too," she said. She added a small, disarming grin.

"And now here we are," he said.

"Yes. Here we are."

They were silent for a moment.

"I bought a little food and something to drink," Moth said. "How about we find one of the picnic tables and talk there."

"Okay," she said.

The first thing he said when they arrived at a shaded table was, "I'm sorry I was so, I don't know, on the phone . . ."

"You were scary. I almost didn't come."

"Half a sandwich," he said. "The fizzy drink is for you."

She half-laughed. "You remembered that. I don't think I've had one of these since . . ." She stopped. She didn't have to say *when we were together* for him to understand it. She pushed the sandwich toward him. "I had lunch already. You eat it. You look like you could use it." Her tone had a tinge of toughness.

He nodded, acknowledging the accuracy in her statement. "But you're still beautiful. Even more beautiful than . . ." He stopped. He did not want to remind her of their breakup, although seeing him would do little else.

She shrugged. "Don't feel beautiful," she said. "Just a little older." Again, she smiled, before adding, "We're both older now."

He took a bite from the sandwich and she continued to stare at him. He thought her look was a little like a funeral parlor director eyeing a newly arrived corpse for a suit of *in the coffin* clothes.

"What happened to you, Moth?" Andy Candy asked.

"You mean . . ."

"Yeah. After we broke up."

"I went to college. Studied hard. Got really good grades. I graduated with high honors. Wouldn't go to law school like my dad wanted. I got started on a graduate program in American History because I didn't know what else to do. Kind of useless, I guess from his point of view—examining past events—even if it's something I love doing . . ."

He stopped. He knew his curriculum vitae wasn't what she was asking about. "I got into trouble with alcohol," he said quietly. "Lots of trouble. I'm what shrinks like my uncle call a binge drinker. Started as soon as I left home. It was like walking a tightrope. Step one: keep up the grades; Step two: get drunk; Step three: write an A paper. Step four: get very drunk—you get the idea."

"And now?" she asked.

"That sort of trouble never leaves you," he said. "But it was my uncle Ed who was seeing me through. Putting me in a better place."

Sometimes a single piercing look is as good as a question. That was what Andy Candy used to make Moth continue.

"And he died. I found his body."

"He killed himself. That's what you said, but—"

He interrupted her. "That's exactly what I don't believe. Not for one fucking instant."

The sudden obscenity was like a window onto some anger that Andy Candy didn't remember in him. She saw Moth look up into the pale blue sky before continuing.

"It's what I told you on the phone: He wouldn't leave me alone. Partners. That's what we were. We had an agreement. I don't know, maybe you could call it an arrangement. A promise. It was convenient for both of us. He'd stay sober helping me. I'd stay sober helping him by letting him help me. It's hard to understand unless you're a drunk. I'm sorry that doesn't make sense, but there it is."

He was a little embarrassed describing himself as *a drunk,* no matter how accurate. He looked over at Andy Candy. She was no longer the girl from high school who had taken his virginity in losing hers. The woman

34

in front of him seemed like the work of an artist who had taken the few lines that sketched out a teenager and added color and shape to create a full portrait.

Andy Candy nodded. She was struck by the notion that it was altogether possible that there was no one in her life she knew better than Moth, and no one who was more a stranger.

"And now?" she asked. "Now you want to kill some mysterious someone?"

Moth smiled. "It does sound ridiculous, doesn't it?"

Andy Candy didn't have to reply to this question, either. She was not smiling.

"But I'm going to."

"Why?"

"It's a matter of honor," Moth said, making a small Elizabethan sweeping gesture. "It's the least I can do."

"That's stupid," Andy Candy said. "And overly romantic. You're not a cop. You don't know anything about killing."

"I'm a fast learner," Moth replied.

Again there was a little bit of silence. Moth rotated slightly so he could look out over the water.

"I didn't expect you to understand," he said. What he wanted to say was, *This is a debt and I'm going to repay it and I don't trust anyone else— especially not some cop or the court system.* He did not say this out loud; he thought he should, then told himself he shouldn't.

Andy Candy looked over to the same distant blue waves. "Yes you did," she said. "Otherwise you wouldn't have called me." She started to stand up. *Get out of here. Leave right now!* The voices shouting within her were like a schizophrenic's unbidden commands: powerful, undeniable. *Walk away right now. The Moth you loved once is gone.*

"Andy," he said cautiously, "I didn't know where else to turn."

Andy Candy lowered herself back onto the bench. She took a long sip of the sweet fizzy lemon-flavored drink.

"Moth, why do you think I can help you?"

35

"I don't know. I just remembered . . ." He stopped there. She watched him turn to the water, then to the sky. She reached out her hand, then abruptly withdrew it. He must have seen the motion, because he pivoted back toward her and put his hand on top of hers. For an instant, she looked down at their hands. She could feel electric memory right through her skin. Then she pulled her hand out of his.

"Don't touch me," she said, quietly, almost a whisper.

"I'm sorry. I didn't mean to . . ."

"I don't want anyone to touch me ever again," she said. These words spilled from her lips, half-despairing, half-angry. She was suddenly afraid that she would start crying and that everything that had happened to her would burst to the surface. She could see Moth trying to comprehend what she was saying.

"I shouldn't have anything to do with you," she added. The words were harsh, but they softened as she spoke them. "You broke my heart."

Moth shook his head. "I broke my own heart, too. I was stupid, Andy. I'm sorry."

"I don't want an apology," she said. She inhaled sharply and slid into an organized, officious tone. "This is clearly, unequivocally a mistake. You hearing me, Moth? A mistake. But what is it you want me to do?"

"I lost my license. Can you drive me a couple of places?"

"Yes. I could do that."

"Come with me while I talk to a couple of people?"

"Yes. If that's all."

"No," he said slowly, "there's one other thing."

"Okay. What?"

"The minute you think I'm completely crazy, tell me. Then walk away forever."

This was the only thing he knew he had to say to her and the only thing he'd practiced on the bus ride over to the park.

She paused. A part of her insisted, *Say that right now—get up and leave and don't look back.* Andy Candy felt like she was sliding down a steep shale rock slope, losing control. She looked at Moth and thought she should do this for him because once she had loved him with fervent teenage intensity and helping him now would be the only way to truly end all the leftover feelings that had lodged within her.

"Finish your sandwich," she said.

4

Eat the gun, she thought.

Not without permission.

Hell, you don't need anyone else to make that decision, no matter what the rules might be. Just eat the gun.

Susan Terry looked across the table at the public defender, who was seated next to his client, a lanky, scared-looking, seventeen-year-old inner-city man-kid who had been caught with a pound of marijuana in his knapsack on his way to classes in his senior year of high school. Beneath the pound of grass was a cheap .25-caliber semiautomatic pistol, of the sort that once upon a time had been called a Saturday Night Special, a phrase now in disuse because in Miami, like every other American city, every night could be a Saturday night.

The public defender was a former nice-guy classmate from law school who had simply landed on the opposite side of the criminal justice assembly line. A decade ago, they had shared a successful moot court argument together, as well as some blow, and Susan knew he was now overworked and overwhelmed. If she were going to cut anyone a break, it would be him. And in Miami, a pound of weed really wasn't a substantial amount, especially in a city that in its heyday had seen *tons* of cocaine seized.

For a moment, she paused, her eyes scanning the arrest documents and initial court pleadings, while her ears absorbed and ignored the near-constant cacophony of angry voices and slamming metal barriers that filled the county jail. A constant music of despair.

The kid had been riding a bicycle. The arresting cop's lame explanation for stopping him and searching him was that he was steering the bike "erratically." That, she thought, could accurately describe *any* teenager riding a bicycle. It might hold up in court. It might not.

And the cop had made another mistake: He had pulled the kid over a block outside the "drug-free" designation of the school district. Twenty-five more yards and the kid would be destined for the state penitentiary no matter how much legal flexibility Susan Terry might have mustered.

More likely, she thought, *the cop spotted the backpack and had a bad feeling about it and didn't want to wait. And it turned out he was pretty much right.*

She and her former classmate both knew this. In her head she was preparing a legal-search-and-seizure argument, just as she knew he was.

The kid had a good record at school. A community college future. Maybe the state university if he just pulled up his grades in math and continued on the basketball team. He had a part-time job flipping burgers at McDonald's and an intact family—father, mother, grandmother all living at home with him. And, most important, he had no prior arrest record—an astonishing detail growing up in the middle of Liberty City.

But the gun—that was a real problem. And why was he taking it to school?

Eat it, she told herself again. *The kid's got a chance.*

Eating the gun was prosecutor slang for dropping the mandatory minimum three-year sentence in Florida for anyone who used a gun in the commission of a felony. The prosecutor's office used the requisite prison term as a cudgel to force guilty pleas, dropping this part of the charge sheet at the last possible legal minute.

The phrase meant something very different to clinically depressed police officers and PTSD-suffering Iraq War veterans.

"Sue, give us a break here," the public defender said. "Look at the kid's record. It's real good . . ." She knew that her onetime classmate didn't get many clients with actual "good" records, and he would be eager—no, probably *desperate*—to find a positive outcome. ". . . And I don't know about that cop's search. I can make a pretty strong case that it was a violation of my client's rights. But anyway, he goes away now, and he'll be right back here in four years. You know what will happen in prison. They'll teach him how to be a real criminal, and you know what he'll do next will be something a helluva lot worse than a half-key of low-grade dope that really ought to plead down to a misdemeanor."

Susan Terry ignored the public defender and stared at the teenager.

"Why'd you have the gun?" she demanded.

The teenager stole a sideways glance at his lawyer, who nodded to him, and whispered, "This is all off the record. You can tell her."

"I was scared," he said.

This made partial sense to Susan. Anyone who had ever driven through Liberty City after dark knew there was much to be frightened of.

"Go on," the public defender said. "Tell her."

The teenager launched into a halting story: street gangs, carrying the marijuana—*one time only*—for the thugs down the block so they would leave him and his little sister alone. The backpack and the gun were for the person who was supposed to move the grass.

She wasn't sure she believed it. There were some truths, maybe, she was sure. But in its entirety? *Not damn likely.*

"You got names?"

"I give you names, they're going to kill me."

Susan shrugged. *Not my problem,* she thought. "So what? Tell you what: You talk to your lawyer. Listen to what he tells you, because he's the only thing standing between you and the complete ruin of your life. I'm going to call in a detective from the urban narcotics task force. When he gets here—I'm guessing maybe about fifteen minutes—you get to make your

decision. Give up all the names of the motherfuckers on your block dealing drugs and you get to walk out of here. Gun or no gun. Keep your
mouth shut, and it's *see yah later*, 'cause you're going to prison. And whatever your momma was hoping you'd grow up to be simply ain't going to
happen. That's what's on the table in front of you right now."

Susan slid effortlessly into tough-girl edginess as she spoke. She particularly liked using the word *motherfucker* because it generally shocked
defendants when it fell from the lips of someone so attractive.

The teenager squirmed uncomfortably in his seat. *The basic, routine,
day-to-day inner-city existential dilemma*, she thought. *Fucked one way. Or
fucked the other.*

Her classmate absolutely knew what her little hyper-harsh performance
meant. He had his own variations on the same stage that he used from
time to time. He clasped his arm around his client in a friendly, reassuring *I'm the only person in the entire world you can trust* grip, but at the same
time he said to Susan, "Call your detective."

Susan pushed away from the table. "Will do," she said. She smiled. *Snake
smile.* "Call me later," she told the lawyer. "I have an appointment right now
I don't want to be late for."

Andy Candy thought, *What am I doing here?* She wanted to say this out
loud—maybe even scream it, high-pitched and near-panicked—but kept
her mouth shut. She was seated beside Moth in the security area outside
the Miami-Dade State Attorney's Office. He was bent forward at the waist
with his hands on his knees, drumming his fingers nervously against his
faded khaki pants.

Moth had said little in the drive over to the state attorney's office, a
modern, fortress-like edifice adjacent to the Metro Miami-Dade Justice
Building, a sturdy, nine-floor courthouse that was no longer modern but
was too young to be antique and had many of the same qualities as a factory
slaughterhouse—an endless supply of crimes and criminals on a conveyor
belt. They had passed through wide doors and metal detectors, ridden
escalators and finally arrived at the security area, where they waited. The

comings and goings of lawyers, detectives, and court personnel kept up a steady buzzing, as sheriff's officers behind bulletproof glass hit the electric entrance system. Most of the people arriving and departing seemed familiar with the process, and almost all seemed in an *I can't wait* hurry, as if guilt or innocence had a timing clock attached.

Both Andy Candy and Moth straightened up when a burly thick-necked guard with a holstered 9mm pistol called his name out. They produced identification.

The cop gestured at Andy Candy. "She's not on my list here," he said. "She a witness?"

"Yes. Assistant State Attorney Terry wasn't aware that I would be able to bring her along," Moth lied.

The guard shrugged. He wrote down all of Andy Candy's information—height, weight, eye color, hair color, date of birth, address, phone, Social Security number, driver's license number—searched her pocketbook thoroughly, then once again made the two of them walk through a metal detector.

A secretary met them on the other side. "Follow me," she said briskly, stating the obvious. She led them through a warren of desks filling a large central area. The prosecutors' offices surrounded the desks. There were small name placards by each door.

They each spotted "S. Terry, Major Crimes" at the same time.

"She's waiting," the secretary said. "Go on in."

Susan looked up from behind a cheap gray steel desk cluttered with thick files and a nearly-out-of-date desktop computer. Behind her, next to a window, was a whiteboard with lists of evidence and witnesses arrayed beneath a case number written in red. On another wall there was a large calendar, updated with mandatory hearings and other court appearances underscored. A single window, which overlooked the county jail, let in a weak shaft of light. There was little in the way of decoration other than a few black-framed diplomas and a half-dozen mounted newspaper articles. Three of them were illustrated with Susan's black-and-white picture. It was an austere place, dedicated to a single purpose: making the justice system work.

"Hello, Timothy," Susan said.

"Susan," Moth replied.

"Who is your friend?"

Andy Candy stepped forward. "Andrea Martine," she said, shaking the prosecutor's hand.

"And why are you here?"

"I needed some help," Moth answered for her. "Andy is an old friend, and I hoped she could give me some perspective."

This, Susan immediately realized, was probably not precisely true, nor completely untrue. She didn't think she needed to care. She fully expected a short, somewhat sad, somewhat difficult conversation, and then her involvement in the uncle's death would be over. She gestured the couple into chairs in front of the desk.

"I'm sorry about this," she said. She reached down and produced a brown accordion file. "I was on duty the night your uncle died. It's office policy that whenever feasible, an assistant state attorney be called to possible homicide scenes. This helps with the legal basis for chains of evidence. In your uncle's case, however, it was pretty clear that it wasn't a homicide from the get-go. Here," she said, pushing the file toward Moth. "Read for yourself."

As Moth began to open the file, Susan turned to her computer. "The pictures aren't pretty," she said briskly to Andy Candy. "There are copies in the file, and here, on the screen. Also the police report, the forensics team report, and autopsy and tox examinations."

Moth began to pull sheets of paper from the file. "The toxicology report . . ."

"His system was clean. No drugs. No alcohol."

"That didn't surprise you?" Moth asked.

Susan responded slowly. "Well, in what way?"

"If he had fallen off the wagon after so many years, maybe then he would have been in such despair he shot himself. But he hadn't."

43

Susan again replied cautiously. "Yes. I can see how you might think that. But there was nothing in any tests that indicated anything other than a suicide. Stippling on the skin indicated the gunshot was from close range— pressed up against the flesh of the temple. The placement of the weapon on the floor was consistent with being dropped from your uncle's hand as the force of the shot pushed him down and sideways. Nothing was taken from the office. There were no signs of any break-in. There were no signs of a struggle. His wallet, with more than two hundred dollars in cash, was in his pocket. I personally interviewed his last patient of the day, who left shortly before five p.m. She was a regular and had been seeing your uncle weekly for the last eighteen months."

She pulled out a notebook. "Detectives also interviewed every other current patient, his ex-wife, his current partner, and some of his colleagues. We could find no evidence of any overt enemies and no one suggested any." She flipped past a couple of pages in the notebook. "A check of his financials showed some stress: He owed more on his condo than it is currently worth—nothing new in Miami—but he had more than enough in stocks and investments to cover being upside down. He wasn't a gambler owing some huge nut to a bookie. He wasn't into some drug dealer for a small fortune. I wish he'd left a lengthy note, which would have been help-ful. But there was one additional thing that contributed to our thinking . . ."

Moth's eyes were traveling haphazardly over words on pages as Susan spoke. He looked up. His mouth opened as if to say one thing, then he shifted about and said another.

"What was that?"

"He wrote two words on his prescription pad."

"What . . ."

" 'My fault,' " Susan quoted. "It's in the photo of the desktop," Susan said. "Do you recall seeing it when you found the body?"

"No."

She handed a photo across the desktop to Moth, who studied it care-fully.

"Of course, we can't tell when he wrote it. It could have been there all day, maybe even a week. It might have been in response to worrying about you, Timothy, because, after all, you called him several times throughout the morning and afternoon—we pulled all his phone records. But it indicated to us a kind of suicidal apology."

"It doesn't look right," Moth said sharply. "It looks like it was scribbled quickly. Not like something he ever meant for anyone to see," Moth added stiffly. "It could mean something else, right?"

"Yes. But I doubt it."

"You said his last patient was at five p.m.?"

"Yes. A little before, actually."

"He told me he had another. An emergency. Then he was supposed to meet me . . ."

"Yes, that was in your statement. But there was no record of another appointment. His calendar had someone coming in the next day at six p.m. He probably just mixed them up."

"He was a shrink. He didn't mix things up."

"Of course not," Susan said. She tried to limit the condescending tone in her voice. What she didn't say out loud was, *Well, he damn straight mixed something up, because he wrote down "My fault" before shooting himself. Maybe not mixed up. Maybe just fucked up.*

Susan looked over at Andy Candy. She had been silent, staring at a crime scene eight-by-ten glossy color close-up photo of Moth's uncle facedown on his desktop, blood pooling beneath his cheek. *She's getting an education,* the prosecutor thought.

Andy Candy had never seen this sort of picture before, other than on television and movies, and then it had seemed safe because it was unreal, a fiction made up for dramatic purposes. This picture was raw, explicit, almost obscene. She wanted to be sick, but she could not pull her gaze away.

"I'm sorry, Timothy, but it is what it is," Susan said.

Moth hated this cliché. "That's only *if* it is what it is," he said, his voice stretching taut. "I still don't believe it," he said.

Susan waved her hand over the documents and pictures. "What do you see here that says something different?" she asked. "I'm sorry. I know how close you were to your uncle. But depression that can cause suicide is often pretty well concealed. And your uncle, given his experience, his training, and his prominence as a psychiatrist, would know this—and how to hide it—better than most."

Moth nodded. "That's true." He leaned back in his seat. "So that's it?"

"That's it," Susan said. She did not add, *Unless someone somewhere comes up with something completely different that says I'm totally wrong so I'm forced to change my mind, which sure as hell isn't going to happen.*

"May I keep this?"

"I made copies of some of the reports for you. But Timothy, I'm not sure they will help you. You know what you should do," she said.

Susan answered the question that wasn't asked. "Go to a meeting," she said. "Go back to Redeemer One." She smiled. "See? The others there even have me calling it by the nickname you invented. Go there, Timothy. Go every night. Talk it out. You'll feel much better."

She smiled, trying to be gentle, but it wasn't hard to feel the cynicism in her advice.

Moth silently collected the package of picture copies and reports that Susan Terry had prepared for him. He took a few moments to examine each picture, letting each one crease his memory, almost as if he could flow into the image and find himself back in his uncle's office. His hand shook a little and he paused as he stared at a photograph of the gun next to his uncle's hand. He started to say something, then stopped. He rapidly flipped through the pictures, until he came to a second one. He stared hard, then shuffled the photos quickly until he came to a third. He took the three pictures and spread them out on Susan's desk. He pointed at the first: *gun on the floor; outstretched hand.*

"This is what I remember," he said. His voice was ragged and dry. "Like, no one moved anything?"

"No, Timothy. Crime scene specialists never move anything until it is photographed, documented, and measured. They're really cautious about that."

Then he pointed at the second picture.

Desk. Bottom drawer. Open perhaps an inch and a half.

"This picture . . . Like nothing was changed?"

Susan craned her head over. "No. That's the way they found it."

A third picture.

Desk. Bottom drawer. Wide open.

A .40-caliber black matte semiautomatic pistol resting beneath some stray papers, encased in a tan leather sheepskin-lined sheath.

"And this . . ." The words were posed as a question.

"I opened that drawer myself," Susan said. "With the technician taking pictures. That's the spare handgun your uncle had registered. He purchased it a number of years ago, when he was doing pro bono therapy at an inner-city clinic in Overtown. He was going in the evenings. A pretty rough area. Not surprising that he toted a handgun to those sessions."

Susan paused. "But he quit that work some time ago. Kept the gun, though."

"Didn't use it, I guess."

"Timothy, lots of people in Miami own more than one handgun. They'll keep one in their glove compartment, one in a briefcase, one in a handbag, one in a bedside drawer . . . You know that."

Moth started to speak, stopped, started a second time, stopped, stared at the pictures, leaned back.

"Thank you for your time, Susan. I will see you at a meeting," he said abruptly. He turned to Andy Candy. "I'm an alcoholic," he said bitterly, as he gestured toward the prosecutor. "But Susan likes cocaine."

"That's right," Susan said coldly. "But not anymore."

"Right," Moth replied. "Not anymore. Right."

Andy Candy was a little unsure what this last exchange meant.

"I guess we'll be leaving now," Moth said.

They all shook hands perfunctorily and Andy Candy and Moth exited the office. He didn't acknowledge the secretary. Instead, as soon as they passed through the outer door to Susan Terry's office he seized Andy Candy's wrist and started to walk quickly, pulling her along as if they were terribly late to a meeting instead of having just finished one. She could see his lips were set, and his face seemed stiff, like a frozen mask.

Through the office, out through security, down the elevator, back through the passageway next to the building metal detectors, out into the sunlight, across the street, until they stood in front of the older courthouse building.

Moth nearly dragged Andy Candy the entire way. She had to almost jog to keep up with him. He said nothing.

Outside, they were hit by a burst of sunlight and heat, and she saw Moth crumble a little—as if struck with a sudden punch—as he stopped in his tracks at the bottom of a wide flight of entry stairs. Trees and foliage had been planted by the access, to give the place a less severe look. This was unsuccessful.

The two of them were quiet for a few moments. In front of them, an old, wizened maintenance man with a water hose and a large push broom was cleaning up what Andy Candy thought was the oddest-looking mess by the curb to the street. She could see feathers and a streak of red-brown on the gray cement. The maintenance man swept up the material into a pile, used a shovel to dump it into a wheelbarrow, then turned on the hose and started to spray the area.

"Dead chicken," Moth said.

"What?"

"A dead chicken. Santeria. You know, the religion that's like voodoo. Someone has a court case inside, so they hire a *brujo* to come sacrifice a chicken in front of the courthouse. Supposed to give them good luck with a jury, or make some judge cut their sentence or something."

Moth smiled and shook his head. "Maybe we should have done the same."

Andy Candy tried to speak softly. She figured Moth was still devastated by his uncle's death and she wanted to be kind. She also wanted to get away. She had her own sadnesses to deal with and she felt caught up in something that bordered on crazy and emotional when she thought that what she needed more than anything was something rational and routine.

"So, that's it?" she asked. She knew he would understand that she wasn't talking about a dead chicken on the steps to the courthouse.

She saw Moth's lip quiver. She thought, *Better help him get through the next bit. Get him to go to that meeting. Then disappear forever.*

Moth said, "No."

She didn't reply.

"You saw the pictures?"

She nodded.

He turned toward her. He had paled a little or else the bright sunlight had washed some of the color from his skin.

"Sit at a desk," he said stiffly.

"Sorry, what?"

"Sit at a desk, just like my uncle did."

Andy Candy plopped down on the steps, then stiffened her back, holding her hands out like a prim secretary. "Okay," she said. Moth instantly sat next to her.

"Now, shoot yourself," Moth said.

"What?"

"I mean, show me how you would shoot yourself."

Andy Candy felt like she was sliding under the surface of a wave, almost as if she was holding her breath and looking through darkening waters as she sunk down. The argument within her—forgotten in the return of Moth to her side—suddenly resounded. *Killer!* she heard in her head. *Maybe you should kill yourself?*

Like a poorly trained actor in some forgettable local production, she formed two fingers and her thumb into the shape of a gun. She lifted it to her temple theatrically. "Bang," she said quietly. "Like that?"

Moth mimicked her actions. "Bang," he said, just as softly. "That's what my uncle did. You could tell from the pictures."

He hesitated. Andy Candy could see pain in Moth's eyes.

"Except he didn't." Moth held his finger-pistol to his temple. "Tell, Me, Andy, why would someone reach down, start to open a desk drawer where he had a gun that had been there for years, maybe pull it partway open, and then suddenly decide instead to use the *other* gun that was on the desk in front of him."

Andy tried to answer this question. She could not.

Moth pantomimed the actions again. *Reaching down. Stopping. Reaching onto a desktop. Raising a pistol.*

"Bang," he said a second time. A little louder.

Deep breath. Moth shook his head. "My uncle was organized. Logical. He used to tell me that the most precise people in the world are jewelers, dentists, and poets, because they worship economy of design. But next in line are psychiatrists. Being a drunk was sloppy and stupid and he hated that part of it. Recovery for Ed meant examining every little action, understanding every step . . . I don't know, being smart, I guess. That's what he was trying to teach me."

Anger mingled with despair in his voice.

"What makes sense about bringing *two* guns to a suicide."

He paused before he took the two-fingered mock pistol from his temple and pointed it out in front of them, as if he was taking aim at heat waves above the parking lot. "I'm going to find him and kill him," Moth said bitterly. The *him* in his threat was a ghost.

5

"I'm really concerned," said Student #1. "No, way beyond concerned. I'm really worried."

"No shit," said Student #2.

"Why don't you add scared out of your mind to that particular algorithm," said Student #3.

"And precisely what do we do about it?" asked Student #4. He was trying to remain calm because everything about the situation seemed to warrant an approach closer to panic.

"Actually, I think we're totally fucked," Student #1 said with resignation.

"Do you mean academically fucked, emotionally fucked, or physically fucked?" asked Student #2.

"All the above," Student #1 replied.

They were seated in a corner of a hospital cafeteria, around simmering cups of coffee. It was midday, and the cafeteria was busy. From time to time they looked nervously about.

"Dean's office. Campus security. Maybe we go to Professor Hogan, because he's the resident expert on explosive personalities and violence. He'll have an *idea what we can do," Student #2 said. She was a hard-edged former nurse in an ICU who had taken night school classes and relied on her fireman husband to watch over their two small children while she battled her way through medical school. "I'll be goddamned if I'm gonna let this situation get any more out of control. We know this is illness. Schizophrenia. Paranoid type. Maybe manic depression—it's one of those. Maybe intermittent explosive disorder. I don't know. So there's a real diagnosis to be made. Whoop-de-do. We just have to take some action before we're all caught up in a mess that impacts our careers. And it's dangerous." Her pragmatism was uncomfortable for the three other members of the psychiatry study group, who were eager to train themselves in the ability to not leap to conclusions and not draw hasty opinions about behaviors, no matter how bizarre and frightening.*

"Yeah. Great plan," said Student #1. "Makes sense until it's us that gets hauled before the faculty board for a clear-cut academic transgression. You can't just call in the hounds on another student without a firm abso-fucking-lutely solid case. And this sure as hell isn't plagiarism or cheating or sexual harassment." Student #1 had seriously considered law school instead of medicine, and had a literal bent to his thinking. "Look, we're just speculating here, about the exact illness and about what just might happen, no matter how dangerous it seems, because all predictions are just bullshit. And you can't turn another student in to administrators just because you think they just might do something terrible and because their behavior is off-and-on erratic, maybe delusional and fits into all these categories that we know about because we just happen to be studying them right now. It's not evidence-based. It's feelings-based."

"Anybody in the group not have those feelings?" Student #2 asked cynically. No one answered that question.

"Anybody not feel in danger?"

Again the group remained silent. Coffee was sipped.

"I think we're screwed," Student #3 said after a long moment. He reached to the chest pocket on his white lab coat. A week earlier he had finally given up smoking, and this was a reflex action. The others noted it—as they were all honing their skills at observation. "And I agree with both of you. But we have to do something, even if it means taking a risk."

"Whatever it is we do, I'm not getting an official reprimand. I don't want something going into my permanent record. I can't afford it," Student #2 said.

"Your permanent record won't mean shit, if . . ." Student #1 blurted out. He didn't need to complete his sentence.

"Okay, right . . ." Student #2 continued. "Well, then I say we go to Professor Hogan for starters, because that's the least provocative thing we can do." Her voice cracked a little. "And we go to see him right damn fast. Or, at least one of us does."

"I'll go," said Student #4. "I'm getting an A from him. But you will all have to back me up if he calls you in to confirm what I tell him."

Heads nodded rapidly. They were all jumpy, nervous—any sudden noise from elsewhere in the cafeteria caused them to shudder. The routine clatter and clank of dishes, the occasional burst of conversation from another table—none of this faded benignly into the background as it usually did. They were all worried that Student #5 was going to walk through the door at any minute, gun in hand.

"I need a list," Student #4 said. "Everyone write down accurate assessments about frightening behaviors. Be as detailed as possible. Names. Dates. Places. Witnesses, and not just that moment where we all saw him strangle that lab rat for no fucking reason. Then I'll take all that stuff and see Professor Hogan."

"As long as there's no delay," Student #1 said briskly. "You guys know as well as I do that when someone's on an edge, they can tumble pretty fast. He needs help. And we're probably helping him out by going to Professor Hogan."

The others stared at the ceiling and rolled their eyes. "Probably," Student #1 repeated.

"Probably. Sure," Student #3 said.

No one actually believed they were helping their fellow student in the slightest, but speaking this lie out loud was reassuring. They all knew that really what they wanted was to protect themselves, but no one was willing to voice this.

"We're agreed, then?" Student #4 said.

Glances across the table as the members of the group eyed one another for support. "Yes," times four.

"All right. I'll see Professor Hogan tomorrow morning before his lecture," Student #4 said cautiously. *"You will all need to get me your lists before then."* This assignment seemed simple. They were students accustomed to hard work, note taking, and outlining under deadline. Doing patient assessments came automatically to them, and this assignment seemed little different. Then Ed Warner glanced at a clock on the wall. *"It's April first, 1986,"* he said, *"April Fools' Day. That will be easy to remember. It's two-thirty in the afternoon and all four members of Psychiatry Study Group Alpha are in agreement."*

Andy Candy lingered a few strides behind Moth as he surged down the hallway toward his uncle's office—only to stop short when he saw the yellow police tape sealing the entrance. There were two long strands with the ubiquitous black "Do Not Enter" message. They created an X that crossed in front of the office plaque: "Edward Warner, M.D. PhD. P.A."

Moth raised a hand, and Andy Candy thought he was going to tear away the security tape.

"Moth," she said, "you shouldn't do that."

His hand abruptly flopped to his side. His voice sounded exhausted. "I need to start somewhere," he said.

Start what? she thought, then felt that perhaps it was wiser not to answer her question.

"Moth," she said as gently as she could, "let's go get something to eat, then I can drop you at your place and maybe you can think all this over."

He turned to his onetime girlfriend and shook his head. "When I think, all I get is depressed. When I get depressed, all I want to do is drink." He smiled wryly, just a light rise at the corners of his mouth. "Better for me to keep going, even if it's in the wrong direction." He raised a finger and touched the police tape. Then he reached for the door handle. It was locked.

"Are you going to break in?" Andy Candy asked.

"Yes," Moth replied. "Fuck it. Truth somewhere. And I'm going to start knocking down every door."

She smiled, although she knew that forcing the door was wrong, and probably illegal. This sounded very much like the Moth she'd once loved.

He would combine psychological with practical with poetic in a stew of action that to her was like honey, sweet and endlessly attractive, but sticky and probably destined to make a mess.

But as he started to reach for the tape, behind them down the hallway another door opened, and they both turned to the sound. A slightly dumpy, dark-haired, middle-aged man tugging on a blue blazer emerged. When the man saw them, he stopped.

"What are you doing?" he asked. "There's no entry there." His accent was tinged with Spanish.

"Going inside my uncle's office," Moth replied.

The man hesitated. "Are you Timothy?" he asked.

"In the flesh," Moth replied aggressively.

"Ah," the man said, "your uncle spoke of you often." He moved toward them, extending his hand. "I am Doctor Ramirez," he said. "My practice has been next to your uncle's for, oh, I don't know how many years now. I am so sorry for what happened. We were friends and colleagues."

Moth nodded.

"I did not see you at the funeral," Doctor Ramirez continued.

"No," Moth replied, and with a fit of nervous honesty that surprised Andy Candy, he added, "I went on a bender."

The doctor looked noncommittal. "And now?"

"I hope I'm back under control."

"Yes. *Under control*. This is difficult. Sudden great emotional blows. I have had many patients in treatment for years, and then the unexpected topples them when they least expect it. But you know, your uncle was very proud of the sobriety the two of you shared. We would often go to lunch between patients, and he would speak with great pleasure and obvious pride about your progress. You pursue a doctorate in history, I believe?"

The doctor had a half-lecturing way of talking, as if every opinion he voiced should be immediately rendered into a life lesson. In some people, this might have been pretentious, but in the almost roly-poly psychiatrist, it seemed welcoming.

"Working on it," Moth said.

They were quiet for an instant, before Doctor Ramirez said, "Well, should you want to speak about matters, my door is open."

"That is kind of you," Moth replied. This was a psychiatric act of grace— *I know you are troubled and the best I can offer is an ear.* "I might take you up on that." Moth thought for a moment, before asking, "Doctor, your office is right next door. Were you there when my uncle . . ."

Doctor Ramirez shook his head. "I did not hear the gunshot, if that is what you are asking. I had left already. It was a Tuesday, and your uncle was routinely the last person on the floor to leave on Tuesdays. Typically a few minutes before six. On Mondays, I have a late patient. Other days, some of the other psychiatrists on the floor stay a little late. There are only five of us with offices here, so we always try to keep each other's schedules in mind."

Moth seemed to process this.

"So, if I had come up to you and asked, 'What evening is my uncle alone on this floor?' you, or anyone else, would immediately have replied, 'Tuesday,' right?"

Doctor Ramirez gave Moth an appreciative look. "You sound like a detective, not a history student, Timothy," he said. "Yes. That is correct."

"Can I ask a personal question, Doctor?"

Doctor Ramirez looked a little surprised, then nodded. "If you like," he said. "I do not know if I will be able to answer."

"You knew Uncle Ed. Did you think he was suicidal?"

Doctor Ramirez thought for a moment, his face marked by a processing of memories and suspicions. Moth recognized this. It was a quality his uncle had, a psychiatrist's need to assess the impact of what he would say, why he was being asked, and what was really behind the question, before responding.

"No, Timothy," he said cautiously. "There were no overt signs of depression that I saw that suggested suicide. I told this to the police who questioned me. They seemed dismissive of my observations. And the mere fact that I noticed nothing does not mean they didn't exist, and that Edward didn't do a better job of hiding them than others might. But I saw nothing to alarm me. And we had lunch the day before his death."

He paused, then pulled out a pad and rapidly wrote a name and address down. "Ed saw this man many years back. Perhaps . . ."

The doctor then reached down into his pants pocket, removed a set of car keys, and sorted through them. He deliberately removed one key from the chain and with an exaggerated, theatrical motion, dropped it to the carpeted floor. "Ah!" he said, with a grin. "The spare key I have to your late uncle's office door. I seem to have misplaced it."

Then the doctor gestured at the door. "If you are going to break in, would you wait until I leave? I would prefer not to be too much of an accomplice here." He laughed a little at his obvious lie. "I'm sorry," he said, slightly apologizing, his tone turning both sad and cautious. "I do not know what you will find inside, but perhaps it will help you. Good luck. I do not ordinarily turn my back on people seeking answers. You can slip the key under my door when you are done."

Doctor Ramirez turned to Andy Candy, made a small, polite bow, and then retreated down the hallway and disappeared into the elevator.

Moth and Andy Candy sat uncomfortably side by side on the couch that his uncle had used for his few remaining psychoanalytic patients. Behind them was a large multihued photograph of an Everglades sunset. On another wall was a bright, abstract Kandinsky print. One wall had a modest bookcase—medical texts and a copy of *The Fifty-Minute Hour*. There were three framed diplomas near the desk. But there was little that said much about the personality of the man whose office it was. Andy Candy suspected this was by design. Moth was staring at his uncle's solid oaken desk, an edgy intensity in his gaze.

"I can't quite see it," he said slowly. "It's like it's right there, and then it fades away."

Andy Candy was caught between trying to guess what Moth was eyeing and trying to imagine what he would do next.

"What are you trying to see?"

"His last minutes." Moth suddenly stood up. "See, he's sitting there. He knows he's supposed to meet me and it's important. But instead he takes the time to write 'My fault' on a prescription pad, reach for a gun that wasn't the one he'd owned for years, and shoot himself. That's what the cops and Susan the prosecutor want to say happened."

Moth paced around, approaching the desk, maneuvering past a single armchair for nonanalytic patients. He nearly choked when he saw the dried maroon bloodstains on the beige carpet and the wooden desktop. When he spoke, his voice was a little shaky. "Andy, what I see is someone in that chair, with a gun. Making my uncle do . . ." Moth stopped short.

"Do what?"

"I don't know."

"Why?"

"I don't know."

"Who?"

"I don't know."

Andy Candy stood up. "Moth, we've got to leave," she said softly. "Every second you stay here, it's just going to make it harder for you."

He nodded. She was right.

Andy Candy made a small wave toward the door, as if to encourage Moth to lead the way. But suddenly an idea occurred to her. She hesitated a second before speaking.

"Moth," she said slowly, "the police and Miss Terry—they would have to be certain this wasn't a killing, right? Even with the gun right there on the floor next to your uncle. So, first thing, they would check out all the usual suspects. *The usual suspects*, just like the movie name. That's what she said they did: They went over his patient list—probably his ex-patient list, too—talked to friends, neighbors, see if he had any enemies, right? See if there was someone threatening him. They made sure he didn't owe money to gamblers or drug dealers. That's what she said, right? They would have ruled out all sorts of things before coming to their conclusion, right? Right?"

She repeated this last word with an icy determination.

"Yes," Moth said. "Right and right."

"So, if it is what you think it is and what they don't think it is, we have to look in the places they didn't look," Andy Candy said. "That's the only thing that makes sense."

She was a little surprised at her logic. Or antilogic. *Look in the places that don't make sense.* She wondered where this idea had come from. She gestured toward the door again.

"Time to leave, Moth," she said cautiously. "If there really was a killer in this room like you said, sitting right there, then they sure weren't going to leave something behind that would make the cops suspicious."

Her practicality astonished her.

6

Two conversations. One imagined. One real.

The first:

"He's holding us all back. We want to get rid of him."

"Well, file a complaint with the dean. But clearly your fellow student is in emotional trouble."

"We don't care how much trouble or stress or difficulty—whatever you want to call it—he's caught up in. So he's sick. Big fucking deal. Screw him. We just want him out, so that our own careers aren't compromised."

"Of course. That makes complete sense. I'll help you."

If it had actually taken place that way it would have made sense for everyone except one person.

And the second:

"Hello, Ed."

First, a moment of confusion: expecting one person but getting someone very different. Then speechless. Jaw-drop.

"Don't you recognize me?"

The speaker already knew the answer because it was evident in the sudden recognition in Ed Warner's eyes.

Then he had slowly and quite deliberately removed his gun from an inside jacket pocket and pointed it across the desktop. The gun was a small .25-caliber automatic loaded with hollow-point bullets that expanded on contact, made a mess, and were preferred by professional assassins. It was the sort of weapon favored by frightened females or uneasy home owners who imagined it would keep them safe from midnight criminal invasions or run-amok zombies, but which probably would do neither. It was also a favorite of trained killers, who liked a small, easily concealable weapon that was easy to maneuver and deadly at close distances.

"You didn't think you'd ever see me again, did you, Ed? Your old study group partner here to visit."

It had gone more or less like the others. *Different but the same*—including the moment he had written "My fault" on a notepad on Ed's desk and then walked out.

One of the things that had astonished Student #5 was how preternaturally calm he'd grown over the years as he'd perfected the act of killing. Not that he precisely thought of himself as a killer in the usual sense of the word. No scarred face and prison tats. No street thug wearing baggy jeans and a cockeyed baseball cap. No cold-eyed professional drug dealer's hit man who could wear his psychopathology like others wore a suit of clothes. He did not even consider himself to be some sort of master criminal, although he did feel a slight conceit in how he'd honed his abilities over the years. *Real criminals,* he believed, *have some fundamental moral and psychological deficit that renders them into who they are. They want to rob, steal, rape, torture, or kill. Compulsion. They want money, sex, and power. Obsession. It's the need to act that drives them to commit crimes. Not me. All*

I want is justice. He considered himself to be closer in style and tempera-ment to some sort of classical avenging force, which gave him significant legitimacy in his own imagination.

He stopped at the corner of 71ˢᵗ Street and West End Avenue and waited for the light to change. A taxi jammed on its brakes to avoid a man in a shiny new Cadillac. There was a quick squeal of tires accompanied by an exchange of horns and probably some obscenities in several languages that couldn't penetrate closed windows. *City music.* A bus jammed with commuters wheezed out pungent exhaust. He could hear a distant sub-terranean subway rattle. Beside him a young woman pushing a baby in a stroller coughed. He grinned at the child and waved his hand. The child smiled back.

Five people ruined my life. They were cavalier. Thoughtless. Selfish. Fix-ated on themselves, like so many preening egotists.

Now only one is left.

He was sure of one thing: He could not face his own death, could not even face the years leading up to it, without acquiring each measure of revenge.

Justice, he thought, *is my only addiction.*

They were the robbers. The killers.

Guilty. Guilty. Guilty. Guilty. One last verdict to go.

The light changed and he crossed the street, along with several other pedestrians, including the woman with the child in the stroller, who maneuvered the curbs expertly. One of the things he liked the most about New York City was the automatic anonymity it provided. He was adrift in a sea of people: millions of lives that amounted to nothing on the sidewalks. Was the person next to him someone important? Someone accomplished? Someone special? They could be anything—doctor, lawyer, businessperson, or teacher. They could even be the same as him: execu-tioner.

But no one would know. The sidewalks stripped away all signs and identities.

In the course of his studies on murder—as he'd come to this philosophical conclusion—he'd spent time admiring Nemesis, the Greek goddess of retribution. He believed he had wings, like she did. And he certainly had her patience.

And so, to launch himself on his path, he'd taken precautions.

He'd become an expert with a handgun and more than proficient with a high-powered hunting rifle and a crossbow. He'd learned hand-to-hand combat techniques and had sculpted his body so that the years flowing past would have minimal impact. He'd finished Ironman Triathlons and taken many speed-driving courses at an auto racing school. He dutifully went to his internist for annual checkups, became a health club and Central Park jogging path addict, watched his diet, emphasized fresh vegetables, lean proteins, and seafood, and didn't drink. He even got a flu shot every fall. He studied in libraries and had became a self-taught computer expert. His bookcases were crammed with crime fiction and nonfiction, which he used to harvest ideas and techniques. He thought he should have been a professor at the John Jay College of Criminal Justice.

I have become a doctor of death.

He continued to walk north. He wore a tailored dark blue pinstriped three-piece suit and expensive Italian leather shoes. A dashing white silk scarf was looped around his neck against the possibility of a chill breeze. The late afternoon sun reflected off his mirrored aviator sunglasses. It was a fine time of day, with fading sunlight slicing through cement and brick apartment canyons, as if picking up momentum as it made its final foray across the dark waters of the Hudson. To any passerby, he must have looked like a wealthy professional heading home from the office after a successful day. That there was no office, and that he'd merely spent the prior two hours happily walking Manhattan streets, did nothing to undermine the image he projected to the world.

Student #5 had three different names, three different identities, three different homes, phony jobs, passports, driver's licenses, and Social Security numbers, and fake acquaintances, haunts, hobbies, and lifestyles. He ricocheted between these. He'd been born into substantial inherited wealth; medicine had been his family's profession, and he could trace the physicians in his ancestry back to battlefields at Gettysburg and Shiloh. His own late father had been a cardiac surgeon of considerable note, with offices in midtown, privileges at some of the city's most prominent hospitals, and a mild disapproval of his son's interest in psychiatry, arguing unsuccessfully that real medicine was practiced with sterile gowns, scalpels, and blood. *"Seeing a heart beat strongly—that's saving a life,"* his father used to say. His father had been wrong. *Or, if not wrong,* he thought, *limited.*

He considered the name he'd been born with to be a sort of *slave* name, so he'd left it behind, discarding it along with his past as he'd shifted trust funds and stock portfolios into anonymous overseas accounts. It was the name of his youth, his ambition, his legacy, and then what he thought of as his abject failure. It was the name that he'd had when he'd first plunged helplessly into bipolar psychosis, been ousted from medical college, and found himself in a straitjacket on the way to a private mental hospital. It was the name that his doctors had used when they treated him, and the name that he'd had when he'd finally emerged—allegedly stabilized—only to survey the wasteland that his life had become.

Stabilized was a word he held in contempt.

Exiting the clinic where he'd spent almost a year, even as a young man he had known he had to become someone new. *I died once. I lived again.*

So, from the day of his release, through each year that passed, he was careful to always take the proper, daily psychotropic medications. He scheduled regular six-month, fifteen-minute appointments with a psychopharmacologist to make certain that unexpected hallucinations, unwanted mania, and unnecessary stress were constantly kept at bay. He was devoted to exercising his body and was just as rigorous in training his sanity.

And this he'd accomplished. No recurrent swings of madness. Level-headed. Solid emotionally. New identities. Constructed carefully. Taking his time. Building each character into something real.

On 121 West 87th Street, Apartment 7B, he was Bruce Phillips.

In Charlemont, Massachusetts, in the weather-beaten double-wide trailer on Zoar Road with the rusted satellite dish and cracked window-panes that overlooked the catch-and-release trout fishing segment of the Deerfield River, he was known as Blair Munroe. This was a literary homage that only he could appreciate. He liked Saki's haunting short stories, which gave him the *Munroe*—he'd reluctantly added the *e* to the author's real last name—and *Blair* was George Orwell's actual last name.

And in Key West, in the small, expensively reconditioned 1920s cigar-maker's house he owned on Angela Street, he was Stephen Lewis. The *Stephen* was for Stephen King or Stephen Dedalus—he changed his mind from time to time about the literary antecedent—and the *Lewis* was for Lewis Carroll, whose real name was Charles Dodgson.

But all these names were as fictional as the characters he'd created for them. *Private investment specialist* in New York; *social worker at the VA hospital* in Massachusetts; and in Key West, *lucky drug dealer who'd pulled off a single big load and retired instead of getting greedy and hauled in by the DEA and imprisoned.*

But curiously, none of these personae really spoke to him. Instead, he thought of himself solely as Student #5. That was who he had been when his life had changed. That was who had systematically repaired the immense wrongs so thoughtlessly and cavalierly done to him as a young man.

Still walking north, he took a quick left to Riverside Drive so that he could steal a look from the park across the Hudson toward New Jersey before the sun finally set. He wondered whether he should stop in a grocery over on Broadway to pick up some prepackaged *sushi* for dinner. He had one death that he had to carefully review, assess, and analyze in depth. *A postmortem conference with myself,* he thought. And he had one more death to consider. *A premortem conference with myself.* He very much wanted this last act to be special, and he wanted the person he was hunting to know it. *This last one—he needs to know what's coming. No surprises. A dialogue with death. The conversation I wasn't allowed to have so many years ago.* There was both risk and challenge within this desire—which gave him a sense of delicious anticipation. *And then the scales will finally be balanced.*

He smiled. *Murder as talk therapy.*

Student #5 hesitated at the corner of the block and stole a glance toward the river. Just as he'd expected, a shimmering slice of gold from the sun's last effort creased the water surface.

Out loud he said to no one and everyone: "One more."

As always, as was his custom with all his plans, he intended to be surgically meticulous. But now he was giving in to impatience. *No lengthy delays. We have saved this one for last. Get to it and set your future free.*

7

The Doctor's First Conversation

The saleslady showing Jeremy Hogan through the nursing home was filled with bright and cheery descriptions of the many features available for residents: gourmet meals (he didn't believe this for a second) served either in one's apartment or in the well-appointed dining area; modern indoor pool and exercise suite; weekly first-run movies; book discussion groups; lectures by formerly prominent professionals who now made their homes there. She coupled this bubbly enthusiasm with more sobering lists of à la carte medical care available—*did he need a daily injection of insulin?*—a dedicated, well-trained, twenty-four-hour nursing staff, rehabilitation facilities located on site, and quick and easy access to nearby hospitals in the case of a real emergency.

But all he could think of was a simple question, which he did not ask: *Can I hide here from a killer?*

In the deeply carpeted corridors, people were relentlessly polite, swooping past him on motorized scooters or moving slowly with walkers or canes.

Many "Hi, how are you?" and "Nice day, isn't it?" inquiries that no one really expected to be answered with anything other than a fake friendly smile and a vigorous nod.

He wanted to reply: *"How am I? Scared."* Or: *"Yes. It's a nice day to possibly get killed."*

"As you can see," the saleslady said, "we're a lively crew here."

Doctor Jeremy Hogan, eighty two years old, widower, long retired, a lanky onetime basketball player, wondered if any of the *lively crew* were armed and knew how to handle a semiautomatic pistol or a short-barrel twelve-gauge shotgun. He imagined he should ask: *"Any ex–Navy SEALS or Recon Marines living here? Combat vets?"* He barely listened to the saleslady's final pitch, outlining the many financial advantages that accompanied moving into the "deluxe" one-bedroom apartment with the desultory second-floor window view of a distant tangled stand of forest trees. It was only "deluxe," Jeremy decided, if one considered polished aluminum rails in the shower and a safety intercom system to be riches.

He smiled, shook the saleslady's hand, told her he'd get back with her within the next few days, wondered about the misshapen fear that possessed him to make the urgent appointment for the tour of the home, and told himself that death couldn't be worse than some kinds of life—no matter what sort of death came visiting.

He expected his to be painful.

Maybe.

And he believed it was closing in on him rapidly.

Maybe.

The part that concerned him wasn't only the threat at the end. It was the pillar on which the threat was built:

"Whose fault is it?"

"What do you mean by 'fault'?"

"Tell me, Doctor, whose fault is it?"

"Who is this, please?"

*   *   *

The curious thing, he told himself as he drove away slowly from the nursing home, *is that you spent much of your career in and around violent death, and now, very possibly facing it yourself, it seems like you don't have a clue what to do.*

Violence had always been an interesting abstraction for him: something that happened to other people; something that took place somewhere else; something for clinical studies; something that he would write academic papers about; and primarily what he talked about in courtrooms and classrooms.

"I'm sorry, Counselor, but there is no scientific way to predict future dangerousness. I can only tell you what the defendant presents psychiatrically at this moment. How he will respond to treatment and medication or confinement is unknown."

This was Jeremy Hogan's standard witness stand response, an answer to a question that was invariably asked in the times he'd been called upon to testify in a court of law as an expert. He could picture dozens—no, *hundreds*—of defendants seated at benches, watching him carefully as he rendered his opinions about what their mental state was when they did what they did that brought them to that courtroom. He remembered seeing: Anger. Rage. Deep-rooted resentment. Or, sometimes: Sadness. Shame. Despair. And the occasional *I'm not here. I will never be here. I will always be somewhere else. You cannot touch me because I will always live in some place within me that is locked away from you and only I have the key.*

And although he knew that *maybe* the person seated across from him wouldn't even notice him droning away under cross-examination, he also knew that *maybe* the person seated across from him would hate him forever with a slowly building homicidal fury.

Maybe was a word he was intimate with.

He had a less formal delivery that he employed in the classroom with medical students delving into forensic psychiatry: "Look, boys and girls— we can believe that all the relevant factors exist that will keep this patient or that patient on a path of violence. Or, conversely, a path where he or she responds rapidly to what we can offer—medication, therapy—and we wonderfully defuse all those violent, dangerous impulses. But we are not equipped with a crystal ball that allows us to see the future. We make, at best, an educated guess. What works for one subject might not work for another. In forensics there is always an element of uncertainty. We may know, but we just don't know. But never say that to a family member, a cop, or a prosecutor, and never under oath in a courtroom to a judge and jury, even though that's the only thing—and I really mean *the only thing*—those folks want to learn."

The students hated that reality.

At first, they all wanted to be in the business of psychiatric fortune-telling—a detail he often jokingly insulted them with. It was only after time spent on a few high-security wards listening to widely varying degrees of paranoia and wildly unmasked impulses that they slowly came to understand his classroom point.

Of course, you arrogant fool, you taught them about limitations but never believed you had any yourself. Jeremy Hogan wanted to laugh out loud. He liked to inwardly mock himself, to taunt and tease the younger self that lived in his memory.

You were right a bunch. You were wrong a bunch. So it goes.

He pulled out of the driveway, leaving the nursing home behind in the rearview mirror. Jeremy was very cautious driving. A patient *left, right, left* look as he merged onto the street. He stuck tenaciously to the speed limit. He was devoted to using his lane change blinker. He braked well in advance of stop signs and never ran a yellow light, much less a red one. His sleek, big black BMW would easily have topped 135 mph—but he rarely asked the car to do anything except meander along at a boring and leisurely pace. He sometimes wondered if the car was secretly angry with him, or frustrated deep in its automotive soul. Consequently he infrequently used the car, which still, after ten years, had a new-car sheen and extremely low mileage.

Usually he employed an old battered truck he kept beside the ramshackle barn at his farmhouse for his occasional forays out for the few groceries he needed. He drove the truck in the same elderly-gentleman manner, but because it was haphazardly dented, its red paint was faded, it rattled and creaked, and one window would go neither up nor down, this style seemed more appropriate to it. *The BMW is like I once was,* he thought, *and the truck is like I am now.*

It took him an hour to get back to his farmhouse deep in the New Jersey countryside. That New Jersey even had *countryside* came as astonishing news to some folks, who imagined it as a paved parking lot and twenty-hour-busy industrial park adjacent to New York City. But much of the state was less developed, acres of rolling, deer-infested green space that sported some of the finest corn and tomato crops in the world. His own place was only twenty shady minutes outside of Princeton and its famous university, set back on twelve acres that abutted miles of conservation land that a century earlier had been part of a large, working farm.

He had purchased it more than thirty years ago, when he was still teaching an hour away in Philadelphia and his wife the artist could sit on the flagstone back patio with her watercolors and fill their home and the collections of wealthy folks with gentle landscapes. Back then the house had been quiet, a respite from his work. Now it wasn't a sensible house for an old man: too many things frequently breaking down; too narrow and steep a stairway; too many overgrown lawns and runaway gardens that constantly needed tending; old appliances and bath fixtures that barely worked; a tired heating system that was far too cold in the winter and far too hot in the summer. He'd routinely fought off the developers who wanted to buy it, tear it down, and build a half-dozen McMansions on the acreage.

But it had been a place that he'd loved once, that his wife had loved as well, where he'd spread her ashes, and the mere notion that there just might—or might not—be a psychotic killer stalking him didn't seem like a good enough reason to leave the place, even if he couldn't get up the stairs without his knees delivering piercing arthritic pain.

Get a cane, he told himself.

Get a gun.

He pulled into the long gravel drive that led to the front door. He sighed. *Maybe this is the day I die.*

Jeremy stopped and wondered how many times he had driven up to his home. *It's a perfectly reasonable place to make a last stand,* he thought.

He looked around for some telltale sign of a killer's presence—an inspection he knew was completely ludicrous. A real killer wouldn't leave his car parked out front, adorned with a "Murder 1" license plate. He would be waiting in a shadow, concealed, knife in hand, ready to spring. Or hidden behind some wall, drawing down on him with a high-powered rifle, placing the sight squarely on his head, finger caressing a trigger.

He wondered whether he would hear the *bang!* before dying. A soldier would know the answer to that question, he believed, but he knew he wasn't much of a soldier.

Jeremy Hogan breathed in deeply, and extricated himself from behind the wheel. He stood by the car, waiting. *Maybe this is it,* he thought.

Maybe not.

He knew he was caught up in something. Periphery or center? Start or end? He just didn't know. He was ashamed of his frailty: *What were you thinking, going to a nursing home? What good would that do you? Did you think that by accepting how old and weak you've become it would hide you? "Please, Mister Killer, don't shoot me or stab me or whatever you plan to do to me because I'm too old and will probably kick the bucket any day now anyway, so no need to trouble yourself with actually killing me."* He laughed out loud at his absurdity. *There's a strong argument to make to a murderer. And anyway, what is so great about life that you need to keep living it?*

He made a mental note to call the saleslady and politely decline the purchase of the apartment—*no,* he thought, *prison cell.*

He wondered how much time he truly had. He'd been asking himself this question every day—no, every second—for more than two weeks, since he'd received an anonymous phone call one night around ten, shortly before his usual bedtime:

"Doctor Hogan?"

"Yes. Who is calling?" He had not recognized the caller ID on the phone

and figured it was some cause or political fund-raiser and he was prepared to instantly hang up before they even got their noxious pitch started. Afterward, he wished he had.

"Whose fault is it?"

"I'm sorry?"

"Whose fault is it?"

"What do you mean by 'fault'?"

"Tell me, Doctor: Whose fault is it?"

"Who is this please?"

"I'll answer for you, Doctor Hogan: It's your fault. But you were not alone. The blame is shared. Bills have been paid. You might examine recent obits in the Miami Herald.*"*

"I'm sorry, I have no idea what the hell you're talking about." He was about to angrily hang up on the caller, but instead he heard:

"The next obit will be yours. We will speak again."

Then the line went dead.

It was the tone, he thought later, the ice-calm words *next obit* that told him the caller was a killer. Or—at the least—fancied himself to be. Raspy, deep voice, probably, he imagined, concealed by some electronic device. No other evidence. No other indication. No other detail he could point to. From a forensic, scientific point of view, this was a stupid, utterly un-supported seat-of-the-pants conclusion.

But in his years as a forensic psychiatrist, he'd sat across from many killers, both men and women.

So, upon later reflection, he was certain.

His first response was to be defensively dismissive, which he knew was a kind of foolish self-protective urge: *Well, what the hell was that all about? Who knows? Time for bed.*

His second response was curiosity: He picked up his phone and hit the "call back" feature. He wanted to speak with the person who'd called him: *Maybe I should tell him that I have no idea what he's talking about but I'm willing to talk about it. Someone is at fault? For doing exactly what? Anyway, we're all at fault for something. That's what life is.* He did not stop to think that the caller probably wasn't interested in a philosophical conversation. A disembodied electronic voice instantly told him that the number was no longer in service.

He'd hung up the phone, and spoken out loud: "Well, I should call the police." *They will just think me a cranky, confused old fool, which might be what I am.* Jeremy Hogan did know one thing: All his training and all his experience told him that there was only one purpose behind making a call like that. It was to create runaway uncertainty. "Well, whoever you are, you've managed that," he said out loud.

His third response was to be scared. Bed suddenly seemed inappropriate. He knew sleep was impossible. He could feel light-headedness, almost a dizzy spell as he stared at the telephone receiver. So he went unsteadily across the room and sat in front of his computer. He breathed in sharply. Even with his stiff-fingered, arthritic clumsiness on keyboards, it had not taken him long to find a small entry in the obituary section of the *Miami Herald* website with the headline: *Prominent Psychiatrist Takes Life; Services Set.*

It was the only obit entry that Jeremy thought could be even remotely connected to him—and that was only by shared profession.

The name was unfamiliar. His initial reaction had been, *Who's that?* But this was rapidly followed by: *Some former student? A onetime resident? Intern? Third-year medical school?* He did some age-math in his head. If the name on the web page was one of his, it had to be from thirty years earlier. He felt a surge of despair—those faces who'd attended his lectures, even those who'd sat in his smaller seminars so eagerly, were pretty much all lost to him now; even the good ones who had gone on to importance and success were hidden deep in his memory.

I don't get it, he thought. *Another shrink a thousand miles away kills himself and that has something to do with me?*

8

Moth did more than a hundred sit-ups on the floor of his apartment, followed by a hundred push-ups. At least he hoped it was a hundred. He lost count in the rapid-fire up and down. He was half-naked—boxer briefs and running shoes but nothing else. He could feel the muscles in his arms twitching, about to give way. When he thought he could not coax one more push-up from his arms, he lay flat on the floor, breathing hard, his cheek pushed against the cool polished hardwood. Then he gathered himself, stood, and ran in place until sweat began to crowd his vision and sting his eyes. He listened to '80s hard rock on his iPod—Twisted Sister, Molly Hatchet, and Iggy Pop. The music had an odd ferocity to it that matched his mood. Uncompromising power chords and relentless cliché-driven vocals crashed through his doubts. He believed he needed to be as determined as that sound.

As he lifted his knees, trying to gain speed without leaving his position, sneakered feet making slapping noises, he kept an eye on his cell phone, because Andy Candy was supposed to pick him up mid-morning so they could go to the first of the three meetings he'd scheduled for that day.

These were not meetings like the one he'd attended at Redeemer One the night before. These were interviews. *Job interviews,* he thought, *except the job I want is hunting down a murderer and killing him.*

Moth stopped. He bent over gasping, grabbed his boxers, and sucked in some stale apartment air. He felt dizzy and shaky, tasted sweat on his upper lip, and was unsure whether this was the alcohol being worked out of his body or the pressing need for revenge.

Moth felt weak, unmanned. He was completely uncertain whether if some well-coiffed, long-legged South Beach supermodel in a black string bikini were to walk into his apartment with an enticing look in her eyes and a welcoming gesture as she undid her bra strap, he could perform. He almost laughed out loud at his potential impotence. *Drink can make you into an ancient old man. Limp. Weak. Didn't Shakespeare write that?* Then he replaced the South Beach supermodel in his mind's eye with Andy Candy.

A rapid-fire series of memories crowded his imagination: *First kiss. First touch of her breast. First caress of her thigh.* He remembered moving his hand toward her sex for the first time. It had been outdoors, on a pool patio, and they were jammed together, entwined on an uncomfortable plastic lounge chair that dug into their backs but seemed at that moment like a featherbed. He was fifteen. She was thirteen. In the distance there was music playing—not rap or rock, but a surprising, gentle string quartet. Every millimeter his fingers traveled, he'd expected her to stop him. Each millimeter that she didn't had made his heart pound faster. *Damp silk panties. Elastic band.* What he had wanted then was to be fast, matching his desire, but his touch was light and patient. *A contradiction of demands and emotions.*

In the solitude of his apartment, Moth gasped out loud. He abruptly tugged the earbuds from his head, switched off his iPod. Silence surrounded him. He listened to his short breath for a few seconds, letting the panting sounds replace his Andrea Martine memories. He told himself that he should studiously avoid quiet. No noise was a vacuum that needed to be filled—and he knew that the easiest, most natural thing to fill this gap would be the drink that would kill him.

He nodded as if agreeing with some lawyerly internal argument, kicked off his running shoes, and dropped his shorts, so that he stood completely naked, sweat glistening across his forehead and on his chest.

"Exercise accomplished," he said out loud, like a soldier giving himself commands. "Don't make Andy Candy wait. Never make her wait. Always be there first. Be ready."

He still did not completely understand why she was willing to help him, but she was, so far, and this seemed the only solid thing in his life, so he believed he needed to regulate himself in a way that would keep her on board, no matter how crazy it all seemed. It was as if he could not allow her the space to actually consider what he was asking of her. *Perhaps,* he told himself, *what we do today will give us an answer or two.*

But he knew it was just as likely to be fruitless. "I need to know," he said out loud, speaking in the same brusque military tone. Moth felt an urgency to get going, and he marched rapidly toward the bathroom, shoulders straight, grabbing toothbrush and comb as if they were weapons.

Andy zipped her small car around the corner, heading toward Moth's apartment building. She saw him standing outside the entrance, waving a greeting.

It looked completely benign: a young woman picking up her boyfriend—in Miami, *su novio*—from the sidewalk so they could go off to the beach or the mall.

As she slowed to a halt, she wondered whether she should tell Moth what she'd done the night before at Redeemer One. She did not know whether she had been right or wrong, if it was a big thing or a little thing:

"You go ahead in. I'll wait for you here."

"Andy, it'll be an hour. Maybe more. Sometimes people really need to vent . . ." Hesitation. *"Sometimes I really need to vent."*

"No. It's okay. I don't mind waiting. I have a book I want to read."

He'd looked around.

"It's in the trunk," she'd lied. "It's a trashy-girls-and-sex novel. Lots of hot passion, unrequited love, and fantastic orgasms. I keep it hidden from my mom the constant prude."

He'd smiled. *"Corrupting your soul,"* he joked.

"The horse is out of that barn," she'd half-laughed.

It was perhaps the first moment of familiar banter and humor that they'd shared since he'd called her.

"Okay. I'm going in. I'll see you in a bit," he said. *"You sure you're okay with waiting? I know someone would give me a lift home . . ."*

"See you when I see you," she said, smiling.

She watched Moth get out of her car, bend down to grin at her through the window as he shut the door, then take off quickly across the parking lot. She saw him join up with two older people, a man and a woman, and enter the church. She waited a minute, then another.

Then Andy Candy exited her car.

A sticky night was dropping swiftly through the stately poinciana trees that guarded the church entrance and she started to sweat instantly. She glanced at the leaves and knew they would flower bright red. This was South Florida and there was more to the ever-present growth than swaying palms and twisted mangroves. There were huge banyan trees that looked like old gnarled men too mean to die, gumbo-limbo, and tamarind. Their roots all stretched into the porous coral rock that Miami was built on, sucking their growth from the water that filtered unseen through the earth. The trees, she thought, could live forever. Anything anyone put in the ground in Miami could grow. Sun. Rain. Heat. A tropical world, one that existed just behind all the construction, building, and development. She thought sometimes that if people took their eyes off the concrete and asphalt around them and let their guard down for just a few seconds, nature would reclaim not only the earth, but the city itself, and all its inhabitants, swallow everything up, and spit it into oblivion.

She moved to the front door, opened it cautiously, and slipped into the church. Cool air and quiet greeted her.

Andy Candy had no plan. All she had was a compulsion: She wanted to see. She wanted to hear. She wanted to try to understand.

She moved stealthily even though she knew there was no real need for caution. She knew if she simply walked into the meeting she would be greeted by everyone—except Moth. She would be welcomed by everyone—except Moth.

It was a little like sneaking up outside some home owner's window like a Peeping Tom. She imagined herself a burglar or a spy. She wanted to steal information. The Moth she'd once loved without hesitation was different now. She had to see how.

The inside of the church was shadowy and empty; it was as if Jesus was taking the evening off. She made her way past wooden pews and podiums, beyond golden crucifixes and marble statues, under the watch of stained glass martyred saints frozen in windowpanes. Andy hated church. Her mother, who sometimes filled in for an absent organist, and her dead father had been regular Sunday service folks, and they'd hauled her to church for as long as she could remember, until the moment she'd fallen in love with Moth and abruptly refused to go any longer. She paused, looked up at one of the images in the windows—Saint George slaying the dragon—and told herself, They would hate me here anyway, because now I'm a killer. *The thought made her throat dry and she tore her eyes away from the stained glass images. She crept forward until she could hear the murmur of voices down a corridor. There were some empty offices on either side of her and a small anteroom at the end. She feared her feet made loud, clumsy clunking sounds, even though the opposite was true. Andy Candy was lithe and athletic. Moth had once called her* My Ninja Girlfriend *because of the way she could sneak from her house after midnight to meet him without waking her parents or even rousing the dogs. This memory made her grin.*

She slipped into the anteroom and saw a wide set of double doors at the rear. These opened into a larger room. There was wood paneling and a low ceiling. She glimpsed leather chairs and sofas spread around a circle at the far end of the room, and she clung to a wall and started to listen just as a round of weak applause greeted someone who'd just spoken.

79

She craned her head and peeked around the corner—drawing back sharply when she saw Moth stand up.

"Hello, my name is Timothy, and I'm an alcoholic."

"Hi, Timothy," came the established response, even though he was no stranger to them.

"I have fifteen days sober now . . ."

Another round of applause and some exhortations: "Good going." "Way to go."

"As many of you know, it was my uncle Ed who first brought me here. He was the one who first showed me my problem and then showed me how to get past it."

Andy Candy could hear the silence, as if the gathering at Redeemer One had caught their collective breath.

"You know Uncle Ed died. You know the police think it was a suicide."

Moth paused. Andy Candy bent to hear everything.

"I don't think so. No matter what they say, I don't think so. You all, everyone here, you all knew my uncle Ed. He stood up here a hundred times and told you how he'd licked his drinking problem. Is there anyone here who thinks he would kill himself?"

No response.

"Anyone?"

No response.

"So, I need your help. Now more than ever."

For the first time, Andy Candy could hear Moth's voice start to quiver with emotion.

"I need to stay sober. I need to find the man who killed my uncle."

These last words seemed high-pitched, as if stretched out and wrung tight before being knotted together.

"Please help me."

She wished she could see the silence in the room, see the reactions on the faces of the people gathered there. There was a long pause before she heard Moth again.

"My name is Timothy and I have fifteen days sober."

She retreated as she heard people begin to clap.

* * *

"How was your night?" Andy Candy asked.

"Okay, I guess. I'm not sleeping great, but that's to be expected. And you?"

"Same."

Moth was about to ask why but did not. He had many questions, not the least of which was why Andy Candy was home when she should have been finishing school. Moth thought he was using up his last bit of reasonable behavior by not asking Andy Candy to share her mystery. He guessed she either would or wouldn't sometime in the future. He told himself to merely be glad—no, *overjoyed*—that she was helping him.

He shifted in the passenger seat. He was nicely dressed—khaki slacks, black and red striped sports shirt—and he had a student's backpack on his lap. Notebooks. Tape recorder. Crime scene reports.

"So, where to first?"

"Ed's apartment. Due diligence." He smiled, before adding:

"Historians like going over and over the same thing. So retrace the cops. Then . . ."

He stopped. *Then* was a notion he wasn't ready to explore. Yet.

9

A Second Conversation

Jeremy Hogan knew there would be a second call.

This belief was not based so much on the science of psychology as it was on instinct honed over years of trying to understand the *why* of crimes instead of the *who, what, where, when* that routinely bedeviled police detectives. *If this killer is truly obsessed with me, he won't likely be satisfied with a single call—unless he has it all planned out, and my next breath is my last. Or close to last.*

He racked through his memory, picturing killers of all stripes. It was a gallery of scars and tattoos, a cavalcade of ethnicity—black, white, Hispanic, Asians, and even one Samoan—of pale men who heard voices and grizzled men who were so cold that the word *remorseless* seemed an understatement. He remembered men who writhed in their chairs and sobbed as they told him why they had killed and men who had laughed uproariously at death as if *nothing* could be a bigger and funnier joke. He could hear echoes of matter-of-fact murder reimagined as littering or jaywalking, reverberating off cinder block cell walls. He could see harsh, unshaded prison lights and gray steel furniture bolted to the cement floors. He could see men who grinned at the thought of their own execution and others who shook with rage or quivered with fear. He remembered men who'd stared at him with an undeniable longing to wrap their hands around his throat, and others who wanted a reassuring embrace and a friendly pat on the back. Faces like ghosts filled his imagination. Some names popped in and out, but most were lost in the flux of remembering.

They weren't important.

What I said or wrote about them, that was what was important.

He took a shallow breath, almost like an asthmatic's wheezy, near-helpless pull at the air, trying to fill stifled lungs.

He admonished himself as if speaking to himself in the third person: *Once you finished your assessment and wrote your report, you didn't think they were worth remembering.*

You were wrong.

One of them is back. No handcuffs this time. No straitjacket. No injection of Ativan and Haldol to quiet psychosis. No heavily muscled armed guard in the corner fingering a truncheon, or watching in an adjacent room on a television monitor. No red panic button hidden under your side of the steel desk to protect you from being killed.

So, one of two things will happen: He will want to kill you right away, because making that first call was the only trigger he needs and he'll be satisfied with getting on with the murder. Or he will want to talk and tease and torture you, prolong the entire performance because each time he hears your uncertainty and fear it caresses him, makes him feel more powerful, more in control—and after he has stretched the limits of your fear, then he will kill you.

He will want to do everything possible to make your death meaningful.

This obvious but subtle observation had taken him several days to reach. But once it flooded him—after his initial fears had dissipated—he knew there was only one real option left to him.

You cannot run. You cannot hide. Those are clichés. You would not know how to disappear. That's the stuff of cheap fiction, anyway.

But you cannot just wait. You're no damn good at that, either.

Help him enjoy your killing. Draw it out and draw him out. Buy yourself time.

That's your only chance.

Of course, he had not decided what he might do with the time he purchased.

And so, he'd taken a few steps to ready himself for the second call. Modest steps—but they gave him a sense of *doing* rather than sitting around patiently while someone planned his death. He made a quick trip to a nearby electronics store to obtain an attachment to his phone, so he could record conversations. This was followed by a second trip to an office supply outlet to acquire several legal tablets of yellow lined paper and a box of Number 2 pencils. He would tape. He would take notes.

The recording device was a stick-on suction cup that picked up both voices in a telephone conversation. It attached to a microcassette recorder. The advantage to the setup was simple: It would not make the ubiquitous beeping sound that legal recordings made.

He wasn't sure what purpose would be served by making a recording. But it seemed like it might be a wise move, and in the absence of any other forms of protection, it seemed to make sense. *Perhaps he'll make some overt, obvious threat and I can go to the police . . .*

Jeremy doubted he would be so fortunate. He assumed the caller would be too smart. *And anyway—what could the cops do to protect me? Park a cruiser outside? For how long? Tell me to get a gun and a pit bull?*

He knew he had great ability to extract information from a subject. This capability had always come easily to him. But he also knew that his examinations had been after the fact—crimes had been committed, arrests made.

He understood crimes from the past. This was the promise of a crime in the future.

Predictions? Impossible.

Regardless, when he sat down at his small desk in his upstairs office, he had a feeling of confidence as he worked out some questions for that inevitable second call. This was frustrating, slow-paced work. He knew he had to do some rudimentary psychological assessments—he had to ask some questions that would ascertain that the caller was oriented to time, place, and circumstances in order to make sure he wasn't schizophrenic and getting homicidal command hallucinations. He already knew the answer to that particular question was *no,* but the scientist in him demanded that he still make certain.

Rule out as many mental illnesses as you can.

But what dragged out his preparation was the realization that he was in uncharted psychological territory.

Danger assessment tools were really designed to help social service systems assist threatened wives to avoid abusive husbands. *Situational context* was crucial—but he also knew that he could comprehend only half of this equation: *mine.* The part that he needed to know was: *his.*

Jeremy Hogan sat in the near dark, surrounded by papers, academic studies, journal copies, textbooks that he hadn't opened in years, and computer printouts of various web pages devoted to risk understanding.

It was night. A single desktop light and his computer screen were the only illumination in the room. He glanced outside his window to take in the sweep of inky isolation that surrounded his old farmhouse. He could not recall whether he'd left any lights on downstairs in the kitchen or living room.

He thought: *I have become an old man. The steady gray fog of aging turns to deep night darkness.*

This was far more poetic than he usually was.

Jeremy returned to his research. At the top of a blank sheet on one of his legal pads he listed:

Appearance
Attitude
Behavior
Mood and Affect
Speech

Thought Process
Thought Content
Perceptions
Cognition
Insight
Judgment

Under ordinary circumstances, these were the emotional domains he would probe before returning a psychological profile. *Of the accused,* he told himself. *But now it's me who stands accused.*

There would be no way to assess *appearance* or anything else that required him to observe the caller in the flesh. So he would be limited to what he could detect from the caller's tone, the specific words he used, and the way he constructed his message.

Language is key. Every word must tell you something.

Thought process is next. How does he construct his desire to kill me? Look for signals that will underscore the meaning of murder to him. When does he laugh? When does he lower his voice? When does he speed it up?

He thought of his assessment as a triangle. If language and thought were two lines, he would need to find a third. That would give him a chance.

Once you know what *he is, then you can start to figure out* who *he is.*

This is a game, Jeremy Hogan told himself. *I damn well better win it.*

He rocked back in his chair, twiddled a pencil in his hand, looked down at his notes, reminded himself to constantly be the part scientist, part artist he believed he was, and found that he wasn't exactly frightened.

Curiously, he felt challenged.

This made him smile.

All right. You've made the first move, Mister Who's at Fault?: a short, cryptic phone call that instantly made me panic like any damn fool who was suddenly threatened. White Pawn to e4. The Spanish Game. Probably the most powerful opening available.

But I can play, too.

Counter with: Black Pawn to c5. The Sicilian Defense.

And I'm no longer panicked.

Even if you do mean to eventually kill me.

When the phone did ring, he was deep in the mixed fog and electric dreams of sleep. It took him several seconds to drag himself from unsettled nether-world into unsettled reality. The ringing insistence of the phone seemed like it should be part of a nightmare rather than wakefulness.

Jeremy took several sharp breaths as he pivoted his feet to the side of the bed. It was cold, but it shouldn't have been.

He inwardly screamed *Composure!* although he knew this was a diffi-cult state to attain. He reached out with one hand for the phone and with the other punched a switch to "record."

The caller ID had read "Unknown Number." A quick glance at a bedside clock told him it was a few minutes after 5 a.m.

Smart, he thought. *He will have been preparing himself for hours, building himself up, knowing he was awakening me and taking me unawares.*

Another deep breath. *Sound dull, befuddled. But be alert, ready.*

He made his voice slow, thick with night. He coughed once as he answered. He wanted to give the impression of age and uncertainty. He needed to sound unsteady and afraid—even decrepit and weak. But he wanted to reply in the same way that he would have years earlier, a physician called in the middle of the night for an emergency. "Yes, yes, this is Doctor Hogan. Who is this?"

Momentary silence.

"Whose fault is it, Doctor?"

Jeremy shivered. He paused several seconds before replying. "I know you believe it is my fault, whatever it is. I should hang up on you. Who are you?"

A snort. As if this question was somehow contemptuous. "You already know who I am. How's that for an answer?"

"Not very satisfying. I don't understand. I don't understand anything, and especially I don't understand why you want to kill me. How long have you been—"

He was interrupted.

"I have been thinking about you, Doctor, for many years."

The reply made him jump.

"How many years is that?"

Damn, Jeremy Hogan berated himself. *Don't be so goddamned obvious.* He listened to the voice on the end of the line. It seemed rough—as if carved out of some frightening memory and sharpened to a point with a dull, rusty knife. He felt nearly certain now that the caller-killer was using some electronic voice-obscuring hardware. *So rule out: accent, inflection, and tone. They won't help you.*

"If I have to die for something I allegedly did . . ."

He restored his own voice to something between irritation and lecture. But as he asked his questions, he listened for the responses.

"*Allegedly* is a great word. It has a nice, lawyerly ring to it . . ."

Jeremy made a note on his legal pad.

Educated.

Then he underlined it twice.

He made a second note:

Not prison-educated. Not street-educated.

He took a chance. "So, you're either a former student or a former subject. What, did I flunk you? Or maybe I wrote some assessment for the court that you think put you away . . ."

Come on. Say something that will help me.

The caller did not.

"What? Doctor, you believe those are the only two categories of people that might harbor ill feelings toward you?"

The caller laughed.

"You must feel you've led an exemplary life. A life without mistakes. Guilt-free and saintlike."

Jeremy didn't have time to reply before the caller added, "I don't think so."

"Why me?" Jeremy blurted out. "And why am I last on some list?"

"Because you were only part of the equation that ruined my life."

"You don't sound like it's ruined."

"That is because I have been successful at restoring it. One death at a time."

"The man who died in Miami, he was a suicide . . ."

"So they said."

"But you're suggesting something different."

"Clearly."

"Murder."

"A reasonable inference."

"Maybe I don't believe you. You sound paranoid, a fantasist. Maybe that death was something you're imagining you had something to do with. I think I should hang up now."

"Your choice, Doctor. Not a wise one, for someone who has spent their life collecting information, but still, if that's what you think will help you . . ."

Jeremy did not hang up. He felt outmaneuvered. He glanced down at his list of psychological domains. *Useless,* he thought.

"And my murder, that will make it complete?"

"That's an inference you are drawing, Doctor."

Jeremy wrote: *Not paranoid. A sociopath?*

He thought: *Not like any sociopath I've ever known. At least—I don't think so.*

"I've called the police. They're all over this . . ."

"Doctor, why would you lie to me? Why don't you make it a better story: *There's cops here now, listening in, tracing this call, and they're going to be surrounding me at any second . . .* Isn't that better?"

Jeremy felt stupid. He wondered: *How does he know? Is he watching me?* A shaft of cold fear dropped through him, and he looked wildly around the room, almost panicked. The caller's steady mocking tones bought him back to the conversation.

"Perhaps you should talk to the police. It will give you a sense of security. Foolish, but maybe it will make you feel better. How long do you suspect that sense will last?"

"You're patient."

"People who hurry to collect their debts invariably settle for less on the dollar than they deserve, don't you think, Doctor?"

Jeremy wrote down: *No fear of authorities.* He thought he should follow up on that.

"The cops—suppose they catch you . . ."

Another laugh. "I don't think so, Doctor. You don't give me enough credit. You should."

Jeremy hesitated as he wrote *Conceited.* He shut his eyes briefly, thinking hard. He decided to take another chance, and to add a slight mocking tone in his own voice.

"So, Mister Who's at Fault, just how much time do I have left?"

A pause.

"I like that name. It's appropriate."

"How much time?"

"Days. Weeks. Months. Maybe, maybe, maybe. How much time does anyone have?"

A hesitation, coupled with that same humorless laugh.

"What makes you think, Doctor, that I'm not outside your door right now?"

And then the line went dead.

10

There was irritating Muzak playing in the elevator as Moth and Andy Candy rode up to the eleventh floor. Both were nervous and the background noise rubbed their thoughts the wrong way. It was an orchestral reinterpretation of some ancient popular rock tune, and both of them hummed along briefly, neither putting a title to the sound.

"Beatles?" Andy Candy asked abruptly. She was on edge, wondering whether she might be tumbling toward obsession along with Moth. When she stole glances in his direction, it seemed as if he wore the look of a mountain climber hanging dangerously from a cliff: desperate not to fall and determined to find a way to lift himself to safety, no matter how frayed his ropes were and how loose the knots holding him in place might be. She could sense wind currents sweeping her along and wasn't sure she should trust them.

"Yes. No. Close. Maybe," Moth replied. "Long before our time."

"But memorable," she responded. "Stones. Beatles. The Who. Buffalo Springfield. Jimi Hendrix. All the stuff my mom and dad used to listen to. They used to dance in the kitchen . . ." Her voice trailed off and she wanted to say, *And now she has to dance alone because he's dead,* but she did not. Instead, she continued, "Now they're just Muzak."

The music distracted Moth. He was unsure how he would react when he saw his uncle's longtime lover. He felt as if he'd completely let everyone down and he was about to be reminded of his inadequacies and failures. But he also didn't know where else to begin his search.

The elevator made a swooshing sound as they reached their floor.

"Here we are," Moth said. Except he knew it wasn't where they needed to be. Andy had said to look where the police wouldn't look—but the only places he could think to start were the same places the police had already considered. *Or trampled,* Moth decided.

"I'm pretty sure it was the Beatles," Andy Candy said, stepping out. Her voice was close to fierce, although she had nothing obvious to be angry about. "'Lady Madonna.' Only screwed up completely with mushy strings and oboes and things."

The door to Moth's uncle's apartment opened before they had a chance to knock. A slight man with sandy hair tinged with gray at the edges smiled at the two of them. But it wasn't truly a smile of greeting as much as an upturn at the corners of the mouth that reflected more pain than joy.

"Hello, Teddy," Moth said quietly.

"Ah, Moth," the man answered. "It's good to see you again. We missed you at the . . ."

He stopped there.

"This is Andrea," Moth continued.

Teddy held out his hand. "The famous Andy Candy," he said. "I've heard about you from Moth. Not much, but just enough, a few years back, and you are far more lovely than he ever let on. Moth, you should learn to be more descriptive." He bowed slightly as he shook Andy Candy's hand. "Come on in." He gestured an entry. "Sorry for the mess."

As they walked inside, they were met with a sheet of bright light. The apartment looked out over Biscayne Bay and Moth could see a huge, un-gainly cruise ship slowly making its way down Government Cut like some overweight tourist, lurching past the high-end, rich folks' playground on Fisher Island. The pale blue of the bay seemed to blend seamlessly into the horizon. The high-rises on Miami Beach and the causeway out to Key Biscayne bracketed the water world. Fishing charters or pleasure boats cut paths through the glistening bay, leaving white foam trails that dissipated rapidly in the light chop of waves. The bright sunshine poured into the apartment through floor-to-ceiling sliding doors that led to a balcony. Moth lifted his hand to shade his eyes, almost as if someone had flashed a light in his face.

Teddy saw this.

"Yeah. Kind of drove us crazy. You desperately want the view, but you don't want to be blinded every morning by that sun coming up in the east. Your uncle tried a bunch of different shades, I mean he must have called up a half-dozen different interior decorators. He got tired of having to recover the couches because they would fade like in minutes. And he had a beautiful Karel Apfel lithograph on the wall that got damaged by the sunlight. Odd, don't you think? The thing that brings us here to Miami causes all sorts of unexpected problems. At least he didn't have to go see a dermatologist and have skin cancers cut off his face and forearms, because for years he liked to take his coffee out onto the porch every morning before heading to work."

Moth looked away from the view toward packing boxes half-filled with art from the walls, kitchen stuff, and books.

"Actually, *we* liked to take our morning coffee out there." This was said with a slight quaver. "I can't stay here any longer, Moth," Teddy said. "Too hard. Too many memories."

"Uncle Ed—" Moth began.

"I know what you're going to say, Moth," Teddy interrupted. "You don't think he killed himself. I have trouble believing that as well. So, in a way, I'm with you, Moth. He was happy. Hell, *we* were happy. Especially in the last few years. His practice was great; I mean, he found his patients to be intriguing, interesting, and he was helping them, which is all he ever wanted. And he didn't care who knew about me—which is a big deal for shrinks, let me tell you. He was just so happy to be *out*, you know. We'd both known so many guys who couldn't reconcile who they are with family, friends, their work . . . Those are the guys that drink themselves to death—which is what Ed was doing so many years ago—or drug themselves or shoot themselves. All the guys who get overwhelmed by a lie that becomes their life. Ed was at peace—that's what he told me, when . . ."

He stopped.

"*When, when, when,* Moth. What a fucking lousy word."

Teddy hesitated before continuing. "But then, Ed always had a mysteriousness about him, an inscrutability, as if there was something clicking and connecting behind his head and heart. I always loved that about him. And maybe that was what made him good at what he was."

"Mystery?" Andy asked.

"It's not uncommon for guys like us. Living unhappily for so long, hiding truths that should be obvious. Gives you a sense of depth, I think. Lots of self-flagellation. It's sometimes worse than that. Torture, really."

Teddy stopped to think for an instant, then said, "I always thought that was what we had in common and that's what pushed both of us to drink. Hiding. Not being who you are. So, we got sober when we met and became who we really are. Armchair psychology, but that's the way it was."

Another pause.

"That wasn't your story, was it, Moth?"

Andy Candy craned forward, waiting for the response.

"No," Moth said. "I would get angry and drink. Or I would get sad and drink. I would do well and reward myself with a drink. Or I would fail, and punish myself with a drink. Sometimes I couldn't tell whether *I* hated me more or *others* hated me more, and so I would get drunk so I wouldn't have to answer that question."

"Ed said his brother put unreasonable . . ." Teddy started, then stopped.

Moth shook his head. "The trouble with binge drinking is that all you need is the simplest of excuses. Not the most complex. And that's the problem. Psychologically speaking, of course. Same armchair you just mentioned."

Teddy pushed a stray lock of hair out of his eyes.

"More than ten years," he said, turning to Andy Candy. "We met at a meeting. He got up, said he had one day, then I got up, said I had two dozen, and afterward we went out for coffee. Not very romantic, is it, Andy?"

"No. It doesn't sound that way." She nodded. "But maybe it was."

Teddy laughed weakly. "Yes. You're right. Maybe it was. By the end of the evening we weren't two drunks nursing lukewarm lattes, we were laughing at ourselves."

She glanced at a wall. A large black-and-white photo of Ed and Teddy, arms casually tossed across each other's shoulders, was the only thing remaining. There were other hooks, but what photos they held had been removed.

Moth was fidgeting slightly, shuffling his feet. He was afraid his voice would crack, especially if he allowed himself to look around again and see his uncle's life packed into boxes.

"Where do I look, Teddy?" Moth asked.

Teddy turned away. He rubbed his hand across his eyes.

"I don't know. But I don't exactly want to know. Maybe I did at first. But not now."

This surprised Andy. "You don't want . . ." she started, but Moth interrupted:

"Tell me something I don't know about Uncle Ed."

His voice was edgy and demanding.

"That you don't know?"

"Tell me a secret. Something he hid from me. Tell me something different from what the cops asked. Tell me something that you don't understand, but seemed odd. Out of place. I don't know. Something outside the understandable, ordinary world that wants Ed's death to be a nice, neat, *sorry, too bad* suicide."

Teddy looked away, out the doors and over the expanse of blue waters. "You want answers . . ." he started.

"No. It's not answers I'm looking for," Moth said quietly. "If it was as simple as a single answer, it would be a question already asked. What I want is a push in some direction."

"What sort of direction?"

Moth hesitated, but Andy Candy jumped in: "A direction of regret."

Teddy looked askance. "I don't know what you mean."

"Uncle Ed made someone angry," Moth said. "Angry enough to kill him and stage a suicide, which I don't think is all that hard. But it will have to be someone from some life that we don't expect, not the life we all knew Ed was leading now. Ed had to know—on some level, somewhere, that there was someone, somewhere, out there . . . ," Moth pointed beyond the picture windows, ". . . gunning for him."

Teddy paused, and Moth added, "And why would he keep a gun in his desk and then use some other gun?"

"I knew about that gun—the one he didn't use."

"Yes?"

"He was supposed to get rid of it. I don't know why he didn't. He said he would, took it with him one day like years ago, and then we never spoke about it again. I just assumed he'd dumped it or sold it or even just gave it up to the police or something until the cops that came here asked me about it. I think maybe he put it in that drawer and forgot about it."

Moth started to ask another question, then stopped.

Teddy made a gesture with his lips, as if Moth's words were hot and he could feel them. Teddy was a small man with a delicacy that made talking about murder seem alien. "If someone was angry at Ed, you will have to keep going back in time to before I met him and we got together."

Moth nodded.

"I wanted to help, you know. I wanted to be able to tell the cops—look at this guy, look at that guy, find me the guy who killed Ed. Bring me his damn head on a platter. But I couldn't find anyone."

"Do you think—" Moth started, but was interrupted.

"We talked," Teddy continued. "We talked all the time. Every night. Over the fake cocktails we would mix up for each other—lime juice and bubbly water on the rocks in a highball glass with a little paper umbrella stuck in it. We talked at dinner and in bed. I've racked my memory, trying to remember any moment he came home scared, uneasy, even feeling threatened. Not once. Not one moment where I said to him, 'You should be careful . . .' If he were afraid, he would have said something. I know it. We shared everything."

Another deep sigh and long pause.

"We had no secrets, Moth. So I can't tell you any."

"Shit," Moth blurted out.

"Sorry," Teddy said.

"So, before he met you?" Andy asked.

"I would imagine so. That's ten years."

"So, we can rule out the ten years you two were together, you think?" Andy persisted.

Teddy nodded his head. "Yes. Correct. But it will be hard," he said. "You will have to go over the hidden parts of Ed's life and go back and back."

Moth nodded. "I'm a historian. I can do that."

This might have been bravado. Moth considered what a historian actually does. Documents. Firsthand accounts. Eyewitness statements. All the collected information that can be pored over in quiet.

"Did he leave notebooks, letters, anything about his life?"

"No. And the cops took his patient files. Assholes. They said they would return them, but . . ."

"Shit," Moth repeated.

"Have you seen his will?"

Moth shook his head.

Teddy laughed, not with humor, but in understanding. "You'd think that your dad, Ed's big brother, would have filled you in. Of course, he's probably pissed."

"We don't really talk."

"Ed didn't speak much to him either. They were fifteen years apart in age. Your dad was the top gun. Your dad is the big tough he-man. Full-contact sports and full-contact business. Ed was the *queer*." This notion made Teddy almost giggle.

Moth heard the rapid description of his estranged father and thought, *That's true.*

"Anyway, Ed was the accident," Teddy continued. "Conception, birth, and every day from then on, that's what he liked to say. Proud."

Andy heard the word *accident* and imagined that it somehow should mean something to her. *I had an accident except it wasn't an accident, it was a clumsy, stupid mistake. I let myself get raped by some guy I didn't even know at a party I shouldn't have been at, but then I killed it.* She turned away to regain the composure that had just slid away from her.

Moth felt himself fill with questions, but he asked only one more. "What are you going to do now, Teddy?"

"That's easy, Moth. Try not to fall off the wagon. Even though I might want to."

He reached into his pants pocket and pulled out a plastic container of pills, holding them up like a sommelier examining a wine bottle label. "Antabuse," he said. "Nasty stuff. Nasty drug. It'll make me sick, and I mean really sick, if I start to drink. Never tried it before. Ed was always into *We have the strength to do this ourselves*—you know that, Moth. But now Ed's gone, goddamn it to hell."

Moth pictured his uncle, still alive, seated at his desk. Moth could see a gun in front of him, and he could see Ed reaching down to the drawer where the second gun was hidden. *Makes no sense.* He was going to say this but as he was about to, he saw tears in Teddy's eyes. And Moth stopped himself.

"Sorry, Moth," Teddy said. His voice quivered, a tuning fork reverberating with loss and sadness. "Sorry," he said a second time. "None of this is easy for me."

Andy Candy thought that was a significant understatement.

"Go away, Moth. I don't want to speak with you."

"Please, Cynthia. Just give me a minute. A couple of questions."

"Who's she?"

"This is my friend Andrea."

"Is she a drunk, too?"

"No. She's helping me out a little. She does the driving."

"Lost your license again?"

"Yes."

"Pathetic. Do you like being a drunk, Moth?"

"Please, Cynthia."

"Do you have even the vaguest idea how many people you've hurt, Moth?"

"Yes. I do. Please."

Hesitation.

"Five minutes, Moth. No more. Inside."

Andy Candy was slightly taken aback by the staccato hostility in Moth's aunt's voice. Every word seemed spoken with black charcoal and burning cinders. She trailed a little behind Moth, who was hurrying to keep pace with his aunt, who marched through the vestibule of the house with military determination.

It was a three-story stucco home—rare enough in Miami—in a southern part of Dade County, surrounded by tall stately palms, manicured lawns, a bougainvillea-adorned walkway, and money. The flat white interior walls were crowded with Haitian art—large, wildly colorful representations of jam-packed markets, weather-beaten fishing boats, and floral designs, all with a homespun, rustic character to them. Andy knew they were valuable; folk art that was exploited in the high-end Miami art world. There were modern sculptures—carved dark woods, mostly free-form, in every corner. The corridors of the house shouted contradictions of creativity and rigid order. Everything was carefully in place, arranged precisely to look magazine-photograph beautiful, make a statement about elegance. Cynthia was dressed to blend in with the high style. She wore a loose-fitting, off-white, silken pair of slacks and matching blouse. Her Manolo Blahnik shoes made tapping sounds against the imported gray tile floors. Andy Candy thought the jewelry around Cynthia's neck was worth more than her mother the piano instructor made in a year.

Moth politely asked, "How is the art business, Cynthia?"

Andy Candy thought the answer was obvious.

Moth's aunt didn't even look back as she replied. "Quite good, despite the overall economy. But Moth, don't waste your five minutes asking me about my business."

There was a man seated in the living room on an expensive white, hand-made cotton couch. He stood up as they entered. He was a few years younger than Moth's aunt, but equally stylish. He was dressed in a nar-row, tight, shiny sharkskin gray suit, bright purple shirt, four buttons open to a hairless chest. He wore his long blond hair slicked tightly back. Andy Candy saw that the man had put white highlights in his hair, the way a fashion model might. Aunt Cynthia walked straight to his side, slid her arm under his, and eyed Moth and Andy Candy.

"Moth, maybe you recall my business partner?"

"No," Moth answered, extending his hand, even though he did. He had met the man once before, and known instantly that he handled Aunt Cynthia's business ledgers and sexual desires, probably with the same degree of extraordinarily cool passion and competence. Moth instantly pictured the two of them together in bed. *How could they fuck without mussing their hair or disrupting their carefully applied makeup?*

"Martin is here in case some legal matter should arise in the next . . . ," Cynthia looked down at the Rolex on her wrist, ". . . four remaining minutes."

"Legal?" blurted Andy Candy.

Cynthia turned coldly toward her.

"Perhaps he didn't bother to inform you, but Moth's uncle and I did not split up on the best of terms. Ed was a liar, a cheat, and despite his profession, a harsh, thoughtless man."

Andy started to reply, but then thought better of it.

Cynthia did not offer a seat to either Moth or Andy Candy as she slumped into a modern leather chair that Andy thought looked more uncomfortable than standing. Martin moved behind her, and placed his hands on her shoulders, either to hold her in place or give her a back rub. Either, Andy imagined, was possible.

"Okay," Moth said. "I'm sorry you think that. Then I'll get right to it . . ."

"Please," his aunt said with a small, dismissive hand gesture.

"In the years that you and Uncle Ed were together, did you ever hear him say he felt threatened, or that someone might want to hurt him, or come seeking revenge of any kind . . ."

"You mean other than me," Cynthia said. She laughed, although it wasn't funny.

"Yes. Other than you."

"I was the one hurt. I was the one he cheated on. I was the one he walked out on. If there was anyone with a reason to shoot him . . ."

She stopped. Then she shrugged, as if it meant nothing.

"The answer to your question is: No."

"In all those years . . ."

"Let me repeat myself: No."

"You mean," Moth started, but she cut him off with another wave of her hand.

"I suspected there were people that he met in his secret life—the one he tried to hide from me—that maybe, I don't know, hated themselves or him or whatever and might have been capable of pulling a gun out and shooting themselves in some drunken bout of self-pity. And sometimes I imagined when he was drinking hard, and disappeared for a couple of days, that maybe something awful had happened to him. But it wasn't likely that some other repressed and closeted gay man that he met in some bar somewhere decided to stalk him years later. Of course it's *possible* . . ." she said, shrugging once again to indicate with body language and tone of voice that it wasn't actually *possible*. "But I really doubt it. And no one ever tried to blackmail him, because that sort of payment would have come up in the forensic analysis of his finances that I had done when we were divorced. And he never came on to some psychotic killer, like in *Looking for Mr. Goodbar*—there's a book you've probably never heard of but was very popular once upon a time—you know, tried to hustle some guy who decided instead of fucking him to kill him. I worried about that for a little bit. But not really."

"So, no one . . ."

"That's what I said."

"Can you think of anyone . . ."

"No."

"In his profession or socially . . ."

"No."

She made another dismissive wave of the hand as if she could simply sweep any uncomfortable memory aside.

"You probably misunderstand something, Moth," she said briskly. "I have nothing against homosexuals—indeed, many of the people in my profession are gay. What angered me was that Ed lied year in, year out, every day we were together. He cheated. He made me feel as if I was worthless."

Andy Candy heard this and wondered how anyone could get something so right and so wrong at the very same instant.

Moth paused. In that brief moment, Cynthia pushed herself up out of the lounge chair.

"So, Moth, as interesting as this little retrospective of my ex-husband's life might be"—Andy Candy recognized this statement for the noblesse oblige sort of lie it was—"I think I've just about answered all your questions, or at the very least all the questions I care to answer, so it is time for you to leave. I think I've already been more generous than I should have been."

Andy Candy shuffled her feet. She did not like Moth's aunt, and told herself to keep her mouth shut, but was unable.

"What about before?"

"Before when?"

"Before you two got together . . ."

"He was a resident at the university hospital here. I was a doctoral candidate in art history. Mutual friends introduced us. We dated. He told me he loved me, but of course that wasn't true. We married. He lied and cheated for many years. We divorced. I don't recall us speaking much about our respective pasts, although if he thought there might be someone waiting around to kill him sometime in the distant future, he would have mentioned it."

Andy knew this too was a lie. It was a lie designed to chop the conversation with the efficacy of a butcher's knife.

"Well, who might know . . ."

Cynthia stared at Andy Candy.

"You want to play at amateur detective. You figure it out."

There was another moment of quiet before Andy Candy let slide, "It doesn't sound like you ever loved him."

"What a stupid and childish statement," Cynthia replied brusquely. "Do you know anything about love?"

She did not wait for an answer, but pointed toward the front entranceway.

Moth spoke quickly. "Cynthia, please. Did he ever say anything, like he was guilty about something, or something happened that troubled him, or anything that you thought was out of place or unusual or wrong? Please, Cynthia—you knew him well. Help me out here."

She hesitated.

"Yes," she said, suddenly brusque. "He was troubled by many things in his past, any of which might have killed him. That's true for all of us."

She waved her hand dismissively.

"One, two, three, four, five. Your time is up, Moth. And you too, miss whatever your name is. Martin will show you out. Please don't call me again."

In the car, Andy was breathing heavily, each gasp ripped from the hot air as if she'd run a race or swum underwater for a great distance. She felt as if she'd been in a fight—or, at least, what she believed a fight would feel like. She almost started to check her arms for bruises and to move her jaw as if it had absorbed a punch. She glanced toward the front of the house and saw Martin the accountant love-slave standing dutifully in the doorway to make absolutely sure they departed promptly. She resisted the temptation to give him the finger. "I wanted to slug her the whole time," she said. "I should have slugged her."

"Have you ever slugged anyone?"

"No. But she would have made a good first."

Moth nodded, but seemed as if a pall had fallen over him. All he could think about was how hard and sad so many years had been for his uncle.

Andy saw the cloud gathering over Moth.

"One more stop today," he said. "I wished we'd learned something by now."

Andy Candy hesitated before replying.

"I'm not sure we didn't," she said, stringing negatives together into a positive. "I've got to think about it a little more, but it seems to me that she told us what we needed to know."

Moth nodded. He stiffened in his seat.

"Bookends," he said abruptly. "One person who loved him. One person who hated him. And then me, the person who idealized him."

"So," Andy Candy said with a wry smile. "Now we go talk to the person who understood him."

Andy thought about what they'd just said. *Love. Hate. Idealized. Understand.* A few other words would fill out the portrait of Ed Warner that they needed.

She put the car in gear.

There are some people, Moth thought, *who sit behind a desk and create an impenetrable wall of authority and there are others for whom the desk-barrier is barely there and almost invisible.*

The man across from them seemed to fit in the latter category. He was an athletic man, with thinning brown hair that fell across his forehead and poked up in back in a cowlick, making him seem younger than his fifty-plus years. He had the habit of constantly adjusting his glasses on the tip of his nose. He wore a neck strap around the spectacles, so occasionally the doctor dropped them to his chest completely, made a point, then lifted them again and replaced them haphazardly, often slightly askew.

"I'm sorry, Timothy, but I don't know how much I can help you and Miss Martine in your inquiries. Patient-physician confidentiality and all that."

"Which doesn't survive a patient's death," Moth said.

"You sound like an attorney, Timothy. That is true. But that would also mean that you had placed a subpoena on my desk, which you have not. As opposed to merely arriving here to ask questions."

Moth realized right then he should be careful.

He also realized he had no idea what being careful would mean. So he began with the question that he'd already asked twice that day.

"Do you know of anyone, did my uncle ever mention anyone, who might hold a grudge or some sort of long-term anger—you know what I'm driving at, Doctor—that finally boiled over?"

The psychiatrist paused before answering, in much the same way that Ed Warner would.

"No. I can think of no one. Certainly not anyone that Ed mentioned in our years of therapy."

"You would recall if . . ."

"Yes. Any element of a conversation that implies a threat is one that we take very good notes on, both for the obvious reason—we want to be sure of safety—and also because how people respond to either real or perceived external dangers is a crucial element of any therapeutic situation. And not to mention that we just might have an ethical obligation to inform the police authorities."

He smiled. "Sorry. I sound like I'm giving a lecture."

The doctor shook his head. "Let me be simpler. No. Did I imagine Ed was ever in danger? No. His risky early behavior, the drinking and anonymous, unprotected sex—that might have created something, I don't know what. But that ended some time ago. He was here merely to understand what he'd gone through, which was a lot, as you know."

"Do you think he killed himself?" Andy blurted.

The psychiatrist shook his head. "I have not seen him in years. But when he completed therapy, there were no suicidal indications whatsoever. Of course, as the police who came to speak with me so quickly pointed out, he would have been more than capable of concealing his emotions, even from me, although I don't like to think so."

This was *cover your ass* talk from the doctor, Moth thought.

The doctor paused again, then added:

"You knew him well, Timothy. What do you think?"

"No fucking way," Moth replied.

The psychiatrist grinned.

"The police like to look at facts and evidence and what will fly under oath in a court of law. That's where they routinely find their answers. In this office, and in your uncle's, the investigation is far different. And for a historian, Timothy?"

"Facts are facts," Moth replied, smiling. "But they slip and slide and change over years. History is a little like wet clay."

The doctor laughed. "Very apt," he said. "I believe so, too. But it is not so much that the facts change as much as it is our perception of them."

The doctor picked a pencil off his desk. He tapped it three times, then started to doodle on a pad.

"He wrote 'My fault' on a paper . . ." Moth started.

"Yes. That troubled me," said the doctor. "It's an intriguing choice of words, especially for a psychiatrist. What do you make of it?"

"It's almost as if he was answering a question."

"Yes," said the doctor. "But was it a question that *had been* asked or was it one that he expected *to be* asked."

The doctor scratched his pencil hard against the pad, making a black mark.

"In the study of history, Timothy, how do you examine a document that might tell you something about your subject?"

"Well, context is important," Moth said.

But what Moth was thinking was: *Place. Circumstances. Connection to the moment. When Wellington muttered "Blucher or night . . ." it was because he understood that the battle hung in the balance at that precise second in time. So, Ed writes "My fault" because those words have a bigger context right then.*

"I have another question," Moth said.

The doctor didn't reply, other than to lean forward slightly.

"Why would Ed own two guns. Or even one gun?"

The therapist's mouth opened slightly. He seemed to think for a moment.

"Are you sure?" he asked.

"Yes."

Another silence.

"That is troubling," the doctor said. "Unlike Ed." He seemed to think hard—as if the two weapons seemed to represent some facet of personality that he'd failed to explore. "And the note—the 'My fault'—where precisely was that on the desk?"

Moth had not thought about this. He replied slowly, cautiously. "Just a little to the left of center. I think."

"Not to the right?"

"No."

The doctor nodded. He reached out, grabbed a prescription pad, held his hand over it as if he was about to write something. Then, he looked down, pointing. "But it was over here . . ." He gestured at the opposite side of the desk. "Perhaps that means something. Perhaps it does not. It is curious, however."

He looked at Andy and then to Moth.

"I think you will need to be more than curious," he said.

This statement seemed to indicate that the interview had ended, as did the doctor's pushing back in his chair.

Andy Candy had been quiet, listening.

"If not exactly who, then what was Ed afraid of?" she asked.

The doctor smiled.

"Ah, a clever question," he said. "Despite his education and training, like many addicts and alcoholics, Ed feared his past."

Andy nodded.

In Shakespeare, she thought, *there are Seven Ages of Man, from infancy to childhood and on to old age and extreme old age. Ed never made it to that stage and the first two are probably hidden, even for a historian like Moth. So, look to the stages where Ed became an adult.*

"Do you know why he came to Miami?" she asked.

The doctor paused. "Yes," he said. "At least perhaps in part. He spent many years fleeing from who he was, trying to escape his family, who had insisted on his medical education taking place amidst all the trappings of prestige that only the Ivy League and similar institutions provide. Timothy, I suspect, is familiar with this pressure. His marriage was the same picture—do what others expect of you, not what you want. This is not that unusual in Miami. I know we're a great place for refugees from all over the world. But don't you think we're an equally good spot for emotional refugees?"

Andy saw Moth lean forward. She recognized the look. *He sees something,* she thought. At least, this was what she *hoped* she saw in his face.

11

Student #5 was on the back deck doing early morning yoga exercises when the bear walked through the rear of the yard. He froze in position so not to startle the animal, holding a pose called *falling butterfly*. He could feel his stomach muscles tighten with exertion, but he refused to lower himself even to the worn wooden floor. The beast would be alert to any odd noise or telltale motion.

The bear—four hundred pounds of lumbering black bear with all the grace of an old Volkswagen Bug—seemed intent on finding a fallen tree and scraping out an *I've just awakened from winter hibernation and I'm damn hungry* appetizer of grubs and beetles, then probably moving back into the thick trees and scrub brush that bordered on Student #5's modest riverside property to find a more significant meal.

An easy shot, he thought. Just inside the house was a Winchester 30.06 deer rifle. *But it would have to be a kill shot. Heart or brain. Big animal. Strong. Healthy. More than capable of running off and dying slowly in the deep woods where I couldn't track him down and put him out of his misery.* He was reminded of the U.S. Marine Corps sniper mantra: *One shot. One kill.*

He was tempted to lower himself to the deck and crawl to the weapon, draw a bead, and fire. *Good practice.*

He watched as the bear inspected and rejected a few of the rotting opportunities, wearing what Student #5 considered a look of bear-frustration coupled with bear-determination. Then, with a visible shrug that seemed to make every inch of luxurious midnight-colored fur twitch, the bear wandered off into the woods. A few bushes quivered as the animal passed by and disappeared. Student #5 thought it was as if the weak, gray, early morning light had enveloped the bear and cloaked him in fog. The dark forest that rose behind stretched for miles, though steep hills and empty onetime logging lands, now set aside for wildlife preserves. His house— actually a ramshackle double-wide trailer perched on cinder blocks with a small wooden deck built off the tiny kitchen—was barely a hundred yards from a bend in the Deerfield River, and the early day hours trapped all the cool night moisture that gathered above the waters.

He listened carefully for a few moments, hoping to catch a fading bear sound—but he could hear nothing, so he lowered himself to the deck. He breathed out sharply, thinking it was like being underwater. He looked out at the backyard area, trying to spot some residual sign of the bear's morning intrusion, but there were none, save for a few damp streaks in the dew where paws had been set down.

He smiled.

I'm the same sort of predator, he thought, *hungry, finished with hibernation, only a lot more lean and a lot more focused. And my tracks fade just as quickly as his do.*

I'm the same sort of predator.

Patient.

In the kitchen behind him an old-fashioned windup alarm clock rang. *End of exercise time.* Student #5 lifted himself up and stretched a little bit before he hustled back inside to dress. Even in a world that bordered on ancient, where a bear was his neighbor, Student #5 prided himself on organization. If he set aside forty-five minutes for physical fitness, then forty-five it was. Not one second less. Not one more.

By mid-morning he was folding donated clothes and stacking canned foodstuffs at a combination Salvation Army outlet and attached free food pantry on the outskirts of Greenfield in a sad strip mall that featured a Home Depot, a McDonald's, and a boarded-up space that had once housed a bookstore that had gone out of business. He volunteered at the outlet whenever he arrived in Western Massachusetts. There were pockets of poverty throughout the rural area he lived in, and the small city had been hard hit by recessions and tough economic times.

To his coworkers he maintained the fiction that he worked at the VA hospital twenty miles away making beds and emptying bedpans—but his enthusiasm and hard work habits kept anyone from asking too many questions. He was always willing to lift some heavy furniture or climb a ladder to reach higher shelves.

From time to time, Student #5 would pause in what he was doing and examine the people who came into the store. There were occasional undergraduates from local colleges looking for bargain winter clothing, and there were other young people who found "secondhand" to be chic, but for the most part there were people to whom the words *hard times* were worn like so many worries lining their faces. These people interested Student #5.

Shortly before his lunch break, Student #5 saw a woman enter the large, warehouse-style building. He wasn't sure exactly what there was about her that attracted his attention—perhaps it was the seven-year-old child in tow, or the slightly confused look on the woman's face. He watched her as she hesitated, just inside a wide set of glass doors. He thought the woman was holding her daughter's hand to steady herself, as if the child was propping her up instead of the other way around.

He was in the men's clothing section, hanging donated suit coats on racks, making sure that price tags were attached to the out-of-style, worn jackets and slacks. There were many odd sizes—anything in a commonplace 42 regular or long was thoroughly dated, with wide lapels and off-putting colors. The suit coats and slacks that were modern tended toward sizes that wouldn't fit anyone save the cadaverously thin or the dangerously obese.

He watched the woman and her child go to the adjacent children's section. He thought she was strangely beautiful—a fashion model's high cheekbones and a haunted look in her eyes—and the child impressively cute in the irrepressible way that children manage to combine shyness with excitement. The child pointed at a colorful, pink sweater that had a dancing elephant embossed on it and the woman glanced at the price tag and shook her head.

Just the act of saying *No* seemed to hurt the woman.

Never thought this would happen to you, he thought. *So, you are new to the world of belt-tightening and unpayable bills. Not much fun, is it?*

Student #5 was about ten feet away, so he barely had to raise his voice.

"We can lower the price," he said.

The woman turned to him. She had deep blue eyes and sandy-colored hair that seemed to him to be as untamed as the thickets behind his trailer. The child was a mirror-copy of the mother.

"No, it's okay, it's . . ." The woman's voice trailed off into the echoes of *Please don't ask me to explain all the reasons I'm here.*

Student #5 smiled and walked over to them. He held out his hand to the child. "What's your name?"

The child tentatively shook his hand. "Suzy," she said.

"Hello, Suzy. That's a pretty name for a pretty girl. You like pink?"

Suzy nodded.

"And elephants?"

Another nod.

"Well, I promise you, Suzy, you're the only young woman we've had in here in weeks that likes both pink and elephants all at the same time. We've had some young women who prefer pink, and we've had a couple who seem to like elephants, but we've never ever ever had someone who likes both."

Student #5 took the sweater from the rack. The yellow price tag read "$6." He took a large black flow pen from his shirt pocket, and crossed out the number and replaced it with "50 cents" and pushed the sweater into the little girl's arms. Then he reached into his pants pocket and pulled out his wallet. He handed Suzy a dollar bill. "Here," he said. "Now you can buy it for yourself, because I really like elephants and I adore that color, too."

The mother stammered, "Thanks, but you don't have to . . ."

He shook his head to cut her off.

"First time here?" he asked.

"Yes."

"Well, it can be a little overwhelming at first." When he used the word *overwhelming* he wasn't thinking about the size of the store. "Do you think you need some groceries, too?"

"I shouldn't, I mean, we're fine . . ." She stopped abruptly, shook her head. "Groceries would be helpful," the woman said.

"I'm Blair," Student #5 said, pointing to a name tag on his shirt that displayed his Western Massachusetts alias.

"I'm Shannon," the woman said. They shook hands. He thought her touch was delicate. *Poverty is always soft,* he thought, *filled with doubts and fears. When you have a job, that's when your grip gets firm.*

"Okay, Shannon and Suzy, let me show you how to maneuver the food pantry. All the stuff there is free—if you can make a contribution, they like that, but it's not really necessary. Perhaps sometime in the future you can come back and make a donation. Follow me."

He leaned down toward the child.

"Do you like spaghetti?" he asked.

She nodded, ducking partway behind her mother's leg.

"Pink. Elephants. Spaghetti. Well, Suzy, you've come to the right place."

Leading the woman and child, he steered them toward the foodstuffs, found a small basket for them to place items in, and walked them down the aisles. He made sure they took two large cans of premixed spaghetti and meatballs.

"Thank you," Shannon said. "You've really been kind."

"That's my job," Student #5 replied cheerily. *Not really,* he thought.

"I'm going to get back on my feet soon," Shannon continued.

"Of course you will."

"It's just things have been . . ." She hesitated, searching for the right word. "Unsettled."

"That's what I would have guessed," Student #5 said. He let a small silence prompt her next reply. *It's remarkable what a little bit of quiet can prompt,* he thought. *I would have been an excellent shrink.*

"He walked out on us," she said, a tinge of bitterness coloring her words. "Cleaned out the bank account, took the car, and . . ." She stopped. He saw her bite down on her lip. "It's been hard," she said. "Especially on Suzy, who doesn't really get it."

"Up at the registers," he said, "they have a list of the state and local social service agencies that can help you. They have counselors. They're really capable. See one. Talk to them. It will help, I promise."

She nodded. "It's been, I don't know exactly . . ."

"But I do," he said. "Stress. Depression. Anger. Sadness. Confusion. Fear. And those are just for starters. Don't try to handle it alone."

When they reached the register, Suzy proudly handed over her dollar bill and carefully counted her two quarters in change. Student #5 reached behind the counter and took a printed sheet of paper from a box. It listed all the numbers for help and names of therapists willing to do pro bono work. He handed it to the mother.

"Make a call," he said. "You'll feel better when you do."

You always feel better when you directly address the root causes of your problems, he told himself.

At the front door, he waved as mother and daughter walked toward a bus stop.

They are the people I was once upon a time destined to help, he thought. *Until all that was taken away from me.*

He glanced around to make sure no one was near enough to overhear him, then he whispered out loud, eyes boring in on the disappearing pink sweater: "Bye-bye, Suzy. I hope you never come this close to a killer again."

12

I looked like a foolish and scared old man, but that was the only choice I had.

When the phone line went dead in the middle of the night, Jeremy Hogan had assumed the man who wanted to kill him *was* right outside his house, and so, acting with all the crazed organization of a person who awakens to the word *Fire!* he'd rushed downstairs to his living room and pulled a single armchair over against a back wall to create a flimsy barricade. He had huddled behind the chair, eyeing every entrance to the room, mostly concealed from a large picture window that he'd instantly assumed would let a killer stare into his home and watch his every motion.

He'd seized a cast-iron poker from the fireplace and braced himself, ready to spring out and assault the murderer he was absolutely certain was coming through the front door at any second. He'd listened intently for a sound—a window breaking, a door lock being sprung. Footsteps. Labored, murderous, Hollywood horror film heavy breathing—anything that might tell him he was about to come face-to-face with the mysterious man who wanted him dead. In his erratic thinking, he'd believed that the killer would know how to bypass the cheap alarm system on the house and that a deadly confrontation was not only inevitable but seconds away. He'd figured he could get in a few swings with the fire poker before dying.

Go down fighting, he repeated like a mantra.

He'd stayed, terrified, frozen in position, until morning light crept in through the window and he'd realized that he was still alive and alone.

His hand was cramped. He looked down at his fingers, clutching the poker handle. They were frozen, and it was difficult to pry them loose.

The poker clattered to the floor, falling from his grip. The noise startled him, and he bent down quickly and retrieved it. He carried it with him, like some hussar with a dueling sword.

"What makes you think I'm not outside right now?"

Jeremy replayed the killer's words. He wondered how carefully they were chosen.

How much of an expert at terror is he?

Jeremy had never experienced this sort of sudden panic before. Images of disaster flooded him: a fireman hearing the sound of ceilings collapsing; a shipwrecked sailor clinging to a piece of debris on an empty, gray, stormy sea; a bush pilot clutching the yoke as the engines behind him cough and fail.

It all left a bitter, dry sense in his mouth as he asked himself: *Did you just survive something? Or did you merely get a taste of what's to come?*

The words he formed in his head seemed to him as if he were speaking them out loud, hoarse, voice cracking, tortured.

More likely the taste, he acknowledged.

As sunlight flooded the old farmhouse, Jeremy found he was still quivering, hands shaking, muscles taut. He wanted to crouch behind every chair or couch, hide in every closet or beneath every bed. He felt like a child awakening from a nightmare, a little unsure that the sleep terrors had truly fled.

He moved gingerly across the room, an old man's measured gait. He clung to the side of the picture window, moving a curtain back so he could peer out.

Nothing. A typical sunny morning.

He maneuvered quietly into the kitchen and stared through the windows above the sink, back across the flagstone patio where his wife would paint, over the small lawn, toward undeveloped conservation land. Each stand of trees, each clump of shrubs tangled together could conceal a killer. Everything that was once familiar and now seemed dangerous.

He asked himself: *How can you tell if someone is watching you?*

Jeremy did not know the answer to that question—beyond the clammy, raw, heart-racing sensation he felt inside—and he realized he'd better come up with one, and soon. He went to the stove and made himself a cup of coffee, hoping it might settle his stretched nerves.

After a moment, he lurched unsteadily back to his office, clutching his steaming cup in one hand and the fireplace poker in the other. He plopped down behind his desk, and grabbed all his papers and research and started scribbling notes, trying to recall details, wondering why they were so elusive. He was exhausted and felt oddly filthy, as if he'd been working in his garden. He knew he was pale. He knew he was sweaty. He ran a hand through tousled hair, rubbed his eyes like a child awakening from a nap.

Did you hear enough to answer another question?

He felt his backbone go rigid.

What question is that, Doctor?

The dialogue in his head echoed.

Are you about to die, or are you going to get another call?

Jeremy Hogan stayed seated. He was not aware how long he remained in place, pondering this. It was as if the open-endedness of his situation, the uncertainty of what he was caught up in was alien, foreign to him. It was like standing on a street corner in some unknown country, hearing a language he couldn't understand, clutching a map he couldn't read. He felt now that he was lost. He pictured the same panicked fireman that had come to his mind earlier—only this time it was his own face he saw hugging the ground, choking down breaths of air, surrounded by explosions and bursts of flames. *No way out.* What's the solution?

Give up.

Or:

Don't give up.

He asked himself whether he could find a way to stay alive, or even if he wanted to.

I'm old. I'm alone. I've had a good run. Done some pretty interesting things, gone to a few unusual places, accomplished much. Had some love in my life. Had some truly fascinating moments. It's been—on balance—pretty damn good.

I could just wait and embrace this killer when he arrives.

"Hi. How yah doin'? Say, could you make this quick, 'cause I hate wasting time."

After all, how much time would he actually be stealing? Five years? Ten? What sort of years? Lonely ones? Years where age steals more and more every passing day?

Why bother?

Jeremy listened to this conversation as if he were seated in an academic auditorium watching a debate on some esoteric subject. *The cons have it; you should just die. No, the pros have it; fight to stay alive.*

He took an unsteady, deep breath. It almost made him dizzy.

But this is my home, and I'll be damned if I'll just let some stranger . . .

Jeremy stopped this thought midway.

He stared at the coffee cup and fireplace poker in front of him. He grabbed the cast-iron poker, spilling the coffee. Then Jeremy stood up and swung it violently in the air in front of him, slashing away at an unseen assailant.

He imagined the weight crashing into human flesh. Coming down hard on a skull. Breaking bones. Slashing skin.

Good, he thought. *But not nearly good enough. You won't be able to get that close.*

If you do, then you are probably already murdered.

He knew he needed help making a choice, but wasn't exactly sure how to ask for it.

Two other men were walking slowly in front of a glass countertop, quietly inspecting the rows of weapons in the case. He presumed everyone coming into the store knew more than he did. On the wall hung at least a hundred rifles and shotguns, each anchored by a steel cord. Each gun seemed more lethal than the last.

It was not a big store—the few aisles were crammed with hunting clothing, predominantly in varieties of camouflage or the electric-orange hue that was designed to prevent some other hunter from mistaking one for a deer. High-tech bows and arrows were on display, along with glassy-eyed, wall-mounted deer heads. Each of the heads sported impressive antler arrays but Jeremy knew nothing about the points on the antlers, the height of the shoulders. He did know enough to find something ironic in the idea that the more prominent a deer got in his own world, the more vulnerable it made him in another.

Jeremy almost laughed out loud. This was a psychiatrist's observation.

Stifling this inner joke, Jeremy walked up to the counter. A single clerk was stacking boxes of ammunition as he helped one of the two other customers, who hefted a wicked-looking black pistol with obvious admiration. The clerk was a middle-aged man, buzz-cut and significantly overweight, with a "USMC" tattoo prominent on a forearm the size of a ham hock. He wore a shoulder harness with a semiautomatic pistol butt protruding and a gray T-shirt that had an old National Rifle Association cliché printed on it in fading red: "If you outlaw guns, only outlaws will have guns."

"Help you with something?" the clerk asked not unpleasantly, looking up.

"Yes," Jeremy answered. "I think I am in need of some proper home protection."

"Everyone is in need of proper home protection these days," the clerk said. "Got to keep you and yours safe. What did you have in mind?"

"I'm not at all sure . . ." Jeremy started.

"Well, you already have an alarm system on the house, right?"

Jeremy nodded.

"Good," said the clerk. "Dog?"

"No."

"How many folks in the house with you? I mean, kids, grandkids visit much? Wife? Does her book group meet at your place? Do you get lots of deliveries from FedEx? Just how much traffic at the front door is there?"

"I live alone. And no one visits any longer."

"What sort of house? What sort of neighborhood? Where's the closest police station?"

Jeremy felt as if he was being cross-examined. The two other shoppers, both now holding unloaded guns, stopped and listened in.

"I live out in the country. It's pretty isolated. Old farmhouse near a wildlife preserve. No real neighbors to speak of, at least none within a couple of hundred yards and none that I'm real friendly with, so no one just drops by. And I'm set pretty far back from the road. Lots of trees and bushes—makes it all scenic. You can barely see my place from the roadway."

"Whoa," said the clerk, grinning. He half-turned toward the other two shoppers, who both nodded. "That's not good. Not good at all." He emphasized the last two words like a teacher might in a grade school classroom. "If the shit hit the fan—if you'll pardon my language—you're on your own, completely. Well, damn good thing you came in here today."

The clerk seemed to assess Jeremy's homestead as he would a potential battlefield. "Let's talk about threats," the clerk said. "What specifically do you think might happen?"

"Home invasion," Jeremy said quickly. "I'm an old guy living alone. Pretty easy target, I'd think, for anyone."

"Do you keep valuables or piles of cash in the house?"

"Not really."

"Uh-huh." The clerk nodded. "But, I'm guessing the place looks pretty nice. High- class. What do you do for a living?"

"I'm a doctor," Jeremy said. "A psychiatrist."

The clerk made a wry face. "Don't get many shrinks in here. In fact, don't think I've *ever* sold a gun to a shrink. Orthopedic guys, yeah. All the time. But not one of you. Is it true you can listen to some dude talk and tell what they're really thinking?"

"No," said Jeremy. "That would be mind-reading."

"Hah!" The clerk laughed. "I bet you can. Anyway, you got a nice car?" This was posed as a question.

"It's outside. BMW."

"Well, that's like posting a big old neon sign outside saying, 'I'm a rich guy,'" chimed in one of the other shoppers, a younger man, long greasy hair pulled back in a ponytail, wearing a Harley-Davidson leather jacket above jeans and a neck tattoo only partially obscured by the collar of his coat.

The clerk smiled.

"So, really what you're saying to me, Doc, is that you live in a nice place, where you're probably surrounded by a bunch of stockbrokers and housewives who do real estate on the side and you give off the look of someone who just might be an easy score."

"Okay," Jeremy said. "True enough. What do you think? A shotgun? A handgun?"

"I think both, Doc, but it's your money. How much do you want to spend for peace of mind?"

Neck Tattoo leaned forward as if interested. The other shopper had turned away to examine other handguns.

"I think I should just listen to the professional," Jeremy said. "Given my situation, and if cost isn't a concern, what would you recommend?" The gun clerk smiled.

"For the shotgun, either a Remington or a Mossberg. Not too heavy. Short barrel for use in close quarters. Simple, efficient mechanism. Won't jam. Won't rust. Can take a lot of combat abuse."

"I've got a Mossberg," Neck Tattoo added. "It's also got a very cool attachment for a flashlight, which is really helpful." He didn't say *why* it was helpful. This seemed obvious.

The clerk nodded. "True. Six- or nine-shot models. And, I think, to really be effective, you should pair that up with a Colt Python .357 Magnum revolver. Put in wad-cutters. Stop an elephant in its tracks. The Cadillac of handguns."

Neck Tattoo started to speak, and the clerk held up his hand. "I know, I know. More rapid firepower with a Glock Nine or a .45." He smiled. "But for this gentleman, I think old-fashioned, easiest to use, just point and shoot and not worry about fumbling around with a clip and chambering a round, that makes the most sense."

The clerk turned back to Jeremy. "A lot of folks see the cops on TV or in the movies and they always use semiautomatics, so that's what they want. But a damn good pistol, I mean, a quality gun—hell, you can drop it in the mud or use it as a hammer when you're doing your weekend chores, and it's still gonna work just fine. That's what I'm guessing will fit you best."

Jeremy followed the clerk down a flight of stairs into the basement along with the two other shoppers. There was a makeshift firing range below the store, with a pair of shooting galleries. The clerk set up the first of the other men, handing all of them ear protectors and boxes of ammunition. Within seconds, the other man was in a slight crouch, expertly aiming and then opening up with a semiautomatic pistol at a target barely forty feet away. A makeshift pulley system ran along the ceiling and there was a built-in table and a single sheet of drywall material that separated the two ranges. The rapid fire from the semiautomatic was deafening, and Jeremy adjusted his pair of ear protectors. They muffled some—but not all—of the reports.

The clerk was yelling instructions, first for the Mossberg 12-gauge, then for the pistol. Loading. Stance. Grip. He gently maneuvered Jeremy into position.

Jeremy snugged the shotgun tightly up against his shoulder. Positioning, the clerk yelled above the incessant explosions coming from the adjacent gallery, was crucial. Jeremy could barely hear, "You don't want to fracture that shoulder!"

The clerk tugged on the pulley system and sent a black-and-white bull's-eye target down to the back wall, in front of a pile of sandbags. Jeremy eyed the target. The shotgun, snugged up against his shoulder, felt like a sudden extension of his body, as if it was screwed into him. In that second, as his finger closed around the trigger, Jeremy felt younger, as if years had fallen from his body. He suddenly felt *equal*. He sighted the target, took a breath, held it as he'd been instructed, and fired.

The weapon kicked back. It was like being punched by a professional boxer, or having the wind knocked out of him. But these sensations fled when he saw that the target had been shredded.

He cocked the weapon, ejecting the spent cartridge, and fired again.

This time the blast seemed more familiar.

He pumped the action confidently, another shell clattered to his feet, and he fired a third time.

The target was almost destroyed. It hung from an old-fashioned clothespin and twisted about, even though there was no breeze in the basement firing range.

"Not bad," Jeremy said. "Worth every penny." He felt a little like a child emerging from a roller-coaster ride. He wasn't sure that the clerk could hear him, so he smiled triumphantly. "Now let me try the handgun."

The clerk handed him the pistol.

In the adjacent gallery, the shopper with the semiautomatic he had no intention of buying paused to reload. He stole a glance at the target blasted into confetti by the shotgun next to him.

Nice shot, Doctor, Student #5 thought. *But you won't get that chance. That's not how this is going to play out.*

He confidently slapped in a full clip as he had done hundreds of times before and fought off the nearly overwhelming urge to laugh out loud because the man just on the other side of the flimsy barrier hadn't recognized him, not even when they'd stood just paces apart. The idea that he'd been able to follow his target right to a gun shop, walk in just behind him, and now was only feet away while the last man on his list uselessly fired a live weapon in the wrong direction was delicious.

You could just turn ninety degrees, Doctor, and solve your dilemma right here, right now. He raised the weapon and aimed. *Of course, so could I. But that's far too easy.* He fired and clustered four shots dead center in his target.

13

The two of them were aware the toxicology report was negative. But typed words on a paper form weren't the same as knowing firsthand. Moth had directed them to the street in front of the high-end hotel.

"Are you sure?" Andy Candy said. "I can go in, ask around. You stay here in the car."

She suddenly believed that part of her job was protecting Moth from Moth. This was a new realization that had just taken root within her.

"No. I have to do it," he replied.

"Okay. Then we'll go in together."

He didn't disagree.

She saw that Moth was already quivering slightly when they entered the hotel's bar. It was dark inside, low light, welcoming textures, soft jazz playing in the background, the sort of place that combined fancy with familiar, paddle fans circling slowly, mirrors, comfortable leather-bound chairs, and low-slung tables. The bar itself was a deeply polished, glistening mahogany, smooth to the touch. Rows of expensive liquors were lined up against the wall, like soldiers on parade. It was a sophisticated place, where the martinis were shaken in gleaming containers and poured into chilled cut-glass goblets with a flourish. It was not the sort of bar where one ordered a Bud Light. It was a spot where wealthy folks came after big deals and celebrated, or where sports stars bought high-priced escorts to sit behind roped-off security barriers and flash jewelry and cash, but without the hype and energy of a South Beach nightclub. Andy Candy knew immediately if she'd asked for champagne, the bottle would be Dom Pérignon.

It was—Moth told her—where Ed had nearly drunk himself to death. He had pointed the bar out to his nephew once, driving by slowly and saying, "Who really wants to die in the mud and dirt with a bottle of rotgut? Might as well go out on silks and diamonds, waving a magnum of Chateau Lafite Rothschild."

Moth and Andy Candy were immediately out of place.

They walked up to the bar uncomfortably. Tending the bar were two young men wearing bow ties, probably a few years older than Moth, and a woman wearing a tight white cotton shirt that was cut low enough to show off an ample cleavage. One of the men rapidly approached them.

"Kind of a dress code in here, guys," he said in a not unfriendly way. He leaned forward. "And it's expensive. Like way expensive. Black-card expensive. There's a pretty nice sports bar two blocks away that's more for college-age types."

Andy Candy leaned forward. Moth seemed tongue-tied, staring at the arrays of liquors.

"Not drinking," she said. "Just a quick question or two and then we're out of here."

She smiled, trying to be as attractive and enticing as possible.

"What sort of questions?" the bartender asked, a little taken aback. "You don't work for TMZ or some sort of gossip site, do you?"

"No," Andy said quickly, waving her hand and shaking her head. "Not anything like that."

"Well?"

"Our uncle . . ." she guessed it would be easier if she adopted Ed as a relative, ". . . has gone missing. Many years ago, this was his absolute number one favorite place. We're just wondering if anyone had seen him in the last month or so."

The bartender nodded. He was experienced at the notion of *missing* and what it really meant. "Got a picture?"

Moth handed over his cell phone, which was opened to a recent photo of a grinning, poolside Ed Warner. The bartender stared at it for a moment, shook his head, then gestured to the other two behind the counter. The three of them craned over the picture.

Three shrugs.

"Nope," the bartender said.

"He would have been drunk," Andy said quickly. She could feel Moth stiffen beside her. "A drunk psychiatrist. And probably not a quiet drunk, either."

Again the bartender shook his head. "One of us would remember," he said. "And one thing you really get to know back here," he added, gesturing the length of the bar. "Faces. Preferences. Regulars. That's part of the drill in serving up drinks. As soon as that first taste of fifty-year-old Scotch hits the lips, no one is a stranger. Even in here. And when folks have too much . . . Well, let's just say we're very discreet. But we remember."

He smiled. "Now, about that dress code . . . *Business casual,* they call it, and you guys . . ."

Andy Candy took Moth by the elbow. "Thanks," she said.

She steered Moth back through the entrance. She felt like some rehabilitation nurse helping a soldier who'd lost a leg in war take a tentative step on a prosthetic device. Moth had not spoken inside.

"I think I need to go to Redeemer One," was all he said.

She hummed familiar lyrics: *If you got bad news, you wanna kick them blues . . .*

It was Susan Terry's habit to arrive at Redeemer One a few minutes after each meeting had begun. This was a curiosity to her—she was doggedly punctual for any prosecutorial conference or court session. But the addiction meetings at the church triggered such complicated feelings within her that she invariably shuffled her feet outside before heading in.

Delay wasn't her usual style.

Impulsive was.

It was the most difficult part of her addiction, she thought, harnessing desire and compulsion—just enough so that she did not indulge in the cocaine she adored, but still had some leftover ferocity for arguments in courtrooms and processing crime scenes. She sometimes wished that she could be just *a little bit* addicted. That might have kept her happy, married and not alone.

She stood by the door to her car. Often in Miami the first few hours of night seem weakly apologetic, as if unsure about replacing the brilliant blue skies of day. She waited a few minutes, watching the other meeting regulars enter the church doors. She was parked near the back, deep in shadows, almost hidden. The church parking lot lights stopped a good two dozen feet from where she had parked. This was antithetical thinking: Most women knew instinctively to pull in close where the lights were strong and where no lingering, faceless threat—even in a church lot— could hide. It was as if Susan enjoyed daring some ski-masked rapist to jump out of the bushes at her.

Defiance and *risk* were another two words that she thought fit her.

Architect. Engineer. Dentist. She watched the others heading into the meeting. Most had a quick pace, bounding up the front steps. They all were feeling the same thing, she realized: *a need to release that big insistent voice held fast deep within.* She kicked at some loose gravel by her feet and watched a pebble nearly strike a tiny lizard, which fled instantly into a nearby tree stump.

She had lost that morning.

Lost, of course, didn't really describe the cascade of emotions that accompanied certain court defeats. Throughout the day she'd had the sensation that she had exited some terribly dire theater, where, as in *Hamlet*, everyone was dead onstage at the end. It had been the denouement of an awful case. A thirteen-year-old boy—fuzzy-cheeked, his voice barely changed—had shot and killed his father with the old man's prized Purdey shotgun. The gun was a $25,000, custom-made-in-England weapon that was supposed to be used in the rubber boot and tailored tweed pursuit of game birds on high-roller ranches and farms set aside in Texas or the Upper Peninsula of Michigan. It wasn't supposed to be used for murder.

At the family's mansion in the exclusive, gated Cocoplum section of Coral Gables, she had been distracted by an uncontrollably sobbing wife and a terrified younger sister who kept screaming over and over in a keening, high-pitched voice, like a record needle stuck in a groove. In the chaos, Susan had failed to realize that two detectives had taken the teenager into a side room and were questioning him aggressively. Far too aggressively. They'd read the juvenile killer his Miranda rights, but should have waited until some responsible adult was able to accompany him. They did not. They'd simply launched into one of the oldest tricks in the police detective's arsenal: *"Why'd yah do it, kid? You can tell us. We're your friends and we're just here to help you. Your dad, he was clearly a bad guy. Let's get it all straightened out right now, and then we can all go home . . ."*

Right. Fat chance.

It was a fine legal line and the detectives had not just crossed it, but trampled on it.

They had seen *killer*. The legal system saw *child*.

That was the precise distinction she had been on the scene to identify and the exact problem she had been there to avoid and she had failed. Dramatically.

So a judge in circuit court that morning had tossed out the kid's cold confession, even though one of the detectives had dutifully videotaped it. And without that confession, proving what had actually happened that deadly night *beyond a reasonable doubt* was going to be hard, if not impossible.

The mother wouldn't testify against her son.

The sister wouldn't testify against her brother.

The whole family's fingerprints were on the Purdey shotgun.

And she knew that the high-priced criminal defense attorney engaged by the family had lined up a series of teachers, psychologists, and school friends—all of whom would happily describe in sympathetic detail the relentless terror that the dead father had brought to that house.

And then that defense attorney would tell a jury it was all an accident. Tragic. Regrettable. Sad. Terrible even. But when all was said and done, an accident.

"The father was beating the mother as he had done a hundred times before and the son tried to threaten him with the shotgun to make him stop. Defending his mother. How sweet. How noble. We'd have all done the same thing. The poor lad, he didn't even know it was loaded, and it went off . . ."

A powerful argument to a deeply moved jury—who would not see the coldness in the son's eyes, nor the glee in his voice as he described patiently hunting the father through the many rooms of the house in much the same way the father had probably used the shotgun to stalk grouse in the fields. He'd ambushed the father in the study when the mother was nowhere near.

Money can't buy you love, Susan said to herself, echoing another song.

Especially when there's a serial abuser involved, she thought. *The dead man might have been a prominent, fabulously wealthy businessman with a big Mercedes and a powerboat tied to his private dock, on every local board, lending his name to every local good cause and needy charity—but he liked to use his fists on his family.*

Fuck him.

And now the kid's going to get away with killing him.

Fuck the kid.

And just maybe fuck me, too.

At the very least, she knew she was due a real chewing-out. At the worst, she'd be spending a couple of months handling DUI cases in traffic court.

She hated complicated crimes. She liked simple ones. Bad guy. Innocent victim. *Bang.* Cops make an arrest. Here's the gun. Here's the confession. An efficient lineup of reliable witnesses. Plenty of forensic evidence. No problems. Then she could get up in a courtroom and point her finger with all the self-righteousness of some outraged Puritan staring at an accused witch.

But even more, she hated losing, even if in losing there was some measure of justice, as there had been that day. And when she lost, especially when she'd been humiliated, she invariably felt the tug of *need*. Cocaine instantly replaced defeat and helped her soar back into the necessary compulsion of being a prosecutor.

When your day is done and you wanna run . . .

So, on this night of failure that obscured truth, she was back at the AA meeting. Susan Terry sighed, thought she'd delayed long enough, started to hum the refrain, *She don't lie, she don't lie, she don't lie . . .* and emerged from the shadows. "Damn it to hell," she said out loud, still thinking of the courtroom that morning. "It was all my fault." The words *my fault* made her pause, because just at that moment she saw Moth hurrying toward the front door of Redeemer One.

Moth was already speaking when Susan slipped quietly into one of the chairs near the rear of the room, hoping that no one noticed her tardy entry. It did not take her long to realize he wasn't talking about drink or drugs.

"Hello, I'm Timothy, and now I've got twenty-two days without a drink . . ."

Soft applause. Murmured congratulations.

"And I'm more convinced than ever that my uncle didn't kill himself. I've been all over his life, and there's nothing suicidal there."

The room grew quiet.

Moth looked around, trying to measure in the eyes of the people in the room how they would react to what he was saying. He knew he should speak carefully, render his words and phrases organized and precise. But he was unable, and feelings tumbled from him like pearls from a broken strand.

"We all know—even me, and I'm the youngest here—what has to happen in order to make that last decision. The *I can't go on any longer* decision. We all know the hole you have to fall into and the one you know you can't climb out of. We all know the mistakes that are necessary . . ."

He emphasized the word *mistakes* because he knew that everyone in the meeting would understand everything that was connected to that single word. *Despair. Failure. Drugs and booze. Loss and agony.* He paused again. Everyone in that room had probably imagined killing themselves even if they had not precisely said the word *suicide* out loud. "And more than almost everyone, we know what goes into that choice."

Moth thought that everything he said had created a slight wind in the room, like an air current, cold, direct on the face. *What do I know more than anything else about my uncle?* Moth asked himself. *The Ed I knew hated secrets. He hated lies. He'd put them all behind him.*

He looked around. The entire point of being in that room right at that moment was to leave deception and dishonesty behind.

"It's not there. Not for Ed. Not in the last few days. Not in the last few weeks. Not in the last few months or years. That leaves only one logical conclusion. It's the same one I reached the minute I sobered up after his death."

He looked around.

"I need help."

When he said *help,* it was as if the room stiffened. Everyone was familiar with the sort of *help* that the meetings typically offered. But Moth was asking for something different.

The meeting slipped into silence. Susan Terry tried to assess the responses of the other addicts in the room to Moth's declaration.

"So, you tell me," Moth said cautiously, "where do I look for a killer?"

Again there was silence, but it was broken when the engineer leaned forward.

"When did he start drinking? I mean, really drinking . . ."

"About three years after he launched into his bad, dumb-ass marriage. He thought he needed a cover-up, or maybe he thought he could not be gay if he was married and he was lying to himself and everyone else about who he was. His practice was starting up, and things should have been great, except they weren't . . ."

"So," the engineer said, "that was when he started to kill himself."

This was a harsh assessment. But accurate.

"And then," the engineer continued, "he stopped trying to kill himself and came here."

"That's right," Moth said.

The philosophy professor half-stood, then sat down and spoke in a determined voice, waving his arms theatrically to underscore his points. "If you go back—to when Ed first became a drunk like me or you or most of the people here—well, why would someone need to kill a person who was doing it to themselves so efficiently?"

A murmur of agreement.

"So, the only way a homicide makes sense today is if the reason for it transcends Ed's drunken days. Sobriety, his life now—all that accomplishment and success—that has to be an affront. A challenge. I don't know, but for someone, it had to be a lot more than just *wrong*," the professor continued.

"Not a robbery. We know that. Not a suicide. That's what you're telling us. Not a family dispute or a sex thing. No triangle of jealousy. Those have all been ruled out. Not money or love. They're off the table. What does that leave you?"

The dentist raised his hand to interrupt. He seemed excited as he rubbed his hands together.

Moth turned to him. He was a slight fellow, with a terrible comb-over and like many in his profession, well versed in suicide. Now he was nodding his head up and down fiercely, and he blurted out: "Revenge."

"That's what I was driving at," said the philosophy professor.

Susan Terry sat ramrod-straight in her chair. Everything she heard seemed half-crazy, half-criminal. She thought she should shout out, tell everyone they were being stupid, it was a closed case and they shouldn't let their imaginations run away with them, shouldn't let Moth's imagination push their own into fantasy.

There were dozens of warnings, denials, objections she wanted to scream. *Why are you all being so stupid?* She glanced over at the dentist. He was smiling, and now he was shaking his head, but not in the way one does if he disagrees—more as one does when he sees some great irony. "I read a lot of mystery books," he said. There was a little laughter, then silence crept into the room again.

"So do I," said the professor finally. "I just don't let the other department faculty know."

There was another low series of voices as the folks at Redeemer One bent heads together. *Revenge* wasn't a word anyone had ever uttered in that setting.

"But for what?" Moth asked.

Again there was silence. Then the well-coiffed lady banker-lawyer spoke softly.

"Who did your uncle hurt?"

They all knew that the lists of people *they* had hurt were extensive for each of them. But quiet dominated the room.

The lady lawyer lowered her voice, but everyone at Redeemer One could hear her clearly: "Or maybe," she said slowly, forming a sentence into what Moth believed was a question, "he did something worse?"

14

Standing beside his next victim had been intoxicating.

Risky—but well worth the thrill: like driving a car too fast on a wet highway, feeling the wheels slipping against the pavement, then magically regaining purchase.

Student #5 was back in Manhattan, at his own desk, less than five hours after watching the newly well-armed Jeremy Hogan pull out of the gun shop parking lot. *Sometimes,* he imagined, *murder seems predestined. It was serendipity that I saw my target exiting his home, good fortune I was able to follow him unobserved, blind luck that he chose to go to the gun store, and then beating the greatest of odds when I stood within arm's reach and went unrecognized.*

He smiled, nodding his head. *This death will be special.*

He loved the danger. *Connect more,* he insisted to himself. *Even if every time raises the threat of detection.*

He had to stop his hand from reaching for his telephone, gathering the small attachment that electronically altered his voice, and dialing Doctor Hogan's number.

Wait. Savor.

Rocking back in his seat, then standing and pacing about his apartment, clenching his hands together, then releasing them, shaking his wrists, as if he could loosen his body, Student #5 warned himself not to get carried away.

Stick to the plan.

Every battle is won before it is fought.

Student #5 kept quotations from Sun Tzu's *The Art of War* on cards that he posted on a bulletin board next to his desk.

Pretend inferiority and encourage your enemy's arrogance.

If you are near your enemy, make him believe you are far from him. If you are far from the enemy, make him believe you are close.

Attack him where he is unprepared. Appear where you are not expected.

It was important not just to know what routes Jeremy Hogan traveled, the hours he kept, the behaviors he couldn't change no matter how much he might want to, but also to be able to anticipate how the doctor might find the emotional strength to *try* to alter familiar patterns in an effort to elude the person hunting him down. He did not believe Jeremy Hogan would be successful at this. People rarely are, he knew. They cling to established patterns because those are psychologically reassuring. In the face of death, people glue themselves to what they know, when in fact what they don't know is closing in on them.

These were all observations he'd gleaned from his studies. They dated back to the days when he believed he was destined to be a doctor of the mind.

Who would have thought that the psychology of killing would be so close to the psychology of help?

He had fought off the temptation to assist the old man out to his car with his brand-new collection of guns and ammunition. It would have been a friendly, neighborly offer—but Student #5 knew he had already risked enough, just in trailing the doctor to the gun store and following him inside. He'd made no effort to try to change his voice when he had asked the proprietor for a weapon to try, subtly watching to see if the word tones might trigger a memory—and then recognition—in the old doctor.

He'd seen none.

He'd expected none.

It made him even more confident.

What great camouflage age is: Add a few crow's-feet and deepen the jowls, put in a touch of gray against the temples, wear glasses to make it seem as if the eyes are weakening—and memory deceives us.

Context, too, was important. The doctor who had betrayed him once when he was young wasn't able to recognize that the nice adult thirty years later holding the store's door wide for him as he struggled with his purchases was the man who was going to kill him.

Because he never considered that I would be right there at that moment.

Sometimes the best mask is no mask at all.

A sudden curiosity overcame him, and Student #5 started to rummage around in his desk drawers, until he came across a small, red-leather-embossed picture album. He flipped it open. There he was, graduating from high school, and then a similar shot—arm in arm with his parents—when he completed college. Grins of accomplishment and black academic robes. Innocence and optimism. These were followed by a couple of bare-chested beach pictures, some candid snapshots of Student #5 with girls whose names he couldn't recall or friends that had faded from his life completely.

He felt a momentary twinge of anger.

Everyone is happy when you are normal.

Everyone hates you when you are not.

Really, they fear you, when it is you that has everything to fear. People don't understand: As you lose your mind, you can also lose your hope.

He took a deep breath. Memory blended with sadness, which re-formed into rage, and he gripped the edge of the desk, steadying himself. He knew that when he allowed the past to intrude on what he was planning—even when it was the past that had created the need—it muddied things.

No one ever came to visit me in the hospital. It was like I was contagious. No friends.

No family.

No one.

My madness belonged solely to me.

There were no pictures from those hospital months, and none taken after he was released. Then he flipped the pages to the picture he knew was the last in the album, but the most important. It had been taken in the quadrangle outside the building that housed the medical school's Department of Psychiatry. Five smiling faces. Everyone wearing the same uniform: white lab coat and dark slacks or jeans. They had linked arms around each other.

He was in the center of the photo.

Were they already planning to ruin my career?

Did they know what they were doing to my future?

Where was understanding? Sympathy?

His hair was unkempt, tangled, a long mess, his look furtive behind the smile. He could see how little sleep he'd had, how many meals he'd skipped. He could see how stress was pulling him across hot coals and plunging him into freezing waters. His shoulders slumped. His chest was sunken. He looked slight, weak—almost as if he'd been beaten up or lost a fight. Madness could do that, just as effectively as cancer or heart disease.

Why did I smile?

He stared at the look on his face. He could see hurt and uncertainty behind his eyes.

This pain was truth.

Their embrace, friendly looks, wide, happy smiles, and camaraderie—those were all lies.

Student #5 removed the photo from the glassine sheaf that held it. He reached out and seized a red marker from his desktop. Holding the marker in his hand like a knife, he rapidly drew an X through each face—including his own.

He stared at the defaced snapshot, then walked swiftly into the kitchen. He found a box of wooden matches in a drawer and went to the sink and struck a light. He let the flame curl over the edge of the picture, holding it sideways, bending it so that the flame would envelop the image before he dropped it into the stainless steel basin. He watched the photo crinkle, blacken, and melt. *Now, all the people in that picture are dead,* he thought.

Killing is making me normal.

Then he waved his hands above the sink.

He didn't want the smoke to set off an alarm.

15

Unsettling dreams and night sweats filled Andy Candy's sleep.

Her waking hours—the ones spent apart from Moth—were riven with doubts. She was suddenly immersed in doing things that might be very wrong, and might be very right; it was hard for her to tell. Complicating matters for her was a residual fury that would overcome her at odd moments, when least expected, during which she would find herself picturing what had happened, trying to ascertain the exact moment when she could have changed everything.

There were times when she thought:

I died that night.

The music had been loud. Brutally loud.

Unrecognizable tunes. Incomprehensible rap lyrics that were about pimps, whores, and guns. Bass heavy, hard-driving, throbbing. Ear-splitting. So loud she had to shout to be heard even an inch or two away and her throat had become raw almost instantly. The frat house had been jam-packed. Even moving a few feet one way or the other had been difficult. The heat had been overwhelming. Sweat, slurred words, gyrating bodies, lights that flickered on and off, red lamps that glowed. Plastic glasses filled with beer or wine being passed overhead. The air was thick with cigarette and marijuana smoke, which mingled with body odors. Occasional shouts, roars of laughter like waves, even screams that might have been joy and might have been panic blended with the relentless music. Hard liquor was swigged from dozens of bottles, shared right and left, guzzled like water.

Not knowing where her date was, she'd fought her way to a side room, hoping to find a little space amidst the press of bodies so she could breathe, all the time telling herself, *Get out of here now because the cops will surely be here soon,* but not listening to her own good advice. The side room was also packed, but the students were jammed back against the walls, creating a small empty space in the center—like a gladiatorial arena. She'd craned her neck to see what everyone was looking at, and as she did this, she heard a wild and unrestrained moan, which was absorbed by cheers, like at a sporting contest.

In the center, a completely naked, heavily muscled boy was sitting on a steel folding chair. His legs were spread wide. She remembered he had a tattoo on one arm—the clichéd Tribal Armband favored by the kids lacking imagination, or else too stoned or too drunk to consider something original when they stumbled into the tattoo artist's parlor. She had stared at the tattoo for a moment, before focusing on the boy's erect organ. It was impressive, and he held it like a sword.

In front of him was a naked girl.

She was dancing, twisting her body provocatively, inches away from the boy who'd moaned.

Andy Candy hadn't recognized her.

As muscular as the boy was, the girl—no more than nineteen or twenty—was statuesque. Flat stomach, large breasts, long legs, and a great mane of dark hair that she shook in time to some inner rhythm. She waved a bottle of Scotch in one hand, poured some of the booze down her chest, licked it from her fingers, then thrust her hips forward as if asking everyone watching to admire her sex, her shaved pubic region. The crowd cheered as she filled her mouth with liquor, then dropped to her knees in front of the boy—gracefully, Andy Candy had thought then, maybe even athletically. She lowered her mouth, letting Scotch dribble from her lips, then pulled back, teasing. The boy had moaned again, straining with his erection toward her. The girl, playing to the crowd, pointed to the erection, then to her lips, as if asking a question. A cheer went up. Cries of *Yes!* and *Do it!* thickened the air. Another frat member circled around the couple, handheld video camera in his hand, getting a close-up as she waved to the crowd like a politician acknowledging a cheering mob, then pitched forward and seemed to swallow the boy whole. This went on for a few seconds, her head moving up and down rhythmically as she fellated him, before she leapt up. She faced the crowd—about two-thirds boys, but a number of young women, too—and bowed. A performance artist. With a flourish, cupping her arms behind her head to display her coordination and strength, she abruptly turned around, and slowly lowered herself onto him.

Her face broke into a smile, and she issued a long *Ohhhhh.*

The young woman had turned to the frat boy with the camera and made a kissing shape with her lips. She was making love more to the crowd and camera than to the muscled boy behind her.

Each thrust, each gyration, raised another wild cheer. People started to clap in time to each up-and-down movement.

Andy Candy had turned away from the show before completion. She wasn't a prude—she'd been to enough out-of-control parties in her college years, and she'd seen sexual spectacles before—but this night there was something in the sweaty abandon she'd seen that unsettled her. Perhaps it was the idea that what should have been intimate and private was being displayed so theatrically. She had wondered if the straining erection and the shaved sex even knew each other's names.

When she turned away, she'd caught sight of the boy who'd ostensibly invited her to the party. He fought his way toward her, glanced over her shoulder, and caught a glimpse of the action in the side room.

"Whoa," he'd exclaimed. "That's intense." His face broke into a grin.

He was a nice enough fellow, she thought, seemed polite, attentive. Sensitive, even. He'd shared his notes on Dickens with her after she'd missed the class on *Great Expectations* with a touch of stomach flu. He came from an expensive suburb. His father was a button-down corporate lawyer and divorced from his free-spirit mother, who now lived with her new family on an avocado farm in California. He'd taken her to dinner once, not a pizza place, but a Chinese restaurant where they'd sat and enjoyed *moo shu* and talked about a writing course they planned to take in the last semester of their senior year. He said he liked poetry. He'd given her a small kiss when he'd dropped her off, and asked her if she might want to go to a party that weekend. Little details—all seemingly benign, and none of which really amounted to who someone was.

"I want to leave," she'd said.

"Yeah. No problem. We'll get out of here. Things might be getting out of hand. But you look like you can use a bit of something strong first."

She'd nodded.

Was that where she went wrong? No. It was going to the party in the first place.

"Here, take mine. I'll get another. It's too hard to fight your way to the bar."

Mine. That's what he'd said. But it wasn't his. It was always for me and me alone.

He'd handed her a large plastic cup filled with ice and ginger ale mixed liberally with cheap Scotch. The same brand probably that the naked girl was drinking.

I hate the taste of Scotch. Why did I take it? Trust.

She'd ignored the first rule of college parties: *Never drink anything that you haven't seen opened and poured.*

She didn't connect the slightly chalky taste with anything suspicious, and certainly not the GHB that liberally laced the drink.

She had gulped it down.

Thirsty. I shouldn't have been so thirsty. If I'd only taken a modest little sip, then handed it back.

The date had smiled.

Rapist. What does a rapist look like? Why don't they wear a special shirt or have a special mark? A scarlet R, maybe. Maybe they should sport a scar or a tattoo—something so I could have known what was going to happen to me after I passed out.

"Okay," he said. "Well fortified. You look a bit pale. Come on—I put your coat upstairs in my room. Let's get it and get the hell out of here, maybe go get a cup of coffee someplace."

No coffee. There was never going to be any coffee.

It took a few minutes to work their way through the throngs, and she was already dizzy by the time they reached the stairs. The music seemed to have gotten louder, all guitars and shrieks and drums pounding out a violent backbeat.

"Hey, you okay?" the nice-guy date asked midway up the stairs.

Solicitous but not surprised. That should have told her something.

"A little woozy," she said. "Feel a little weird. Must be the heat going to my head."

She'd slurred her words, but she wasn't drunk. She remembered that detail afterward.

She'd steadied herself with the handrail.

"You need some fresh air," he said. "Here, let me help you."

Nice. Polite. Gentlemanly. Thoughtful. *He said he liked poetry.* He took her arm to help her, except they were heading upstairs, not outside.

She knew she needed the air.

She didn't get any. Not for some time.

I should have turned him in. Called campus security. Filed a complaint. Gone to the police. Hired a lawyer.

Why didn't you?

I don't know. I was lost. I was confused. I didn't know what happened to me.

And so, you let him off the hook.

Yes. I guess so.

* * *

This, too, she remembered: nausea overcoming her in the morning. Violent, dizzying, gut-wrenching nausea. And then again—the same sickness repeated, slightly more than a month later.

And one additional memory: the nurse at the clinic kept calling her *dear* as she helped her up and fitted her onto the examination table. The instruments were stainless steel, but glistened so brightly she imagined she might have to shade her eyes. They had knocked her out with anesthetics, and told her she wouldn't feel any pain.

Physical pain, that is.

The other kind was constant.

The guilt made her cry. Less as the days went by, but she could still feel her eyes filling at what she imagined were random moments. Right and wrong blended within her into an unmanageable tension, and even if it was dissipating, it was slow to leave her. She told herself that there had to be a faster way out of the spider's web of emotions that trapped her.

Yes, Andy Candy thought, *maybe I should go back to school and kill the frat boy. Moth will help me, after we kill whomever it is he wants to kill.*

That would make things even for everyone.

Moth was waiting for her outside his apartment. He looked hesitant, as if he was trying to make up his mind about something.

She pulled to the curb but Moth didn't immediately get into the car. Instead he leaned down, and she lowered the window. A blast of hot air penetrated the car interior.

"Hey," she said softly. "Where to today?"

He shook his head. "I don't know." Then he added, "I'm not sure I'll ever know."

They walked. Side by side. They would have appeared to anyone to be a young couple deep in discussion, probably talking about some momentous decision, like renting an apartment together, or if this was the right time for one of them to meet the other's parents. But a casual observer would not have noticed that as close as they seemed pressed together, they did not touch.

Andy Candy thought Moth sounded defeated. He was glum, filled with a sudden pessimism. The energy that had characterized their first days together seemed to have fled.

"Tell me," she said softly, using a delicate tone that a current, not former, lover would employ. "What is it?"

The sun was beating down on them, but Moth's look was overcast. They were heading into a small park, trying to find some shade beneath trees. Children were playing on swing sets and jungle gyms in a nearby exercise area. They were loud, in that unrestrained way that children having fun have, and it only seemed to make Moth's voice sound more discouraged than it already did.

"I'm stuck," Moth said slowly.

She had the sense to know something else was coming and she kept quiet as they walked a few more strides. Moth kicked at a dead brown palm frond that had fallen and littered the sidewalk. Then they sat together on a small bench.

When he did speak, it was like listening to a tortured soliloquy by a new professor giving his first lecture on a subject he was uncertain about.

"When a historian looks at a murder, it's either assessing politics—when that anarchist shot the archduke in Sarajevo and somehow managed to trigger the First World War—or it's social, like when Robert Ford gunned down Jesse James from behind while James was hanging a picture in his home. There's a clear-eyed, cold-blooded way of deconstructing all the factors, leading to a conclusion about the murder. A squared plus B squared equals C squared. Algebra of death. Even if there are eleven thousand documents that get analyzed. But Uncle Ed's killing, it's all backward, although maybe that's not the right word. I see the answer—he's dead—but not the equation that results in that conclusion. And I don't know where to look."

"Yes we do," Andy Candy said slowly. She thought she should take Moth's hand and squeeze it, but she did not. "It's in the past."

"Yes. Easy to say. But where?"

"What makes sense?"

"Nothing makes sense. Everything makes sense."

"Come on, Moth."

He hesitated. "I don't know where to look, or how to look."

"Yes you do," Andy Candy said. "We're looking for hate. Big-time, out-of-control hate. The kind of hate that lasts for years." *Will I have that hate?* she wondered suddenly.

"Not out of control," Moth said. "Or sort of out of control, but out of control after years of planning, if that makes sense." He stopped. He laughed a little. "I have to stop using that word," he said.

"What word?"

"*Sense.*"

She smiled with him. She watched him lift his eyes and stare across the park toward the frolicking children. "I've been thinking about when and why I drink. It's always moments like this, where I'm unsure what to do. If I had an assignment, a paper due, a presentation, you name it, no matter how tense or stressed, then I was always okay. It's when I got, I don't know, unsure about things. Then I found a drink. Or ten. Or more, because you stop counting pretty fast."

Moth laughed, but not because anything was funny. "First filled with doubt, then filled with booze. Pretty simple, Andy, if you think about it. Uncle Ed used to tell me that there are many things people can handle in life, but uncertainty might be the hardest."

Moth turned to Andy Candy.

"What about you, Andy," he said slowly. "Are you unsure about what you're doing?"

She was unsure about everything, but shook her head. "You mean helping you?"

"Yes."

Andy Candy realized both *Yes* and *No* would be the same lie. "Moth, there is nothing certain in my life right at this minute, except that maybe my mother's dogs still love me. And probably she still loves me, although she's leaving me pretty much alone right now. And my dad would still love me, but he's dead. And so here I am. I'm still here."

Moth nodded. "So where next?"

"Where can someone learn to hate you?"

Andy Candy thought right then about the frat boy. *Why couldn't she have seen that smile for what it really was?* Aloud, she said, "Ed at college. Ed at medical school. Because we can't see anyone in the present-day Ed's life that would want to kill him except maybe his ex-wife, but she seems too tied up in Gucci to bother."

Moth laughed. "True." Again he paused. "Adams House," he said. "Adams House at Harvard—that's where he did his undergraduate work. He had two roommates. We should call them. But medical school . . ."

His voice trailed off, then regained strength. "I'll have to think about that," he said. Andy Candy stole a sideways glance at Moth. He was sitting straighter on the park bench than before and was twisting his right fist into his open left palm.

16

Susan Terry sat behind her desk tapping a pencil against a stack of files spread out in front of her. A gas station clerk shot, a pair of armed robberies, a domestic dispute homicide, and three rapes—more than enough to occupy her for weeks on end. She tossed the pencil down, watching it clatter off the desk and fall to the floor, where she left it. She stood up, went to the window, and looked out. She saw a breeze ripple palm fronds, looked up higher, eyes tracking a jumbo jet descending into Miami International Airport. She turned her gaze toward a nearby parking lot, where she hypnotically followed the route of a black Porsche making its way out to the highway. When the sports car disappeared she gripped the edge of the windowsill and began swearing under her breath—an abrupt torrential downpour of disconnected *god damn its, sonofabitches,* and *fuck fuck fucks* until she was almost out of breath.

She said out loud: "He's got absolutely no right or reason to think the way he does." Picturing Moth at Redeemer One made her increasingly angry. "Doesn't he get it? Closed case. Suicide. We're all sorry. Tough luck, kid. Put some flowers on your fucking uncle's grave and get on with life and sobriety."

There is something dangerous in what he's doing, she insisted inwardly, but precisely what was so dangerous eluded her. Her experience with murder tended toward the explosive—the drug deal gone wrong, the husband or wife who suddenly decided they were fed up with being constantly nagged and coincidentally had a gun in their hand.

The dead uncle's file was on top of some cabinets in a corner of the office. She had placed it on a cart that one of the secretaries rolled by every day, *files to be filed,* but for some reason had pulled it back and stuck it on top of all the homicides, robberies, and other sundry felonies crowding her schedule. Typically, hard copies of paperwork on closed cases were shredded, and electronic copies kept in some pile of bytes hidden in a computer.

For a moment, she imagined sending a homicide detective over to talk to Moth. A righteous *Come to Jesus,* one-sided, tough-edged conversation:

"Look, kid, stop fucking around with things you don't understand. We were all over this case. And now it's closed. Don't make me come see you again. You getting what I'm saying, kid?"

She could do that, no problem. She also knew that this sort of minimally strong-arm tactic wouldn't go over well at Redeemer One. And she ruefully acknowledged she needed that place as much as she needed anything in her life—because she didn't have anything else in her life other than her job—even if she rarely spoke at the meetings, and tried to hide in the corners. She surprised herself by recognizing how much she needed to just listen.

"All right," she said again, with a near-lecturing tone of voice to no one in the room. "No cops. Do your job, even though it sucks and this is a complete waste of time. Make yourself a hundred percent certain."

She went over and retrieved the file and plopped down behind her desk.

Autopsy. Toxicology. Crime scene analysis.

All said the same thing.

She reread each detective's interview report. Ex-wife. Live-in lover. Therapist. The detectives had also contacted everyone on Ed Warner's current patient roster. They were thorough enough to go back a few years, even speaking with some ex-patients. She herself had read through Ed Warner's computer files and office visit notes, searching for any telltale sign that what was obvious wasn't. There wasn't even an abrupt termination— some patient that couldn't be helped or failed to pay on time—and she matched everyone who was seeing or had seen Ed Warner with his carefully notated diagnoses. One upper-class neurosis after another: lots of angst; rampant depressions; some drug and alcohol abuse. But no signs of uncontrollable rage.

And absolutely no murder.

Susan Terry hunched over, looking through all the documentation, then patiently looking through it a second time.

With the last page, she leaned back, suddenly exhausted.

"Nothing," she said. "Nada. Zilch. *Rien du tout.*"

She admonished herself: "An hour you could have spent doing something worthwhile."

The papers were strewn about her desktop, so she began gathering them, sticking all back into an accordion-style folder with "Ed Warner— Suicide" and the date in black ink. The last item into the folder was the autopsy report. She was shoving it in, along with the rest, when she had a sudden idea.

"I wonder," she said, speaking out loud again to no one except herself. "Did they . . . I bet they didn't—Jesus . . ."

She removed the autopsy report and flipped through it for what had to be the millionth time. The report was a combination of entries—blanks filled in on a standardized form—alongside clipped, dictated narrative: "*Subject presents as a fifty-nine-year-old male in otherwise good condition . . .*"

"Shit," she blurted. What she was looking for was not there. "Shit, shit, shit." Another torrent of obscenities clouded the room.

Simplest of tests.

Gunshot residue. GSR in prosecutor parlance.

A swab of the dead man's hand. A quick chemical concoction. A conclusion: Yes. His hand displayed signs of a recently fired weapon.

Except they hadn't done it.

Susan inwardly argued with herself.

Of course not. Why bother? The gun was lying on the floor right by his out-stretched fingers. It was obvious. No need to work extra hard on something so clear-cut.

She stood up, paced around her desk twice, then sat down heavily.

Look, she told herself, *it doesn't mean anything. So they neglected one test, and not all that important a one, either. Big fuckin' deal. Happens all the time. The preponderance of the evidence all points directly to one inescapable conclusion.*

She suddenly had trouble convincing herself of this.

Susan Terry tried to make herself put the file back on the cabinet where it could wait for the secretary to take it in the morning, shred the paper, and electronically file each report away in some storage space where Susan would no longer have to think about it and it could grow whatever the modern electronic equivalent of moldy and forgotten is.

Fuck me, fuck me, fuck me, she inwardly repeated. She placed the file back on her desk.

"Someone who hated Ed back in college so much he would carry a homicidal grudge over decades? Not a chance. Larry, what do you think?"

"Ludicrous."

Moth and Andy Candy had set up a conference call with Ed Warner's two Harvard roommates. Frederick was an investment banker in New York and Larry was a professor of political science at Amherst College. Both claimed to be *busy men* but had agreed to speak out of respect for their dead college friend.

"But," Moth persisted, "didn't he have any conflicts, arguments, I don't know . . ."

"Ed's only problem stemmed from his own inner conflicts over who he was," said the political scientist. This was a euphemism for homosexuality. "His friends all knew or suspected and frankly, even though the times were different then, didn't much care."

"I would concur," said the investment banker. "Although it was clear that if there was some element of anger, you know, something that might cause a murder, that would have come from Ed's strained relationship with his family. He didn't like them and they didn't like him. Lots of pressure to succeed and make a name for himself, that sort of distant but insistent and often crippling demands. At Harvard, that wasn't uncommon. Saw it all the time. And, at our age then, it led to a fairly regular type of rebelliousness or a tumble into depression."

He paused, then added. "Should have seen our hair. And the music we listened to. And the unusual substances we ingested."

The voices on the telephone were tinny, but filled with the flush of memory.

"Ed was no different from the rest of us," the political science professor said. "There were some undergraduates who really struggled with the pressures at Harvard. Some that dropped out, some that got strung out, some that took the saddest way out. Suicides and attempted suicides weren't unfamiliar events. But Ed's issues weren't that much more profound than anyone else's and nothing he did spilled over into some sort of grudge-type anger like you're hunting for."

There was some silence, while Moth tried to think of another question. He could not. Andy Candy could see the blank being drawn on Moth's face, and so she thanked the two roommates and hung up.

Can you wear discouragement like a suit of clothes? she wondered, because she could see it written all over Moth's face. Another dead end.

The abrupt thought arrived within her unbidden: *Don't let him give up. It will kill him.*

So before Moth could say anything, she said, "Okay, on to medical school. That makes more sense to me anyway."

Moth used an efficient lie.

My uncle has passed away and I'm trying to reach out to his classmates at medical school to let them know about his death and possibly help contribute to an educational fund at the university, which he was eager to establish. It's in his will.

Andy Candy duplicated this falsehood at the Miami hospital where Ed Warner had done his residency in psychiatry.

The dual calls resulted in a helpful list provided by an alumni office secretary of 127 names, along with e-mail addresses and some medical practice websites. Ed had subsequently joined a group of first-year psychiatry residents in Miami.

The two sat next to each other in a study carrel in the main library at Moth's graduate school. They each had a laptop computer open and easy Internet access.

"Lots of names," Andy Candy whispered. There were other students working nearby, and anything spoken was hushed. She grabbed a piece of scrap paper and wrote down: *surgeons, internal medicine, radiologists—killers?*

Moth took his pen and drew a line through each subspecialty and then wrote *only shrinks.* He understood this actually made no sense, from the historian's perspective. A proper assessment of any era precludes no factors, and he guessed that an orthopedic surgeon could be a killer as readily as a dermatologist. But it made the most sense to focus on Ed's profession. *A good historian,* he thought, *starts close and works outward.*

He wrote: *Match Day.*

Andy Candy nodded. The medical school had provided a list of where each graduate had been matched for their residencies. Ed's name was near the end with the abbreviation *psych* following it. She went back, listed thirteen other names that were designated the same way and the hospitals they were sent to train at. Ed was the only newly minted doctor to be sent to Miami.

She took six. He took seven. They started a Google search on each name. Odd bits of information came up—practices, awards, fellowships, a driving–under-the-influence arrest, a divorce that landed in court.

But these details didn't interest them.

What did show up made Andy Candy want to shout out loud, but that would have aroused everyone in the library.

She'd turned toward Moth and seen that he was rigid, ramrod-straight, next to her. His face had paled a little and she saw his fingers quivering above the keyboard of his laptop.

"What are the odds . . ." he'd whispered so softly she could barely hear him, as he turned the computer toward her and pointed, "that out of fourteen names, four are already dead?"

Low, she thought. *Impossibly low. Improbably, incredibly, unbelievably low.* Andy Candy stifled her desire to scream and wondered if it should be: *homicidally low.*

17

A Third Conversation

Jeremy Hogan had spread a deadly array of weaponry on the dining room table: shotgun, handgun, boxes of ammunition, the fireplace poker, a selection of kitchen carving knives, a six-battery black steel flashlight that he thought could effectively double as a club, and a ceremonial replica of a Civil War–era cavalryman's sword that he'd been given after a speech fifteen years earlier at a military college in Vermont. His subject that day had been post-traumatic stress disorders in victims of crime. He wished he could remember what he'd said. He wasn't sure whether the sword was sharp enough to actually penetrate skin, although it might be intimidating if he waved it around.

He practiced loading and unloading the revolver, and then the shotgun. He wasn't quick, sometimes fumbling the rounds, and he feared he would shoot himself in the foot or leg. When he ejected one live cartridge from the 12-gauge's magazine, it fell to the floor and rolled underneath an antique sideboard. It took him a few minutes to extricate it, finally using the ceremonial sword, still in its tasseled scabbard, to reach to the back. The cartridge and the sword came up covered with dust.

Mid-morning, he constructed a makeshift target, stuffing an old shirt with rags, frayed towels, and rolled-up newspaper. He added some kindling wood from the fireplace to give the target heft and retrieved a broken dining room chair from the attic to prop it all up. He took the target outdoors, across his flagstone patio, into the yard that led to thick deer-infested forest and onetime farmers' fields that stretched behind his house. It was not lost on him that he was putting the chair in the middle of the landscape his dead wife had once loved to paint in vibrant watercolors.

After retrieving the weapons from inside, he paced off a ten-yard distance and squared up. Handgun first. He raised the weapon, realized he'd forgotten his earplugs on the table inside, put the gun down on the damp grass (hoping the moisture wouldn't harm it), trotted back inside and fitted the ear protection, then went back out again and assumed the firing stance the gun store owner had demonstrated. He thought he got it right. Two hands on the weapon, feet slightly apart. Knees slightly flexed. Weight on the balls of his feet. He bounced a little, trying to find the right position, one he'd be comfortable in. The gun store owner had emphasized this.

Deep breath. Odd thought: *How can I be comfortable if I'm facing someone who wants to kill me?*

He fired three rounds.

All missed.

Maybe this is too great a distance, he considered. He moved several yards closer. *I mean, isn't he likely to be only a few feet away? Or maybe not. What sort of Wild West shoot-out do you think is going to happen?*

Jeremy pursed his lips together, held his breath again, took significantly more careful aim, and fired the remaining three rounds. The gun jumped and bucked in his hand like an electric current, but this time he managed to control it a little better.

One shot winged the shirt collar, one missed, and the third smashed into the center, knocking the target over.

Good enough, he told himself, knowing that this was a lie.

He set the Magnum down, walked over, and lifted the target back into position, then returned to his ten-yard firing spot. Again mimicking the position he'd been shown the day before, he snugged the shotgun to his shoulder and fired.

The blast staggered him slightly, but he saw the target absorb the brunt of the shot. The shirt shredded, some of the kindling and paper flew in the air, and the whole thing toppled backward and sideways.

Jeremy lowered the weapon.

"Not bad," he said. "I do believe I'm becoming dangerous."

The shotgun is better. Don't need to be nearly so precise.

He worked the plugs out of his ears and felt a tingling in his shoulder. For a moment, he was confused, because the force of the shotgun's explosion seemed to be echoing, and then he realized that the phone was ringing inside his house, muffled but insistent. Clutching his weapons, he hurried inside to the kitchen.

As before, the caller ID was blank.

I know who it is.

He did not pick it up. He simply stared at the receiver, as if he could see the ringing.

It went silent.

I know who it is.

The phone rang again.

Jeremy reached for the receiver, but stopped his hand. *One ring. Two rings. Three.*

Most routine, ordinary callers would give up. Leave a message. Telephone solicitors don't allow more than four or five rings before they irritatingly decide to try later.

Six rings. Seven. Eight.

When I was a child, when people had a telephone on the wall—like I do in the kitchen, or sitting on the desk; like I do upstairs—one had telephone manners. Before auto- answering machines and cell phones with an "ignore" button and video conferencing, before cloud data storage technology and all the other modern things we take for granted, it was considered polite to let the phone ring ten times before hanging up. No longer. Now people get frustrated after three or four.

Nine, ten, eleven, twelve.

The phone kept ringing.

Jeremy smiled. *I just learned something. He's very patient.*

But then, a second, chilling thought: *He knows I'm here?*

How? He can't.

Impossible.

No, not impossible.

He picked it up. *Thirteeenth ring. Was that bad luck?*

"Whose fault is it?"

He'd expected that question. Jeremy took a deep breath, mustered years of knowledge, and replied rapidly.

"It's *my* fault, of course. Whatever *it* is. Disagreeing with you on this point makes no sense. Not any longer. So . . . Any chance that by conceding your position, apologizing profusely, offering up some sort of mea culpa in a public forum, maybe donating a large sum to your favorite charity, I can avoid being murdered?"

His own question—a little rushed, spoken like an academic lecturer—was almost flippant, maybe even a little ridiculous. He'd thought hard about the right tone. Every decision he made was a gamble. Would sounding unafraid make his killer act precipitously? Would he live longer, be able to find a way to protect himself, if he sounded cowed, terrified? Contradictions flooded him. Which would draw out the process of murder? What would buy him the time he needed?

Clutching the phone tightly, Jeremy raced through options. Every word he spoke was a decision.

An actor on the stage *becomes* one person or another, wears his emotions outwardly as he speaks his lines. *Method acting. Become what you have to portray.*

He breathed in sharply.

What do the poker players say? All in.

There was a slight hesitation over the phone line, then an equally slight laugh.

"If I were to say, *Yes there's a chance*, how would you respond, Doctor?"

Jeremy could feel his entire body quivering. His fear was profound. It was almost as if he could feel the presence of his murderer in the room with him. The darkness in the man's voice overcame all the mid-morning sunlight streaming through the windows, the benign blue sky above. Talking to this man intent on killing him was a little like descending into a shadow that enveloped him.

Do not let terror creep into your voice.

Provoke him. Maybe he will slip.

"Well," he said cautiously, as if he'd had time to think about his reply, "I suppose then we could have a reasonable conversation about what you would want me to do. Charities we could consider for donations. Actions I could take to try to balance this wrong you imagine I've done to you."

Jeremy paused, then added, "Of course, this conversation could only be defined as *reasonable* if you aren't some fantasy-obsessed near psychotic and all your talk and threats aren't merely a product of your overwrought imagination. If that's the case, I can easily prescribe some medications that will help you, and certainly recommend a good therapist you can see to work through these issues."

He said all this in a clipped, *not amused* doctor voice.

Let's see how you react to that, he thought.

Another pause. A short laugh. A bemused question:

"Do you think I'm psychotic, Doctor?"

"You might be. Probably on an edge—even if you do manage to conceal it in your voice. I'd like to be able to help you."

He won't expect that tack, Jeremy believed.

"You know, Doctor, you sound a little like those white-collar criminals you see on the news, who stand all contrite before a judge, all eager to serve up soup to homeless folks in a shelter instead of going to prison for the millions they stole and the lives they wrecked."

Jeremy licked his lips. He wondered why they were so dry.

"I'm not them," he replied.

Weak. Weak. Weak. He berated himself inwardly.

"Really? It's an interesting question, Doctor. Tell me this: What is the right punishment for someone who ruined another person's life? What does one do with the person who stole every hope and dream, every ambition and every opportunity? What's the proper penalty?"

"There are degrees of guilt. Even the law recognizes that."

Impotent. Mealy-mouthed. Crippled.

"But we are not in a court, are we, Doctor?"

Jeremy suddenly thought he saw an opportunity.

"Did I put you in prison with an assessment? Did I testify against you in a trial? Do you think I misdiagnosed you?"

He regretted his bluntness. Ordinarily he would try to elicit answers more subtly. But the caller made that difficult.

"No. That would be too simple. And anyway, even a psychotic would probably recognize that you were merely doing your job."

"No they wouldn't," Jeremy responded. He was thinking hard, trying to add each word the caller made into a picture. *It wasn't in court. What else might it be?* He saw an answer: *Teaching.*

But before he could act on this idea, the caller responded with another laugh. "Well then, Doctor, I guess we have the answer to your inquiries about whether I'm a psychotic."

Outmaneuvered. Come on, think!

Again the caller paused. "It's interesting talking with you, Doctor. Curious, isn't it? Relationships: father and son, mother and child, lovers, coworkers, old friends. New friends. Each connection has its own special qualities. But here, we're in very significant territory, aren't we? The relationship between a killer and his victim. Puts weight on every word."

He sounds like me, Jeremy thought.

Then abruptly: *Follow that.*

"Your other victims—if there really are any; I can't be sure, you know—did you create a connection with each?"

"Astute, Doctor. You challenge me to prove that I've killed before. That might help you figure out who I am. No such luck. Sorry. But this is what I would say: I think in any killing there are at least two levels of conjunction. There's the level that exists that *caused* the need for killing. Then there is the moment of death. I would think those were arenas that you probed in your career."

Jeremy found himself nodding.

"Have you spoken to your other victims before you killed them?"

"Some yes. Some no."

Okay. That's something, Jeremy thought. *In some situations Mister Who's at Fault needs direct confrontation. In others, who knows?* He kept probing.

"Which situation gave you more satisfaction?"

A snort. "They were equally satisfying. Just in different ways. You would know that, Doctor."

"Do you kill us all in the same way?"

"Good question, Doctor. Police, prosecutors, professors of criminal justice, they all like patterns. They like seeing obvious connections, being able to add details together. They favor crimes that are a little like those paint-by-numbers kits that you might give a child. Fill in blue in number 10. Red in 13. Yellow and green in 2 and 12. And suddenly what you're painting becomes clear. I'd think you'd have figured that I'm smarter than that."

Smarter than most of the killers I've met. What does that tell me?

A hesitation, then the caller added, "Keep trying, Doctor. I like a challenge. One has to think clearly if one intends to be both oblique and specific at the same time."

Jeremy imagined a grin on the caller's face.

"So everyone has died in a different way?"

"Yes."

He realized that he'd gripped the phone so tightly his fingers were white against the black plastic surface. He guessed the conversation was like steering an out-of-control car down an icy hill. He was careening, sliding, trying to will the tires to regain purchase on the slick road, at the same time that hundreds, perhaps thousands of small inputs were being processed by his brain. Reason battled panic within him.

"Were all of us equally at fault?"

The caller had clearly anticipated this, because he answered without hesitation, "Yes."

But then, after a pause, he added, his voice slipping into an almost conversational, friendly tone, "Let me ask you a question, Doctor: Suppose you agree to help rob a convenience or a liquor store with your two buddies. Gonna be an easy job. You know, wave around a handgun, collect everything from the register, and get away scot-free. No big deal. Happens every night somewhere in America. You're sitting outside, behind the wheel, engine running, picturing what you're going to do with your share of the cash, when you hear gunshots, and your two buddies come racing out. They tell you that they panicked and blew the store owner away. Your nice little easygoing robbery just became felony murder. You drive fast, because that's your job, but not fast enough, because you look up and see cops behind you . . ."

Again a small laugh. "Now, Doctor, are you as guilty as your two buddies?"

Jeremy could feel his throat go dry. But he worked hard to process what he heard.

"No," he said.

"Are you sure? In most states, the law makes no distinction between you in the car and your friend pulling the trigger."

"Yes," Jeremy said. "But . . ."

He stopped. He could see the point. It stifled him.

He felt frozen, as if all his knowledge and understanding and years of experience were just beyond his reach.

He felt old. He looked over at his weapons. *Who am I kidding?*

No, he said to himself. *Fight back. No matter how old you feel.* He took a deep breath. *Why this story about some run-of-the-mill crime, now?*

He felt an electric surge inside. *That's a mistake. That's maybe his first mistake.*

Jeremy took a deep breath and tried to capitalize.

"So, what you are now saying is that I unwittingly drove a car to a crime that others committed, and this is going to cost me my life now. You would not have used that example if it didn't in some way mimic your own feelings. Interesting."

This time he could *feel* a hesitation on the other end of the line. *That struck a chord,* Jeremy thought. He persisted:

"So, Mister Who's at Fault, your point is that I should look at things I contributed to, not something I might have done exactly. That's a difficult bar for me to reach. I mean, after all, we're considering over five decades of experiences here. If you really want me to comprehend what I've done, you're going to have to help me out a little more."

Another pause, before the caller continued:

"More help from me will just hurry this process."

Jeremy smiled. He had a small touch of confidence.

"That would be your decision. But it seems to me that this relationship—you and me—only works for you if I have a grasp on the *why* behind your desire."

Touché, he thought.

A cold response:

"I think that's true, Doctor. But sometimes knowledge means death."

This time, Jeremy didn't glibly answer.

The caller continued. Voice low, clearly electronically masked, but containing so much venom that Jeremy almost looked to his hands for the telltale wounds from a rattler's bite.

"The ethics of violence are intriguing, Doctor, aren't they? Almost as intriguing as the psychology of killing."

"Yes."

Beyond agreeing, he didn't know what to say.

"Your fields of expertise, right, Doctor?"

"Yes."

Words were suddenly failing him right and left.

"It's frightening, isn't it, being told you're going to be murdered."

Yes. Don't lie.

"Yes."

A question came to Jeremy, and he blurted it out. "Did all the others react like me?"

"Again, a good question, Doctor. Let me put it to you this way: My relationship with each death was unique."

Jeremy thought hard, trying to anticipate the weave of the conversation. As in a tapestry, each thread meant nothing individually, but everything in unison.

"Did you tell each of us you were going to kill us?"

"A better question. The answer is: not necessarily."

"So, you're talking to me, but you didn't talk to all of us before . . ." he paused, before adding, "you did what you did."

This was neither grammatically correct not forensically specific.

"That's right. But in the end, you all get the same deal. A death that belongs all to you."

"Yes, but isn't that true for everyone?" Jeremy replied, trying to keep his voice flat and unemotional. The same tone he used in hundreds of interviews with hundreds of killers, but which now seemed useless. "We all have to die someday." *Obvious. Stupid.*

"True enough, Doctor. If a bit of a cliché. We like the uncertainty of hope, do we not, Doctor? We don't know when we're going to die. Today? Tomorrow? Five years? Ten years? Who knows? We fear that moment when some date is set, whether we're in our cell on death row or in some oncologist's office, when he looks at our latest scans and test results and frowns— because whether we hear it from the warden of the prison or the warden of disease, suddenly a date has been set. In life we embrace certainty about so many things. But when it comes to ourselves, and the moment we have to die, well, uncertainty is what we prefer. Now, I'm not saying it isn't possible to come to grips with that death date. Some patients and prisoners manage. Religion helps some. Surrounding oneself with friends and family. Maybe even creating a bucket list. But all those things simply obscure that gnawing sensation within, don't they?"

Jeremy knew he was supposed to answer, but could not. He did concede inwardly, *Well, that's where my fear comes from. He's right about that.*

He suddenly turned and grabbed his revolver off the kitchen table, as if it could comfort him. It seemed heavy and he was unsure whether he had the strength to lift it and take aim. In the same instant, he realized he'd neglected to reload it. He looked around wildly for the box of ammunition and saw it all the way across the room, sitting on a table where he couldn't reach it.

Idiot.

But he did not have enough time to berate himself further.

"You think you can protect yourself, Doctor. You can't. Hire a bodyguard. Go to the police. Tell them about the threats. I'm sure they will be interested . . . for a time. But eventually, you will be back on your own. So, maybe build a fortress. Run to some forgotten, hidden place. Try to give yourself some hope those ways. All wastes of time. I will always be beside you."

Jeremy spun around. *He can see me!* Then he shook his head. *Impossible. Or, maybe it isn't.*

Nothing was ordinary. Nothing was as it should be. He could hear his own breath getting shallow, sickly. *I'm dying* he thought. *I'm being killed by fear.*

The voice on the phone interrupted his thoughts.

"I have enjoyed talking with you, Doctor. You are much more clever than I ever remembered, and I've said things I probably shouldn't have. But all good things must come to an end. You should prepare yourself, because you don't have much time left. A couple of hours. Maybe a day or two. A week, possibly."

The caller hesitated.

"Or maybe it's a month. A year. A decade. All you need to know is that I'm on my way."

Jeremy interjected. His voice was high-pitched, almost girlish. "Tell me what the hell you think I did."

Another small silence, before the caller replied, "Tick-tock. Tick-tock. Tick-tock."

Jeremy blurted out, "When?" But this question went into a dead line.

The phone was silent. It was almost as if the man was a ghost, or Jeremy had been the dim-witted, naïve-rube subject of a Las Vegas magic trick. Poof. Disappeared.

"Hello?" he asked. This was a gut reaction. "Hello?"

Why had disappeared from Jeremy's lexicon. *That was it,* he thought. *No more calls. What did I say?*

He listened to the quiet. Even knowing his killer was no longer there, Jeremy repeated what had become the only relevant question: "When?"

And finally a third time, very softly, more for himself than for the man coming to kill him: "When?"

18

One, two, three, four . . .

"No answer."

"Keep trying."

"Okay."

Five, six, seven . . .

"No answer. I don't think he's home."

"No answering machine. That's weird. Keep trying."

Eight, nine, ten, eleven, twelve . . .

"Where—" Moth started.

"I didn't think you would call again." The voice edgy, near anger, fully strained.

"Doctor Hogan?"

Pause.

"Yes. Speaking. Who is this?"

Clipped words. Curt tone. Moth stammered his response, surprised to be talking, taken aback by the intensity of the disembodied voice.

"My name is Timothy Warner. I'm sorry to disturb you at your home but this was the number I got. I'm seeking some information about my late uncle. Ed Warner. He was a student of yours many years ago. He took your lecture course on forensic psychiatry."

Another pause. Silence crept across the phone line, but it was the sort of silence that was filled with hidden, explosive noise. Moth waited. He thought he should say something, but the distant doctor spoke slowly.

"And now he's dead," Jeremy Hogan said.

"Yes," Moth blurted out. A single word, but one that carried so much surprise that, watching him, Andy Candy imagined that he'd heard something shocking. Moth's face seemed to freeze.

"It's not my fault," Jeremy Hogan said slowly. "None of it was my fault. At least, I don't think so. But apparently it was. Whatever it was."

My fault made Moth stiffen in his seat. His throat was suddenly dry and he waved his hand almost like someone trying to reach out and touch something that was just beyond his grasp. He looked toward Andy Candy and nodded, signaling something to her that made her own pulse accelerate, and she too leaned forward in her seat.

"You remember my uncle?"

"No," Jeremy replied. "Perhaps I should, but I do not. Too many classes, too many students, too many grades and recommendations and test scores and classroom talks. After all those years, the faces all blend together. I'm sorry."

"He became a really good therapist."

"Not my field. Now look, young man, what did he do? What was he to blame for?"

This question was spoken with urgency.

"I don't know," Moth answered. "That's what I'm trying to find out."

"And his death," the old psychiatrist started, "what can you tell me about his dea—?"

"He committed suicide, or, at least that's what the police believe," Moth interrupted, speaking too fast.

"Yes. I know. In Miami. I read about it."

"Why did you—?"

"Someone told me to read his obituary."

"I'm sorry. Someone told you? Who?"

Jeremy hesitated. In a situation that seemed already beyond bizarre, this call from a dead psychiatrist's nephew seemed to fit right in place.

"I don't exactly know," he said slowly.

Moth felt like the phone in his hands was red hot.

"My uncle . . ." he started, words picking up momentum, "I think he wasn't a suicide. I think he was killed."

"Killed?"

"Murdered."

"But the paper said . . ."

"The paper was wrong."

"How do you know that?"

"I knew my uncle."

Moth said this with so much conviction that it defied doubt.

"And the police think . . ."

"They also say suicide. Everyone says suicide. That's the official word. I say faked."

Another pause.

"Yes," Jeremy Hogan said, choosing his words cautiously. He was drawing connections in his head. *Suicide* made little sense. *Murder* made complete sense. "That would make things significantly clearer. I believe you are correct."

Moth fumbled, trying to think of what to say next. It was as if questions were choking him like hands around his throat. He needed to ask, but couldn't spit out words. Many voices had suggested he was on the proper track, but none had carried any proof or authority. This voice seemed different. It had weight.

"Perhaps we should speak in person," Jeremy Hogan added. His voice had changed, suddenly pensive, soft, and almost regretful. "I do not know what your uncle and I shared, but something linked us together. Can you come up here? You will have to hurry, because I'm expecting to be murdered soon, too."

*   *   *

She barely said a word to her mother, but took the time to rub some dogs' ears and affectionately scratch some dog throats. Then Andy Candy went to her room, found a small suitcase, and threw clean underwear and a few toiletries into it. She had no idea how long she would be gone. She found jeans and sweaters and a warm coat. It wasn't like packing for school, or packing for a vacation. She had no idea what packing for a conversation about killing required.

"You're going someplace—"

"Yes. With Moth. Shouldn't be long."

"Andy, are you sure—"

She interrupted for the second time. "Yes." She knew she should say much more, but every aspect of her sudden trip north suggested much wider, more difficult talks, which she was unwilling to have. So she adopted a laconic, curt, angry-teenager tone that she hadn't used in years and that didn't invite her mother in. For a moment she wondered which was the real Andy Candy. *Who are you?*—the most common question for people her age. Answers, however, are tricky. Happy. Sad. Possessed. She added up all the rapid changes she had gone through in the past weeks. The Andy Candy who was outgoing, quick to laugh, friendly, and eager to join in all sorts of activities had been closeted away. The new Andy Candy was bitterly quiet and absolutely unwilling to share details.

"Well, at least tell me where you're going," her mother said, exasperated.

"New Jersey."

Hesitation. "New Jersey? Why . . ."

"We're going to see a psychiatrist." This was a statement of fact that was wrapped in a lie, she thought.

Another hesitation. "Why would you go all that way to see a psychiatrist?" her mother asked. *Plenty of psychiatrists in Miami.* Doubt was riveted to her voice.

"Because he's the only person left who can help us," Andy replied.

Her mother did not ask, nor did Andy volunteer an answer to the obvious question: *Help with what?*

19

A Fourth Conversation, Very Brief

The key to all his killings was deceptively simple: no recognizable signature.

Ed Warner's death had been a clever puzzle to plan. Finding a way to be seated across from him in conversation had been the clear choice, but still required cautious design. It mimicked a typical therapeutic session. The only difference had been that the handshake at the end had been replaced by a close-range gunshot—an idea he'd stolen from the forty-year-old movie *Three Days of the Condor.* Robert Redford, Faye Dunaway, and Max von Sydow. He suspected that no modern cop, not even one who liked slightly dated adventure flicks, had seen it. But Jeremy Hogan presented different problems.

I told him far too much.

He's not stupid. But he will be unsure what the next step he can take might be.

Act before he can act.

Winchester Model 70, 30.06 caliber. Weight 8 lbs.

Five rounds 180-grain ammunition.

Leupold 12X scope.

Effective range: 1,000 yards.

But he knew that would be a military-trained sniper making an extraordinary kill shot, compensating for wind, atmosphere, humidity, and the flattening trajectory of the bullet over the terrain.

Exceptional range: 200 to 400 yards.

That would be a highly skilled and experienced big-game hunter. A shot to boast about.

Typical range: 25-50 yards.

This would be a weekend-warrior type, falsely persuaded about his hunting prowess, fantasizing he was some new-day Davy Crockett descendant, armed to the gills with expensive equipment that got used maybe a couple of times a year and spent the rest of its time locked in a closet.

The doctor was the last death on his agenda. He was unsure whether he'd done enough to make it ring true. He feared coming so far over so many years, only to fall emotionally short. *That's the biggest danger,* he told himself. *Not arrest, trial, conviction, sentencing, and being shunted off to prison to await a date with an executioner. Far worse would be failure after coming so far.*

"That's a strange thought for a killer," he said out loud, as he rolled this notion over in his mind.

The only answer lay in the last act.

He returned to the busy task of preparing. Duffel bag. Camouflage clothing, including a carefully constructed ghillie suit that he thought rivaled those he'd seen professional soldiers create. Heavy boots with a distinctive waffle tread, a complete size too small—he'd cut extra space in the toes. Backpack with emergency headlamp, entrenching tool, water bottle, and PowerBar. All these items had been transported from his trailer in Western Massachusetts—where they didn't attract attention the same way they would in New York City.

Student #5 paused and picked up a hand-drawn map of the interior of

Jeremy Hogan's house, along with an hour-by-hour schedule of the doctor's daily routine. He wondered: *Does he know he goes to the bathroom at the same time every morning? Does he realize he sits in the same chair in the living room to read or watch the few television shows he likes? British comedy-dramas on PBS, naturally. He also sits in the same position at his desk, and in the same place at the dining room table when he eats his microwaved dinner. Does he see that? Does he have any idea how regular his routines are? If he did, he might be able to save his life. But he doesn't.*

Each routine was a possible killing moment. Student #5 had considered each moment from this perspective.

Gutting knife. Disposable cell phone. He double-checked the weather report, examined the GPS track he'd established, and for the third time went over the time the sun set in the West and calculated how many meager minutes of light he would have between death and total darkness.

Like any good hunter, he thought.

He used an old deer-jacking, out-of-season trick: a small salt lick placed a week earlier in a tiny forest clearing. He was deep in a wooded area, a little over a mile from Jeremy Hogan's home through rough but manageable territory. Though it was early in the afternoon, damp cold seeped into his clothing, but he knew that once he started moving he would warm rapidly. He remained motionless, downwind from the salt lick, concealed by camouflage, rifle snugged up against his cheek, barrel resting on deadfall to steady his shot. From time to time he would fiddle with the adjustment screws on his scope, making sure the image was clear and the crosshairs were perfectly aligned.

He was lucky this day. Only ninety minutes had passed when he caught the first movement through the thick branches.

Shifting his weight ever so slightly, he readied himself.

Solitary doe.

He smiled. *Perfect.*

The deer moved cautiously into the open space, lifting its head to pluck scent or sound from its world, alert to potential threats, but unaware that Student #5 was drawing a bead.

Death memories distracted him and he forced himself to concentrate on the deer moving tentatively toward the salt lick.

"I want to help you," Ed Warner had said.

"You missed your chance. I needed help when we were young. Not now."

"No," the psychiatrist had persisted, voice a little unsteady with tension, "it's never too late."

"Tell me, Ed," Student #5 had persisted, "how will you explain this? What will it do to your practice when the world knows that you couldn't even prevent an old friend from killing himself right at your feet?"

A wonderful lie he'd designed.

He had stood up then, his gun placed up against his temple, pre-suicide. It was persuasive theater. Student #5 knew that Ed Warner would read all the body language, hear the hoarse tension in his voice, and the picture he would create in his mind was that his onetime classmate meant to kill himself in front of him right at that moment, just as he'd promised. Shakespearean drama. Or maybe Tennessee Williams. Student #5 had moved around the side of the desk, closing in on his target. He had rehearsed the necessary movements a thousand times: finger on trigger, bent over slightly; then, suddenly, before Warner could recognize what was truly happening, shove the gun directly against the psychiatrist's temple.

Head shot.

Squeeze.

And fire.

He fixed the crosshairs on the deer's chest. He imagined he could see it rising and falling with each hesitant breath. It was wary. Afraid. It had every right to be so.

Heart shot.

Squeeze.

And fire.

* * *

The deer's carcass was still warm, and a small trickle of blood dripped down his jacket. *Sixty pounds,* he thought. *Hard. Not impossible. You trained for this moment.*

Before slinging the body over his shoulders, Student #5 had used a small folding entrenching tool to cover up the remains of the salt lick. Then, following a trail through the woods that he'd trudged several practice times carrying a heavy backpack to simulate a dead deer, he set out for Jeremy Hogan's house. Light was just beginning to shallow up and flatten out, but he believed he had enough left. It would be close, but manageable.

Killing was like that, he reminded himself. It was never exactly as precise as one hoped for nor as sloppy as one feared.

His slung rifle bounced uncomfortably against his backside as he maneuvered through thickets and deadfall. He wished he could've brought a machete to clear some of the tangled bushes away, but he didn't want to leave an obvious path through the woods that some crime scene expert might identify. He knew he was leaving tracks, but the mis-sized boots—cramped and painful as they might be—created imprints that seemed haphazard and erratic. This was important.

The sky above was sullen gray, thick with clouds and the threat of cold rain. This was good. Rain would help cover any signs of his presence.

A thorn tugged at his pants leg.

He was breathing hard. Exertion. Weight. Excitement. Anticipation. He told himself to slow down, be careful. He was getting closer.

When Student #5 spotted the location he'd selected, he forced himself to hesitate with every step. No abrupt, attention-seizing motion.

Stealthily, he moved to the very tree line.

He kept his eyes on Jeremy Hogan's home, perhaps forty yards of ill-kept lawn from the edge of the forest.

He's there. He's inside. He's waiting, but he doesn't know how close he is.

Student #5 lowered the deer carcass from his shoulders just at the last tree before civilization and grass took over.

The body thumped against the soft ground.

He made sure that the carcass appeared as it did when he'd first shot it. *A collapsed-in-death deer. Not a carefully arranged deer.*

Crablike, crouched to lower his profile, he backed away from the deer shape, carefully maintaining his sight line, letting the scrub brush and foliage hide him. Perhaps twenty yards back into the forest he stopped at an old oak tree. Right at his shoulder height there was a notch where a branch had broken off. It formed the perfect shooting position.

The forest in front of him created a tunnel-like window straight to the house. No stray limbs that might deflect his shot ever so slightly and throw it off. The dead deer on the ground was directly in the path his bullet would travel.

He lifted the rifle and eyed down the scope.

He hesitated, inwardly asked himself:

What will the cops see?

A simple answer:

A murder that isn't a murder at all.

Student #5 reached for his throwaway phone.

He was so focused that he did not hear the car pulling to the front of the house, and from where he was poised he could not see it.

Jeremy Hogan was at his desk, feverishly writing notes on a yellow legal pad. Every snatch of conversation, every impression, anything that might help discover who Mister Who's at Fault might be. He scrawled words across the page, disorganized and hurried and lacking all the scientific precision he'd developed over the years. He had no idea what might help him, so every random thought and observation flooded the pages.

He looked up only when he heard the car come down his drive.

"That's them. Got to be," he said out loud.

Jeremy glanced out the window and saw a young couple exit the nondescript rental car.

He smiled. "She's beautiful," he whispered. It had been a long time since he entertained a young woman as striking as the one hesitating in his driveway. He had the odd thought that the young woman was far too pretty to talk about murder.

Grabbing the yellow legal pad, he jumped up and hustled to the front door.

Neither Andy Candy nor Moth knew what to expect when the door swung open. They saw a tall, lanky, white-haired man, clearly both pleased and nervous as they greeted one another.

"Timothy, Andrea, delighted to meet you, though I fear the circumstances are problematic," Jeremy Hogan said rapidly. With a small wave, he ushered them into the house. There was a small, awkward moment.

"This seems very nice," Andy Candy said, just being polite.

"Lonely and isolated, alas," Jeremy replied. "All alone now." He looked over at Moth, who shifted, unsettled.

"I suppose we should get right to it," the doctor continued. He held up his legal pad, filled with notes. "Been trying to get organized, so we'd have a place to begin. Sorry it all seems so confusing. Let's go into the living room and sit." Before they could agree, the phone rang.

Jeremy stopped. The corner of his mouth twitched.

"He's called me," Jeremy said slowly. "Several times. But I don't think he will call again. Our last conversation . . ."

His voice faded, as the phone continued to ring.

The old psychiatrist turned to the young couple.

"Odd," he said. "Ironic? The phone is either a killer or some damn fundraiser for yet another worthy cause."

He pushed his notes to Andy Candy.

"Wait here," he said, leaving them in the entry.

They watched as he walked into the kitchen and stared at the caller ID on the phone. It read *Anonymous*. His first instinct was to ignore it, but instead he picked up the phone.

Student #5 sighted down the rifle barrel.

He heard Jeremy's voice: "Yes?"

Now there was no more need to conceal his voice with an electronic scrambler. He wanted the doctor to hear the real him.

"Now, Doctor, listen very carefully," he said slowly.

Jeremy gasped. Surprised. He felt frozen in position.

In the crosshairs of the scope, Student #5 could see Jeremy's back. He adjusted slightly, keeping the phone to his ear, finger caressing the trigger.

"A history lesson. Just for you." As he'd expected, Jeremy didn't reply. "A couple of decades ago, four students came to you and wanted your help in getting the fifth member of their study group dismissed from medical school because they thought he was dangerously crazy and threatening their careers. They wanted to sacrifice him so they could get ahead. You did their bidding. You were the enabler. The facilitator. I was the person who suffered. It cost me everything. What do you think it should cost you?"

Jeremy stammered. His words were misshapen. Incomprehensible. The only word that he was able to choke out that made any sense was, "But . . ."

"The cost, Doctor?"

Student #5 knew Jeremy would not respond.

He had thought hard about what he would say. Ending with that question had a specific design: It would hold the doctor in position, confused, hesitant.

"That's a fine blue shirt you're wearing, Doctor."

"What?" Jeremy asked.

A poor choice for a final word, Student #5 thought.

He dropped the cell phone to the soft earth at his feet, steadied his left hand against the rifle stock.

He took a single breath, held it, and gently pulled the trigger.

Familiar solid recoil.

Red mist.

The immediate death thought: *All these years and now I'm free.*

The only thing that surprised him was the sudden piercing scream that followed. There should have been deep silence marred only by the fading echo of the rifle's report. This unexpected noise troubled him—but he still had the internal discipline to pick up the cell phone, make a quick check of his surroundings for any telltale evidence he might have left behind, and start his rapid retreat through the darkening woods. His first few strides were accompanied with the belief: *It's over. It's over.* Then each subsequent step was marked by the whispered Bob Dylan song lyric to carry him away: *It's all over now, Baby Blue.*

And then a last word that fed his fast pace: *Finally.*

PART TWO

Who's the Cat?
Who's the Mouse?

20

Moth lied.

Sort of. What he found was a way of answering questions that created an impression of truth while obscuring the larger falsehood. He was surprised at how easy this was for him. So much of maintaining sobriety stemmed from being aboveboard, he was a little frightened at how easily dishonesty fell from his lips.

The doctor's home was suddenly crawling with cops and EMT personnel. Moth had been taken into one room, while Andy Candy was put in another so they could be questioned separately. From where he was standing, he could no longer see the doctor's body.

"So why were you here, again?" the detective asked.

"My uncle passed away recently—a suicide down in Miami," Moth answered. "We were very close. Doctor Hogan was one of his important teachers in medical school. I'm trying to gain some understanding for the reasons behind my uncle's death and I was in contact with the doctor the other day. He invited me to come speak with him. I gather he felt he was too old to travel and whatever he was going to say wasn't appropriate for a telephone conversation."

"Did he say anything about any sort of threats . . . ?" the detective persisted.

"Well," Moth said hesitantly, "we intended to talk about my loss—and I believe he thought he might be able to help me come to grips with it. He was a prominent psychiatrist, after all. Maybe he was just being polite. Maybe he was lonely because he was living here all alone, and he wanted visitors. I didn't ask."

Moth looked at the detective. Nothing in the way the man was standing, sounding, questioning made Moth think, *This is the moment to tell this person everything.*

"This is a long way to travel for a single conversation."

"My uncle was really important for me. And I got a cheap fare."

Andy Candy lied, too.

It left an odd taste in her mouth, as if her fictions were sour foods, but at the same time it quickened her pulse, because with every falsehood she felt she was surging into an adventure.

"And exactly where were you standing when you heard the shot?" The detective, a young woman only a half-dozen years older than Andy Candy, affected a tough-gal, no-nonsense tone, wielding her notepad and pen with the same authority as she might the weapon strapped to her waist.

Andy Candy hesitated, pointing first, then actually walking to the position she'd occupied when Doctor Hogan died. "Right here. Then here after we heard the . . ." She didn't finish this statement instead, continuing instead with, ". . . Then I went into the kitchen." She breathed in hard and imagined it was a little like rewinding a tape recording, because she replayed in her mind's eye what she had seen and heard.

Gunshot.

Distant. Muffled. Barely registered: *What was that?*

Split second.

Look up.

Glass fracturing.

Then: a sight that was as loud as any noise—the back of the doctor's head exploding in a red cascade of brains and blood.

A sickening *thud* as the elderly psychiatrist pitched forward, slamming into the wall, driven by the force of the bullet. The phone in his hand crashed to the floor. He made no sound as he slid down—or none that she could hear, because in that moment she screamed: a high-pitched banshee-wail of immediate panic, shock and fear wrapped together in some primitive, desperate cry. It blended with Moth's great shout of astonishment and surprise to create a harmony of terror.

It all happened so quickly that it took Andy Candy some time to comprehend what had taken place, and to collect all the disparate pieces of the killing and process it. It was a little like waking up from a nightmare of blistering heat, thinking, *Boy, that was a nasty dream,* and then recognizing that the house around her was actually on fire.

The detective questioning Moth was stocky, middle-aged, wearing an ill-fitting suit. "And what exactly did you do, after you realized the doctor had been shot?"

Moth tried to picture his actions, assessing what to put in—heroic—and what to leave out—panicked. What he had done was leap back, like a person coming upon a snake in the grass, before twisting and grabbing Andy in a bear hug and pushing her to the side of the entryway. As the doctor had crumpled to the floor, Moth had cowered beside Andy Candy, hovering over her as if shielding her from falling debris.

Then a different side of him took over, and he let her loose and rushed into the kitchen. All the elements of violent death were being sorted out in his head, and instincts he did not know he possessed were taking over. It did not occur to him that he was exposing himself to a second shot. He bent down, like a battlefield medic, only to pull his hands back sharply. He immediately recognized there was nothing he could do. No tourniquet. No clamping an artery. No CPR or mouth-to-mouth. Deep red blood was already pooling on the floor, marred by pieces of bone and viscous gray brain matter, and he could see the nightmare vision of gray hair matted by death, skull destroyed.

Out of the corner of his eye, he saw the array of weaponry on the table, and with a warrior's cry of defiance, he jumped over, seized the shotgun, did not bother to check to see if it was loaded—which he wouldn't have known how to do anyway—found himself tugging at the back door, losing seconds to a dead-bolt lock that he fumbled with, then racing crazily outside. He raised the shotgun, swinging it right and left, finger on the trigger, but could see no target. Some vague notion of protecting Andy Candy and himself penetrated his fear. He held his breath.

He stood stock still for what were only seconds, but which seemed to draw out into some indistinct, massive length of time. Night seemed to drop around him, cloaking him in darkness. He wanted to shoot something, or someone, but there were nothing but shadows surrounding him, stretching out of the nearby forest across the doctor's backyard. Mocking him.

So, he went back inside.

"It's okay," he said to Andy, although how he could reach this conclusion eluded him, as it did with what he said next. "Whoever it was has disappeared."

Andy Candy thought she should cry. She felt tears in her eyes, but an almost iron stiffness throughout her body. She lingered in the doorway to the kitchen, frozen, eyes fixed on the doctor's body, her hands covering her mouth, as if anything she might say would only add to the fear ricocheting within her. She imagined her feelings were as pale as she was sure her face was.

"Did we," she stammered, "who, I mean . . ." She stopped. The *who* part she thought she knew. The *did we* part seemed ridiculous. Her words were so dry they scratched her throat.

Moth seemed cold, robotic. "We know who it was," he said bitterly, putting sound to the thought that passed into her head. He laid the shotgun on the table.

Andy could feel sweat beneath her arms, although she shivered as if

186

cold. She could not tell whether she was hot or freezing. "Moth, let's get out of here," she said. "Let's just go. Right now."

Run, she thought. *Escape.*

Then: *From what?*

And: *Where to?*

"I don't think we can do that," Moth replied.

At the moment she had no idea what was right and what was wrong, and she doubted that Moth did either. She could only imagine that another window was going to explode and a sniper's bullets seek her or Moth out. She suddenly felt she was in terrible danger, that every second she lingered might give the assassin time to reload, draw a bead, and end her life.

Andy Candy lurched back, unsteady. One hand shot out and she grabbed at the wall. She felt dizzy and believed she might pass out.

"Help," she whispered, although what sort of *help* she was requesting evaporated in the room. She had the odd thought: *People think death is the end. It's only the beginning.*

Moth wanted to walk over, throw his arms around her, hold her tightly, stroke her hair, and try to comfort her. He had a cinematic vision of what a hero should do in a moment like this one, but he stumbled as he moved toward her, and then stopped a few feet away.

He saw Andy reaching for her cell phone. *911. Of course,* he thought.

But he said: "Wait a second." *Comforting Moth* disappeared, replaced by *Thinking-like-a-killer Moth.* He turned back to the weapons on the table. He replaced the shotgun, and picked up the .357 Magnum and all the boxes of shells for the handgun.

"We're going to need this. And that, too." He pointed at the legal pad with the doctor's hand-scrawled notes. Andy Candy had dropped it to the floor in the entranceway.

"Wouldn't the police . . ." she started, and then she understood what Moth was saying. She picked it up and handed it to him. She did not recognize the step she took for the immense danger that it represented, although she was vaguely aware that the two of them were stepping over lines and crossing boundaries that no rational person would.

187

"All right," Moth said, tucking the legal pad under his arm. "Now, make the call."

She dialed. "What do I say?"

"Tell them there's been a death. Gunshot."

She twitched, tension in every movement. "And when they get here, what do we say then?"

Good sense would have dictated that they instantly turn over all they knew, which wasn't much, and all they imagined, which was a great deal, to the police, who were properly equipped to deal with homicide. In the same instant, both decided not to. The words *It's up to us* flooded both of them. The idea of trying to turn over trust to some cop seemed not only stupid, but dangerous. So many deaths were jumbled in their minds that the ability to see matters rationally evaporated. Moth felt iron inside. All he could imagine was revenge.

He said coldly: "An accident?"

If everything around her was a merry-go-round of death and crazy, clinging to something that seemed to make sense when it actually didn't was all Andy Candy could muster.

"All right," Andy said. "An accident or something, or maybe we just don't know." This seemed awkward to both of them, but for different reasons. Moth found himself thinking, *This is my fight.* Andy Candy thought, *Whatever it is you've started, you have to finish.* Both failed to see these beliefs for the naïve romantic foolishness that they were.

"Just tell them what we heard and saw and that's it," Moth said. He paused. He felt like a pretentious theater director giving an actor her instructions. "Andy . . . Don't act calm."

She looked down at the doctor's body. She could feel tears welling up in her eyes. *What a strange request,* she thought. But that was the extent of her ability to process anything happening around her.

"That's easy," she said. There was so much hysteria circling around her, reaching out and seizing some to parcel onto a phone call to a police dispatcher seemed simple.

But just hearing her own voice seemed to help her regain some control over her racing emotions. She had the odd thought, *So that's what it's like to see someone murdered.*

She punched the numbers on her phone, all the time thinking she was caught up in some strange out-of-body experience. Moth pushed past her, walking out the front door to the rental car. Then the clipped dispatcher's voice came on the line, and she heard herself giving an address, although it seemed like it was someone else, someone reliable and unfazed, summoning the police.

"When you ran outside, did you see anyone or anything?"

Moth had hesitated before shaking his head. He asked himself the same question and realized "Nothing" was the only answer. Or maybe, "Nothing out of the ordinary." Except that a 180-grain deer slug had exploded in the doctor's head seconds earlier. That wasn't ordinary. But Moth realized that nothing in his life any longer was ordinary. He hoped Andy Candy recognized the same.

"No. I'm sorry. Nothing."

The detective wrote down every word Moth uttered.

There were other questions for both of them. Routine questions, like, "What flights were you on?" and "Did the doctor say anything before being shot?" There were photos taken and crime scene technicians called, just as there had been when his uncle was killed. There was some commotion when a detective walking the bullet path came across the murdered deer and someone said "Hunting accident," which didn't seem totally convincing—though Moth and Andy Candy heard it repeated several times. There was a lot of "How do I get in touch with you?" exchanges of e-mail and cell phone numbers. Neither Moth nor Andy Candy could tell exactly what the policemen thought about the psychiatrist's death, even when they asked the obvious question:

"Do you know of anyone who wanted to kill the doctor?"

And both replied:

"No."

They didn't have to agree beforehand about this lie. It just came naturally.

21

The scream bothered him immensely.

It was out of place and unexpected.

Little in any of his killings had gone wrong. Then—as he replayed the scream in his memory—it transformed systematically into a concern. And concern quickly changed into a completely new consideration that went beyond simple curiosity, into something akin to worry, which was a feeling utterly alien to him. And this worry deepened with each passing moment. It made him feel decidedly strange, almost light-headed, his pulse accelerating, and his skin tingling, as if he was getting a small electric shock. These were all new sensations in the process of murder, and he didn't like any of them.

There should have been silence.

Silence and death. That was how I'd planned it.

Maybe some rustling sounds from tree branches as I retreated. That's all.

Who screamed?

Who was in that house?

No one was supposed to be there.

Cleaning lady? No. *Neighbor?* No. *Cable repairman?* No.
I should have gone back.

Student #5 canceled his next-day flight to Key West, where he'd intended to vacation, leisurely drinking a Cuba libre at the bar at Louie's Backyard restaurant as he'd plotted out the remaining, nonlethal phase of his life. He had lately been indulging in pleasant fantasies—perhaps finding a job in the therapeutic community to take advantage of all his long-dormant psychological expertise. Maybe he'd work in a halfway home for former patients, or answer phones at a suicide prevention line. He didn't need to make money. He needed to fill his remaining life with the deep satisfactions he'd expected when he'd first gone to medical school so many years earlier.

He'd even considered reconnecting with what relatives he had left— scattered cousins who believed him dead. He liked to envision the shock and surprise as news traveled around the family: *He's alive!* He would be like one of those Japanese soldiers discovered on abandoned Pacific Ocean islands, still thinking the war was being fought thirty, forty years later, unable to bring themselves to surrender, being greeted as heroes with parades and medals when they returned in confusion to their strange and modern homeland. Possibilities had seemed endless. He could regain his name, his identity, and more critically, his potential—and no one would ever know how he'd achieved this.

It should have been like being young again.

Suddenly the new history that he'd thought was magically going to be delivered to him by freeing himself from his old history was threatened.

Rage instantly filled him.

Son of a bitch. Goddamn son of a bitch. A goddamn scream.

He had already spent some hours gathering all the elements of Jeremy Hogan's murder together and disposing of them all: Computer hard drives and handwritten notes. Pictures, maps, schedules, routes. Weapons. Ammunition. Electronic voice-masking devices and throwaway cell phones. All the detailed information, personal history, and daily routines that he'd used preparing for and executing the psychiatrist's death. He had hoped that when he'd destroyed each link to the murder, he could finally start in on a new life.

God damn it to hell. Wasted time.

He told himself to be rational and begin investigating that scream, but this admonition made his breathing even tighter.

Late at night, in his New York apartment, Student #5 forced himself to once again turn to his computer. It took him a few minutes to install a brand-new hard drive, time he spent cursing wildly.

His first visit was to the website for the *Trenton Times,* the largest local paper in the nearest city. It carried only a single story: *Retired Doctor Killed in Apparent Hunting Accident.*

He read the half-dozen paragraphs thinking, *That's right, that's exactly right*—but the story didn't contain enough detail to diminish his nervousness. Indeed, the article quickly degenerated into a listing of Jeremy Hogan's professional accomplishments beneath a single police lieutenant's quotation: "There are indications that the doctor might have been a victim of an out-of-season hunting mishap."

"Mishap," he blurted out loud, on the edge of outrage. "Mishap?" He was staring at his computer screen and wanted to punch it. "No shit."

Student #5 looked up and out his window. Manhattan night's glow greeted him. He could hear traffic out on the streets, the usual combination of cars, trucks, horns sounding, and occasional sirens. Everything was just as it should be and yet, something seemed decidedly wrong. All the sounds that should have reassured him in their normalcy did no such thing.

Like any scientist reviewing data from his latest experiment, Student #5 went back over every aspect of the kill. Even more than some of his others, this one had seemed to be perfect—right down to the final bit of conversation, the hesitation before he'd caressed the trigger. He recalled the solid pressure against his shoulder and the small image he'd seen through the scope. He'd been 100 percent certain that Jeremy Hogan had experienced the absolutely necessary moment of fear and recognition and known at the very end he was about to die and who it was that was doing his killing—even if he didn't remember the name. Just a heart-stopping second or two for Hogan to flood with terrible and completely deserved memories, feel terror in his stomach, and realize he was lost despite every precaution he'd taken. And then, deliciously, as all these things flooded him, his brain exploded.

An ideal murder.

One to envy. One to savor.

Except for that scream.

Student #5 went over the sound in his head.

Female. High-pitched. *Was there a secondary sound?*

Damn it, damn it, damn it. The plan had been so simple:

Dial.

Speak rehearsed lines.

Aim.

Shoot.

Quickly check for any leftover clues inadvertently left behind.

Retreat.

And he'd stuck precisely to it. Just as he should. Just as he had every other time.

Except, this time he should have waited.

He cursed, gripped the edges of his desk tightly, stood up abruptly, paced about, pounded one fist into an open palm, then dropped to the hardwood floor and started doing sit-ups. At fifty, sweat glistening on his forehead, he stopped.

Telling himself to remain calm and focused, Student #5 returned to the computer. He decided to try the website for the *Princeton Packet,* a twice-a-week suburban paper that covered the area. What he immediately saw were lots of stories about zoning board meetings, leash laws, recycling efforts, Little League baseball tryouts, and school projects. With a little mouse-click persistence he found: *Apparent Hunting Accident Claims Prominent Professor's Life.*

The story was similar to the prior one, but it had a few more details, including the dead deer and the phrase: *The doctor's body was discovered by houseguests.*

He thought: *No one ever visited the doctor. Not in years.*

So who are they?

Student #5 barely slept. Most of the rest of the night he spent staring at the story on his computer, half-expecting other words to form on the screen.

10 a.m.

Use a throwaway phone. Stick to the story.

The line was ringing and he had scripted the most reasonable lies in his head.

"Hello. *Princeton Packet.* This is Connie Smith."

"Ms. Smith, hello. I'm terribly sorry to bother you at your office. My name is Philip Hogan. I'm calling from California about the recent death of my cousin. Distant cousin, unfortunately, both in miles and relations. The whole thing has taken us all by surprise. Now we're just trying to find out exactly what happened, and I can't seem to get a straight answer from the local police. I mean, what sort of accident was this? I was hoping you might be able to fill me in on a few details."

"The cops are usually pretty tight-lipped until they sign off on the whole thing," the reporter replied.

"Your story said a hunting accident? My cousin wasn't a hunter, at least, not that we knew of, so . . ." He let his voice trail off, endowing each word with a question mark.

"Well, yeah. I'm sorry to have to say this, but the 'accident' part is dicey. It appears a stray shot from some out-of-season idiot using a far-too-powerful rifle killed your relative instead of a deer. Or in addition to a deer. The cops are looking for the hunter—maybe he's facing a manslaughter charge in addition to a pile of wildlife violations—but no success so far. That's why they won't cooperate."

"I see. That sounds terrible. I never met my cousin, but he was a quite accomplished psychiatrist. And he was home when this happened?"

"Yes. Answering a phone, apparently. I mean, just bad luck, really, as best as I understand it. But you shouldn't rely on what I've been told. Eventually the police will issue a final statement, which is likely to be more accurate than the hearsay and rumor I've picked up on."

"Oh," Student #5 said, filling his voice with as much phony concern as he could muster, "how awful."

"Yes. I'm sorry for your loss. It was a lousy break."

"It seems that way. What a tragedy, but, at least, he was getting on in years. And I think Cousin Jeremy lived alone, ever since his wife passed away. He must have been sad and lonely."

"I wouldn't know," said Connie Smith.

"Do you have funeral home information?"

"The paper will publish an obit after the coroner releases the body, so check back in a day or so."

"Okay. Will do. Oh, one other question, and I really thank you for your help . . ."

"No problem."

"How was he discovered? I mean, he didn't suffer, did he?"

"No. Death was probably instantaneous . . ."

This Student #5 already knew. *The suffering came earlier.* But he wanted to ask questions that fit the image he was trying to create in the reporter's mind. *Distant. Modestly concerned. Mostly just curious.*

"But how . . ." he continued.

"Apparently a young couple had come to visit him. Coincidence, really, a cop told me off the record. They weren't relatives. There had to be some other reason they were there, but it wasn't in the initial police report and I don't know what it might be. Probably a medical student looking up a professor emeritus, but I'm just guessing."

"Did you speak with them?"

"No. By the time I got to the scene, they'd already cleared out. They had to be scared out of their minds. Come to visit and . . ." The reporter stopped. She was probably afraid of being insensitive.

He was cautious. *Don't sound eager,* he reminded himself.

"Oh, perhaps I should try to connect with them, then. Do you have names, numbers, anything that might help me get in touch with them?"

"I've got their names," she said. "But no numbers. The cops, I guess, didn't want me calling them up before they finished their investigation. Typical. Probably they don't want you calling them, either, but hell. They wouldn't be too hard to track down."

"But you haven't . . ."

"No. Don't see much to report here, unless the cops come up with the stupid hunter's name. Then there will be an arrest and a follow-up story."

That won't happen, he thought.

He listened carefully and asked the reporter to spell the *houseguest* names out twice. Student #5 stared hard at the letters in front of him. They seemed to waver, dancing like heat above a highway on a scorching day. Boy. Girl.

Girl meant nothing: Andrea Martine.

Who are you?

But the boy's name meant much: Timothy Warner.

I know who you are.

He knew he should be angry with himself because he'd missed a connection. But he let his subterranean fury dissipate into the prospect of more research, thinking that study would help calm him down and maybe make the nasty sensation of . . .

He paused as if he could make his thoughts hesitate, like reining in a runaway horse, as he considered what he was feeling. *A sensation of what? A threat? A failure? Danger?*

"Hope I've helped," said the reporter.

"Yes. Thank you. Immensely," Student #5 replied.

A part of him wanted to laugh. *Suburban reporter. Inexperienced. You're talking to the absolute best story ever to cross your desk. Only you don't see it.*

22

On the airplane returning to Miami, Andy Candy fell asleep—exhausted by a sort of tension she'd never experienced before—and her head drooped onto Moth's shoulder. He thought this was probably the sexiest moment he'd experienced in years. It reminded him of the first time she had ever touched him with intimacy. What had actually been groping and unco-ordinated had turned silken and smooth in his memory. He desperately wanted to stroke her cheek, but did not.

He luxuriated in the scent of her hair and tried to concentrate on what had happened to them. The occasional turbulent bump conspired to interrupt the most contradictory of emotions: murder and desire.

Jet engines droned. A stewardess walked the aisle. She smiled at Moth as she passed by.

He was glad to see us. Relieved. Eager to help.

An awful picture formed in Moth's imagination: the doctor, hand outstretched, welcoming them into his home. *How long did he have left? One minute? Two?*

And then the phone rang.

Moth breathed in sharply. *Blood was everywhere. Andy screamed.*

He pictured the doctor reaching for the phone.

There was a countdown going on: Five, four, three . . .

Something was being said.

Two, one . . . murder.

Moth realized that Doctor Hogan had merely listened, frozen in place. He'd said nothing to indicate who it was on the other end of the line.

How close were we to dying? Suppose we'd followed him into that kitchen and were standing at his side?

Instead, we were ten feet from death.

Moth stiffened in his seat, refusing to shift even an inch because he didn't want to do anything that would make Andy Candy inadvertently move her head away from his shoulder. He started to look around the plane wildly, imagining that his uncle's killer had followed them on board. It took him several seconds to calm his racing pulse, insisting, *Don't be crazy. He's not here.*

At least, not yet.

Moth closed his eyes, listened to the engines.

Before today, murder was an abstraction, he thought. *Even when I saw Uncle Ed's body, it was still a killing that had happened, not a killing that was happening.*

Verb tenses that underscored death.

We're learning. Fast.

Fast enough?

He wasn't at all sure about this.

What they saw, what they heard, what they felt, how they reacted all combined into a stew of violent death. The burgeoning academic in Moth wondered whether all these sensations put together were what soldiers on a battlefield experienced.

And then they have nightmares, he thought. *Even with all their training, what they get are night sweats and paranoid anxiety. What protects us?*

He stole a look at his right hand, imagining that it should be quivering with a drunkard's shakes. Then he watched Andy Candy and counted each regular breath she took, trying to see if somewhere on her relaxed face was the beginning of some nightmare.

What do we do now?

For a moment, he had a distant thought, something way on the periphery of what he was trying to process: *Am I going to kill her by asking for her help?* But as quickly as this idea intruded he dismissed it, because he selfishly knew how much he needed her.

Andy Candy awakened on the final approach into Miami and realized that she was suddenly wrapped up in a tapestry of killings and that anyone in their right mind would flee the instant they touched down before they got woven any deeper into the fabric. She'd formulated this opinion before. But on those times, it had seemed an intellectual conclusion, like something obvious to any good student taking an advanced English literature course. No longer. Reason battled against something deeper than loyalty. She could feel Moth's presence in the seat next to her and even if she wouldn't turn to look at him, she knew that he would be lost without her. *Blinded,* she thought. *That's what he would be.* She replayed Doctor Hogan's death in her mind's eye, and understood that the two of them were naïve and probably foolish to think that they could contend with the sort of threat that fired that rifle.

She had an odd thought: *People celebrate the climbers that risk death to reach the peak of Everest. People wildly criticize the climbers that make some small error in judgment or planning and die on the route to the top of Everest. But people don't remember the climbers who recognize their limits and turn back toward safety just yards from the summit. They may be alive. But they are forgotten.*

Their flight landed without a problem. They went to baggage claim. Moth had checked his small suitcase, and he paced around nervously waiting for it to arrive on the conveyor belt. Andy Candy was a little taken aback by his behavior until she realized that he'd put the doctor's gun in his bag, and he was afraid some X-ray machine had spotted it.

* * *

199

Five dead psychiatrists.

Four students. One professor.

What did they have in common?

His first instinct was: *a shared class?*

Forensic psychiatry. That was what Jeremy Hogan taught. But none of the four dead students specialized in that field. They were a research psychiatrist, a therapist, a child psychiatrist, and one who specialized in geriatric psychiatry. And only Ed had actually taken Doctor Hogan's class.

Andy Candy had set up a workspace in Moth's tiny galley kitchen, perched on a stool by the counter, hunched over her laptop, and surrounded by coffee cups and notes—including the scrawled entries on Doctor Hogan's legal pad. She knew these should have been turned over to the detectives in New Jersey, but also felt certain they would have been ignored. Moth was seated behind a small desk, also working on a computer. It was midday, bright sun flooded through the windows, but Andy Candy thought they were working as if it were closing in on midnight.

Moth stared at the names in front of him: *five unique deaths.* There was no single element that shrieked, *This is the how they died, and that will tell you the why.* They lived in different parts of the nation. They had different career arcs, different types of families. Their histories were wildly different.

What they had in common was a third-year program years earlier when they all decided to go into psychiatry. That told him this: His uncle's killer was either someone they all treated as students, someone who taught them, or someone in the program with them.

He wondered: *Why would a teacher kill his onetime students?* Moth removed that category.

Thirty years after graduation: His uncle died from a handgun fired at close range into his temple.

Thirty years after graduation: He and Andy Candy had witnessed a death from a distance, a shot fired from a high-powered rifle. But of the five deaths he was examining, these were the only ones where guns were involved.

One student. One professor.

"All right," Moth said to Andy. "We know about two deaths. We have to do a little basic research into the others." She nodded.

Another ex-student. A phone call to a rich widow:

How did he die?

Twenty years after graduation:

"Stupidity, really. Stupidity, but it became a big-time lawsuit. A young and inexperienced nurse filling in for someone home sick that day— she'd never worked in the ICU before—misread a heart surgeon's post-op medication instructions, and so the injection he got . . ."

Moth listened to a story of scrawled notes on a chart and medication that should have been *point five zero milligrams* unfortunately becoming *fifty milligrams*. This was the most common of ICU mistakes and probably happened more often than any hospital wanted to let on. The widow seemed resigned to the story. "The surgeon was tired and hurried, and though he denied making a mistake on the chart, well . . ." She hesitated, and added, "Well . . . well, well . . . you know doctors' handwriting." The woman sighed deeply. "There was a little mark on the chart—the lawyers showed it to me. It almost looked like his pen had run out of ink, or somehow it got erased, like some liquid spilled on it, and he claimed it was the missing decimal point. At least, that's what he would have said in a trial, but it never got that far. Argue this, argue that, but he was still dead. The hospital attorneys were eager to settle."

Another sigh: "Think about it. You die because of a little mark on a paper that may or may not be there. A damn decimal point. It was ten years ago. I've moved on."

Moth thanked the widow, apologizing for disturbing her, and thinking that nothing in the tone of her voice supported the contention *I've moved on*. But as he spoke, he thought, *A medical student would know about dosages and ICU errors. He would know about a decimal point.* He wondered about the word *erased* that the widow had used.

Another ex-student. A phone call to a state trooper in charge of auto accident reconstruction:

How did she die?

Eighteen years after graduation:

Gruff, no-nonsense voice: "The doc liked to walk her dog in the evening, right around dusk, on a little two-lane, real narrow country road. No sidewalks. No shoulder. Not smart. And she was walking on the wrong side. Should be facing oncoming traffic, but she wasn't. She and her husband had split up and he had the kids for the weekend, so there was no one around to call the police when she didn't return home. When we measured skid marks, checked weather and light conditions, it appeared she was hit from behind on a blind curve just a little after dark, dragged about ten feet before being knocked into a drainage ditch, where she was out of sight from any subsequent motorists passing by. Suspect vehicle was traveling at least fifty miles per hour on impact. Couldn't find any brake marks until yards past the point of collision. It was morning before someone spotted her down there—and that was some schoolkids walking to a bus stop who didn't know what to do, so it was even longer before we were on scene."

The trooper paused.

"A lousy death. Impact didn't completely kill her. It was the combination of blood loss, shock, and hypothermia. Got damn cold that night, like upper twenties. Maybe took a couple minutes, maybe a couple hours. Couldn't tell for certain. Son of a bitch hit-and-run driver killed the dog, too. A golden retriever. Sweetheart of a dog. From time to time, she used to take the dog into a psych ward where she worked. People said the dog was better for the patients than any therapy."

"And your investigation?"

"Went kind of nowhere," the trooper said. "Very frustrating." Moth could hear the shrug over the phone line.

"We put out a BOLO—a Be on the Lookout—for the car, once we'd identified it from a paint chip that stuck to the dog's leash. We notified body shops in a three-county area—you know, look out for anyone with left front end damage. Pulled all sorts of rental records, auto sales, registrations—the works—looking for the car. But it didn't show up for six months, and then . . ."

The trooper's voice trailed off a bit, before coming back on strong.

"Burned out. Torched. Way back in the woods. Forensics pulled the VIN number off it, but all it did was match up with a vehicle stolen from a mall parking lot in the next state over four days before the accident."

Again the trooper hesitated. "There was one detail that really stuck with me. Seen it before, seen it again, but it's still pretty damn nasty."

"What's that?" Moth asked. He sounded like a reporter collecting facts; the more terrible, the more flat and sturdy he sounded.

"There were some signs in the leaves and other debris around the doc's body that the hit-and-run driver stopped, got out, went and stood next to the doc—you know, checked out what he'd done—before taking off."

"In other words . . ."

"In other words, made absolutely certain she was dying and then left her."

"And?"

"And that was that. Dead end. Some lucky bastard got away with a ve-hicular homicide, unless you can tell me something I don't know."

Moth considered this request. There was a lot he could say. "No," he said, "I was just trying to get in touch with the doctor to inform her about my uncle's suicide. They had been classmates together, and there's a memorial fund. When I found out she was dead, I just got curious. Sorry if I've wasted your time."

"No problem," said the trooper. Moth could hear suspicions in the man's voice. He didn't blame him.

But at the same time, he wanted to pound the table. *What is there in a hit-and-run that speaks about the study of psychiatry?*

Nothing he could readily see—except that telling statement: *made absolutely certain . . .*

Another ex-student. Two calls.

How did he die?

Fourteen years after graduation:

First: a college-age son.

"Dad was alone at the summer house up on the lake. He liked to go up there early in the season, before anyone else showed up—get the place open, putter around, be by himself . . . You know, it's really hard for me to talk about it. I'm sorry."

Second: Taylor-Fredericks Funeral Home in Lewiston, Maine.

"I'll have to check my records," the manager said. "It's been a long time."

"Thank you," Moth replied. He waited patiently.

The man came back on the line. He had a whiny, nasal voice, almost a caricature of a funeral home director's.

"Now I remember . . ."

"Boating accident?" Moth asked.

"Yes. The doctor had a small sailboat that he typically took out every day in the summer. But this was early April—you know, ice melt was just about finished, house-opening season. No one was around. He must have put the boat in the water, decided to take a little spin. The weather wasn't that mild and he shouldn't have been out on the lake. People don't want to hear it, but in April there's still a lot of leftover winter in these parts. He shouldn't have done that."

"But what exactly killed him?"

"Sudden gust, probably. At least, that's what the county coroner sort of figured. Boom must have caught him on the side of the head. Knocked him into the lake, probably unconscious already. Water temperature was maybe forty-five degrees. No, probably lower. Can't last long in that. Ten minutes, they tell me; that's it. Anyway, it was forty-eight hours before divers found his body, and that was only because some other home owner spotted the overturned boat out in the lake and called the cops. Coroner noted some damage to the back of his head—but the body had been in the water, so hard to say exactly what happened. And the boat flipped after he went out—at least that was what folks guessed—so anything left behind was gone. Sad story. Family had him cremated and his ashes spread on the lake. I gather it was a special place for him."

Very special, Moth thought. *The place he was murdered.*

But the leap from *murdered* to *how?* eluded Moth. And there was nothing in what seemed like a random accident that spoke of medical school thirty years earlier.

"God damn it," Moth whispered, hanging up his phone.

Suicide. Hunting accident. Hit-and-run. Hospital mistake. Boating accident. Each death either spread out over years or jammed together a few weeks apart. None of it seemed to occupy any realm of probability; but it might start to make sense if seen from the perspective that Moth alone occupied.

He looked over at Andy Candy. *Maybe not completely alone,* he hoped.

" 'My fault,' " Moth said.

Andy lifted her head. "That's what Doctor Hogan said. Same as your uncle. Sort of."

"Five people are dead. There was a reason. Let's find out what they shared."

Andy Candy nodded. "This is what we have," she said, pointing at Jeremy Hogan's scribbled notes. "It doesn't seem like much. But it is, really."

"Why do you say that?"

"He was the only professor. The others were all students. So . . ."

"So we know *when* whatever it was they were to blame for happened. We just have to find out what it was."

Andy Candy used her most persuasive voice, the one in which she mingled a young-girl, bright-eyed innocence with the persistence of a veteran investigative reporter. No one in the current dean's office at the university's medical school had been on the job thirty years earlier, and they were reluctant to give out contact information for retirees.

But *reluctant* didn't mean they wouldn't. She obtained a phone number for a doctor long gone from the university.

On the fourth ring, a woman answered.

Andy quickly went through the cover story—Ed's suicide, the memorial fund. She was halfway through when the woman interrupted.

"I'm sorry. I don't think we can contribute."

"Can I speak with the doctor?" Andy Candy persisted.

"No."

This was so abrupt she was taken aback.

"Just for a minute or two."

"No. I'm sorry. He's in hospice care."

The woman's voice seemed to be coming across some vast space, and she stifled a small sob.

"Oh, I'm sorry . . ."

"He only has a few days, they tell me."

"I didn't mean to . . ."

"It's okay. It's been expected. He's been sick for a long time."

Andy Candy was about to create some quick excuse and hang up. She could sense the woman's pain over the phone line, almost as if she were standing next to her. But as Andy pawed at words, she found herself tightening, almost overcome with a sudden determination.

"Did the doctor ever speak about anything—I believe it would have been the class of 1983—anything unusual? Anything out of the ordinary with the students?"

"I beg your pardon?"

"It was my uncle's class," Andy lied. "And something happened . . ."

The woman paused. "What's this about?" she demanded.

Andy Candy took a deep breath and continued lying.

"When my uncle died, he referred to some event back in his med school program. We're just trying to find out what he meant."

This seemed like a reasonable explanation.

"I can't help you," the woman said. "My husband can't help you. He's dying."

"I'm sorry. But—"

"Call one of the people who went through the psych program. That program was always the most problematic of all the disciplines. More trouble for the administration than it was worth, I think. Every year there were fifteen admitted. Maybe one of them didn't end up crazy. Perhaps they can assist you."

And then the woman hung up.

Andy Candy looked down at her list. The distraught woman hadn't said anything she didn't already know—and yet, she had.

Fifteen admitted.

She counted graduates.

Fourteen graduated.

Four dead.

One missing.

Someone came in, but did not come out.

There it was, and so simple it frightened her.

Andy Candy shivered. Moth must have seen something in her face, because he bent toward her. Andy had difficulty putting what she understood in that second into some articulate statement of discovery. But inwardly she suddenly felt as close to death again as she had in the moment she saw Jeremy Hogan's head explode and she'd screamed. She wondered whether she was doomed to spend the rest of her life screaming. Or more likely, waiting to scream.

23

Susan Terry made a point of sitting beside Moth at Redeemer One that night. When it was her turn, she declined to speak. She gestured to Moth, who also shook his head, which seemed to surprise everyone, and testifying was passed on to the engineer, who methodically outlined his latest Oxy struggle.

When the session broke up, Susan placed her hand on Moth's arm, holding him in his seat for a moment.

"I have someone waiting," Moth said.

"This will only take a minute," Susan responded.

She watched as the others filed out of the room or milled over by the coffee and soft drink table.

"You've missed some of these meetings," Susan said.

"I've been busy."

"I'm busy too, but I've been here. You're too busy to show up and talk about addiction?"

This was blunt and to the point.

"I was out of town."

"Where?"

"North."

"*North* is a big place. They have bars in the *North*?"

She hoped that a little sarcasm would loosen him up. Sarcasm makes people angry, and angry people shoot their mouths off. This was an equation she'd learned in her first day as a prosecutor and that she hoped would work with Moth.

"I suppose so. Didn't go to any."

Susan nodded. "Sure," she said, making a single syllable sound like a dozen. Any interrogation, even the most offhanded one, relied on probing weaknesses. She was well versed in Moth's greatest weakness, because she shared it. "So, what exactly did you do, up in the great wide North?"

"I went to see a man who knew my uncle when he was younger."

"Who was that?"

"A retired psychiatrist who was one of my uncle's teachers."

"Why him?"

Moth didn't answer.

"I see," Susan said. "So, you're still convinced there's some mysterious master criminal out there?" She continued her sarcasm, trying to needle Moth into saying something concrete. She ricocheted between doubts and certainties about the uncle's death: *doubts* that were her own, brand-new ones and which she wanted to disappear as readily and quickly as possible, and *certainties* reflected in Moth's steadfast and, to her, completely irritating insistence.

Moth faked a laugh. "Yes," he said. "But I wouldn't know how to characterize him. You think there is someone—some sort of Professor Moriarty that battles Sherlock Holmes? You think that's what I'm doing? But what happens to them? Reichenbach Falls. Anyway, in this case *master criminal* seems a little premature."

He thought this was lying with truths. And he liked using the word *premature.*

"Timothy," Susan said, trying abruptly to soften her tone, which was usually another effective technique, although she was beginning to believe that Moth might be immune to most routine approaches. "I'm trying to help you. You know that. I warned you that going off half-cocked on some wild-goose chase was dangerous. Tell me, in your trip north when you visited this man your uncle knew like dozens of years ago, did you find out anything?"

Moth could not stop himself. The word exploded from his lips, though it was spoken in a whisper.

"Yes."

They were both quiet for an instant. Susan Terry shook her head, unconvinced.

"What exactly was that?" she demanded. This question was spoken in a tone that was unequivocal: a professional prosecutor's not subtle insistence.

"That I'm right," Moth said.

Then he rose and walked quickly toward the exit, leaving Susan behind on the couch watching him, anger mixing with curiosity in a dangerous cocktail.

In the car outside Redeemer One, Andy Candy waited for Moth and busied herself making more phone calls.

Right about the time she thought the meeting would be winding up she dialed the number for a psychiatrist in San Francisco. He was the third name on her list of surviving graduates and seemed to be in private psychoanalytic and therapeutic practice. He had a mixture of responses on Angie's List, half of which seemed to canonize him, and half that implied he should be indicted or imprisoned or consigned to the Seventh Circle of Hell. Andy imagined that this range would probably constitute flattery to most shrinks.

She was surprised when the doctor answered his own phone. She stammered briefly as she went through the now-memorized bit about Uncle Ed and a memorial fund.

"A memorial fund?" the doctor asked.

"Yes," she said.

He hesitated. "Well, I suppose I could kick in a small amount."

"That would be great," she replied.

Again he hesitated. His voice seemed to take on a different pitch. "That can't really be why you're calling," he said decisively.

She tried to rapidly form some sort of excuse or explanation, but could not. "No. Not exactly," she said.

"Then, please, what is it?"

"We . . . I . . . uh, don't think Ed committed suicide. We think there's some incident way in his past that . . ." She paused, unsure how to continue.

"An incident? What sort of incident?"

"Something that connects his past with his present," Andy replied.

"That is about as simple and accurate a description of psychiatry as you could possibly come up with," the doctor said with a small, disarming laugh. He continued, "And my part in this?"

Again she paused. "Third year, medical school."

Now it was his turn to be silent for a few seconds.

"The best worst year," he said. "What's the cliché? *That which doesn't kill you makes you stronger.* Whoever thought that foolishness up never spent three hundred and sixty-five days as a third-year medical student and certainly knew nothing about mental illnesses."

"Do you remember Ed?"

"Yeah. Maybe. A little bit. He was a good guy. Smart and incisive, I remember. We shared a class or two, I think—no, we had to have. We were in the same field, heading in basically the same direction. But that's not the point, is it?"

"No."

"I'm not accustomed to speaking with people about sensitive matters over the telephone," he said.

"We need help," Andy burst out.

"Who is the *we* you refer to?" The doctor was being cautious.

"Ed's nephew. He's my friend."

"Well, I don't know how much I can help."

Andy Candy remained quiet, figuring he would continue. She was correct.

"What do you know about the third year of medical school with a concentration in psychiatry?" the doctor asked abruptly.

"Not much. I mean, it's when you make a decision—"

"Let me interrupt you," he said sharply. "It is . . ." He paused, considering what he was going to say. "There was a movie. *The Year of Living Dangerously*. A nice descriptive phrase. That's what it was for all of us."

"Can you help me understand?" Andy Candy asked, thinking that was a good way to keep a psychiatrist talking.

The doctor paused.

"Two things. First the context: third year. Then what happened, although I'm not sure I know too much about anything. There were some rumors, I recall. But none of us had the time to pay any attention to rumors. We were all too concerned with what was right in front of us."

"Okay." She was trying to lead him.

"Third year is filled with stress for any medical student. But psychiatry provides a different stress, because of all the disciplines in medicine, ours is the most elusive. There's no rash on the skin, trouble urinating, difficulty breathing, or unexplained cough to help us out. It's all about interpreting unusual behaviors. Third year, we were all physically exhausted, half-psychotic ourselves. We were vulnerable to many of the diseases we were studying. Crippling depressions. Doubts. Sleep deprivation and hallucinations. It's a very difficult time. The demands were relentless and fears of failure very real."

"So . . ."

"I hated that year and loved it, too. In retrospect, it's a year that brings out the best and worst inside you. A defining year."

"Did you take a course with Professor Jeremy Hogan?"

The psychiatrist hesitated again.

"Yes. His lecture course on forensic psychiatry. It had a great nickname: *Reading Killers*. It was fascinating, even if outside my interests."

"Ed Warner was in the course too, and something connected Doctor

Hogan to Ed and some other students . . ." She quickly read off the names of the other dead psychiatrists.

The doctor paused again. "To the best of my memory—remember, we're going back decades here—those were probably the members of Study Group Alpha. I can't be sure, understand? I mean, it was many years ago. In third-year psychiatry, there were three study groups: Alpha, Beta, and Zeta. That was a joke in Latin—first, second, and last. There were five of us randomly assigned to each group. Some natural rivalries arose—every group wanted the best GPA, wanted the best Match Day results. But there was a problem in Alpha."

"A problem?"

"One student seemed to be trapped in psychosis. At least, that was the story that went around. Of course, with the stress, the decisions, the never-ending course work, plus the fear that we'd make a diagnostic mistake, every group had members on edge. Breakdowns weren't uncommon . . ."

The psychiatrist paused again.

"His was."

A Short, but Dangerous Conversation That Actually Happened

"Doctor Hogan, I'm sorry to disturb you . . ."

"What is it, Mister, uh . . . Warner, correct?"

"Yes, sir. I'm here on behalf of my fellow study group students . . ."

"Yes? I have a class scheduled and not much time. Can you get directly to the point?"

Ed Warner: Deep breath. Organizing thoughts quickly. Shuffling feet. Sensation of doubt.

"Four members of Study Group Alpha are concerned with the behavioral patterns of the fifth member. We sincerely believe that he presents a genuine threat, either to himself, or perhaps to us."

Jeremy Hogan: A pause. Rocking in a chair. Tapping a pencil against teeth. Scheduled class mentally postponed.

"What sort of threat?"

"Physical violence."

"That's quite an accusation, Mister Warner. I hope you can back this up."

"I can, sir. And coming to speak to you was, all of us felt, the last resort."

"You understand an accusation like this can impact all of your careers?"

"We do. We've taken that into consideration."

"And why have you brought this to me?"

"Because of your expertise in explosive personalities."

"You believe your fellow student is on an edge that might result in . . . precisely what, Mister Warner?"

"Over the last weeks, this student's behavior has grown increasingly erratic, and—"

"Exams are approaching. Many students are on edge."

Ed Warner: Another deep breath. A quick glance at sheaves of paper from each member of the group, outlining impressions.

"Last week he strangled a lab rat in front of all of us. No reason. He just seized the rat and killed it. Flat affect as he did it. It was like he was demonstrating his ability to kill without remorse. He constantly talks to himself, in a rambling, disjointed, usually incomprehensible, but frequently angry manner—especially as it relates to his family pressures and then, about us. He is isolated, but threatening. He claims to own weapons. Guns. Every effort we have made to engage him, maybe defuse the situation, get him to seek help, has been rebuffed. Sometimes his facial expressions are labile and disconnected to recognizable context—one second he will laugh inappropriately, then a second later he will burst into tears. Last week he took a scalpel from a surgical theater and sliced the word kill *into his forearm in front of all of us, while we were holding a pre-exam cram session. I'm unsure that he either felt any pain in that second, or realized what he was doing. Whenever anyone in the study group seeks to correct him, point out a difference of opinion, even suggest a different type of answer to an academic question, he is likely to suddenly scream in their face, or else stare hatefully at them. Sometimes he writes down our names, the date, and a description of the dispute in a notebook. It's like he's not taking notes for class, but taking notes on us. Preparing a case, I think, to internally justify an act of violence . . ."*

Jeremy Hogan: A nod of the head. A genuine look of concern.

"You must take your situation immediately to the dean's office and inform him of everything you've told me. You should do this without delay. You are absolutely correct. Your fellow student sounds to be in significant trouble. He may need hospitalization."

And then the brief exchange that started everything:

"Can you help?"

"Him?"

Ed Warner: Hesitation. Honesty.

"No. Us."

"I will call the dean right now and tell him you are on your way to his office. He will want to see chapter and verse. You are correct, Mister Warner. The symptomatology you present includes several recognizable elements of certain sorts of dangerous explosions. I would think acting quickly in this situation is crucial."

"Should we contact campus security?"

"Not yet. The dean should do that."

Then Jeremy Hogan reached for the phone on his desk with very much the same motion he would use thirty years later in the precious few seconds before he died.

Andy Candy waited for the psychiatrist in California to continue. She could hear him gathering his breath.

"There was a physician in our department—a research guy—studying early-childhood attachment disorders, who did much of his work with rhesus monkeys. National Institutes of Health grant, I recall, not that it's important."

"Monkeys?"

"Yes. They're great subjects for psychological studies. Very close in social behaviors to you and me, even if the churchgoing public doesn't want to believe that."

"But what—"

He interrupted her. "Just rumor, you know. Innuendo. Whatever actually happened got covered up by the university really fast, probably because the administration didn't want it impacting their *U.S. News and World Report* ranking. But the sort of story that stays with you, even if I haven't thought about it in years and years. No one has ever asked me about this. And, you must recognize that as sensational as it seemed to be then, there was no time for any of us to digest it, assess it, what have you. We were all swept up in all that third-year tension."

"I understand," she replied, although she doubted that she did.

"The research psychiatrist came in to his laboratory one morning. Door had been forced open. He found five of his prize monkeys arranged in a circle on the floor. Their throats had been sliced."

Andy Candy gasped.

"But what . . ."

"Dead monkeys. No, *slaughtered* monkeys."

The psychiatrist hesitated. "Now, did that have some connection to the troubles in Study Group Alpha? No, one ever proved that, at least not that I know. And it wasn't as if that research doc hadn't made more than a few enemies. He was notoriously cruel to his assistants, and prone to yelling at them, firing them, and screwing up their futures. Not hard to imagine that one of them went looking for a little payback."

"You don't think that?"

"I never knew what to think, and had no time to think it anyways," the psychiatrist continued. "That wasn't what bothered me."

"What was that?" Andy asked, slightly afraid to formulate this question.

"It was the number. Five—as in five dead monkeys. There were twelve others that were untouched. Sometimes, when one examines acts, particularly acts of violence—it makes sense to try to connect dots. Why weren't all the monkeys killed? Or perhaps, just one?"

Andy Candy stammered again, making some grunting sound that came out instead of a question. The only word she could come up with was "And . . ."

"And that's all. I always thought that the lab incident had something to do with that psychotic student. A matter of timing, I suppose. A hearing. Dismissal. Back of an ambulance heading to a private psychiatric hospital. Goodbye, so long, and that was it. One minute he was there, the next gone. And there was no obvious connection to that particular laboratory. Like, he wasn't studying with that professor. But, like all of us, he knew about it, and he knew how to get in and out. So maybe the Freudian in me wants to see a link, but a detective wouldn't."

"Why not?"

"Four people testified at that dean's office hearing: the members of the study group. Curiously, though, there were five slaughtered monkeys. Four versus five . . . which threw it all askew."

"What about Doctor Hogan?"

"He wasn't at that hearing. All he did was what any faculty member would do: contact the dean's office. The rest was up to the members of Study Group Alpha. So I can't really see what he has to do with this."

"I see . . ." Andy Candy said, although she didn't know if she did.

"Of course, this all might be just conjecture. Sounds like far too much Hollywood, if you ask me. And perhaps it was the overinflated and overheated suppositions of a too-tense and stressed-out imagination, so I wouldn't put that much credence in it. Even in medical school rumors were inflated, exaggerated, and bandied about like junior high school dating rumors. But the dead monkeys—those were very real."

Andy Candy felt her mouth go dry and she choked out her question: "Do you remember the name of that student?"

The doctor hesitated.

"Interesting," he said after a momentary hesitation. "You would think that recalling a detail like monkey murder would automatically mean that I would remember the name as well. But I do not. Totally blocked. Intriguing, huh? Perhaps if I think about it for some time, it will come to me. But right now, no."

Andy Candy thought she should have a thousand additional questions, but she could not come up with any. She looked out the window of the car and saw people starting to emerge from Redeemer One. She realized suddenly that the hand holding her cell phone was slippery with sweat.

"Sorry. I don't know if I've helped you or not," the doctor continued. "That's all I recall. Or, possibly, that's all I care to recall. You let me know where I should send that contribution to the memorial fund."

The psychiatrist hung up.

24

Gotta love Facebook.

Student #5 was getting to know Andrea Martine from a distance. He was staring at an electronic array of her wall pictures and reading captions and comments, lots of silly, inconsequential words that concealed some important elements: *dead father the vet; music teacher mother; happy college times that seemed to stop abruptly; no posts for weeks. I wonder why.* Bits of information flooded him as he carefully sorted through the typical teenager-to-college-student chaff in his search for hidden details that would help him plan. He had an odd thought: *Did Mark Zuckerberg ever imagine that his social network could be used to make a decision whether to kill someone?*

He smiled and had an added thought: *It's a little like preparing to go on a blind date, isn't it?* He imagined himself seated across a restaurant table, exchanging pleasantries with Andrea Martine. He spoke in a nice, friendly voice: *"So, you like adopting animals, do you? And reading Emily Dickinson poems and Jane Austen novels both for class and in your spare time? Isn't that interesting . . .*

"It sure sounds like you have a fascinating life, Andrea. Full of possibilities. I would be so sorry to have to cut it short."

This dialogue made him laugh out loud. But the burst of humor didn't manage to conceal troubled thoughts that were lurking in the back of his imagination.

He read through everything, then read it all again, revisiting photos and archived materials. He looked closely at a single picture of a grinning Andrea arm in arm with a dark-haired, thin boy. No name. This picture had the caption *EX* beneath it.

Student #5 noted frequent use of a nickname: *Andy Candy.*

Interesting construction, he thought. *Sort of like a porn star's nom de sex.*

He thought Andy Candy was pretty and recognized that she had a disarming smile and a lanky, sleek figure. He guessed that she was devoted to her studies and a good student. He imagined she was outgoing, friendly, not overly social but no wallflower either. She had posted pictures showing her drinking beer with friends, riding a two-person bicycle, bikini-clad on vacation dropping from the sky harnessed into a parachute towed behind a speedboat. There were pictures of her on a soccer field and playing basketball during her teenage years. There were baby pictures, with the obligatory question written beneath: *Wasn't I a beauty?* She wasn't at all like anyone he'd killed—up to this point.

One old person. Four middle-aged psychiatrists. Study Group Alpha.

But Andy Candy went into a different category. *This would be a killing of choice. This would be a killing to protect your future and to hide what you have done.* Uncertainty made him pause. Made him slightly unsettled. *What's she guilty of?*

Student #5 eyed one particular photo. He guessed she was in her late teens when it was taken. Andy Candy was cuddling on a fluffy sofa with a mutt—and dog and girl were looking directly at the camera, cheek to cheek, each wearing a slightly skewed baseball cap from the University of Florida and a wide grin, even if the dog did look a little uncomfortable. The picture went directly into the young person's category of "cute." There was a joking caption underneath the picture: *Me and my new boyfriend Bruno getting ready for freshman orientation Fall 2010.*

Innocent, he thought.

He bent toward the computer screen. "What were you doing in Doctor Hogan's house, young lady?" he asked, a stern schoolteacher wagging a finger under the nose of a miscreant classroom cutup. "What did you see? What did you hear? What do you mean to do now?"

He almost expected one of the pictures to answer him. "Don't you understand what it means?" Silence filled the room. "I might just have to kill you."

Student #5 shut down the Facebook page and turned his attention to Timothy Warner. No social network site for him—but there were other sources of information, including police records.

Timothy Warner showed up twice for driving under the influence. There was a district court adjudication—six months' nonreporting probation and loss of license.

He found some other entries for Timothy Warner: magna cum laude from the University of Miami, undergraduate degree in American History, and the recipient of a prestigious award. This news release from the university conveniently included a picture and the information that Timothy Warner was continuing at the university to obtain a doctorate in Jeffersonian Studies.

He fixed his eyes on the picture. "Hello, Timothy," he said. "I think we're going to get to know each other."

The *Miami Herald* website listed Timothy Warner in the "survived by" category following its obituary report on his uncle's suicide. Some additional quick clicks on the keyboard, and within a few seconds he had addresses and phone numbers for both Andy Candy and Timothy the nephew.

Student #5 rocked in his chair like an eager sub hoping to be called to go into a game.

He knew what they looked like, and he knew where to look for them, and he believed that whatever blanks he had left on his *Do I need to kill them both?* list could be filled without too much trouble.

He split his computer screen and put up the picture captioned *EX* next to the university press release of Timothy Warner. This interested him. *Did love bring them back together?*

He shook his head.

More likely: death.

25

Andy Candy thought they had entered into some weird parallel universe. Where they stood, the morning sun was insistently bright. The air was warm. Gentle breezes stirred palm fronds into a rhythmic, benign dance.

And now what connected the two of them was murder.

And fear, too, she thought. But she wasn't quite able to gather all that anxiety up into a neat package and describe it to Moth the way she had related all the details of her conversation with the West Coast psychiatrist the night before. When she told Moth all that the doctor had said, she imagined herself some sort of executive secretary of killing. Details had flooded her afterward, and she'd tried to sort through them all: *You go to a college frat house party and it becomes death. You get a call from your old high school boyfriend and it becomes death. You fly to talk to an old psychiatrist and that becomes death.*

What's next?

Too many things were conflated together inside her head. She wanted to grasp something solid, but nothing seemed quite real to her any longer.

Dead monkeys in a psych lab thirty years ago.

Was that real?

Names of dead people on a page in front of her. Accident, accident, suicide.

Were they real?

The baby she'd aborted.

Was it real?

Andy looked over at Moth. *No,* she suddenly thought. *It's not a parallel universe. It's the theater of the absurd and we're both eagerly waiting for Godot.*

"Are you hungry, Andy?" Moth called out.

He was standing at a counter, collecting Cuban coffees for the two of them.

They were outside a window-front restaurant on Calle Ocho, the main thoroughfare through Little Havana, engaging in a Miami tradition: dynamiting oneself awake. A line of folks—from businessmen in dark suits to mechanics in greasy overalls—were sipping small cups of sweet, frothy, strong coffee and eating pastries. Andy Candy and Moth were both on their second cup of the brew, which they knew was more than enough caffeine to keep them going for hours.

"No, I'm okay," she replied. She waited until he joined her on a small cement bench.

Moth did not believe he was proving to be much of a detective. His working knowledge of police work was limited to what he'd seen on television, which ranged from the incredible to the gritty with a good deal of mundane mixed in. His approach was a typical student's: He considered reading modern cops-and-robbers fiction and wondered whether he should spend some time absorbing true-crime accounts of famous killings as well. He scoured the Internet assessing scholarly papers on DNA testing and forensic website entries describing varieties of killers. These ranged from deranged moms who drowned their children to cold-blooded serial killers.

None of what he learned seemed to help him.

Everything he'd done seemed backward. *Cops start with details that create questions and get answers that paint a clear-cut portrait of a crime. I started with a certainty that has been replaced by doubt. Their approach is to eliminate confusion. Mine has only created it.*

Andy Candy could see the troubled look on Moth's face.

"Moth," she said briskly, an idea occurring to her. "We should watch a movie."

"What?"

"Well, maybe not the movie. Do you remember what the assignment in Mrs. Collins's tenth-grade English class was?"

"What?"

"The main reading for the fall semester. I know it was the same for you even if you were ahead of me, because she never changed a thing, year in, year out."

"Andy, what are you . . ."

"I'm serious, Moth."

"Okay, but what has it got to do—"

She interrupted him with a wave of her hand.

"Come on, Moth. The book that fall . . ."

Moth lifted his small cup, smelled the aroma, and smiled.

"*The Count of Monte Cristo.* Alexandre Dumas."

"Right," Andy replied, with a small grin. "And what's it about?"

"Well, lots of things, but mainly revenge that is exacted years later."

"And your uncle's death?"

"Revenge that was exacted years later."

"That's what it seems."

"Right. That's what it seems."

"So, the next step is we get a name from medical school way back then. The fifth student in that study group. Then we track that person down."

"Edmond Dantès," Moth said.

Andy Candy smiled at the literary reference. "Kind of," she said. "Shouldn't be that complicated. The schools keep records. But we just find him. Heck, Moth, we could just subscribe to one of those *Find Your Classmates* websites and they'd do most of the work for us. I know we can do that."

"I've always thought those sites exist so that people can reconnect with some crush they had in high school and have adult sex," Moth said. "But you're right. Let's get that name. That's the obvious next step. And then . . ."

He stopped.

Andy Candy nodded, but said:

"And then we have a choice to make."

"What's that?" Moth asked.

"Either we're finished . . . or we're just starting." This was a question wrapped in a statement.

Moth took the time to sip more coffee before responding. "I get the impression that this is not the sort of case a Miami cop is eager to handle," he said. "But, hell, what do I know? Maybe. I'll bundle it all together and take it to Susan Terry. Put it on a platter and serve it up like barbecue. She'll know what to do . . .

"Except why do I still get the feeling she will just laugh at me if I try to explain it to her?"

And then Moth laughed. False laugh.

Andy Candy joined him. The same false laugh.

But in that moment they both realized that nothing was really humorous about their situation. It was more a moment of intense irony, overcoming the two of them as quickly and efficiently and totally as the strong coffee hitting their bloodstreams.

She had said *we* but in reality she meant *I,* as Andy Candy had perfected her telephone style with registrars and alumni offices. Moth listened to her work the phones, inquiring, pleading, and finally cajoling. He watched her face, as it changed from smiles to frowns and back to a satisfied grin. He thought she was a performer on a stage, a one-person show, able to run through and express emotions with speed and accuracy.

When she got *the* name, she first wore a smug *That was easy* look. But then, as she wrote down details, Moth saw her look change. It wasn't precisely fear that crept back into her eyes, nor was it anxiety that began to make her voice quaver. It was something else.

He wanted to reach out for her, but did not.

She hung up the phone.

For a moment she looked down at a scratch pad, where she'd taken some notes. "I have the name," she said. Her voice seemed thin. "Study Group Alpha. Student number five. Asked to take a leave from school in the middle of his third year. Never went back. Did not graduate."

"Yes. That's the guy. Name?" Moth knew he sounded eager and that this enthusiasm was somehow inappropriate.

"Robert Callahan Jr."

Moth breathed in sharply. "Well. There we go. Now we get started on where . . ."

Moth stopped. He saw Andy Candy shaking her head.

"He's dead," she said.

26

Before heading for the South, Student #5 rode the subway down to the Lower East Side of Manhattan and took a long walk. He ended near Mott Street, at the edge of Chinatown where it blends into Little Italy, creating a confusing mishmash of cultures on streets crowded with delivery trucks, open-air markets, and tidal flows of people. It was a fine morning, sunny and mild—a turned-up collar on his suit coat and a white silk scarf were all he needed to stay warm. He stood out a bit—in his expensive suit and tie, he looked like a hedge fund manager. He was surrounded by folks wearing jeans, work boots, and hooded sweatshirts with sports teams' logos, but he enjoyed this distinction. *I've come a long ways.* This was a nostalgic walk for Student #5. It was where he'd first moved years earlier after being released from the hospital, and where instead of trying to return to medical school he'd performed the identity legerdemain he enjoyed now.

A horn blasted. High-pitched Asian voices argued over the price of live fish swimming in dingy gray tanks. A yuppie couple with two children in a high-tech stroller pushed past him.

Lots of life, he thought. Vibrancy everywhere. *But it was where I went to die.*

This sort of sentimentality was unusual for Student #5—but not unheard-of. He sometimes felt weepy when watching a trite rom-com. Some novels pitched him into spells of depression, especially when favorite characters were killed off. Poetry often made him pensive in an uncomfortable way—although he continued to read it, and actually subscribed to *Poets & Writers* magazine at his Key West house. He had developed techniques to rid himself of unwanted emotions when they occurred—changing *Love Actually* or *Mr. Smith Goes to Washington* on his Netflix queue to *300* or *The Wild Bunch.* He would replace misty eyes with gore. With novels and poetry, whenever he felt bubbling emotions he would set the words aside and exercise furiously. With sweat running down his eyes and his biceps aching from exertion, he was less likely to think about Elizabeth Bennet's nineteenth-century problems with Mr. Darcy and instead focus on his own death designs.

He stopped outside a nondescript redbrick building on Spring Street— one of seemingly millions of similar buildings in the city. A part of him wanted to go up and ring the buzzer for number 307, and ask whoever was living there now what they had done with his furniture, his clothes, and every knickknack, kitchen item, and art piece he'd put in that apartment—and then abruptly left behind. He doubted that the tenants were the same after decades—but curiosity threatened to consume him.

Leaving his artwork had distressed him a little, but he had known how critical this was. He'd always been handy with a pencil or paintbrush as a child and it was something he'd returned to in the hospital. *Express yourself,* they'd told him. *It's part of getting better.*

It was also a window into who he was. Every brushstroke, every penciled line on a page makes a statement. Draw a flower, and maybe they think you're getting better. Draw a knife dripping blood, and you were likely to be locked up another six months. Or until you were smart enough to start drawing flowers.

Because he understood these things, he had made absolutely sure that everyone in the hospital—doctors, therapists, ward nurses, and security personnel—and everyone in his family knew how important his drawings and paintings were to him. That way, when he abruptly left those things behind, it would say something critical to the people who came to search for him—whether they were family, police, or even some dull and dogged private eye. "He'd never leave his artwork behind."

Yes I would.

He remembered the day he'd disappeared into his new existences. He'd left everything, along with a precisely drawn map showing every street he might travel and noting three good places to throw himself into the East River. Bridge. Dock. Park. At the top of the map he'd scrawled, *I can't take it any longer.* He'd liked that phrasing. It could mean almost anything, but it would be taken just one way.

People want to believe in the obvious, even when something is a mystery. They want rational explanations for aberrant behaviors, even when these are elusive and difficult to pin down.

So, it had been simple: *Leave behind a couple of clues that point in the same direction, so that even without a body, they would all reach the same conclusion—two plus two equals four; he's dead.*

Especially when it isn't true. And he was proud of his self-control: Not once since he'd left the apartment had he picked up brush and paint and indulged his sense of artistry.

The doorway beckoned him. He started toward it, then forced himself to stop. He thought: *This is like looking at the place where I was born and where I died.*

The street hadn't changed all that much with the passing of years. There was a new Starbucks on the corner, and what was once a deli was now a high-end boutique selling women's clothing. But the dry cleaner mid-block was the same, as was the Italian restaurant three doors down.

Student #5 slowly reached into his suit pocket and removed the pictures of Andy Candy and Timothy Warner. *They were babies when I lived here,* he thought. *Up to now, the people I've killed, I knew. Not really fair,* he thought, *to kill without familiarity. That would make me little more than some punk sociopathic criminal.* He quickly listed some of the diagnostic criteria for *antisocial personality* in his head: failure to conform to social norms; impulsivity; reckless disregard for safety; consistent irresponsibility; lack of remorse.

Not me, he reassured himself—although he wondered about that last category, a thought that brought a grin to his face.

27

Andy Candy was pushing some papers around on her makeshift workspace in Moth's apartment. She stacked them in a neat pile in front of her before clicking a few keys on her laptop computer. A four-paragraph story arrived on her screen. It was from the *New York Post* and dated slightly less than two years after one member of Study Group Alpha was asked to leave medical school: *Police Seek Missing Med Student in River.*

Another couple of clicks bought up another story, this from the archived obituaries of the *New York Times*: *Plane Crash Claims Life of Surgeon and Wife.*

She highlighted a single statement near the bottom of the story detailing a private plane being piloted by the surgeon that landed fatally short on a rural strip near the family's vacation home in Manchester, Vermont. The highlighted sentence read: *Doctor Callahan and his wife left no immediate survivors. Their only son disappeared five years earlier in an apparent suicide.*

Andy kept bringing up entries from various websites—including a New York State Surrogate's Court declaration of death for one Robert Callahan

Jr. It was a determination five years after the disappearance of the son, and it preceded the plane accident by six weeks. As best as she could tell from the paperwork, the parents had sought to have their son declared legally dead. She guessed this had something to do with estate planning, but she couldn't be certain. She imagined that the plane crash too was murder, but in this case she couldn't see how. She had discovered an FAA report on the crash that blamed it on inexperience and pilot error. Robert Callahan had obtained his pilot's license only four weeks earlier and promptly gone out and purchased a single-engine Piper Cub.

She rolled her eyes over all the windows open on the computer screen and thought, *Dead, dead, dead. It's all about death.*

"What do we know?" Andy Candy asked.

Moth leaned over, took a few minutes to read over what she'd put up on her screen. "We know who. We know why. We know a little bit of how, if not precisely. We know when. We have all sorts of answers," Moth replied deliberately, almost defiantly.

"What does it add up to?" Andy Candy asked firmly.

She knew the answer to this question: *everything and nothing at the same time.*

Moth considered this question for a moment or two before offering a reply that almost made it seem he could hear her thoughts: "I don't think we should ask that quite yet."

"Well," she said, gesturing toward the words collected on the screen, "what we do know is that the person we've identified as your uncle's probable killer reportedly died a quarter century or so ago, like right when you and I were being born, even if his body was never found. So unless he's some ghost or zombie, he's probably not someone we can just go *click, click, click* and find. So much for that *Find Your Classmates* website. I mean, to get that declaration from the state, somebody had to do some research and come up empty. Papers had to be signed and notarized and made all official."

She looked over at Moth. She wanted to do something sensitive, like touch him on the arm, something reassuring. But instead, she rocked back and forth in her seat, and said, "He's dead, he's dead, he's dead. Except he isn't, is he?"

Moth nodded. His only comment was, "Andy, how hard is it to disappear in this country?" And then he answered his own question. "Not very."

Andy Candy tapped on the computer screen with her index finger. *What are we doing?*

She had another frightening thought: *How many people does Edmond Dantès kill along the road to revenge?*

And then a worse thought: *It will never end.*

The word *end* filled her like a heavy meal. It was electric in her head—*end, end, end*—and so she turned it around and used it in her next statement.

"That's the end, Moth," she said quietly. "I don't know what else we can do."

Ghost killer, she thought. For an instant she had the same sensation that she'd had in Jeremy Hogan's house. *Run! Get away!* She pictured the doctor's body on the floor, the puddled blood, the destroyed head. She believed that she had shut away the most terrible images into some distant spot, as if she had not seen these things happen, and that they actually took place in some realm that was neither real nor dream.

Unsettled, unsure, she tried for certainty. "It's over, Moth. I'm sorry. It's over. We're at a dead end."

The words she chose were not all that dissimilar to those he'd used and regretted, years earlier, when they broke up.

High school heartbreak: He was excited, heading off to college. She had two years to go before doing the same. Long phone call. Apologies. Tears. Sick in the stomach with emotions. Then emptiness, followed by some anger. "I never want to see you again!" Of course, that was a lie. When Andy thought back on the end of their romance, it seemed so mundane and unexceptional that it almost frightened her.

"Dead end," she repeated.

Moth, barely hearing anything Andy Candy was saying, felt trapped. Facts, details, connections—all the underpinnings of everything that had driven him to this point were arrayed in front of him, either on Andy's computer, in notes, in articles, or in their own recollections. The burgeoning historian within him knew that the time had arrived to piece it all together in a coherent way and turn it over to the proper authorities.

This was precisely what a responsible, reliable, not alcoholic or drug-addicted individual would do—look at all they'd done, take some pride in what they'd uncovered, give themselves a pat on the back, and then walk away, leaving it in the hands of professionals. Then they could look forward to the day it all landed in court, or perhaps the day they were interviewed by some heavy-handed reality-based television show that hyper-focused on cold crimes. Nancy Grace would have a field day. It would no longer be about his uncle's murder. It would become a part of lowbrow culture: a news story. *"Determined young students uncover thirty-year trail of murder and revenge! Footage at eleven!"*

This thought stabbed him. He looked up and saw that Andy Candy had rotated back toward the computer screen.

I'm going to lose it all, he realized. *Andy. Uncle Ed. Sobriety.* Everything seemed tied together, knotlike.

But what he said contradicted everything he felt: "You're right, of course, Andy."

He dragged more words from a dark spot within him. "I think we should put it all together, everything we've found out, and I'll take it to Miss Terry. I'll hate doing that. I mean, I got into all this because it was up to me to get to the truth of Uncle Ed's murder . . ." His voice trailed off, then returned with energy. "That would be the right thing to do."

"You've done a lot," Andy said.

"Not enough."

"And you know the truth," Andy Candy said.

"You think that's adequate?" Moth asked, sounding very much like some professor.

"It will have to be," Andy replied.

Neither of them believed this.

"Okay. Susan Terry," Moth said. "She will know what the next step is."

He did not trust Susan Terry. He did not even like her. But he did not see an alternative, because he realized that if he had said something else to Andy Candy right at that second, then the moment that he'd feared from the beginning just might arise. It was one thing to say, *I'm going to kill* when he didn't know whom he was talking about. It was a different thing to say that now.

What did I tell her at the start? As soon as she thinks I'm crazy she should walk away.

He wanted to keep her near him for a little longer—and the word *kill* threatened that.

The two of them worked hard the remainder of the day preparing what seemed a little like a term paper or a junior high school science project. They listed everything they'd done, and everyone they'd spoken to. They included numbers, addresses, descriptions, and every detail they could remember from every conversation. They wrote a time line and printed out newspaper articles. They were as organized as a pair of top-notch students could be. They worked hard for a *just the facts* approach—otherwise, as Moth kept saying, Susan Terry would immediately dismiss the entire narrative.

Late in the afternoon, Andy Candy stretched her arms wide. "We should take a break, Moth," she said. "I haven't worked this hard since school."

"We're almost done," he replied.

"Well, clear our heads a bit, then finish strong."

"Is that what you would do at college?"

She smiled. "Yes."

He smiled, too. "So would I. A little walk, then?"

"Some fresh air would be good."

The two of them pushed away from the computers and papers. Andy glanced down as she stood. She pointed at the yellow legal pad filled with Jeremy Hogan's scribbles. "We haven't really gone over these," she said.

Moth shook his head. "We'll just turn it over to Susan and see if she can see something." He shrugged, and added, "And we haven't used that, either." He pointed at the .357 Magnum and a box of hollow-point bullets that he'd put on a kitchen counter. "I should get rid of it," he said.

Andy Candy nodded. Guns, depression, loneliness, and alcoholism created a potent mix. Leaving the gun with Moth was a scary thought. "Just chuck it," she said. "Some Dumpster somewhere, or maybe throw it into one of the canals when no one is looking."

"I can do that," Moth said. "I bet half the canals in Miami are cluttered with guns that bad guys have tossed." He did a couple of deep knee bends and grinned. "I haven't gotten much exercise. Stiff as all get-out."

Outside, the sun was still warm, but the breeze had picked up. There were some gray-black thunderheads collecting to the west, over the Everglades—but the threatened storm seemed to be a few hours away, even with the strong winds rattling the palms.

They walked fast, stretching their legs. They did not speak much, until Andy Candy asked Moth, "Are we going to Redeemer One tonight?"

And Moth answered, "Yes."

"If you see Susan Terry . . ."

"I'll tell her I want to come to her office to see her. She'll be okay with that, I guess."

In the distance, they could hear the afternoon rush-hour traffic starting to build. They crossed a busy street and started down a deeply shaded residential area. The sidewalk was uneven—some of the slabs of concrete had been pushed up and sideways by the roots of trees. They picked their way forward gingerly, making sure they didn't trip. The street was shadowy. It was a little like walking amidst variations of black.

"Do you think it's over, Moth?" Andy suddenly blurted out.

He felt a disjointed sadness. "Almost," he said.

Logic would have suggested that they then talk about themselves, but they did not. Neither of the two of them felt like that was a subject it was safe yet to pursue.

* * *

Nor were either of them alert to the person trailing a safe fifty yards behind them, shadowing every turn they made.

Remarkable, Student #5 thought as he easily kept pace. *One can learn an immense amount about people simply by close observation.*

Of course, he knew that was an inherent tenet of the career he was once precluded from joining, but he was inordinately pleased that the capabilities he'd displayed so many years earlier hadn't disappeared. Indeed, he happily realized, they'd been honed and sharpened to a truly razor point.

28

He watched as Andy Candy waited in her car and Moth went into Redeemer One.

Student #5 thought: *Serendipity. It's almost as if some totally wayward, completely badass, and decidedly psycho-killer deity absolutely wants me to kill them.*

He had been following the two of them since they'd unexpectedly emerged from Moth's apartment earlier that afternoon, only a few minutes after he'd arrived at the same location, which was a short time after his plane touched down in Miami, and before he'd even checked into the four-star hotel where he'd made a reservation. He was certain they remained unaware of his presence.

He scrunched down in his rental car seat and settled in to watch. Eyes firmly fixed on Andy Candy, once Moth disappeared inside Student #5 made his mind as much of a blank as possible. He told himself to clear aside preconceived notions, prejudices, and opinions. *Curious college dropout and lost kid with a drinking problem.* That's what he knew, and he didn't think it was much. *People always talk about important, accurate first im-*

pressions. Bullshit. He shifted about, trying to find a comfortable position to keep watch. He was about twenty yards away from Andy Candy, not far from the entrance to the church. If anyone were to notice him, he had decided to say that he was there for the meeting, but had second thoughts about going inside—which would be enough to satisfy any curious sort. But he did not expect to need this explanation. *Drug addicts and alcoholics are inherently unsteady and unreliable.*

Not hard to imitate that, he thought.

From where he was parked, he could see Andy Candy poring over some papers. His curiosity was nearly hypnotic. He wanted to get closer. He continued to watch her, thinking he was extraordinarily patient, but knowing that whatever decision he was going to make, it had to be made quickly.

Inside the Redeemer One meeting room, Moth looked around for Susan Terry, but did not see her. *Well, I guess she's not as dedicated to sobriety as she said she was,* he thought cynically. He slid into a seat on a leather couch, nodding to the other regulars. The meeting began with the usual slow-paced welcome. Then the leader gestured to the first person to his right in the loose circle that they formed. This was the middle-aged corporate woman lawyer. She straightened her designer skirt as she rose.

"Hello, my same is Sandy and I'm an addict. I have one hundred and eighty-two days now."

Moth joined the others with the greeting, "Hi, Sandy." This was said in unison, like a responsive church reading. All of the folks at Redeemer One knew Sandy, knew her struggles, and were relieved to hear that she was continuing to stay on track.

"I've managed to make some progress with my ex and with my kids," she said. "They're going to take me out to dinner this week. It's like a little test, I think. Plop that bottle of nice red wine in front of me and see what I do. Ignore or guzzle."

She said this with a wry smile. There was a smattering of applause.

"It could go either way," Sandy continued. She hesitated, then looked squarely at Moth. "But I think here tonight, what we all truly want is to hear from Timothy."

She fixed Moth with an uncompromising stare as she resumed her seat. There was a long silence in the room. A few people shifted about. The engineer stood up. "My name is Fred, and I have two hundred and seventy-two days now. I agree with Sandy. Timothy, it's your turn."

The session leader—a onetime alcoholic assistant minister who liked to sport dark turtleneck shirts even in Miami's heat—tried to interrupt. "Look, it's Timothy's choice. No one should be forced . . ."

Moth stood. "It's okay," he said, even if it wasn't. He looked around the room. He took a deep breath. "Hello," he said slowly. "My name is Timothy and I have thirty-one days now, although it's been thirty-four since my uncle was killed."

He paused, looking around the room. People leaned toward him. He could sense their interest.

"Everywhere I go, someone seems to die," he said.

Susan Terry was kneeling on the carpet beside the coffee table in the living room of her apartment. It was a glass tabletop and directly in the center, right past where a half-empty bottle of Johnnie Walker Red rested, there were two narrow lines of white cocaine powder. She gripped the edges of the table with both hands, as if an earthquake were violently shaking the building and she was hanging on, trying to keep steady.

Do it. Don't do it.

It was the blood. There was so much blood.

She could feel sweat gathering beneath her arms, lining the top of her temples. For an instant she wondered if the air-conditioning in her building had suddenly gone off, but then she recognized the sweat for what it was: the physical manifestation of a terrible decision.

With an almost impossible feat of strength, she pulled her right hand off the table edge and reached into her pocketbook. Never taking her eyes off the lines of coke, she rummaged in the satchel and finally pulled up the .25-caliber automatic she customarily carried whenever called to a crime scene, or when forced to leave her office after dark. The gun was an important part of Susan's *I won't be a victim like the people I see in court* bravado.

Breathing hard, like someone held underneath the waves seconds too long, she chambered a round in the pistol. Then she placed it in front of her, next to the cocaine.

Might as well kill yourself faster, she told herself. Still half-frozen in position, she eyed the two alternatives.

Shoot the dogs. These words slipped into her head, and she repeated them out loud. "Shoot the dogs, God damn it. Shoot the dogs. Just shoot them now. Shoot them both. Watch them die." She swayed a little unsteadily and whispered, "Shoot the dogs shoot the dogs shoot the dogs."

The last crime scene she had been called to, early that morning, just before the sun rose, pulled out of bed by a homicide detective's flat voice that didn't successfully conceal his sad anger, had produced two things: a small vial of cocaine and the promise of a nightmare. It was a crime scene that had shattered her composure and her carefully balanced tough-gal persona.

"Ms. Terry?"

"Yeah. Jesus. What time is it?"

"A little before five. This is Detective Gonzalez, Miami Homicide. We met once before on that—"

She interrupted. "I remember you, Detective. What is it?"

"We've got an unusual murder. I think you should be here. We're in Liberty City . . ."

"Drugs?"

"That's not it exactly."

"Well, what exactly is it?"

She asked this as she was swinging her feet out of bed, reaching for some jeans and a jacket, thinking mainly about coffee.

"Death by dog," the detective said.

The last gray-black licorice tendrils of the night were still wrapped around the morning when she headed out for Liberty City. Up on the interstate, past her usual turn toward the prosecutor's office, and then down a highway ramp into one of Dade Country's poorest sections, an area made famous decades earlier by riots and upheaval. The curious thing about Liberty City—as most residents of the area knew—was that it was the highest, most solid ground for miles. It was only a matter of time and rising sea levels before developers figured out it was the safest place to build. And that would re-form the area. Maybe a hundred years—but the likelihood of the poor folks being pushed out and the rich folks moving in seemed a good bet.

The night obscured some of the worst of the poverty. There is a blanket-like sensation to the last of the dark in Miami—between the heat, the humidity, and the richness of the inky sky tones, it feels a little like the loose wrappings of a funeral shroud.

Susan steered her way down quiet streets of small, bedraggled white cinder-block houses and low-slung, cheap apartment buildings. There was debris on the roads, cars up on blocks, scattered broken appliances, iron bars on windows, and chain-link fences everywhere. It was like a whole section of the city was rusted.

Even with the gun in her satchel on the seat next to her, she would never have willingly driven alone down any of these streets. *We like to imagine we are color-blind,* she thought, *but come here alone and the first thing that jumps out is race.*

She saw the glow from police strobes two blocks away.

When she got closer, she spotted a coroner's vehicle, a half-dozen marked patrol cars, and several unmarked—but unmistakable—detectives' vehicles gathered in front of two cinder-block houses jammed close together, separated only by one of the ubiquitous chain-link fences. A small crowd of the curious milled in the shadows. There was also a yellow Animal Control truck pulled inside the police perimeter, and she saw two green-uniformed wildlife officers animatedly talking with some of the regular police.

No one stopped her as she parked and approached: *Young, white woman who isn't a cop? Has to be a prosecutor.* She spotted Detective Gonzalez and walked aggressively up to him.

"Hey, Ricky, so what is it?"

"Ms. Terry. Sorry to get you up in the middle—"

"No need to apologize," she interrupted. "It's my job, too. What've we got?"

The detective shook his head in a world-weary way, said "Thought I'd seen everything," and pointed to the back of the Animal Control truck, giving a small wave. One of the green-suited officers standing adjacent opened the truck's double-wide rear doors, exposing two steel-reinforced cages inside. The cages were designed for wayward wild panthers and aggressive alligators.

Or pit bulls. Two of them. Heavily muscled, scarred faces, thick chests. Frothing, snarling, beyond savage, they instantly threw themselves against the cage barriers, shaking the truck, howling banshees, frantic in their desire to get free.

"Jesus," Susan recoiled a step and blurted out. "What the hell . . ."

And then Detective Gonzalez told her a story. It was a midnight story, with a touch of Poe or Ambrose Bierce and typical of South Florida.

A solitary older man—crippled in an industrial accident years earlier so that he now limped on a deformed leg—whose primary source of income was occasionally training dogs for illegal underground fights unfortunately happened to live next door to a family whose two young boys taunted him mercilessly. Fed up, the old man had invented a fast-release lock on the caged area where he kept his dogs and stopped chaining the dogs securely. Slipknots and weakened links. The boys stopped in front of his house this past night, decided to throw rocks at the dogs they believed were safely locked up, threw other rocks at the old man's windows. Woke him up. Called him names. Just a little bit of local nastiness on a night that was far too hot, far too humid, and destined for something terrible.

The old man assumed that his wire fence in front would hold the dogs in, and he triggered the pulley system he'd designed, freeing two of the animals. He'd figured that the sight of two seventy-pound dogs flying across the yard, teeth bared, would do an adequate job of putting the right sort of fear in his tormentors. The fence would stop the dogs, the kids would be terrified, and he'd have a measure of satisfaction without even bothering to take the usual Dade County approach, which was brandishing a handgun.

He'd been wrong in all his assumptions.

Both dogs slammed into the fence. It buckled, gave way, and they scrambled through the opening.

Both dogs had easily run down the panicked youngsters.

Both dogs had rapidly ripped the life from the children before the old man could get loops and chains around their necks and get them under control.

End of story. She could feel weakness in her core. *Awful. Not tragic. Just sick.*

"You don't want to see these bodies," Gonzalez said to Susan.

She choked at the thought of mauled children. "I have to . . ." she started.

"The dogs," the detective said. "Are they, like, weapons that we should impound? What sort of homicide is this? We talking a strange sort of Stand Your Ground law thing here? I mean, after all, the kids were throwing rocks. But these dogs, well, are they evidence? Seems like a bunch of legal questions, Counselor. If it was up to me, I'd shoot 'em right here. But I wanted to consult with you first."

Susan nodded. She knew what she wanted to say: *"You're a hundred percent right. Shoot the dogs. A little instant street justice.* She did not say this. "Seize the dogs. Have Animal Control maintain a constant record, just like if they were a gun or a knife at a murder scene, so we have proper chain of evidence to produce in court. Make sure you take sworn statements from those officers about how dangerous the dogs are and make sure you get some of that . . ." she gestured toward the back of the truck, where she could still hear the dogs slamming against their restraints, ". . . on video. Arrest the old man, read him his rights, and charge him with first-degree murder. Have Crime Scene make sure they keep that locking system intact, so that we can present it in court. Get pictures of the fence, where the dogs broke through . . ."

She took a deep breath. The orderly prosecutor inside her was shaken. "Jesus," she added.

"I've seen bad," Gonzalez said. "But this one. Those dogs, they go straight for the jugular. Trained killers. Hell, they're worse than some professional hit man and twice as efficient. Kids didn't have a fucking chance. People think, it's just a dog, how hard could defending myself be? They've got no clue."

He took her arm and steered her farther into the crime scene. One body was in the side yard. The other was just outside the front door. Susan took another deep breath. *That one almost made it,* she thought. She paused when she saw an assistant medical examiner. Even in the flashing lights, she thought he looked pale. He was poised above a small body. She looked down at the kid's bright blue high-tops, not his throat. Then she forced herself to lift her eyes.

That was Susan's morning.

Mauled, half-eaten child; it had played some terrible chord deep within her and she'd tripped. Stumbled. Fallen. Failed. *Evil is relentless and routine,* she thought.

Every addict knows two numbers to call when they see something or do something or learn something that makes them totter on that edge that they thought was far away, but is really right beneath them all the time; when something happens that suddenly strips away all the facades of normalcy and reestablishes all the pain that resides hidden inside. One number is for a sponsor, to talk them out of doing what they want to do. The other number is the dealer, who will provide the alternative.

I wouldn't have called if it hadn't been for dogs and dead kids' bodies. I thought I had it all beat. I was back to being the tough prosecutor with the knife edge and granite surface. Things bounced off me. That's what I thought. No more desire. Except for tonight and all that children's blood.

Susan believed if she were truly smart she would be able to look at her life and say to herself: *Oh see, I wasn't loved enough as a child and that's why I'm an addict.* Or: *I was beaten and abandoned and that's why.* Or: *I was weak when I should have been strong, lost when I should have been found, hurt when I should have been healthy.*

In possession of understanding, she would be armed against herself.

It didn't work that way.

Instead she was back in her apartment hours later, drinking hard and staring at the choice on her glass tabletop. Gun and coke. Coke and gun. *Shoot the dogs. Shoot yourself.*

One death or another.

When the phone rang behind her, she jumped.

First there was silence.

Moth looked around at the others gathered at Redeemer One and doubted they'd ever heard a story like his before. It wasn't a story about the types of compulsions they were all familiar with.

He didn't have to wait long before the group burst into a chaotic mishmash of questions, comments, fears, and suggestions that all came flying at him as he stood in front. It was like being buffeted by a strong wind. The usual Redeemer One decorum and orderly processes of sharing were instantly shattered. Voices were raised. The air was electric with opinions. Arguments, sarcasm, even some shaky doubts all reverberated around him.

"Call the police."

"Like 9-1-1? That's nuts. Some cop will show up and have no clue what to do."

"Well, then how about the cops that already investigated Ed's suicide?"

"Yeah. Call them and tell them how stupid they've been. That will work."

"Well, how about hiring a private detective?"

"Better yet, hire an attorney who employs a private detective."

"That makes some sense, except how many attorneys know how to deal with some revenge killer? How do you look up that category in the phone book? Where is it? Somewhere between defending DUIs, divorces, and estates and wills?"

"You have to speak to Ed's family and his partner. They need to know what you've discovered."

"Right. And how exactly will they help?"

"Why not call the *Miami Herald*? Tell an investigative reporter, put them on the story. Or *60 Minutes*. Or someone who can independently look into it."

"Don't be silly. The press would just screw it up. And have you read the *Herald* lately? It sure as hell ain't what it used to be twenty years ago. They can barely get the details of a zoning board meeting straight. I say go back to New Jersey and hand it over to the state police."

"What will the cops up there do? They've got no jurisdiction down here. And anyway, Timothy doesn't have evidence—he has connections. He has suppositions. He has some guesswork and some possibilities. He has a motive for murder, and even that is pretty far out there. And he's got a lot of coincidence. What else?"

"He's got more than that."

"You sure? The sorts of facts that would stand up in a court? I don't know about that."

"I think Timothy should write a book."

"Great. That will take a year or two. What should he do right now?"

"I wish Susan the prosecutor were here. She's a professional and she would know what to do."

Moth answered this last comment.

"I can call her. She gave me her card, with her home number." He reached into his wallet and pulled out Susan Terry's business card.

This made the room grow quiet again. Heads nodded in agreement.

Sandy the estate lawyer reached into her purse and produced a cell phone. "Here," she said. "Call right now, while we're all here." This was said with maternal insistence. It also reflected the widespread understanding at Redeemer One that promises to call someone weren't the same as actually calling them.

Moth started to dial, but stopped when the University of Miami philosophy professor—who had up to this point been oddly noncommunicative—finally leaned forward, holding up his hand like a student in one of his classrooms.

"Timothy," he said slowly, "something occurs to me that seemingly hasn't been noted by the others. I actually believe you've heard some good suggestions here, and you should follow up on them," he stated in the same tones he would use in a faculty meeting. "But what I fear is something different."

Moth paused. "What's that, Professor?"

"If this person, this former medical student you've identified that apparently has been so proficient at killing . . . so good at it that he's committed, what? Five killings without being caught . . . ?" Again he drew out his response in a pedantic fashion. "What makes you think he doesn't know about you?"

Silence.

The regulars at Redeemer One were frozen in position.

"Well, I mean how . . ." Moth stammered.

He stopped, knowing that this was about to become a question neither he nor anyone else there could successfully answer.

Another silence.

"Dial that number," Sandy the estate lawyer said. Her voice was steel.

Moth looked about the room. People were leaning forward in their seats, expectant, energized.

Not the typical meeting tonight by any means, Moth thought wryly.

He resumed dialing, as the professor continued:

"And, Moth," he added softly, "if he does know about you, what will he do about that?"

29

"Put it on speakerphone," someone said.

"Susan, everyone can hear us," Moth spoke loudly.

"Why aren't you here tonight?" asked the philosophy professor pointedly.

Susan Terry did not answer this question. She held her phone in one hand and put the other to her forehead, stroking her temple aggressively, as if that motion could help massage away the fears spread out on the coffee table. For a nervous moment, she imagined that everyone at Redeemer One could see the array in front of her, disapproving looks on their faces. She was slumped down against a cheap, uncomfortable couch, wearing a sweat-stained white tank top and baggy gray sweatpants. *Cocaine-snorting clothes,* she thought. *Clothes to escape in.* Her dark hair was bedraggled, sticking to her neck. She knew her makeup had run, giving her a raccoonlike look around the eyes. She wore no shoes, and she wiggled her toes, almost like a person afraid she'd damaged her spine might, to reassure herself that she still had the ability to stand up.

"I had an early morning call," she said. This was truthful. "I was exhausted and fell asleep." This was a lie.

Holding the cell out like a religious offering so that everyone could hear her, Moth looked around. He was unsure how many of them believed Susan right at that moment. Every meeting combined layers of disbelief warring with blind acceptance, a combination that shouldn't logically work, he thought, but somehow managed to.

Susan could feel sweat between her breasts. It was clammy. But she adopted the tones of the put-together, no-nonsense prosecutor. She wondered where that person had disappeared to. She didn't know if she could handle any feeling of being judged, because she knew she would come up short.

"Why are you calling?" she asked abruptly.

Moth was about to answer, but was cut off by Sandy the corporate attorney. "He's calling because we all insisted he call. Every one of us," she said loudly enough for the phone to pick up every word, like a mother calling children to the table. She made a hand gesture to encourage the others, and there was a general murmur of assent from the gathering.

Fred the engineer added, "He has been explaining everything that leads him to believe his uncle was killed by someone. We think he makes a compelling case. Very circumstantial, we concede, but still compelling. Fascinating, actually. You are the only person we could all agree to reach out to."

The voices coming across the cell line were tinny, almost hallucinatory. Susan leaned back, hesitating. *Closed case. Maybe. Doubts. Open case. Maybe. Doubts.* "His uncle's suicide has been thoroughly investigated and closed. Timothy and I have gone over this extensively—" she started.

"He's not the only one," Moth interrupted sharply. He kept his eyes on the crowd in the room.

Susan rocked a bit on her apartment floor, leaned her head back as if exhausted, felt like her tongue was growing thick. What she wanted was to bend over the table, snort the remaining lines of coke, and embrace everything that meant, or else pick up the automatic and finish everything that remained of her life all at once. *I'm dying,* she thought. *I'm all alone and I'm always all alone.* She squeezed her eyes shut, but heard a voice that sounded strangely like her own speaking firmly, almost as if there were another her in the room.

"You think there have been other suicides . . ."

"No. Not suicides. Murders," Moth replied. "Murders designed to look like something else. Like accidents and mistakes."

Redeemer One remained hushed. No one had moved from their seats, but Moth felt like they were all crowding around him, pushing him forward; he could almost feel their hands on his back. For the first time in many days, he wished Andy Candy were there, so he could introduce her to everyone in the session. This, he knew, was a crazy thought, and he shed it as quickly as he could. It was a room for addicts, and she wasn't exactly one of them.

"All right," Susan said slowly. "Timothy, let's meet again. We can go over it all another time. You can tell me what you've learned. Can you come to my office tomorrow?" *That is, if I have a tomorrow,* she thought.

Moth looked out at the others. Sandy, Fred, the philosophy professor, and the others were all shaking their heads in unison.

"Tonight," Sandy said in a stage whisper.

The heads all started to nod.

"No delays," said Fred. "We all know what happens when you delay doing something important."

He wasn't speaking about anything other than addiction.

"Tonight," Moth said.

"All right," Susan said. But what she thought was, *I guess I'll live a little longer.* How much longer she couldn't say. She forced herself to her feet, knowing she had to clean up some to meet with Moth. She stared at the two remaining lines of cocaine. *Not nearly enough,* she thought. Her cell phone was in her hand, and she scrolled through her contacts until she saw the name of her dealer. *Meet Moth. Meet the dealer.* She continued to eye the small amount she had left. She suddenly didn't know whether she should leave the cocaine behind on the table, or leave the gun. Or perhaps she should take both with her. For a woman who prided herself on the ability to make wise decisions in a timely fashion, this doubt was as fierce as any desire.

On her lap were Jeremy Hogan's handwritten notes.

Like any good scientist, he had tried to organize them in an easily understandable fashion, but Andy Candy wasn't a doctor and so she both struggled and was fascinated. There were headings following each conversation the old psychiatrist had with his killer, and then key words scrawled on pages, along with abbreviated and truncated analyses. Some phrases had been underlined, others starred, and some circled. It seemed free-form, and she was reminded of reading the cantos of Dante's *Divine Comedy* in a course on Renaissance literature. School seemed suddenly very far away from her. She had an odd thought: *These notes are like the poetry of death.*

She saw that his initial conversation with the man who would kill him was brief. At the top of one page he had written "Initial Talk." And below that he'd scribbled: *Fault. Last account.*

Beneath these entries his scrawl continued:

"Others"? Means I am part of a group.

Rule out: Killers I testified against. Individual acts.

Unless "group" includes prosecutors, arresting police, judges, juries, forensic specialists—everyone associated with criminal prosecution.

Very possible. How to check?

Rule out: Ex-colleagues.

Any longtime hatreds, academic slights that might prompt murder?

Unlikely. But possible.

Rule out: Students? Did you flunk someone?

Slight possibility. Go over school records?

Likelihood of finding person that way: Small.

Then he'd written:

Essential: Assess what sort of killer he is.

That was the final entry on the first page.

On the second page of notes, Doctor Hogan's handwriting seemed hurried, and Andy Candy guessed that he'd been writing as he spoke, cupping the phone in the crook between shoulder and ear, pen in hand.

She saw:

Educated. Not prison or street. Not self-educated.

Product of Ivy League—like Unabomber?

Controlled obsession. Manages his compulsions. Puts them to his use. Intriguing.

Not disoriented. No mood/affect influences in speech patterns. No colloquialisms. No accent.

Not paranoid. Organized.

She paused and considered a notation that had been both underlined and circled:

Sociopath. But none like I've seen.

The word *none* was underlined three times.

At the bottom of the page, Doctor Hogan wrote in block letters:

He will want to look me in the eyes before killing me. Prepare for that moment. My best chance.

She took a deep breath.

"Wrong about that, Doc," she whispered. "I'm sorry. But you were wrong about that."

She hesitated. An idea crept into her head.

"Were you wrong?"

Maybe he'd already . . .

She stopped herself. It was suddenly hot in the car—no: *stifling*—and she flicked on the ignition and rolled down the windows. She drank in some of the humid air that slid in, hardly different from the stale air inside the car. It was like the distinctions of night had dissipated around her. She had the same uncontrollably nervous sensation that she did when reading some unsettling thriller, or watching a scary movie. She was absolutely certain that if she lifted her eyes and started staring into the night, even in the safety of the parking lot, she would start to see ominous shapes and those shapes would morph into ghostlike killers. So, instead of looking out, she lowered her eyes back to the entries in front of her.

She flipped over to the last page of notes.

She read Jeremy Hogan's final entry over and over again, unable to stop herself.

He's already won. I'm already dead.

"Timothy, just tell Susan what you told us. Tell her the same way. She'll believe you."

"Or, at least, believe enough to take the next step, whatever that is. She's a state employee. Hell, she'll at least want to cover her ass."

"But Timothy, be careful. You don't know what you're dealing with."

Admonitions ringing in his ears, Moth fairly jumped down the stairs outside Redeemer One and jogged through the shadows in the parking lot. He saw Andy Candy lift her head as he approached. She had a furtive look about her, but seemed relieved that he had returned.

"We have another meeting tonight," he said as he slid into the passenger seat.

Andy Candy nodded, started up the car, and backed out of her parking spot. Around them other cars—ranging from the philosophy professor's small hybrid to the corporate attorney's big Mercedes—were pulling out of the church's lot. She paid no attention to the car that headed out in the same direction as them.

"No," Susan Terry told the waitress, "just ice water for all of us." She also ordered sushi for the table, although she was absolutely certain that the raw fish would make her violently ill.

The waitress departed, probably mentally adjusting her tip without a liquor tab added in, and Susan turned to Moth and Andy Candy. "Okay," she said. "Lay it out for me."

She looked across the table with as tough a glance as she could muster. "No bullshit," she added. "This isn't a game or like doing some college paper. Don't waste my time."

Moth knew this was a lot of posturing, but said nothing. Andy looked down at the sheaf of handwritten notes from Jeremy Hogan that was rolled up in her hand. Moth shifted in his seat. Both of them thought Susan looked terrible. The change from the prim, put-together prosecutor they'd seen in her office, in charge and organized, to the jean-clad and scraggly-haired, pale and slightly shaky person in front of them was striking. That Susan was able to sound the part—her voice steady and demanding—only made the contrast more profound. Moth instantly recognized what the change implied. Andy Candy had a terrible thought: *She looks like I must have when I came out of the abortion clinic.*

There was a momentary quiet, while Moth tried to organize his words. But what he finally said was designed to have the maximum impact.

"Four days ago, in rural New Jersey, Andy and I witnessed a murder," he said.

Student #5 *hated* sushi, so after seeing the trio get seated he'd walked over to a nearby fast food restaurant and got a sandwich to go. He was something of a health food nut, and it was rare for him to ever eat anything made at a counter or that came off a fryer. But things seemed oddly different for him this night, as if he was suddenly going to have to make all sorts of changes, and this made him anxious.

He walked back to a bench that was just down the street from the sushi restaurant, a vantage point that would allow him to see them all leave. It was hot, humid, and he felt oddly short of breath. He could no longer actually watch Andy Candy and Moth and the person they were speaking to, but he had an adequate idea of what was being said. He just didn't yet know who they were saying it to—although he knew instinctively that he would be following her later that night. He needed to achieve at least that small bit of certainty as he was making his mind up. *Whoever it is,* he thought, *she is probably dangerous.*

His food seemed ashen in his mouth, as if every slice of cold cut, every tomato, and every piece of lettuce had spoiled, the bread was stale, and his diet soda was watery and flat. He tossed the sandwich after a couple of bites.

30

Student #5 was stretched out on the floor of the Biltmore Hotel in Coral Gables, in an executive suite. It was just before midnight, he couldn't sleep, and he was naked, doing one-hand push-ups on the carpet. *Ten with the right. Ten with the left. Ten with the right. Ten with the left.* Sweat burned his eyes. The hotel was hosting a tech company start-up convention, and out on a patio a rock band doing '60s covers was entertaining the young executives. The music seemed out of place to him. What should have been modern hip-hop or rap became leftover Jefferson Airplane, Steppenwolf, and the Rolling Stones. Screeching guitar and power vocals wafted up to his room, which overlooked the hotel's immense pool and adjacent golf course.

Between rasping breaths, he listened, then said out loud, his up-and-down exertions keeping time to the music, "Absolutely right: I clearly, unequivocally, can't get *no* satisfaction." *A conundrum,* he thought. There's *a clever word to describe my situation.*

The word made him want to spit.

He had always liked to think of himself as an intellectual killer, someone who understood the psychological chapter and verse of murder, who saw the profound emotional depths that killing another person explored. *Killing is like spelunking,* he thought as he continued to snap off push-ups. *Dark caves, mysteries, and each step takes me farther into the unknown.*

Not only had revenge killing freed him, he believed it had made him psychologically larger. He imagined himself part Buddhist, a Zen master of death, part James Bond—the book spy, not the movie action hero— who delivered simplicity of decision with a Walther PPK. Killing, to him, was an important process, not something spur-of-the moment or rushed. *No drive-bys or convenience store, gas station, or liquor mart holdups with gunfire for me.* It was artistic, like sculpting a shape out of stone, or filling a canvas with color. The deaths he'd created had reason—and not anything as mundane as money, power, madness, or cruelty. That was why, he inwardly insisted, *his* killings weren't easily categorized, and, indeed, weren't really murders at all. He thought everything he'd done belonged in a special definition that was unique but highly appropriate.

Others would do the same.

If they only could.

How many times has a person said "I'd like to kill that guy . . ." and it made complete, total sense. And then they didn't act? Foolishness. You can either go through life crippled by what others do to you . . . or you can take charge.

Up, down. Up, down: *Thirty-one, thirty-two, thirty-three. Don't stop.*

When he reached fifty, he dropped to the floor, breathing hard.

It took a few minutes before he rose, muscles burning, and went to his laptop computer. Google Earth gave him bird's-eye and street-view visions of three addresses: The Nephew's. The Girlfriend's. The Prosecutor's.

This last bit of information had been the result of some clever computer searching after he'd watched the woman he now knew was Susan Terry walk into her condominium building. He'd tailed her deep into the night, a little surprised at the obvious drug connection she'd made before she'd returned home. He'd taken the address, compared it with recent sales and tax rolls, easily obtained a name, then discovered that there had been more than one mention of Susan Terry in the *Miami Herald.* He'd read several articles and said, "Well, young lady, you seem to be on something of a courthouse losing streak. Need to do better for us taxpayers, 'cause we're paying your salary. Do you think that little boost of nose candy is going to help you win cases?"

Major Crimes. That was the section she worked in—and even if she was as incompetent and drug-addled as he guessed, she still couldn't possibly be a total fool. He was not the arrogant sort of killer who automatically assumed all police detectives to be dull-witted incompetents until the moment some cop sat across the table with a notepad, a recording device, and the arrogance of knowing they had the absolute goods.

He went to the window, stared out across the night. The lights from Coral Gables and South Miami gave the distance a faint glow across the dark expanse that he knew was the golf course, but which looked in the ink dark to be an ocean. Below him, the music finally stopped. *"Don't you want somebody to love? Don't you need somebody to love?"* were the last words he could make out as he watched the party dissipate. "No," he said, "I do not need someone to love." *You could sleep now,* he thought, knowing this was untrue. No sleep until he'd made some decisions.

Take charge, he admonished himself. *Figure it out. Dissect what you know.*

"If you kill The Nephew, even if it looks like an accident, what happens?"

Full-scale murder investigation. No delay. His suspicions about his uncle's death immediately gain complete credibility. Inevitable: newspaper and television headlines.

"If you kill The Girlfriend, what happens?"

Same. Added idea: Young Timothy will become more obsessed with me.

"If you kill The Prosecutor, what happens?"

The full weight of the Miami investigative services will descend upon that crime. The FBI will get involved. And The Girlfriend and The Nephew will tell them precisely where to start looking. Those cops and agents will never quit until they find me.

"Suppose I just disappear?"

I have to do that anyway. He traced rivulets of sweat still running down his chest. *Nor would I ever know for one hundred percent certain that I was free. I would have to constantly monitor those three people, God damn it to hell.*

He thought hard, and the beginnings of an idea started to form in his head: *Death for death.* "Bring them closer. Close enough to kill."

"And how do you do that?"

"Fear and weakness." *People think that fear causes someone to run away and hide. In actuality the opposite occurs.* He went to a bathroom mirror and stared into his eyes, nodding his head in agreement.

He could see dangers everywhere, and he wondered whether he had enough time to properly plan it out. Designing sudden death was something he enjoyed and took pride in. A delicious idea crept into his head. It relaxed him, and he believed it was almost time to finally go to bed. This day was nearly over.

Andy Candy felt like she was late, although no specific time had been agreed upon, so she was hurrying through morning rush-hour traffic, weaving aggressively from lane to lane down South Dixie Highway. She figured that if she were pulled over by a trooper, Susan Terry could get her out of any ticket the cop might write. This sudden sense of automotive impunity made her grin, and she was almost laughing when her cell phone rang.

She had a hands-free connection in her car, so she pressed the button on the radio panel, assuming it would be Moth, telling her about the next scheduled session with Susan Terry. "Hey, I'm on my way," she said, cheerily. "Be there in a few."

"You may think you are on your way, Andrea," an unfamiliar voice said coldly, "but you will not arrive at the destination you want."

She nearly swerved off the highway. "Who is this?" she asked, voice rising.

"Who do you think?"

"I don't know."

"Yes you do. We were very close, only a few short days ago, at our mutual friend Jeremy Hogan's house."

Cold plunged through her at the same second that heat exploded around her. She could feel her heart suddenly racing. For an instant she thought the car had spun out of control, but then she realized the highway was dry and it was her head that was spinning. "How did you get . . ." she stammered, ". . . *this number*" getting lost in her panic.

"Not a challenge."

Her throat went suddenly dry. Words formed behind her lips, but they became sand on her tongue.

"I need to ask you a question or two, Andrea," the voice continued. "Or should I call you *Andy Candy* like your closest friends?"

She croaked out a sound. *My nickname. He knows my nickname.* She looked around wildly at the other cars cluttering the highway, as if someone could help her. She felt wedged in, hammered into place. Crushed.

"First question, very simple, easy to answer: Have you ever spoken with a killer before?"

She could feel her breathing tightening. The sensation was like what she had always imagined as having a boa constrictor wrap itself around her chest and starting to squeeze.

"No," she coughed out, the word scouring her throat. *Was that my voice? It seemed like someone else speaking.*

"Didn't think so. So this will be new for you. Okay, second question, significantly harder: Are you willing to die for your old boyfriend?"

She nearly choked. Cars ahead of her were slowing down and she had to force herself to remember to hit the brake at the last minute, avoiding rear-ending the vehicle in front of her by only inches, tires squealing. She felt dizzy, hot, and feverish. As her car jerked to a stop, she felt like she was still moving, actually picking up speed, racing pell-mell down the street. She did not know how to answer. *Yes. No. I don't know.*

She started to say *Why?* but then she realized that the phone line had been disconnected. "Wait," she blurted to no one. Behind her, cars started to honk. She did not know whether to go forward or to stay stock-still.

Andy Candy wanted to scream, and her mouth fell open. For an instant, she thought maybe she already had screamed but had not been able to hear herself, suddenly deaf. She was unsure of everything.

31

9 a.m. Miami-Dade State Attorney's Office.

Susan Terry behind her desk, trying to figure out what her day held. Loud knock at the door.

Susan: "Come in."

"Hello, Susan."

Quick scramble to her feet. Firm handshake. It wasn't often that the head of Major Crimes came to her office.

"Hello, Larry. I'm sorry for the mess. I was working and didn't expect anyone—"

His hand up in a stop sign.

"That's not why I'm here."

Momentary silence. The stop sign became a gesture to resume her seat, and the head of Major Crimes drew up a chair and plopped himself down. He hesitated briefly, staring directly at her, before continuing. Susan thought: *The way he's looking at me should tell me something. Or everything.*

"Susan, have you looked in a mirror at yourself?"

She had, instantly guessed what it was that he'd seen, but she said nothing in reply.

"We both know what's going on, right?"

"I . . . no . . ." she stammered.

"You were warned when this happened before. This office cannot, under any circumstances, have people engaged in illicit drug activity. You know that. For crying out loud, Susan, we're the people who prosecute drug crimes and put the bad guys in prison! So, you are being suspended. I'm sorry."

"Please . . ."

"No *pleases*. No excuses. No debate. Suspended. And truly fortunate that I'm not saying *fired*. Late last night Narcotics got a goddamn unusual anonymous tip and went out and arrested a man I think you know and know goddamn well, because those were the first fucking words out of his mouth when detectives arrived at his place and caught him cutting up a key of coke. He's not lying, is he? Don't answer that. I don't want to hear any crap. And he says he recently sold you a dime bag. He was specific about that. And then another last night—which tells me you already went though the first. That's not a lie, either, is it? Again, don't answer. That's what the smug bastard told those cops and they were nice enough to call me in the fucking middle of the night before making any sort of official report with your name prominently displayed in it. You caught a big break on that."

"That's . . ." she started, then stopped short. She understood how stupid anything she said would sound. *Who made that call?* she wondered, only to realize the question was irrelevant.

"You want to keep your job?"

"Yes."

"All right. Then either check yourself into residential rehab, or start going to meetings regularly and see a shrink that specializes in addiction or find an outpatient program—I don't give a shit, as long as it's a plan and you can stick to it and it works. You're taking a leave of absence. Maybe a month. Maybe two. We'll see. Then you can come back to work under supervision and with routine unannounced piss tests. That's the best deal I can give you. Or you can quit right now, hang out a shingle, try to go into private practice, see how that works for you. I mean, maybe somebody out there wants to hire a lawyer who spends their spare time doing lines of coke. I wouldn't know. Or maybe you can just become a junkie. Up to you."

This sarcasm sliced her skin.

"My cases . . ."

"Reassigned. This will create some additional work for your colleagues, but they'll manage."

She nodded.

"You're not to have any contact with anyone associated with this office. We're going to have to give your drug dealer buddy a helluva deal to keep his mouth shut about you, and I don't like doing that. If the press ever heard—Christ, what a mess that would be; I can see the headline: *State Attorney Cover-up for Addict Prosecutor.* Jesus. Anyway, what you're going to do is go get straight and then we will see where we are."

"Shall I . . ."

"Out of here in an hour. I'll make up some story for everyone. Like I'm putting you on a special assignment. Everyone will know the truth, but it's a reasonable lie. Cover asses. Save face."

She wanted to say something. Again she did not.

"That's it. And Susan . . ."

"Yes."

"I really hope you can pull yourself together. You want the names of some rehab specialists? I can get you those. And I want you to check in with me every week. Not with anyone else. Call my private line. I want to hear the rehab plan by the end of this week. By the end of next week I want to hear how it's going. And so on. And I will want names of doctors, sponsors, whatever, so I can call them and speak with them myself. Got that?"

"Yes."

"Susan, everyone here is pulling for you."

He did not add *Don't fucking let us down again* but she knew that was implied. She wished that her boss had sounded more angry, outraged even, but he had not. Mostly he'd just sounded weary and resigned.

It took her an hour to stack her current cases on her desk in as orderly a fashion as she could manage, and leave behind some notes so that which-ever prosecutor took them over wouldn't be hopelessly lost from the get-go. Then she took her badge and her handgun and slid these into her briefcase.

The only file she didn't leave behind was ED WARNER—SUICIDE.

Near hysteria, verge of panic, tears and clammy sweat, quaver in the voice, quiver in the hands. Moth saw all the fear in Andy Candy's eyes, face, and body and thought it was like delirium tremens after an alcohol bender, or the pallid, near-dead look of someone coming down off a two-day crack cocaine binge. He was familiar with the looks created by substances, less accustomed to the looks created by terror.

Andy's voice was plaintive, trapped. "What do we do now? He knows who we are." A pause. "What do you think he will do?"

What she wanted to say was *Kill him, Moth. Kill him for me.* She did not say this and did not know why she didn't because it made sense.

Moth wanted to pace aggressively around his apartment, like a general planning a siege, at the same time that he wanted to sit beside Andy Candy, throw his arm around her, and bring her head to his shoulder.

Andy dropped her face into her hands, and very much wanted to be comforted except that she doubted there was anything Moth could say right at that moment that might comfort her. She was actually a little sur-prised that she'd managed to drive the remaining blocks to his apartment with the killer's words ringing in her ears. She seemed to ricochet between sobbing breakdown and cold, determined resiliency. Any sensation of toughness surprised her and seemed new. She wasn't sure what to make of it, but hoped it would stick with her.

She looked up at Moth. *He's afraid for me.* She thought he looked stricken, like she imagined she must have looked on the day her father was given his deadly cancer diagnosis. *No brave words, no stiff-upper-lip, let's-keep-our-eye-on-the-ball-and-we'll-get-through-this bullshit,* she thought. *Just murder waiting in the doorway, ready to push inside.*

Cancer and abortion and murder all blended together in her imagination as if they weren't all different moments in her twenty-two years, but were somehow combined into a single entity.

"All right," Moth said, his voice even-keeled. "We talk to Susan Terry and see what she says." He smiled wanly, trying to encourage Andy Candy. "Call in the cavalry. Bring in the Marines. Whatever will keep us safe. Susan will know exactly what we should do."

But she did not.

"Christ," Susan blurted.

The three of them were standing in the parking lot adjacent to the Miami-Dade Office of the State Attorney. It was late morning, nearly noon, heat was building, and the steady drone of nearby traffic punctuated their conversation. Moth could see a line of sweat forming on Susan's forehead. She seemed pale to him, as if she was sick or hadn't slept. He thought Andy should be the pale one. Or maybe him. Their threat was real. But it was Susan who seemed shaky—more shaky than she'd been in the sushi restaurant—as if something was terribly out of kilter. He thought he recognized this for what it was, but said nothing—although the words *up the nose* fixed in his head. He wasn't sure whether Andy Candy saw the same integers that added up to a single quotient: *cocaine.*

"Go through it again," Susan said, because she couldn't think of anything else to ask.

"What he said was: Had I ever spoken with a killer before? Of course not. Scared the hell out of me." Andy Candy tried to minimize the frantic tone in her voice. She wanted to seem in control when she felt anything but. "Still scares the hell out of me. Susan, what do we do?"

Moth had said nothing up to this point. He'd hidden his surprise when Susan told him to meet her outside.

Moth finally spoke, filling his voice with no-nonsense demands: "Look,

Susan, we need protection. Like round-the-clock bodyguards. We need the cops to take over. We need to open a real investigation and find this guy before he . . ." Moth stopped there, because he did not want to start suggesting what this anonymous killer might be capable of.

Susan nodded, but said, "I don't know if I can help."

There was a momentary silence.

"What the fuck?" Andy Candy blurted.

Susan looked at the two young people. *Tell the truth? Find a convenient lie?* She swallowed hard. *Timothy will know,* she thought. *Can't fool another addict.* "I've been suspended. All I'm supposed to do is—"

Moth interrupted her. "Get straight."

"That's right."

"I fucking knew it," Moth said, turning his head away so that Andy wouldn't see the frustration there.

"But you could call someone, right?" Andy said. "Someone else who could help us."

This simple request didn't compute with Susan. *Call her boss and say what exactly? "I'm sorry I'm suspended but there's this killer or maybe not because it's a case I already cleared. So I fucked up more than once. Like fucked up squared."*

Or maybe I should call some homicide detective who will think hearing from a suspended prosecutor with a cocaine habit and a pressing need for a big-time favor is precisely the last thing in this world he wants on his plate and who will kiss me off so fast I won't even feel it happening. Like a razor cut, Susan thought. *I'm radioactive.* "No," she said slowly. "I think the only thing is to handle this ourselves. At least until I can . . ." She stopped. *Can what?* She knew this was a singularly stupid approach. She did not see an alternative.

"Then what," Moth said abruptly, "is our next move?" He hesitated, then added, "And it should be some move that keeps us all alive." He racked his brain trying to envision one.

"Right," Susan said. She did not add, *"And what move might that be?"*

Andy felt her imagination crowded: *Doctor Hogan wasn't safe. Uncle Ed wasn't safe. None of the others were safe.*

"We should do what he has done," she said.

"What do you mean?" Moth asked. 'We can't toss away who we are, like he did."

Andy Candy turned to him. "That's not what I meant," she said. She reached out and grabbed his hand, the same gesture someone might make to lead another into an embrace.

She wanted to form her words cautiously, but they came out in a rush. "What we know is that someone thirty years ago went to medical school, fell into a psychotic episode, got kicked out, was hospitalized, got out, allegedly died in Manhattan's East River a suicide, except he didn't, and then he devoted the remaining years right up to this moment arranging deaths that didn't exactly look like murders. Five people are dead. So, this killer had to become *somebody*. There's a trail there, and we have to find it. Then we can protect ourselves. Look, there's a mistake. Gotta be. Somewhere. I mean, no crime is perfect and no criminal is always a genius. Right, Susan?"

Susan nodded, although she thought even that small reassuring gesture was a lie.

Moth thought Andy's plan to find the killer's trail would be nearly impossible to accomplish.

He also realized that it was exactly what they needed to do.

Two blocks away, Student #5 was thinking very much along the same lines, only from a different perspective. *Create a trail they can follow, and bring them to your doorstep. Flypaper—hangs seductively from the ceiling, the perfect place for flies to land. Except it kills them.*

32

By the end of the day, Student #5 had grown increasingly weary, over-heated, and a little bored with following The Nephew, The Girlfriend, and The Prosecutor around. The afternoon sky was cloudless, so the tropical sun beat down constantly and he didn't think the three of them were doing much of any relevance. They spent a good deal of time inside Moth's apartment. There was a trip to an office supply store and another to a pharmacy. Late in the day, Andy Candy had gone out and returned with two bags of groceries. Takeout. It was all totally predictable.

But he told himself that it was necessary to be like the hound in a hunt, relentless once the fox's scent was picked up. So when the three *targets*— that was how he was beginning to think of them—arrived at Redeemer One in time for the evening meeting, he tucked his car in shadows well away from where he knew The Girlfriend would park.

He waited until the last addict or drunk hurried through the front doors, checked on The Girlfriend, who was scrunched down in her seat as if she was hiding, then exited his car. He rapidly crossed the night, cutting through the darkness like a hot knife through bread crust—

following a path of curiosity that he didn't realize mimicked one Andy Candy had taken.

Student #5 ignored the somber religiosity of the church, made a small waving gesture toward the Christ figure at the head of the pews—just a cynical acknowledgment of *Look who's here* and *you can't stop me*—and proceeded toward the back, where the meeting was already getting started.

As Andy Candy had, he hesitated just outside, peering in, trying to memorize faces.

He turned suddenly when he heard footsteps behind him.

It was the engineer. A little late, hurrying.

The engineer stopped. He smiled at Student #5.

"It's open to anyone with a problem," he said. "Want to come in?"

Student #5 smiled. *Perform like an addict.* "I think I'd just like to hang here and listen," he said.

"We can help you," the engineer continued. "That first step is the hardest. We all know that."

"Thanks," Student #5 said. "Let me think about it. You go ahead."

"Well, okay. But you want help, it's inside that door," the engineer said. Lively, hopeful. Optimistic. Welcoming.

"I know," replied Student #5.

As the engineer walked past him, he slunk back a little into a nearby shadow. *I truly know,* he thought. *Yes, that first step is the hardest. In killing.* Delightful irony in that.

He decided he didn't need to hear or see anything else. Quietly, he retraced his steps back through the church.

By the time Student #5 returned to his car he was churning with ideas. In the fairy tale, Hansel and Gretel leave a trail of bread crumbs through the forest because they want to be able to find their way home. But the trail disappears when the birds that follow after them devour every crumb. *That's the kind of trail I need to create: one that is obvious enough for them to see but vanishes.*

He looked around, as if he could see past the nighttime, the trees and bushes, streets, buildings, people—the entirety of the city. *Cannot act here,* he told himself. *This is where they are known. This is where they have whatever strength they have left. Relatives. Friends. Cops. Hell, the people in that meeting. All these elements create resources.*

So where don't they have resources?

In my worlds. But, which one?

He recognized this would probably mean he would have to give up one of his carefully constructed lives, and this troubled him.

New York City was out of the question, even with the delicious day-to-day anonymity the city provided. *Killing there is a big mistake.* Inviting some really sophisticated detective—a Vinnie Italian Last Name or a Patrick O'Something—into a truly unique crime scene, with all the forensic sophistication available to that police force, was a poor idea at best. *The cops in New York know what they are doing. Seen a lot. Done a lot. Not much fazes them. They're determined, experienced, and damn hard to fool.* And he loved the city. *Noise. Energy. Confidence. Success. That's what New York offers. Can't give that up.*

The trouble was, he loved his other homes as well. He'd just had his kitchen in Key West expensively remodeled and new ecologically conscious solar panels placed on the roof. When this was all over he wanted to take a vacation there.

That left the bears and the ramshackle trailer.

As much as he liked living there, Charlemont was a good place for a killing, with its local cops adept only at solving teenage drinking and reckless driving cases and low-rent burglaries where someone's snowmobile gets stolen. By the time they got professional investigators in from the Massachusetts State Police, he could be long gone.

He felt some regret about having to make a choice, which seemed unduly unfair to him, so he shifted the blame onto The Nephew, The Prosecutor, and The Girlfriend. It would help him to learn to hate them, he realized. *Makes killing easier.* "You three have fucked me up," he said bitterly. "But now I'm going to fuck you up."

He looked over to where The Girlfriend had parked. He could just barely make out her profile from where he sat.

"Okay. Let's toss out Crumb Number Two, thank you *Hansel and Gretel*."

He picked up one of the many throwaway cell phones he'd acquired, dialed a number—thinking, *Not calling you this time. That was Crumb Number One, even if you didn't realize it at the time. Interesting crumbs on the path.*

"Hi," he said briskly, in as friendly a tone as he could manage. "I'd like to schedule an appointment for tomorrow."

As he spoke, he looked over toward The Girlfriend. A sudden burst of excitement exploded within him. *She's getting out of the car!*

Why is she doing that?

But he kept his voice as even, steady, and outgoing as possible as he finished up his phone conversation and watched Andy Candy walking toward him through the evening shadows.

Inside Redeemer One the meeting had rapidly devolved into arguments and cacophony.

"Jesus H. Christ," Fred the engineer half-shouted, "you realize what sort of danger you're in?"

"Or might be in," someone corrected loudly. "You don't know."

"None of us knows, for Christ's sake."

"But God damn it, they need to take precautions."

"Like what?"

The assistant priest who ran the meetings frowned. "Please," he said, holding his hands wide in some sort of supplication, "try to remember where you are."

He meant *church* and was probably uncomfortable with obscenities and the Savior's name being bandied about, but this was immediately lost on the others.

Susan was still standing in front of her seat. Moth was next to her. She

273

had started the session by sharing the standard: "Hi. My Name is Susan, and I'm an addict. I have one day sober now . . . actually, barely twenty-four hours . . ."

The philosophy professor interrupted, which was frowned upon at these meetings but under the circumstances seemed appropriate. "So, when we called you the other night . . ."

Susan nodded, ashamed. "I was high. Or in the process. But that's not important right now. What's important is that there is a strong likelihood that Timothy here is correct about his uncle's death . . ."

This statement gathered a murmur, but one that instantly tumbled into a deep, attentive silence as Susan had continued, "So, yes, there very may well be a serial killer out there." She'd paused at that moment, thinking, *A pretty odd serial killer, by any stretch of the imagination. Not like any I've ever seen before.* As she spoke, she looked like an actress on a stage looking for the greatest portent in her words, as she added: "And I can't do anything, not one damn thing, about it."

That conclusion was what tripped the cacophony. In a room devoted to thoughtful sharing of troubles, expressed patiently, one at a time, everyone seemed to have something to say at once.

"That's not right."

"Of course you can."

"Can't you call the police?"

"That makes no sense whatsoever."

"You can't just stand around and let some killer kill again."

"Why do you think there's nothing you can do?"

This last question was the one she decided to answer. "Because I fell off the wagon and now I've been suspended. I'm not allowed to have any contact with anyone in law enforcement. Until I get straight."

Another silence. Susan peered around. "Maybe someone here wants to make that call?"

More silence. It lasted seconds, during which Susan felt as if she were being dragged into darkness, as if the lights around her were slowly being dimmed. The philosophy professor finally spoke:

"You have no friend in a homicide office you can approach informally?"

She shook her head. "Right now, the only friends I have are here," and she was unsure even about that.

The philosophy professor—sandy-haired, wearing old-fashioned wire-rimmed glasses, tall and lanky but with the sort of look that seemed to indicate he would clumsily drop a basketball if one were handed to him—nodded his head, as if agreeing with a brilliant graduate student.

"So, they're on their own?"

"*We* are on our own."

Out of the corner of her eye, she caught Moth nodding his head.

The philosophy professor leaned forward. He spoke to Susan, but actually addressed everyone in the room. "Well," he said, wearing a wry smile. "This is a support group. So, how can we support you?" Then he smiled. "I have an idea or two."

"Two important concepts to embrace," the professor continued. He leaned forward, lowering his voice, but kept his eyes directly on Susan, probing her. She looked around and saw that the others in the room were fixed on her with the same intensity. *Can't hide addiction from those looks,* she realized.

Moth had risen from his seat and was standing beside her. "What concepts are those?" he asked.

"The first is sobriety. Don't let drugs or drink do the job of some serial killer," the professor said. This might have been a cliché, but inside Redeemer One it was repeated endlessly with genuine passion.

Moth nodded. He could hear a murmur of assent through the room. He didn't dare look over for Susan's response.

"And one other important idea," the philosophy professor continued.

The room grew silent.

"Be ready to kill before you are killed," he said brutally.

The immediate torrent of responses from the room was like a waterfall of words splashing down on Moth's head, but in all the confused answers he grasped a single ironic notion. *Frontier justice from an academic philosopher.* He suspected that Susan did as well, although he didn't trust her to be able to act. At least, not act in the same way that he could.

It is, Andy Candy thought, *stifling.* It was the excuse she used to escape the cage of the car.

Weak cones of high-intensity light from haphazard overhead fixtures illuminated the church parking lot. Bushes and trees surrounded the perimeter, creating a moat of shadows. Although the church's front door was brightly lit, suggesting safety, the spot felt unsettling, dangerous.

She paced forward aggressively, as if she determined to reach a specific destination. Then she stopped, hesitated, pivoted first to her right, then her left, looking suddenly lost, as if she'd taken too many steps in the wrong direction.

Stop thinking, she told herself. She wanted to put on earbuds and blast brain-numbing hard rock music. A part of her wanted to sprint back and forth across the parking lot, dodging from light to light, until she was exhausted with effort. She contemplated holding her breath like a blue water diver. One minute. Two minutes. Three. Some impossible length of time that would take over all her senses, feelings, abilities and eradicate all the fears that resounded within her.

A part of her was drawn toward the meeting inside the church. *They're safe in there,* she thought, although she realized that merely by being there everyone acknowledged how much danger they were in. But it was a different sort of danger, she understood. *They fear themselves. I fear someone else.*

Andy Candy nearly dropped to her knees, suddenly weak. She reached out and steadied herself with a hand against the trunk of a car. Everything in her life seemed to require toughness.

She knew she had it. Somewhere. She was unsure whether she could find it. She had no idea whether she could actually use it effectively, if she did discover it. She wanted courage and determination. But wanting and acquiring are different things.

She looked around. She felt her knees weaken again, almost buckling beneath her. She had the sensation of being adrift.

She breathed in sharply. She could feel her pulse racing just as if she was facing a threat. But in the darkness around her, she could see none. Or many. She was unsure.

In that second she understood: *I no longer have a choice.*

This unsettled her, but then she burst out in a sudden, wild, braying laugh. Nothing was funny. The sound she made was simply a release. When she looked up she saw Moth coming out of Redeemer One and felt a surge of relief.

Student #5 also saw Moth emerge from the church.

Sins completely expiated? He sneered.

He was only feet away from Andy Candy. In the rearview mirror, he could see her hand steadying herself against his car. He didn't move, remained frozen in his seat, fighting the overwhelming urge to reach out and touch her. *Only one thing more intimate than love,* he thought. *Death.* That she hadn't spotted him seemed miraculous. *A miracle from the God of Murder,* he thought. Barely breathing, he watched Andy peel away from the side of his rental car and make her way toward Moth: *Like lovers rushing to greet each other after a long absence.* With each stride she took, he exhaled a little more, until his heartbeat returned to normal. He sniffed the night air. Wild scents, flowers, musky growth, all carried on the black, humid air, filled his nostrils. With so many different smells, he figured, the familiar and utterly unmistakable scent of killing would surely be hidden.

33

Roll the wrists.

Flex the fingers.

Back straight. Sit upright.

Both thumbs lightly touching middle C. First play all the C notes going up with the right, then the same going down with the left.

Student #5 dutifully listened to the instructions, followed each prompt as carefully as he could, while at the same time measuring, observing, and absorbing as much as he could without ignoring Andy Candy's mother's pleasant admonitions.

"You say this is your first time at the piano?" she asked.

"Yes, indeed," he replied. This was a lie. It had been years since his childhood lessons, but years passing didn't mean he wasn't lying.

"I'm impressed. You are doing well."

He tried a simple scale, and was a little surprised that what he played actually sounded like music. It was like a basic movie sound track to planning a killing. No John Williams swelling orchestra, just single, deadly sounds. Generic killing tones. The real notes weren't being played on the piano—they were in the photographs on the wall, the layout of the home, a careful assessment of where Andy Candy came from and who she seemed to be. There were also some sharps and flats that indicated where she hoped to go—but Student #5 realized those would be discordant.

"Do you live here all alone?" Student #5 abruptly asked.

This question was designed to be totally inappropriate. Unsettling. He could hear Andy Candy's mother inhale just a little more sharply than before.

"Concentrate on the notes. Try to make your hands move fluidly."

"I guess if you are a piano teacher, you have to open your door to just about anyone." He said this with a half-laugh, a subtle tone of nastiness, while bending toward the simple sheet music in front of him. "Even if it's Ted Bundy or Hannibal Lecter who wants lessons." He did not have to look at Andy Candy's mother's face to imagine the impact those names had. All he had to do was feel the way she shifted about uncomfortably on the piano bench.

"I think I would hate to be alone with strangers so much of the day," Student #5 said. "I mean there's no telling who could come walking through that door. It's not unreasonable to think even some killers want to learn to be musicians."

He enjoyed sounding so thoughtful, and bent toward the keyboard. "Like, what keeps you safe? Not much, I guess." He nodded toward a crucifix on the wall. "Not even faith, I bet."

Student #5 didn't expect an answer to that provocative question. He doubted there was anything else he could say that would make the mother any more nervous, except his next question, as he rippled through a set of notes:

"Do you keep a gun in the house?"

He heard her cough. Again no answer. This wasn't a surprise, although he imagined she was churning with replies: *Yes, I keep a Dirty Harry .44 Magnum at my side at all times*" or *"No, but my neighbor is a cop and he watches out for me,"* or *"My dogs are savage and trained to attack at my command."*

It was amusing.

The lesson lasted thirty minutes. At the end, Student #5 shook hands with Andy Candy's mother, who handed him a *So You Want to Learn the Piano* textbook and several handwritten exercises for his next session. But at the same time, she said, haltingly, "You know, I usually don't do adult lessons. Mostly just young kids and teens. Can I recommend someone you can continue with?" She was half-gesturing, half-pushing him toward the door.

"Are you sure you can't? I've enjoyed this time so much. I feel like we've connected. I'd really like to see you again."

"Yes, I'm sure," she said. "Sorry. I think my next lesson is here."

"But you advertise 'Children and Adults' on the web, when your page comes up . . ." he persisted falsely.

"I think you need someone with more expertise than me," she said, trying to sound as final as possible. The more stern her tone, the more nervous it meant she was. This was precisely the sensation that he'd wanted to create. *Crumbs.*

"Okay," he said slowly. "But I feel like we were just getting to know each other." He put a special emphasis on the word *know.*

Can't be any more creepy than that, he thought. He reached abruptly for his wallet, a really quick motion that made Andy Candy's mother recoil slightly, as if he was going to produce a knife or gun and torture, rape, and murder her right then and there. But this was part of his sleight of hand. *Houdini would smile,* he thought.

As he removed three $20 bills, Student #5 dropped his Massachusetts driver's license to the floor at Andy Candy's mother's feet. Like any polite person—even a scared one—she reached down and picked it up. Anything to hurry him out of her home. But he fumbled with his wallet some more, head down, ignoring the license in her outstretched hand, to give her time to examine the front.

"Massachusetts is a long ways, Mister Munroe," she said, eyes fixed on the license. *Just long enough to get his name, maybe register the town of Charlemont.* "I thought you said your name was . . ." She stopped abruptly, then said, "I thought you said you were local . . ."

He snatched the license from her hand as if it was on fire. Again, she took a half-step backward. *What an actor. I should have been on Broadway.*

For the last part of the night, Student #5 parked a half-block away from his destination. It was a neighborhood of modest, cinder-block homes, flat-tiled red roofs, and as many chain link fences as there were palm trees.

He waited.

The first order of business was to make sure there were no cops around. Nor did he want his voice to be picked up on a bug planted in a ceiling light fixture or a telephone wiretap, nor some infrared observation *trap* camera to identify a heat signature and start clicking frames. What he wanted was a few private moments.

Waiting patiently, Student #5 kept his eyes on a single home.

If I were a drug dealer, he thought, *what would I do to guarantee my safety? Especially after being arrested, then unarrested and released.*

I would have video monitoring cameras mounted by the front door and the rear entry, a high-tech alarm system. Surely I would have invested in tempered steel bars on windows and doors and a state-of-the art intercom. Lots of electronics in a nondescript, modest house.

What else? A variety of weapons placed in key locations inside. A handgun. A 12-gauge shotgun. Maybe an AK-47. Good for all situations.

Bodyguard? Hired muscle?

Not for the ordinary transactions. I would keep some names on speed dial if an occasion presented itself where I needed some imposing backup, like if I developed a supply or bill-collection issue and needed some intimidation at my side. But for routine business I would rely upon my electronics and my state-of-the-art locking system.

Student #5 wondered whether any of that had been seized or damaged when the police broke in the other night—following his anonymous tip. *Probably. But don't count on it. And repair services in Miami that cater to these sorts of needs work around the clock.*

Looking about, up and down the street, as if measuring the depth of night darkness, Student #5 fixed a cheap wig to his head. A maroon baseball hat emblazoned with the letters "UMASS" and a logo of a colonial Minuteman brandishing a musket was scrunched down on his head to hold the wig in place. Then he slid on large aviator sunglasses.

The street outside his car was empty. He exited and walked briskly to the dealer's house. At the front door, he rang a buzzer and waited.

It took a moment for the answer to come from inside.

"Not doing business right now."

Student #5 replied: "Not here for that."

A pause. "Give me your name, remove your hat and sunglasses, and look up into the camera above your left shoulder."

"No," Student #5 said firmly.

"Then get the fuck out of—"

He interrupted: "Don't you want to know who dropped the dime on you?"

A tease that couldn't be ignored.

Another hesitation. Tinny, intercom reply: "I'm listening."

"Call this number: 413-555-6161. Make the call from a secure phone, and not one that the cops have tapped. Better figure that every line you've got, including the cell phones you purchased today at the mall, are being checked, so get out of your house. You've got thirty minutes to make the call."

He was guessing about the cell phone purchase. Keeping his head down, Student #5 rapidly retreated from the front door.

He won't go far to make the call.

There are many different types of drug dealers. Hip-hop-styled, gold-chain-wearing, full-entourage-of-hangers-on street types; white-jacketed pharmacists who like to have a little extra sideline; and this guy—a suburban, ex-business-school sort who thought he could make some good cash and fly under the radar by living modestly and staying away from shiny cars, leggy women, and flash. Regardless of the type—they are all smart enough to be armed. A 9mm Glock stuck in his jeans waistband. He's not Cuban, but he will still wear a loose guayabera shirt to conceal the gun. A preferred drug dealer handgun.

He will be wary. But curious.

In a world that relied on disposable cells like the number he'd given, finding a freestanding telephone could be a trick. Student #5 had spent a little time that day reconnoitering the ten-block area around the drug dealer's home and had identified four different locations where old-fashioned pay phones still operated. *He will either go to the Mobil station on Calle Ocho or to the McDonald's on Douglas Road. Both are well lit and busy, even late at night. He will feel safe in either. Maybe.*

This made Student #5 smile. Things were reversed: *The criminal with the gun will feel he's in danger. Mister Helpful—that's me—is in control.*

He thought a little harder and then drove toward the gas station. The McDonald's was likely to attract cops needing coffee.

He was correct in this supposition. He parked on a side street after seeing the dealer pull into the station. Within seconds his phone rang. He let it ring twice, smiling. *That 413 area code won't be lost on him. Western Massachusetts.*

"Okay, I'm listening," the drug dealer said. "Secure line. So, no bullshit."

"What do I get for giving you a name?" Student #5 asked.

"What do you want?"

"Cash and some blow."

"How much of each?"

"How much do you want the name?"

"I want the name. But how do I know you've got the right informa-tion?"

"You don't. But it is."

"Fuck you. I don't believe you. Made me come out for nothing."

Student #5 was already enjoying the conversation. It was an unusual match of wits. The dealer was sophisticated about the mechanics of crime— but not as sophisticated as Student #5 was. "Not nothing," Student #5 said.

"You a cop?" the dealer demanded.

"That's a stupid question," Student #5 replied. "I can say *no*. I can say *yes*. You're not going to believe either answer."

"The law says you have to identify yourself if . . ."

"I don't really adhere to many laws," Student #5 said. "Of course, that could be true for all sorts of people. Good guys. Bad guys. Rogue cops even."

The dealer hesitated. "Okay," he said. "Then give me a plan."

Student #5 took this moment to pause, as if he was thinking, when he had already decided what he was going to do: make himself seem greedy. "Two ounces and five grand cash."

"That's a lot."

"Not really. The amount of coke is low enough so even if I'm stiffing you, you can easily make it up by cutting your next batch a little more carefully. Same for the cash. Not a huge sum. Hell, in a legitimate business it would be a tax write-off—like taking some executives out to a fancy dinner and ordering an expensive bottle of wine—and the government would end up paying a third of it when it came off your tax return. Think of it the same way. And you can afford it, even if I'm lying. Which I'm not."

"Okay, if I agree, how do we . . ."

"Same place where you are standing. In twenty minutes. I'll call that line."

"Twenty minutes isn't nearly enough . . ."

"Sure it is. I figure you've got that much cash lying around your house. And don't be stupid enough to bring anyone with you—even if you could get some muscle out of bed and hustle over here in twenty minutes. Hurry home. Grab the coke. Grab the cash. Hurry back. This transaction is going to take ten seconds. You hand me an envelope and I give you a name. Then we never see each other again."

The dealer paused again.

"This sounds like a scam. I think maybe fuck you."

"That would be your choice. But just how many people know you got pinched and then released so fast it would make your eyeballs spin? Not too many, I bet. Other than the cops, the guy who turned you in, and me, who else knows your business ventures took a little side trip to the Dade County Jail? I suspect you would prefer to keep this blip on your financial horizon quiet. Too easy for your clientele to say 'So long, thanks for everything' and find someone who *isn't* on the police radar."

This was an argument that Student #5 believed would ring true. Economics of drug dealing in Miami: There was always someone ready to step into an artificial void.

"Tell you what," the dealer said cautiously. "One grand. No blow. You give me the name. It pans out, and I'll fix you up with the rest."

"Now who needs to trust whom?" Student #5 said. *Not stupid*, Student #5 thought. *Handing over that much cocaine is a felony and he still thinks I just might be a cop or a DEA informant. Handing over cash isn't anything.*

"My lawyer will get the informant's name."

"If he could, he already would. Tell you what," Student #5 said. "One ounce. Two grand and that's it. Just enough for me to have a little party."

"Can't do the blow," the dealer said. "You should know that when the cops showed up they seized my whole supply. Wiped me out. So it's cash only for the name."

Student #5 hesitated, to give the impression that he was thinking, when he'd expected this. "Okay," he said slowly. "Two grand. And a taste. Oxy. Grass. Something for a party."

"Where do we meet?"

"Right where you're standing now."

"Twenty minutes, and back here," the dealer said. "Twelve hundred and whatever I can dig up and we have a deal."

The *taste* would be some very small amount of something that looked like but wasn't actually OxyContin. Probably over-the-counter antihistamines. He didn't care.

"Done," Student #5 said. "Clock is starting now."

Hang up.

Dealer gets back in his car. A black Mercedes, as familiar in Miami as palm trees. Pulls away. Moving fast, but not fast enough to attract unwanted attention.

Wait seven minutes.

Walk across to the Mobil station. Approach the exterior phone from an angle where the only attendant inside behind the counter can't see.

Drop the baseball hat on the concrete beneath the phone.

Walk away.

It took twenty-two minutes for the dealer to return. From his vantage point, Student #5 watched him hurry to the pay phone. Student #5 dialed the number and saw the dealer seize the receiver.

"You were late," Student #5 said.

"No I wasn't," the dealer replied.

"Not worth arguing over," Student #5 said. "Here's what you do: Look down . . . see the hat on the ground?"

The dealer did as he was told. "Yes."

"Okay, you're going to put the agreed-upon elements of all this into that hat and turn it over so it's hidden. First, though, hold up the cash so I can see it. And you should figure that from where I'm watching you, I can even read the serial numbers on the bills."

Student #5 saw the dealer smile. "You sound like someone who's done this before. Makes me think this is bullshit."

"Just don't be stupid, like put the stuff in, get the name from me, and then pick it all up and try to leave. That would anger me immensely, and I have some resources."

"You threatening me?"

"Yes."

The dealer laughed a bit.

"So, we're not going to meet?"

"You want to?"

Again, he saw the dealer smile.

"Not really."

The dealer removed an envelope from his pocket. He fanned a few bills in front of his chest: $100s.

"How's that?"

"Good," Student #5 said. "Now in the hat." *He can hardly miss that logo on the front. Don't see too many University of Massachusetts Minutemen logos in South Florida. Plenty of University of Miami Ibis, University of Florida Gators, Florida State University Seminoles, but not Minutemen. Hard to forget that logo.*

"Done." He saw the drug dealer toe the baseball cap into a shadow. "Name?" the drug dealer demanded.

"Timothy Warner."

A pause.

"Who? Who the fuck is that? Never heard of him."

Student #5 felt a great sense of accomplishment. "Just drop that name on Susan Terry, your prosecutor client. See how she reacts."

He disconnected the line and watched the dealer. He could tell the man was torn—didn't want to leave whatever fake drug and real cash was lying on the sidewalk. *Are you the sort of man that honors a deal?* Student #5 wondered.

To his surprise, the dealer was. With only a slight hesitation and a single glance back, the dealer returned to his car and drove rapidly away.

Student #5 watched the next three cars pull into the gas station to fill up at the pumps, to see if one of those drivers was looking at the abandoned hat. *Possible. But irrelevant.*

He put his rental car in gear and also started to drive away, slowly. He had never had any intention of obtaining anything from the dealer, but he had enjoyed the back-and-forth. *Someone will get a happy surprise,* he thought. *Maybe the underpaid gas station attendant will spot it.* Student #5 didn't care.

He won't call The Prosecutor until tomorrow morning but he won't wait much longer than that. He will do a name search on his computer first, just as I did, find out many of the same things about young Timothy. Maybe then he'll call his lawyer, try the name out on him before calling The Prosecutor. And while he's doing all that, I will have time to leave one more trail of crumbs before going home.

34

Two phone calls and an argument—each upsetting in its own way.

The first call came to Moth, mid-morning. He thought it would be from Andy Candy, just as Moth was beginning to worry about her being a little late. He snatched up his phone—but the caller ID came up *Anonymous* and he paused before answering. His first thought was that the killer who had called Andy was now calling him and he tried to prepare something to reply. He felt abruptly naked—yet was unable to *not* answer.

"Yes?"

"Timothy?"

He vaguely recognized the voice, but didn't place it instantly.

"Yes."

"This is Martin from your aunt's office." Cold. Flat. Atonal.

Moth was taken aback. He stammered, "Yes, Martin, ah, how can I—"

"I thought your aunt was totally explicit when you spoke with her."

"Explicit?"

"Yes. I believe she made herself abundantly clear."

Moth gathered himself. "Yes. She didn't seem to want any contact, especially if it had something to do with Ed . . ."

"I think she meant Ed—or anyone else."

"Yes, okay, Martin, but I don't see . . ."

Deep theatrical sigh, followed by a chilled voice. "Your aunt does not like to be threatened."

Moth was confused. "Threatened?"

"Yes. Threatened."

"Martin, I'm not following you . . ."

Martin the art purchasing assistant, sex provider, and all-around factotum business partner continued in an irate, indignant, irritated tone that told Moth that he had rehearsed his speech.

"Let me explain so there is absolutely no confusion. Shortly after we opened the gallery this morning we received a call from some thug. Let me repeat his words precisely so you will know exactly how angry we are: *'Tell your fucking nephew Timothy to stop fucking around with me or else I will fuck him up, but I will also fuck you and your business up and maybe do a lot worse. Got it?'* Nice question to end on. Of course I quote *got it* end quote."

Moth reeled back. He wanted to say something to the obnoxious assistant, but his mind went blank.

"So, Timothy, your aunt Cynthia would like me to say the following to you: 'Whatever drunken or drugged-up mess you are now in, please don't involve her, or else you will hear from her lawyers, who will be equipped with a restraining order and will make your miserable life even more miserable.' Is that perfectly clear?"

Couldn't make that threat any more pretentious, Moth thought. It was a pretty clear contrast from the other threat—not guns, knives, and murder, but *lawyers.* Typical of his aunt. But her threat was minuscule. He knew who had made that call. He just couldn't see *why.* Moth suddenly felt awash in a sea of danger. He tried to gather himself, maintain a non-panicked sense of understanding. He wished Andy Candy were there because he respected her rational side and her ability to see the larger picture.

He felt blind. *This is all part of a plan. It has to be.* This thought wasn't reassuring. He admonished himself: *You need to figure out what is going on.*

Moth took a deep breath. "Yes, but Martin—"

"Is it clear?"

"It is."

"Then we have nothing more to speak about."

"Martin, please, was there any indication *who* was making this call?"

The assistant paused briefly. "You mean, Timothy, there is more than one person who might be angry enough with you to go around threatening innocent people?" This was said in a fake-incredulous voice.

"Please, Martin. Help me out here, so at the very least I can make sure that whoever it is doesn't bother you or Aunt Cynthia again."

This was a false promise. Moth actually wished for one evil second that he could find a way to steer the killer in his aunt's direction. *Fuck them up as promised. That would be great.*

Martin seemed to hesitate. "Well, no, no indication, except for one thing."

"One thing?"

"Yes. The caller's accent."

"Accent?"

"Correct. I would have expected this thuggish talk from someone different . . ." Martin began.

Moth knew that Martin—whom he imagined was an utter racist—meant *black* or *Hispanic* when he used the word *different*. Moth wished he could use that moment to display all the contempt he had for his aunt's assistant and his aunt, but he did not.

"Yes," Moth replied.

"Clearly, this fellow wasn't from around here. Broad *a* sounds and dropped *g*'s. Reminded me of . . ." Martin hesitated. Moth could sense the assistant's shrug over the phone line before he continued. ". . . my days as an undergraduate in Cambridge. You know: *'Pahk the cah in Hahvahd Yahd.'* That's it. Very New England accent. Sounded like a character from some violent movie like *The Departed* or *The Town*. Could have been Maine,

New Hampshire, Vermont, or Massachusetts, but certainly not Miami or anywhere in the South. I hope this narrows your choices down. Regardless, this conversation is now over."

Martin hung up. Moth pictured the smug, self-important look the man would have on his face, but then this portrait dissipated and he began to pace around his apartment aimlessly, on edge, his feet driven by a sudden wave of questions.

The other phone call was equally curt.

Susan Terry was just out of the shower, drying her hair, unsure what the day held for her, unsure what her next step was—either with Moth and Andy Candy or with her addiction—when her phone rang. She answered casually, befitting her semidressed state.

"Yes, this is Susan Terry."

"Miss Terry, this is Michael Stern. I represent—"

She knew whom the lawyer represented. The man who sold her drugs and then sold her name to detectives for his freedom.

"Yes. This is my private home line," she said, snapping rapidly to attention, like a soldier on parade.

"Your office informed me that you are on special assignment."

"I'm not at liberty to discuss my current job."

This was a statement designed to cut this conversation off quickly, even if she had a slight curiosity as to why this lawyer was calling her this morning. The attorney hesitated, clearly already angry with her snippy tone.

"Perhaps you would like to tell me who Timothy Warner is," he demanded. "Of course, if you would prefer, I can go to your boss and ask him. Would Warner be someone from the University of Massachusetts, perhaps? Or does he simply like their hats?"

Susan's mouth opened but no words came out. A few seconds passed before she managed to croak, "What? Hats? What are you talking about?"

"Timothy Warner. The confidential informant who implicated my client unfairly in felony charges that have already been dropped."

"How did you get that name?"

The lawyer mocked her. "I'm not *at liberty* to discuss my sources."

Susan took a deep breath. "Neither am I, then," she said. She had dozens of questions flooding her, but didn't ask any. "I do not think I care to speak with you any longer," she said. Her voice had a confidence and a haughtiness that was pure performance, because she felt the exact opposite. *Why would Moth know anything about my dealer?* she wondered. *How would he know his name?* She tried to remember if she'd ever used the dealer's name at Redeemer One but she knew that she had not. *And why would Moth call Narcotics? What would he gain by turning me in and making a mess of my life?*

God damn it. And what the fuck was that about a baseball hat? And Massachusetts?

She had never been to Massachusetts. She didn't think she knew anyone from Massachusetts. But clearly it was important, although how and why eluded her.

No reason occurred to her, except she understood that *no reason* could say as much as something clear and to the point. She was unable to control her gathering fury.

The argument—as so many arguments do—started off innocently enough: a conversation that began with, "I had a terrible day. A real creep wanted a lesson."

Andy Candy's mother said this, trying to penetrate the immensely thick emotional walls that her daughter seemed to have erected. She was willing to talk about anything—her music students, the weather, politics—if it would lead into a discussion about Moth, or about Andy Candy's secretive, nervous behavior, or what plans she might be making to finish up her degree at the university and get on with her life. Andy Candy's mother, though blissfully unaware of how dangerous it was, was aware that her daughter was trapped in the midst of something.

For her part, Andy felt caught on some sort of hellish merry-go-round—but maintaining silence on all subjects having to do with murder seemed to her to be the only way she could protect her mother from any harm. It was as if by *not* speaking, she could bifurcate her life. Safe part—home, mother, dogs, fluffy comforter on her bed, happy memories of childhood. Deadly part—school, rape, Moth, the murdered Doctor Hogan, some ghostlike killer who seemed no farther away than a phone call. Keeping these two lives separate seemed crucial.

"What do you mean *a real creep?*" Andy Candy asked, aware that since the killer had called her, everything in her dual existences was electric. She could feel her skin tingle.

"Guy calls out of the blue, wants a lesson right away, then when he gets here, lies about his piano experience and starts asking inappropriate questions, like 'Do you live alone?' and 'Do you have a gun?' And I caught him staring at the photo of you hanging on the wall, like he was trying to memorize it. Made me uncomfortable, but you shouldn't worry, I refused to allow him back for another lesson."

Shouldn't worry. In Andy Candy's mind, this went well beyond irony. "Who was it? I mean, what name . . ."

"Oh, he lied about that, too."

Andy Candy exploded. High-pitched, sweat-driven, furious questions rocketed from within her. She bombarded her mother, trying to determine *who* it was that had occupied the piano bench, and *why* he had come there. Every answer she received made her anger more frantic and pushed her deeper into uncertainty, which felt very much like a black hole opening up beneath her feet.

When she'd heard everything—*Munroe, driver's license, some town up north that started with a* CH—Andy Candy raced unapologetically from the house and drove hard for Moth's apartment, leaving her mother both confused and teary-eyed. In that tire-squealing, run-the-stop-sign moment, Andy Candy didn't think she would be safe at her home any longer. She didn't know if there was anyplace safe for her. But at least she knew Moth would understand the danger, even if she had no idea what they could do about it.

* * *

293

Student #5 decided to fly north first-class. *Totally deserving,* he thought. He used a credit card to pay—one assigned to his Key West persona. It was a slight indulgence, he could easily afford it, and it would be a welcome reward for what he was already thinking was a *damn good* bit of work. All his years of careful planning directed toward his other killings had given him confidence about the seat-of-the-pants deaths he was now constructing. He thought of an athlete who spent years drilling proper form and technique into his muscles, called upon once again to remember all those hours of lessons and pitch a ball, throw a pass, shoot a puck. *It never leaves you.*

Nothing he'd created would tell The Prosecutor, The Girlfriend, and The Nephew anything concrete—other than the idea *I'm close. Very close.*

It would cause them to argue with each other, probably confuse them, and possibly even scare them. Everything they would experience was designed for one result: *They will think they know just enough to hunt me down. It will not occur to them that it's me hunting them.*

The stewardess arrived and asked him if he wanted a drink. He did. Scotch on the rocks. The bitter, seductive taste flowed into him. He liked Scotch because the liquor was relentless.

One sip. Two. The plane was lifted up past the bright Miami skyline toward its cruising altitude and he leaned back, closing his eyes. A memory of a favorite childhood book came to him: *Uncle Remus*—fried-chicken-and-chitlin tales from a happy-go-lucky, benign Old South that never actually existed, stories that were totally politically incorrect with obvious racist undertones.

One in particular was psychologically astute: Br'er Rabbit speaking in a deep, Southern-tinged voice that right at the moment seemed oddly like his own, pleading piteously for hunters to *not* do precisely the thing he wanted them to: *"Please don't throw me into that briar patch."*

Then a second story came to mind, equally sophisticated, and probably a little closer to what he intended. This tale revolved around a doll named Tar Baby.

35

Moth and Andy Candy lay on his bed, wrapped together like spoons. They were fully dressed, but touching as if they had just had sex. They had not, although it had occurred to both of them. Andy held Moth's hand tightly between her breasts. Moth rested his head against her back. Their breathing was raspy, shallow, but driven more by unsettled fear than anything else. They whispered to each other like the childhood lovers they once were, but it was a conversation that seemed to contradict the way they held each other.

"What are we going to do?" Andy asked, except this was a rote question and she already knew the reply.

"What we started out to do," Moth answered. "What else can we do?" Again, this was an expected response.

Neither really understood what they meant by this. They had more or less the same thought: what had begun as a bit of barely controlled bravado and revenge fantasy had progressively become more and more real. They had seen one man die, and now they knew that someone else had to die. It's one thing to say *I'm going to kill someone* and another thing altogether to actually do it. Neither—although they would not share this doubt—believed they *could* kill someone. They had moments where they imagined it might be possible—others where they had zero confidence.

In a world that seemed to take violence and killing for granted, they were naïve about methods of murder. No military or police training. No mafia or drug cartel culture of killing. They weren't psychopaths or sociopaths who could flick off death like an unwanted bug landing on an arm. They were *normal*—even if Moth's alcoholism and Andy Candy's victimization and subsequent abortion made them feel unique. Secretly, both longed for the simplicity of teenage days past that seemed to have suddenly been stripped away from them.

"We have a gun," Moth said. "And we have someone who knows about killing. At least, intellectually."

For a moment Andy Candy stiffened, and then she realized that Moth was referring to Susan Terry. *A law school understanding. An after-the-fact comprehension that went along with being a prosecutor,* Andy Candy realized. *Can Susan pull a trigger? Hell if I know.*

"What will happen to us?" Andy Candy asked.

Moth smiled, stroked her hair. "We will get through this, grow old, fat, and happy, and never think about it again. I promise."

He left out the word *together*. And Andy Candy didn't actually believe the word *promise*.

"Well, if we do nothing, we know what will happen," she persisted.

"Do we?" Moth replied.

The two of them began to unfold, and within a few seconds were seated side by side, upright on the edge of the bed, like a pair of wayward children being disciplined and forced to sit still as punishment.

"Maybe he thinks he can just scare us into silence."

Andy Candy nodded. "That would be great. Except how would we ever know? Silence for how long? He took years and years to kill off the other people. Who's to say we wouldn't look up fifteen years from now—you know, living some nice suburban, soccer mom and coach dad life—and suddenly be staring at a gun. *Bang!* That's what he did to the others."

"What the fuck good does silence do for either him or us?"

Moth rose from the bed and began pacing around. "You know, the great men I study in history—they were always trapped into decisions. They never knew with absolute one hundred percent certainty if any course was right. But they believed that failing to try was worse than actually failing."

Andy Candy smiled wryly as she watched Moth travel back and forth, gesturing with his arms with each point made. It reminded her a bit of the moody but energized Moth of high school, somehow grown into someone familiar but different. Moth liked to drift into lecture tones. *He will make a good academic,* she thought. *He will have a nice life performing in front of a classroom—but only if he lives through this.* "Except—what does *failing* mean for us?" This question chilled the room.

"In a way, the same thing that it did for them," Moth replied, trying to force a smile. "What they faced was a loss. Maybe humiliation. Freedom. Gallows. Firing squad. Prison. I don't know. High stakes. That's what we know."

"Doesn't seem all that different for us," Andy replied. "Hit-and-run. Fake suicide. Hunting accident."

"No, it doesn't."

"What do you suppose he will invent for us?"

Moth didn't answer. His mind reeled with possibilities, none of them good.

Another pause. The practical Andy Candy started to emerge: "Shouldn't Miss Terry be here?"

"Yes."

Susan Terry remained in her car, parked outside Moth's apartment. She was on the twin edges of rage and despair, unsure about both.

What she craved—more than anything else—was to descend into more drug use and instantly forget everything that had happened to her in the past few days. After that morning's phone call from the lawyer she had immediately fueled herself with the last dregs of coke she had left, wondering only once why she hadn't flushed it down the toilet in the wake of her suspension and her trip at Timothy's side to Redeemer One. She took a deep breath. *I don't care what I promised those assholes,* she aggressively lied to herself. The siren song of cocaine seemed to pledge a lotuslike forgetfulness: *You won't have to worry about your job or your career. You won't have to worry about some killer. Every promise you made to everyone everywhere can be ignored and forgotten. Every pain you feel can be erased.*

In her satchel by her side was her semiautomatic. *Did you turn me in, Timothy? Why did you want to ruin my life?*

That this made absolutely no sense didn't diminish her fury. Susan Terry was balanced between the organized and rational state prosecutor who accumulated facts and evidence and the bad girl and drugged-up near criminal she had descended into. She had little idea which side of her was going to win out. But in that second, anger nearly overcame her, and she seized the satchel, exited the car, and rapidly made her way to the apartment.

When she knocked, Moth foolishly opened the door without first looking through the peephole.

Susan instantly thrust the automatic into his face. The hammer was cocked and a round was chambered, and the words "You little motherfucker . . ." stood for a greeting. Moth staggered back in shock, but Susan pushed after him, so that even with his frantic retreat the gun barrel still lurked inches from his eyes.

He choked out, "Wait, what, please," but couldn't come up with another word. He was confused, panicked—not that he hadn't expected someone to kill him, but this was the wrong person entirely. He thought of trying to find his own weapon and fighting back, but it was unloaded, on a bureau top, useless.

"I want the truth," Susan said coldly. "No more fucking around."

Andy Candy gave out a little half-shout of surprise and froze in position on the bed. She had more or less the same frightened thought: *This is wrong. Susan isn't the killer, is she?*

"Truth?" Moth asked. His voice was suddenly dry, and the word groaned like metal bending under immense pressure. He tried to raise his hands, partially in surrender, partially to deflect the shot he was certain was coming. He felt fear punching him in the stomach, choking his throat.

"Why did you drop the dime on me?"

Drop the dime sounded incomprehensible in a moment where her finger toyed with a trigger.

Moth continued to reel back, but stopped when his rear butted up against his desk. "What?" he coughed out. He looked at Susan Terry—hair disheveled, eyes wide, edgy tone to everything she said, hand quivering, frantic, in pain, strung out—and he realized that whatever resistance she had to pulling the trigger and killing him hung in some balance between rational and drugged. The apologetic, *I want to be sober* woman who had accompanied him to Redeemer One had been replaced by a stranger. And then, he realized, the Susan with wild eyes and a gun wasn't a stranger at all. It was just that the same person could actually be two people. He knew this was just as true for himself.

He took a deep breath, trying to find a grip on control. When he spoke again, he realized that in his shock, his voice had grown high-pitched.

"Tell me what you think I've done," he pleaded.

"Why did you call the cops? Give them my name and then my dealer's name. You know what you've done to me?"

Moth forced tightness into every muscle. He tried to will his pounding heart to slow down. He straightened up, tried to look past the barrel of the gun, and replied, "I didn't do anything like that. I don't know what you're talking about."

Susan Terry wanted to kill. More than anything, right in that second, she wanted death. But *whose* death eluded her. She stared at Moth. "Then who did?"

He swallowed hard. "You know."

She could feel every muscle in her body, and especially the muscles in her hand and finger, tightening on the trigger. The noise around her was roaring, like a jet taking off, and then she realized the room was filled with silence and that the deafening noise was coming from deep inside herself.

Someone—it couldn't possibly be her—screamed from within: *Make a choice!*

Moth gathered every tactic he'd ever learned at Redeemer One and quietly said, "Susan, do you know what you're doing?"

It took an immense effort to lower her gun to her side. *Choice made.*

"I'm sorry," she said. "Pressure."

This word seemed as good an explanation as any. But what was really true was that cracks and fissures were forming inexorably throughout her life.

In the momentary hesitation in the apartment, Andy Candy told herself, *Move!* Before she realized it, she'd risen to her feet and stepped in between Moth and Susan Terry.

"What's going on?" she demanded.

Inwardly, she thought, *I'm the one that's supposed to be terrified. The killer called me! And then he went to my house! What the hell is all this?*

Susan Terry leaned back. "I think I need a cold drink," she said.

"Water," Moth said. "With ice." *Odd,* he thought, *how one is able to endow a simple word like* water *with utter ferocity.*

Romance novels with happy endings; Victorian era literature, with bows and curtsies and infinitely intricate emotional back-and-forth. Sweeping Russian novels from the nineteenth century—*War and Peace.* Hemingway and Faulkner, John Dos Passos and Steinbeck's *The Grapes of Wrath.* Novels of manners, novels about spies who came in from the cold, novels about star-crossed lovers. Andy Candy racked her memory, tried to recall all the books she'd read as a literature major, trying to find the one that would steer her toward the right thing to do.

Nothing leapt out to her.

She looked over at Susan Terry. The prosecutor was hunched over at a table, two hands wrapped around a glistening glass of ice water, her weapon in front of her, her eyes staring off into the distance.

The phrase *thousand-yard stare*—she thought she'd first come across it in a memoir about Vietnam—came to her.

Moth had moved over to his desk and was shuffling through papers. After a moment, he looked up. "I think the problem is—everything we know about him is in the past. Everything he knows about us is in the present."

Andy nodded, then said, "Not exactly. I mean, we know a little."

"He knows who we are. Where we live. What we do."

Susan was still looking off into the distance.

Andy Candy rose, went over, and picked up one of the notepads she used for sorting her way through information. But this was mostly a prop, to help her organize the ideas in her memory. "We have a name—even if it is a phony one—that my mother saw. And she saw his license. Massachusetts."

Susan finally looked up. "Area code for the phone—413. And a hat with a UMASS logo on it."

Andy Candy didn't ask *how* Susan knew these details.

Andy continued. "The town name my mother saw. It began with *Ch.*"

Moth had turned to his computer. *Chicopee. Cheshire. Chesterfield. Charlemont.* He mumbled these town names out loud.

"Charlemont," Andy said. "Like Charlemagne, only . . ." She stopped.

Susan shook her head. "Why would you think he's gone home—even if one of those towns is his home? Why isn't he right outside, right now? He seems to like killing in Miami."

The three of them were silent for a moment. Moth spoke first. "Why should we wait around to be killed?"

The others looked at him.

"If we're going to hunt him down, then shouldn't we start there? How else can we get ahead of him?"

Susan nodded—but she didn't really know why.

Andy Candy went over and squeezed Moth's hand. She didn't think of him as much of a protector or a hero, but she thought the two of them together had always been a formidable couple. *Once upon a time.* She hoped she wasn't deluding herself.

But at the same moment the literature major within her bubbled to the

301

top of her consciousness: Enough of Dumas, Edmond Dantès, and *The Count of Monte Cristo*. Instead she recalled *Beowulf.* The hero first lies in wait for Grendel. Though he knows it will cost lives, maybe even his own, he can see no other way to fight. But even after the pitched battle and arm-ripping victory, there is a greater threat he hadn't foreseen. And he must pursue that threat right into its own lair.

36

He didn't like to think of himself as an overly cruel person, although in the wake of all that he'd accomplished, he was certain that some hard emotional times had been created for children, relatives, maybe even friends of the people he'd killed. This was rudimentary psychology and he wanted to be empathetic. *Nobody suffered too damn much: funerals with tears, fine elegies, and somber black clothes. Not much else.*

But when he pictured Timothy Warner, he grew angry—a pulse-accelerating, red-faced, teeth-gritted sort of half-fury. Cold, but in control, while recognizing that he was on the verge of explosion.

He thought: *This fucking kid has no right to be putting me in this situation. I should be all finished with killing. Getting on with things.*

Stupid boy. If you hadn't pursued me, you would live.

Stupid boy. You are taking your friends down with you.

Stupid boy. You should have learned to leave well enough alone.

Stupid boy. Pursuing me is like committing suicide.

He did not think he could hate Andrea Martine or Susan Terry in the same way.

But he was more than willing to kill them. Spectacularly.

What does the military call it? Collateral damage.

He busied himself, in a flat-out hurry, collecting items, planning. What he had in mind for The Girlfriend, The Nephew, and The Prosecutor was significantly more elaborate than his usual design. What he expected was closer to art than it was to murder, although he doubted anyone besides another truly sophisticated killer would ever be able to appreciate that distinction—and he had little respect for other killers, who seemed to him to be mostly gangsters, sociopaths, and thugs, and beneath contempt.

Sometimes, when in New York City, he went to late night midnight shows or off-the-beaten path grimy East Village art galleries to watch performances that blended theater with painting, film with sculpture, forms that used all sorts of avenues to create a visual experience. *Very trendy stuff,* he reminded himself. On other occasions, he drove his old pickup truck to the Massachusetts Museum of Contemporary Art. There, in faded jeans, uncombed hair, and dirt-encrusted work boots, he examined some of the more exaggerated styles that cutting-edge artists invented.

In Key West he would from time to time attend the drag queen shows on Duval Street, where he would nurse a Key West Sunset Ale and appreciate not merely the cabaret-style singing, Broadway dance numbers, and exotic outfits, but the fact that the shows displayed the ability of people to change who they were into something utterly different. *Chameleons singing show tunes. I wonder if they would appreciate what I am about to put together.*

Student #5 was driving a little too fast, heading to a half-dozen different hardware stores for containers—the same containers, at stores spread all over the valley he lived in. Cash each time. He also planned a trip to a Radio Shack for an old-fashioned tape cassette recorder. On the list he'd written, he'd scheduled a stop at Home Depot for electrical switches and wires, a large floor fan, cans of spray odor eraser, bungee cords, Velcro strips, and sixty-pound-test fishing line. All typical purchases for someone living in this rural area.

Student #5 was deeply concerned that he hadn't left himself enough time to prepare, so he avoided conversation, even pleasantries, as he collected his items. He kept a baseball cap tugged down on his head, wore sunglasses. He didn't have any real concern that a security camera might pick him up on video, but overpreparation was an important consideration. He didn't want to forget a simple item that might derail what he had in mind.

At a wilderness store, he purchased a secondhand one-person kayak. It was orange and slid easily into the back of his truck with his other gear. At a hunting store, he obtained the cheapest-model shotgun he could— there was irony in his choice, he thought, because he wasn't like Jeremy Hogan, purchasing a top-of-the-line gun that did the dead psychiatrist absolutely no good.

He made a plane reservation. He made a reservation with a rental car company—the company that advertised, *"We'll pick you up!"*—and got their smallest vehicle, promising to drop it off at the airport.

Two thoughts plagued him:

How long before they arrive?

A different me must greet them at the door, and that different me will have to remain with them forever.

He knew the answer to the first was: *soon*. He was confident he had left enough disparate clues in Miami to get them to Western Massachusetts. *They will put dropped license and baseball cap and area codes all together.* The idea, he knew, had been to create fear—but the sort of fear one is inexorably drawn toward, not the sort that causes one to run away screaming.

You show someone a door and invite them inside. This was basic psychology. *Compulsion.*

He was counting on Timothy Warner's inability to stop when he got near. *Think you are closing in. Think all the answers you need are right behind that door. Think that no matter what the danger might be, you must enter. Think that you are steps away from success.*

You will be.

Just not how you expect it.

He was troubled by only one element of his plan. The *different me* was a definite challenge. But he knew where to go to find what he hoped would serve as a reasonable facsimile of his self.

None of the three packed much: a change of underwear, a couple of pairs of socks, a gun.

At Miami International, Moth had the odd thought that he was retracing the killer's steps. He wondered whether the same ticket counter attendant had helped his quarry. He wondered whether he was standing in the same position, having the same conversation: *Any bags to check? No, nothing except reason and intelligence.* Andy Candy, on the other hand, was preoccupied with the sensation that she was leaving much more than a city behind, that each stride she took was sending her deeper into some jungle of uncertainty.

Susan Terry—having cleaned up as best she could—was being practical. She used her state attorney's office badge to explain why she had two weapons—Moth's .357 Magnum and her own .25-caliber semiautomatic—in her small overnight suitcase. She had been surprised when Moth had told her about bringing his weapon back from New Jersey, underscoring how much of the safety the flying public assumes is actually nonexistent. Susan did not inform the flight personnel that her badge was suspended, and she was relieved that this detail hadn't shown up on a perfunctory computer search.

They boarded their flight and sat quietly together. Moth found it interesting that they didn't speak or read or watch the tiny television sets implanted in the seat-backs in front of them. None of them needed any distraction other than their thoughts.

Andy spent the entire trip looking out the small window at the expanse of night beyond. The darkness seemed mysterious to her, filled with shades of uncertainty and unusual, unrecognizable shapes. Occasionally, she would reach over and touch Moth's hand, as if to make certain that he was still at her side. Midway through the flight she realized that it wasn't the night that was threatening, it was all the doubt concealed by the black sky.

* * *

More or less at the same time that the trio was boarding their flight from Miami, Student #5 was perched on a small rise near the parking lot of a Friendly's restaurant. On the other side of the lot was an access road that led to a large grocery store. At the intersection with a main road, there was a stoplight and a small traffic island.

The island was a favorite place for the out-of-work, alcoholic, or drug-addicted and homeless to stand. They would fashion handwritten signs out of cardboard: "Will do odd jobs." "Anything will help." "Homeless and Alone." "God Bless You."

This evening, there was one man holding a sign and begging from pass-ersby in grocery-laden cars whom Student #5 watched carefully. Most people ignored the man. A few rolled down their windows, offered some spare change or a stray dollar bill.

There are places like this in every town and city in every country around the world, he thought.

Student #5 waited until the traffic coming from the grocery diminished. Light was fading around him at the end of the day—but not so much that what he intended to say wouldn't make some sense. He went back to his truck. On the floor by the passenger seat were two cheap bottles of booze—Scotch and gin. There was also a six-pack of the most inexpensive beer he could find. He drove over to the sign-holding man, who seemed resigned to failure and was probably starting to wonder where he'd find a warm spot to sleep.

Rolling down his window, Student #5 said to the man, "Hey, you want to make fifty bucks?"

"You bet," the homeless man said eagerly. "What do you need?"

Student #5 knew this opened the door to anything, from lawn mowing to a blow job. He had expected this up-for-anything reply. The homeless man was already a victim—of society, his own needs, mental illness, or perhaps just bad luck—and this made him vulnerable.

"Got some cut wood I need loaded in the back of my truck. I've been at it all day and my shoulders are killing me. Just got one or two more loads to do. You do the lifting for me and I'll give you the fifty. Okay?"

"You got it, boss," the man said. He tossed his sign aside and hurried to the passenger seat, pulling open the door and jumping inside. Student #5 saw the man spot the alcohol on the floorboards, eyes quickly widening.

He took a quick look around and saw that they were alone. *No security cameras on that street intersection,* he thought. *And no one anywhere, paying any attention at all.* "Hey, you want a beer or two, help yourself," Student #5 said pleasantly.

37

They spent the night at a cheap motel not far from the airport because Susan Terry insisted that showing up long after dark at the home of a killer suspected in multiple deaths clearly wasn't the wisest of ideas. She also pointed out that this killer seemed capable of just about anything, and was obviously skilled with weapons and would likely react like a cornered wild animal when they confronted him. None of them had ever actually faced a cornered wild animal, so this admonition had an Animal Planet documentary feel to it.

Susan had been put through a rudimentary police combat course several years earlier when she first joined the prosecutor's office, but neither Andy Candy nor Moth had any weapons training—anything that actually equipped them for what they believed they were facing. The only equipment the three of them shared was the two handguns and a shaky sense of determination. They knew that at the end of their trip lay a very dangerous man who had woven himself deeply into their lives. But none thought that removing him would be anywhere near as simple as plucking a loose thread from a sweater.

Moth clung to his fantasy of revenge, though it was fading. He just wasn't sure what he could replace it with yet.

Andy Candy wanted to lash out, conflating fear and anger. She wanted safety above all else, although she didn't know what she would do with it if she found it.

Susan Terry imagined some sort of *Ask hard questions/extract a confession/ make an arrest* scenario that would manage to restore her sense of self-control and simultaneously return her to the good graces of her boss in the Miami-Dade State Attorney's Office. *"Hello, sir. Not only am I put together and sober and happily going back to meetings, but see here, I've also apprehended a really unique serial killer. Perhaps a raise is in order?"*

There were two beds in the small, run-down room they checked into. At first, all of them exhausted by tension, Susan Terry and Andy Candy shared one bed and Moth plopped down in the other. But midway through the night, unable to sleep, Andy Candy slid from her side and crawled in beside Moth. In their high school romance days, they had sex, but never actually spent the night together in a bed. Their couplings had been furtive—in cars, at homes vacated by parents out on a movie date, on the beach. For a few moments she appreciated his even breathing and the touch of his cool skin—wondering how he could be so calm—but then she, too, dropped off, hoping that she wouldn't be awakened by nightmares.

Student #5 surveyed his trailer and thought it all looked very complicated for something that should be so simple. After all, it could be reduced to *Bang! Boom! Death.* So he asked in a satisfied worker's drawl:

"What d'you think, Homeless Guy. Will it work?"

The homeless man made some sound that wasn't a scream, but went way beyond a grunt, squarely somewhere in the panic spectrum and devolving into a helpless gurgle.

"I think it will. Not that many moving parts. Did you know that I based this setup on a system that has been made famous, like in movies and books? Mafia hit men and characters from the *Saw* franchise. Not all that hard to put together for someone who knows knots and lines. And a little ingenious, too, if I must give myself some credit."

He kept his voice light, as if he were a handyman talking about something no more important than fixing a plumbing problem. He looked over at the homeless man.

"Don't squirm. Don't move at all. Otherwise—well, isn't it obvious?"

The homeless man whimpered.

Student #5 believed that was an appropriate sound, given the circumstances.

The homeless man was secured on a cheap wooden chair, bound hand and foot with long thin strips torn from a cotton towel and smeared with a paraffin-like gel, pulled so tight they dug into his flesh. A single piece of duct tape covered his lips. His back was to the only door to the room. A solitary window let in some weak dawn light. It was early, the night had been long, and Student #5 knew he still had preparations to make.

Be quick but don't rush. There will be time for rest later. Stay alert.

The homeless man was staring forward and slightly down into the barrel of the shotgun. It was on a small angle, pointed up about a foot below his chin, propped on some two-by-fours and wedged into position by books and pillows. A single strand of fishing line was tied to the trigger, then run through a small pulley—the type used to raise and lower curtains—taped to an adjacent table.

Student #5 wanted to apologize in advance: *"I'm sorry, fella. Clearly life has been pretty cruel for you. That sucks and this is a tough way to go out. I do appreciate your help in this, and I'm truly disappointed that it will cost you your life, but you're not alone. A few people are dying today."*

But he didn't say this. Instead he removed the piece of duct tape that was covering the homeless man's mouth. The homeless man gasped, and choked out a raspy "Please, buddy, I didn't do nothing . . ." but Student #5 ignored this. It was to be expected. *No one ever thinks they did anything to deserve dying for, when the exact opposite is generally true.*

He did reply, "Look, Homeless Guy, I understand you are innocent in all this. I could explain what's going on, but it's really a long story and I wouldn't want to use up our remaining time."

The man's eyes followed every movement Student #5 made.

"I mean we do have some time left. Not exactly sure how much; remains to be seen. But using these minutes to swap sad stories seems like a waste. It would be interesting, I'm sure. But what would we actually gain?"

Student #5 was doing a psychological equation in his head. He knew, *Keep this man impersonal. Objectify him. He doesn't know it, but someday, he will be famous.* Student #5 smiled. *When I'm ninety and finally write my memoir.*

He double-checked his knots. He knew enough to maintain constant levels of uncertainty, confusion, and doubt. Those three elements needed to be like background music. His plan very much relied on the homeless man's comprehending only what little he could see in front of him:

Shotgun. Death.

He adjusted a small microphone clipped on the man's shirt and said, "Okay, I would like you to say the following. I want you to repeat the words over and over. I want you to change your inflection—plead, cry, shout, scream; use a whole lot of different tones. You have to really cut loose. Don't hold back. Make it completely believable—actually, Homeless Guy, I imagine that's the easiest bit of the performance."

The man's eyes went wide with terror.

"You are onstage, Homeless Guy. Can you do that?"

The homeless man nodded, very carefully.

"Okay. I want you to call for help. I want you to call out, *'In here!* Say *Please help me!'* And *'Help! Help! Help!'* I want you to make sure that someone on the other side of the door hears your cries and will immediately respond to them. Nothing more. Just call for help. Got it?"

The homeless man looked confused.

"You need to be persuasive for whoever is on the other side of that door."

The man still seemed blank.

"Look," Student #5 added, "do you want to get rescued? In a short time, people will be here who can cut you free. Doing what I say is your only hope of getting out of this alive. This is your best and only chance, so make it work. You've got to try to help yourself. You can do that; I know you can. I'm just trying to make it easier for you."

Actually, there is no hope. He knew that the *no hope* realization had to arrive at the final instant, because without some psychological edge to cling to, people behaved erratically and wouldn't do what they were asked. They shut down. Abandoned effort, curled into a fetal position, gave up, and accepted death. He didn't want that to occur prematurely. *Let's keep up appearances.*

The homeless man's lips seemed cracked, and Student #5 knew the man's throat would be parched by fear. It hadn't been hard to get him drunk the night before, to the point of unconsciousness. There was some humor in this, he realized, because Timothy Warner was undoubtedly familiar with the same stupor. Student #5 believed there were both irony and intellectual symmetry in using a drunk to kill a drunk.

He popped open another beer and held the cold bottle to the man's lips. The homeless mad slurped wildly at the drink.

"Better?"

The man nodded.

"Want a chaser?"

Student #5 held up a large bottle of cheap whiskey.

The man nodded again, and Student #5 generously poured some into the man's mouth. He wondered, *Is he thinking, If I have to die, I might as well go out drunk? Probably. Makes sense.*

"Do what I say, and there will be more."

The man looked eager.

"A good performance. That's what I want. I need you to continue for five, no, at least ten minutes. That will seem like a long time, but keep it up. No breaks. Do you understand?"

The man's eyes twitched a *yes.*

"Think of it this way: You are calling for help. That help will save you.

So I'd put heart and soul into it. It's your best chance." The homeless man seemed ready. "Okay. Start . . . now!" He pushed the "record" button on the old-fashioned tape machine and glanced down at his wristwatch.

The first *Help!* was croaked, a word spoken with sandpaper.

Student #5 used his arms to gesture, like someone mimicking an orchestra conductor. The words started to flow, genuine, sincere, totally panicked, rising like an aria of despair.

38

The drive from the motel near the airport outside of Hartford, Connecticut, to Charlemont, Massachusetts, took nearly two hours, but more than the time involved, it was the change from urban to rural that kept Andy Candy's eyes on the passing scenery. For the last twenty minutes or so, they paralleled the Deerfield River. It glistened in the morning sunlight. Moth was familiar with the history of a famous massacre that had taken place nearby back in the 1700s—local Native Americans doing in some settlers in unpleasant fashion—and started to mention it, until he realized that bringing up centuries-old ambush killings might not be the right tone for this day.

They passed rolling hills covered with thick stands of tall fir trees. The Green Mountains of Vermont loomed in the distance. It was the antithesis of Miami—which was all neon, glowing lights, concrete, and palm trees, a go-go atmosphere. This was a far different America, different even from the farmland and forest that they'd seen in New Jersey when they went to see Jeremy Hogan. This seemed almost antique. Andy Candy couldn't have said exactly how it was different—but there was an odd feel to the isolation they were driving into. *A good place to hide,* she thought, and this made her shift about with growing tension.

The town of Charlemont was even smaller than they expected it would be. A bedraggled gas station. A pizza place. A general store. A church. It lacked most of the romantic New England qualities of slightly more substantial old towns. No grassy common and stately white clapboard homes built in the 1800s. Instead, it was spread along both sides of a road, near the river, with some whitewater outfitters and a nearby modest ski area that offered zip-line trips in the off-season. To say it was quiet would have been an exaggeration.

Susan Terry was driving. She pulled into the parking lot in front of a redbrick building with a large old-fashioned bell tower rising in its center. There was a sign: "Town Offices."

"Just follow my lead," she said as she parked.

Inside it was cool, shadowy. A town directory pointed them toward the Charlemont Police Department. Susan Terry saw that it listed only four names—and one was designated "river patrol." She guessed this was the officer best equipped to deal with folks who got into trouble canoeing on the water without life jackets.

There were two people in the office, both in uniform, a middle-aged man and woman. They looked up when Susan Terry entered, trailed by Andy Candy and Moth.

"Help you?" asked the man pleasantly. Andy Candy assumed he was accustomed to helping strangers out with routine messes. In the fall the area was likely filled with leaf peepers traveling to see the foliage.

Susan Terry produced her badge. She smiled. Friendly. But focused. "Sorry to show up without advance warning," she said. "But we need a little assistance. I'm with the Miami-Dade County Attorney's Office, and a resident of your fine town is a potential witness in a felony case we have down in Florida. He might be reluctant to give me a statement—and I think we will need an officer to accompany us to his home so we can question him appropriately."

She lied easily. Moth knew this capability went hand-in-glove with drug use and alcoholism. When one was so accustomed to lying to oneself, it wasn't hard to lie to others.

The Charlemont policeman nodded. "Don't get this sort of request too often," he said. "Sure you wouldn't prefer a state trooper? There's a barracks not too far away."

"Local jurisdiction is better from the legal point of view."

"Okay. What sort of felony are we talking about?"

"Homicide."

This made both officers hesitate. "We've never had a murder here, at least none that I can remember," the man said. "Don't know if we've ever even had someone connected to a murder."

"We have them all the time down in Miami," Susan said lightly.

"Who are these young folks?" the policeman asked, gesturing at Moth and Andy Candy.

"The other witnesses. It's important that they get a look at the fellow up here."

"He a suspect?"

"Not precisely. Just a person of interest for my case."

"You expect trouble?"

Susan smiled, shrugged. "No one's ever all that eager to help out in a criminal case, especially one that's out of state. That's kind of why we're here unannounced."

The cops nodded in agreement. This made sense. "So you want us to . . ."

"Drive up. Knock on the door with me. Give me some backup if I need it. Encourage a conversation. Just a little muscle-flexing."

She made it sound like this was nothing more complex than a discussion over unpaid parking tickets. Susan's mind churned with possibilities. She imagined flight and absence. Or perhaps door-slamming refusal. The possibility of gunfire. In truth, she had no idea what to expect, but having a uniformed officer was undoubtedly going to help. A part of her would have preferred a detachment of Marines. She'd faced many criminals, but always with an upper hand—in a courtroom or when they were already behind bars. Still, she believed she had the advantage here of surprise and numbers, It did not occur to her that she might be wrong.

"We can do that. Where we going?"

"Fellow's name is Munroe, lives out—"

"In those old trailers on Zoar Road, near the catch-and-release trout management area. We know it," the woman cop interrupted.

"You know him?"

"Not really." The male cop took over seamlessly. Andy Candy figured they were husband and wife. "See the guy in his truck from time to time. This is a small town, so you get to know all the names. He's not there too much, which makes me think he's got some other home somewhere, although he don't look like he's got any spare change lying about to help him maintain more than one place. Definitely keeps to himself. Can't recall ever going out there on any call of any sort."

The cop turned to the woman policeman. She tilted her head.

"Me neither," she added. "I hate those old trailers. Fire traps and big satellite dishes. Total community eyesore. Wish the town would condemn them. And when we do get called out there, it's usually domestic disturbances—you know, someone drinking too much, starts beating on their spouse or the kids. Very poor folks for the most part—and it isn't like this is a rich community, like Williamstown."

"When were you looking to knock on his door?"

"Now."

The man nodded. "Well, the young guy—our newest officer—is on patrol and he's probably bored already. I'll give him a call. Donnie's just two weeks on the force—hell, there's only four of us anyways—but he can use the experience."

"That would be great," Susan Terry said. She had the distinct impression that newly minted officer Donnie would catch all the pain-in-the-butt assignments for some time.

Moth and Andy Candy kept quiet.

* * *

I didn't want to take this way out, but after all that's happened it seems reasonable. None of it was MY FAULT. But those whose fault it was have all been taken care of.

Student #5 had painstakingly written each word with his left hand before leaving the single sheet of paper on the dashboard of his truck. He doubted that a real forensic handwriting examiner would be fooled, but he also doubted whether the local cops would have the money in their tight budget to hire some big-city expert. Before heading back into the trailer, he also took the time to spread around a dozen bright red tablets of pseudoephedrine on the floorboards and leave an open, half-empty box of baking soda on the passenger seat.

He heard a muffled cough from the bedroom. He didn't turn that way; instead he continued to keep his eyes focused on the roadway down to his trailer. He had tried to invent some early-warning system, but hadn't been able to come up with something that he thought would be reliable, so he was forced to keep watch, even though he was tired and his muscles ached both with strenuous work and tension.

Timing, he knew, was critical.

Three minutes. Maybe four. It could be a little less. Not much chance it would be more. *They will pull in. Stop. Get out. Survey the front. Then approach. One one thousand, two one thousand, three . . .* He counted seconds in his head, envisioning the scene in front of him.

He went over each detail. It was a little like the orchestration of a play in football. This player goes this direction while another takes a different route, everyone following a specific plan. Offensive success. Defensive confusion. He smiled. Coaches in football forever admonished their players, *Do Your Job.* The cliché was, *Everyone on the same page.*

Student #5 had pantomimed every action he expected to take, carefully clocking each motion until he was at four minutes. He was a little nervous because there didn't seem to be any leeway for the unexpected— and one thing killing had taught him was to always keep the unexpected expected.

He reassured himself: *You've prepared wisely. It will happen as you imagine it will.*

The day before he had purchased seven canisters of propane—the sort used for outside gas grills. He had also acquired a half-dozen five-gallon plastic containers of gasoline, some plastic tubing, and glass bottles. He had carefully placed all of these in locations throughout the trailer where they couldn't be immediately spotted. The large fan he'd obtained was to shift scents and fuels through the trailer rapidly.

Home becomes fake meth lab. Meth lab becomes bomb. Simple. Effective. The sort of basic plan that someone living in this run-down world might come up with. He had a sudden memory of the late, great Jimmy Cagney in *White Heat* standing on the roof of the burning oil tank: *"Top of the world, Ma!"*

When he looked up, he saw two cars approaching. The first was a marked Charlemont patrol car, the second a small rental. He could see three shapes in that second car.

Now! he told himself.

Without hesitation, he spun into action.

Young Donnie was a local boy less than a month out of police training academy after two tours in Afghanistan, unsure of whether he'd made the right decision in joining the hometown force instead of holding out for the more sophisticated and adventurous duties of a state trooper. The Charlemont Police Department job consisted primarily of giving out speeding tickets to folks who failed to notice that the town's limit was 25, rousting local high school kids from hanging out and smoking pot behind the church, and occasionally acting as a referee in a beer-fueled husband-wife argument. He looked at his future and saw a thickening waist, a modest house, a day care operator wife, two kids, and the same old thing day in, day out. He didn't like this vision.

When he'd received the radio call to accompany a big-city Miami prosecutor to a potential homicide case witness's house, he'd leapt at the chance. This task seemed much more in line with what he'd hoped becoming a policeman would entail.

He'd never been to Miami. He imagined it to be always sunny and warm and filled with unusual crimes, drugs, guns, desperate criminals, and cops who frequently unholstered their sidearms. Shoot-outs, supermodels and high-speed chases—a television-show version of the city that while not precisely accurate, wasn't exactly untrue, either. So he made a point of reminding himself to ask the lady prosecutor about policemen's job opportunities down in Dade County after she finished interviewing the man in the trailer. *Get out of Sleepytown and head to Dodge,* he told himself.

He was driving slowly so that the trio in the car behind him could keep up.

On his radio, he called the main office. "Hey, Sergeant," he said briskly. "We're arriving at that location now."

"Ten-four," came the curt response.

This was, he thought, the most interesting thing that had happened to him in days.

Turn on the fan. It oscillated back and forth. Humming.

Spill the gasoline containers. Liquid sloshed across the floor.

Open the propane tanks wide. They hissed as the gas leaked out.

Kill the pilot lights on the stove. Rip out the flex tube that carried more propane from the large old tank outside. Kitchen explosion imminent.

Dash to the bedroom with a gallon jug of 100-proof vodka. Pour it over Homeless Guy. Open the propane tank Homeless Guy can't see from his position, tied into the chair. More gasoline. On the bedding. On the floor. On the walls.

Fast. Fast. Fast.

"Okay, Homeless Guy, this is the big moment," Student #5 said. Before the man had a chance to respond, Student #5 jammed a gas-soaked rag into his mouth, gagging him. *Now you will understand: No chance; there never was a chance.* He didn't look to see—although he knew it was there—panic in the man's face.

He took four votive candles and lit them with a safety match, hoping that the fumes instantly filling the room wouldn't explode in that moment. He breathed a small sigh of relief when they didn't. He balanced the candles on the man's quivering legs.

"I wouldn't let those drop," Student #5 said.

Of course, that was an impossible suggestion. They would fall. It was inevitable.

He switched on the tape recorder.

Cries of *"Help me!"* filled the room.

Then he took the fishing line attached to the shotgun trigger, carefully tied it to the back of the door handle, and closed the door behind him.

Move! he told himself. *They will be approaching the front door.*

One minute. Two. Three. He had lost track of the time and hoped that his practice runs were close to the real thing. He felt a little like a sprinter in a track meet: hours, days, months, and years of training for ten seconds of flight.

At the rear kitchen door, he didn't look back.

He let himself out the back as quietly as he could. No scraping, sliding door noises. No hurried footsteps on the deck. *Stealth.* This was the only moment he truly feared. He doubted the visitors would have the sense to cover the rear exit. Any professional would know to do this—but not a history student and his ex-girlfriend. *They're not killers. Nor are they cops.* The Prosecutor might know—if she was arriving at the trailer with an army of policemen. But she wasn't.

Across the yard. Into the brush. Stick to the right. Stay low. Stay quiet. Stay concealed. He remembered the bear he'd seen in the yard. *None of that noisy lumbering about,* he told himself. Tree branches and thorns plucked at his clothes, but he fought his way forward. *Find the kayak where you hid it in the bushes by the river's side. Paddle downstream to the picnic area where you parked the rental car. Rub yourself down with perfumed cleaning wipes—*

eradicate any lingering gas smell. Put all your clothes and especially the shoes into a double-sealed plastic bag. Remember to drop it into the big Mc-Donald's Dumpster close to the interstate highway that gets picked up every day. Change into the blue pinstriped business suit in the suitcase on the back-seat. Drive away nice and slow and remember to wave at the volunteer fire department trucks that will be flying by in the opposite direction.

Goodbye, Mister Munroe. You were a good person to be for many years, but your time has come. You've been used up. Passed the "sell-by" date. Turned the last page on your story.

Goodbye, old, sad trailer, and goodbye, Nephew, Girlfriend, and Prosecutor. Out of the old forever.

Hello, new.

39

In the car, Susan Terry chambered a round in her pistol.

She was filled with righteous fury, half-derived from the way the man inside the ramshackle trailer had screwed up her life, half from the burgeoning sense that she was close to a killer who'd gotten away with multiple crimes and that she was about to corner him.

"Stay behind the cars," she said. "Keep low, whatever happens. If this guy has done what you've said he has, then he can shoot distances accurately. Don't give him a clean look."

"What are you going to do?" Andy Candy asked. Her voice was dry.

"Find out who he really is," Susan replied. "And after that, take him into custody. And then the pressure will get to him."

If this was not exactly a plan, Moth still felt swept up in something that he had started. Now that it was about to become much more real than he'd ever envisioned, he was unsure what to say or do. He began sorting through moments of decision for great men, trying to see how a Washington or a Jefferson, a Lincoln or an Eisenhower, might react. This was absolutely no help and no reassurance whatsoever.

"One more thing," Susan said. Her voice was edgy, chilled. "If everything goes to hell, use the cop's radio and call for help. Whatever happens, don't let this guy get away."

She looked them both in the eyes. "Got that?" she asked in a way that meant it wasn't really a question, it was a command.

They exited the rental car.

Donnie the cop was already standing outside his patrol car, looking across to the front door of the double-wide trailer. It seemed quiet, and his first thought was, *Abandoned and empty.* He immediately replaced this with an Afghanistan-born sense of alertness. He pivoted toward Susan— and saw the pistol in her hand.

"Whoa," he grunted out. "What the hell . . ."

"This man may be dangerous."

"I thought you said *witness* . . ."

"Yeah. That. And maybe more."

Donnie immediately removed his own service weapon. He too chambered a round. "I should call for backup if you're expecting trouble. Do you have a warrant?"

Susan shook her head. *This is my show and I'm not willing to share it. In a few minutes, everything in my life will be back on track. Or something else.*

"We're going to knock. See what happens. But be damn careful."

Donnie looked a little wide-eyed and shook his head. "I don't know about this," he said.

"We're here. We're going to do this," she replied firmly. "We walk away, and we might never have this chance again."

In her experience, killers rarely believed in shooting their way out of a situation when they could just as easily talk their way out. This thought was buttressed by the notion that this killer *knew* there was little evidence against him. And this, she believed, would make him arrogant.

And talkative.

She was further armored by the belief that he would *never* expect them there in front of his house. "All right," she said. "Let's go."

Susan glanced back and saw that Moth and Andy Candy were crouched behind the rental car. She could not see the .357 Magnum in Moth's hand—but she expected it was there.

Donnie the combat vet was suddenly aware that there seemed to be no cover anywhere, and he wasn't happy about this. He was accustomed to clear-cut, well-defined missions, being led by highly trained professional military men, and suddenly everything he was doing seemed small-town stupid and wildly inexperienced.

He also didn't see an option. He knew he wanted to impress Susan Terry and act like he imagined a veteran Miami cop would act. So the only thing he did that made sense was to call his sergeant back in the tiny town offices.

"Sarge? Donnie here . . ."

"Go ahead."

His shoulder radio was tinny, and crackled with static, which hid some of the nervousness creeping into his voice. "This might be a little more complicated than just talking to a reluctant witness," he said.

"You asking for backup?"

"Let's go," Susan said impatiently. She was staring at the trailer, looking for any signs of activity.

Donnie nodded and spoke into his radio: "Just stand by." He was a man who followed orders, and he was being given one.

The two of them cautiously approached the front door. Susan wondered whether there was a rifle aiming directly at her chest. She expected death, and a part of her was absolutely okay with that. Moth's uncle, she thought, would recognize her rash behavior for the suicidal impulse that it was. But that was as far as she got in reflection. She replaced all these thoughts with a single-minded focus on the man inside. *Killer. End of the line. For someone.*

She was far more composed than she had any right to be.

Donnie, on the other hand, felt cold sweat beneath his arms and half-imagined he was back in combat and approaching some dusty clay-and-brick hut in the middle of godforsaken nowhere, not knowing whether some smiling kid would poke his head out the door wanting a piece of candy or an AK-47 would suddenly open up. But with each step he took forward, Donnie grew more collected, each nerve end on edge, every sense he had—hearing, sight, smell—sharpened. *You've been trained,* he told himself. *This isn't any different.* This gave him some confidence.

He huddled to the side of the front door—*Don't let someone fire through the woodwork into your chest*—and was about to knock when he heard: "Help me! Help me, please!"

The words were faint, but unmistakable, coming from somewhere within. He looked at Susan Terry. She too had heard the plea. She craned forward, and heard it again.

"In here! Please help!"

"Son of a bitch," Donnie said.

Instead of knocking, he reached for the door handle.

Unlocked.

He twisted it and pushed the door open six inches. He remembered his police classes. "Police officer!" he bellowed. "Come on out!"

The only response was the continued muffled pleas.

He pushed the door a little wider. "Police!" He tried to think of something else to say, something dramatic, but nothing came to mind. "Show yourself!" was the best he could do.

Donnie pushed the door open wide. It was then that the smell hit him. Gasoline and rotten eggs. At first he thought it was the pungent smell of a body left in the sun after being toasted with high explosives, then he recognized it for the more suburban smell it was: leaking propane. "Jesus," he said.

"Help me!" came the voice.

Donnie looked over at Susan Terry. "Hang back," he said.

"No fucking way," she replied. She placed one hand over her mouth and nose, the other on her weapon.

In a half-crouch, two hands on his weapon, Donnie stepped into the trailer. He saw the fan moving back and forth, but that wasn't the motion he was trying to find—human motion: a gun being raised, a knife brandished.

"Please, please, please . . . ," came the cries.

He could tell they were coming from what he guessed was the bed-room. Still hunched over, he went to the door, stepping past typical clut-ter and debris, almost choking with the smell.

Carefully, Donnie put his hand on the door handle. With his gun hand, he gestured Susan Terry to a position behind him. Then he slowly pulled the door open.

Gunshot.

First explosion.

Andy Candy half-shouted, half-screamed. The sound was not a recog-nizable word. Moth stiffened, nearly frozen in place, ducking down, partly shielding Andy with his body.

A second explosion ripped the air with a ferocity that astonished them.

Moth realized he was yelling, a torrent of obscenities fueled by shock and fear. If his first instinct had been to cower and cover Andy Candy, his second was to lift his head, driven by fascination: Whatever was happen-ing seemed almost like something on a movie screen in front of him.

He could see that the rear of the trailer was billowing smoke and that flames were shooting out of the roof. Windows were shattered.

Moth hesitated, almost as if he was hypnotized. Then he shouted, "Stay here!" and shocked himself by rising up from the relative safety provided by the car and racing toward the burning building. He tossed his arms over his head, as if he expected fallout from the explosions to rain down on him.

Andy Candy didn't do what he said. As soon as Moth dashed forward, she ran in a crouch to the passenger door of the patrol car and jerked it open. The radio microphone was hanging from a hook in front of her. She bent in, throwing herself across the seat, seized it, pushed down on an ac-tivation switch—just as she had seen done in dozens of television shows—and began shouting:

"We need help! Help!"

A voice immediately came over the radio. "Who's this?"

"We were there this morning . . . with the officer out at the trailer by the river . . ." Her words were jumbled, confused, but there was no mistaking her tone.

"What's happened?" It was a woman's voice, but she seemed calm, which shocked Andy.

"An explosion. There's a fire. We heard a gunshot . . ."

"Where is the patrolman?"

"I don't know. He's still inside."

A third explosion shook the air.

"Are there injuries?"

Andy Candy didn't know, but there had to be. "Yes. Yes. Send help now."

"Stay where you are. Police, fire, and ambulance on the way," said the disembodied radio voice.

Andy looked up. What she saw was Moth fighting his way into the flames licking around the trailer's front door. "No!" she shouted, as he disappeared from sight.

The first blast had driven Susan Terry back, slamming her viciously against a bureau, fracturing her arm in two places, leaving her dazed. The second explosion seemed to scorch the air above her, superheated with flames, turning the inside of the trailer into a furnace. She realized she was in immense pain and almost on her back. Everything she could see was spinning, obscured by smoke and fire. At first she thought Donnie the policeman was dead, a few feet away from her. She reached out for him, but her right arm wouldn't move, and her left waved uselessly in the air. She wondered, *Am I dying? Here? Now?*

Things were moving in slow motion, and she saw the policeman stir, as if he'd been able to fight off unconsciousness. She saw him push to his knees. This was an astonishing act of strength, she thought, because she knew she couldn't do this. She wanted to close her eyes and give in to the heat and the rising noise echoing in her ears. Freight trains and jet engines.

When he crawled toward her, she had trouble deciphering what was happening. She knew she was in shock, but what that actually meant eluded her. She choked on smoke, coughed, thought she could no longer breathe, and wondered whether she had screamed. She could see the policeman's lips moving, and he was clearly shouting something important, but what it was seemed impossible to figure out, as if every word was in a different language.

And then she felt herself move.

This confused her, because she knew she hadn't been able to give her arms, legs, body any directions. None of her muscles were responding to anything. She felt limp, rubbery, as if every tendon in her body had been severed by the force of the first explosion, and she imagined that perhaps she was already dead.

It took her a moment to realize that Moth had seized the back of her shirt and was tugging her toward the entranceway. The pain in her arm was suddenly violent, as if someone was pounding her relentlessly, hammering sharpened stakes into her skin, and she howled. The sudden hurt mingled with her cries, redoubling when Donnie the policeman grabbed her shoulder. Almost like a pair of lifeguards rescuing an exhausted swimmer caught in the waves, he and Moth dragged her toward safety. Susan could not see the doorway. All she could see were red and yellow flames racing like meteor showers across the trailer ceiling, a Jackson Pollock of fire.

Death, she thought, *can be beautiful.*

She had no understanding that in that instant her life was actually being saved.

40

One of the cops called him a hero, but he didn't think that was true. *Fool* was probably closer to the truth, although when he had a second to think about it, Moth was unable to identify the exact moment when his foolishness began. It certainly preceded running into the burning trailer and helping to haul Donnie the policeman and Susan Terry out of the flames. Perhaps, he considered, it dated to when he'd gone to see Jeremy Hogan, but that didn't seem right, either. For a moment, Moth decided that his journey into naïveté started when he had called Andy Candy, but neither was that completely correct.

He continued to work backward through all that had happened, and he decided it must have been triggered the moment when he found his uncle's body and immediately fell so precipitously off the wagon. This idea made him shake his head, and finally he insisted to himself that everything had begun when he broke up with Andy Candy in high school so many years earlier. That was where his foolishness had taken root and flowered—although he noted ruefully that Uncle Ed the shrink would undoubtedly have dated its start much earlier and blamed it on demanding, absent, and unwittingly cruel parents.

A young woman EMT with a pleasant smile and confident manner bandaged his hands and told him that even though they didn't seem that bad, he should see a doctor promptly because burns were tricky.

He doubted he would do this, except that Andy Candy, standing beside him, said, "I'll make sure he goes."

"There might be some scarring," the EMT said.

Of this, Moth was certain. But he was thinking of the sorts of scars that weren't visible on the skin. *Ed's kinds of scars.*

Nearby, an ambulance siren started up. This vehicle held Donnie, who had been reluctant to leave the scene until ordered to by his sergeant. He had burns that would heal and smoke inhalation. Moth caught him sitting on the step to the ambulance sucking in oxygen through a mask and grinning as state troopers and his fellow local cops, EMTs, and volunteer firemen all took the time to clap him on the shoulder and tell him he'd done *goddamn* well.

Nothing, Moth thought, *quite as delightful as being alive when you should be dead.* Susan Terry was already being transported to the ER—and then probably to surgery for her shattered arm, he realized.

Moth felt Andy put her arm loosely across his shoulders in a curiously possessive movement. He breathed in, and leaned back against the side of a patrol car. For an instant, he closed his eyes, wishing it were night and he could sleep, but it was midday and the sun was flooding the area. When he opened them, he saw three men approaching. One wore the white-brimmed helmet of a fire chief. The other was the Charlemont sergeant he'd met that morning. The third was a state trooper with a small plaque on his shirt above his name tag that read: "Homicide."

"Mister Warner," the trooper began slowly, "you feel up to answering a few questions?"

"Sure," Moth said.

"You know there's a dead body inside?"

The trooper gestured toward the smoldering shell of the trailer.

"No," Moth said. "Who . . ."

"Probably Mister Munroe, the owner. But it will take the coroner and Forensics some time to make a real determination, assuming they even can. The body was burned pretty badly. And our officer says that the gunshot he heard came from inside the back room, where the fire apparently started, before all the propane and gasoline containers went up. I've never seen a homemade meth lab go up before. Makes a helluva mess. Anyway, that gunshot might have been a self-inflicted wound."

"How would you know that?"

"We found a note in the guy's truck. Autopsy will probably reveal twelve-gauge pellets."

Moth nodded. *It's over?* He didn't believe it. It seemed far too simple. "Meth lab?" he asked.

The trooper ignored the question. "So, why are you here?" he asked. He looked over at Andy Candy. "So, why are *both* of you here?"

Questions. Answers. Doubts. Sworn statements. Lies and half-truths. There is a bureaucratic processing of violence that parallels the more familiar and drawn-out forensic analysis of a crime scene. It seems as if ubiquitous yellow tape marked "Police Crime Scene—Do Not Enter" encloses more than just space. It encircles a sorting through and categorizing, where what someone says is joined with what some scientist determines to create a portrait of what happened, how it happened, and why it happened. But within these pictures there are always gaps and blank spots; frequently there are mismatched colors and contradictory images. On occasion, a crime scene becomes an immense trompe l'oeil—where what seems to be something, isn't—in which misdirection dominates.

"Hello, Stephen."

Pause.

"Hiya, Steve."

Hesitation. Sly smile.

"Hey, Steverino, how yah doin'?"

Not bad. Not bad at all. Thanks for asking.

Student #5 was staring at himself in a mirror above the sink in his small refurbished and remodeled house on Angela Street in Key West. The house was directly across from the cemetery—which was, at nine to eleven feet, one of the highest places in the town, affording nearby residents some modest sense of hurricane security. The house was what locals called "a cigar maker's" home—back when it was built in the 1920s it had been occupied by Cuban refugees who had fled one of that island's frequent upheavals, emigrated ninety miles, and perfected the art of rolling fine tobacco cigars for the Daddy Warbuckses of the state. The houses were small, single-story, narrow places, built out of the local pine that was relatively impervious to weather and termites and which had, over the decades, become wildly popular with well-heeled types looking to build vacation cottages. Their cost often exceeded seven figures—but Student #5 had astutely purchased his many years earlier and sunk money into metal roofing and central air-conditioning and granite kitchen counter-tops—so he knew he would double, triple his money were he to market it.

He had no intention of doing so.

He turned up the collar on his sport shirt and slipped on a pair of expensive Ray-Ban sunglasses. He wore shorts that were frayed around the edges and tattered old running shoes that had seen many better days. It would be moist and warm when he went out, and he knew he would be sticky with sweat by the time he'd traveled a single block.

"So, Stevie-boy, do you feel safe?"

"Now that you mention it, I do, indeed. Yes, I feel very safe."

"I thought the little signs of backwoods drug manufacturing were very clever."

"Me, too."

"And that dead body . . ."

He was reminded of a line uttered by the character Winston Wolfe in *Pulp Fiction*: *"Nobody who will be missed."*

Student #5 believed he'd created a substantial number of conflicting elements in his trailer. This would establish confusion—police would not know what sort of crime they were investigating. And, by the time they sorted any of it out—if they ever did—they would discover a ghost, a man that didn't exist. And nothing linked the fictitious and now-dead Blair Munroe of Charlemont, Massachusetts, to retired drug dealing entrepreneur Stephen Lewis of Key West, Florida.

He had sort of hoped that the explosions at the trailer would take The Nephew, The Girlfriend, and The Prosecutor up along with Homeless Guy. He had been checking local news feeds, which still provided breathless accounts of the conflagration and reported the fact that there was at least one fatality—he knew that—and others hospitalized. So some doubt had crept in: *Too bad. Tough luck. Hurt but not dead.*

That's the trouble with using explosives. They make the requisite destruction, but they lack the necessary intimacy and certainty of a bullet.

It made no difference. He had drawn an ending. That it was the second ending he'd been forced to create was now only an irritation. He had vanished, and like a newborn, was looking at the world for the first time.

Well, if they did survive . . .

An inward smile.

Something to think about.

He glanced down at his watch. It would take him fifteen to twenty minutes to get out his rusty old one-speed bicycle—a preferred means of travel in Key West—and ride at a leisurely place down to the evening freak show at Mallory Square. The dramatic setting of the sun in the west was celebrated nightly by contortionists, fire-breathers, guitar players, and anyone else who figured they could make a buck off cruise ship tourists by doing something weird, like posing for pictures with an iguana perched on one shoulder and a boa constrictor wrapped around the other.

Like most Key West residents, he generally avoided this nightly ritual. A celebration of the kitsch and laissez faire that emblemized Key West: too many people jammed into a small area; traffic backed up on the side streets. It was a moment of serenity expressed loudly. But this evening he was set to participate. It was the best spot Student #5 could think of to say goodbye to a nonexistent persona who had treated him well over many years.

Not unlike the sun setting—a huge, glowing ball of reds and yellows dropping into an expanse of shimmering blue void—Blair Munroe was disappearing.

He would have a drink. Toast the name. Then move on. Possibilities were endless. Choices were his. Horizons were clear.

Intense pain followed by a cloak of drugs to hide it. Looking up into a bright, unforgiving light. Counting backwards. Sleep. Awaken. More pain. A steady drip from an IV. Pain fading, like the volume on a stereo being turned down. Again sleep.

Then awakening to something that went beyond a mess and touched on felony. When Susan Terry emerged from her postoperative fog, she was glad to be alive. Maybe.

A nurse came into her hospital room, opened up some shades.

"What day is it?" Susan asked.

"Thursday morning. You came in on Tuesday."

"Jesus."

"Are you in pain?"

"I'm okay," Susan replied. Clearly she was not.

"There are a lot of people who want to speak with you," the nurse said. "There's a line that starts with the state police. Then your boss back in Miami. And there's this young couple that has been in at least a half-dozen times, but you've been out of it each time."

Susan leaned back on the bed. There was a slight smell of disinfectant. She glanced over at the IV tube running into one arm. The other was encased in white wrappings. "What am I getting?" she asked.

"Demerol."

Susan breathed in. "Great stuff," she said. She gathered some inward strength and spat out: "But I can't have it. I have an addiction problem."

The nurse's eyes opened wide. "I'll get the attending," she said. "Talk to him about it."

What Susan suddenly wanted more than anything else was that drip. She wanted to luxuriate in the fog of morphine-based painkillers. She wanted to let it coax her into half-sleep and forgetfulness. She wanted it to keep all the people who wanted to talk to her at bay—maybe even prevent them from ever talking to her.

She also knew that it would kill her—probably more effectively than propane and gasoline tanks exploding in a homemade bomb could.

Susan gritted her teeth together. "Send in the attending, please," she said. As soon as the nurse turned her back, Susan yanked the IV needle out of her arm. It was, she thought, the best she could manage right at that moment.

41

Of course, they weren't completely believed.

In fact, they were barely believed at all. There were contradictions in their stories, aspects that raised questions instead of answering them, a few outright lies that created numerous doubts and suspicions, and, when they had each completed being interviewed, so many holes that it would have taken a grave digger with a backhoe hours to fill them all.

But Massachusetts State Police investigators had no obvious reason to detain them any longer. The detectives knew there were crimes involved— but they couldn't see what the three of them had done that broke the law.

Andy Candy had been given a particularly difficult time.

Investigators figured that she would be the weakest link. She was the youngest. She was the only one uninjured, although Moth's burns were healing rapidly and not, it turned out, significant. Her connection to the man in the exploding trailer seemed the most tenuous. Consequently, her questioning had been harsh—ranging from the typical *"We're your friends"* to *"We know you are lying to us and we want the truth"* to *"You understand that withholding evidence in a murder case is a felony and do you really want to go to prison to protect your boyfriend and some suspended prosecutor?"*

She'd replied: *"What do you think I'm protecting them from?"*

They'd persisted: *"So, why are you here?"*

Andy surprised herself by maintaining an irritating calm that frustrated her interrogators and sticking to her half-assed story: *"The man in the trailer maybe had a connection to Timothy Warner's uncle's death, which was a suicide, but questions have arisen, and we were here to try to get some answers but before we could ask any, the whole damn thing went up. I think it's because the guy in the trailer saw the uniformed cop outside and figured it was a drug bust and he was going to prison for the rest of his life, so he blew himself away and set the whole thing on fire just to say 'Fuck you' to all you guys. That's what I think. Wish I could be more help.*

"Really. I do."

But she didn't.

Delta Air Lines upgraded them all to first class when the woman at the ticket counter saw the cast and sling encasing Susan Terry's right arm.

They were quiet most of the flight south to Miami. Susan popped over-the-counter Tylenol with regularity, which only did a little to control the gnawing postsurgical pain. She was proud of herself for avoiding instant junkie-hood, although she would have preferred a prescription for Tylenol laced with codeine. She thought she could use the throbbing sensation in her pinned-together arm to help her through the addiction battle. Every time she *didn't* take a narcotic it reminded her that she was sober, which on balance was a good thing. She ignored the pain shooting through her arm and the sweat dampening her forehead as best she could.

Shifting about in her seat, she looked across the aisle of the plane to Andy Candy and Moth. It was dim in the cabin; the engines droned steadily. The man next to her had dozed off. It was uncomfortable for her to move but she leaned toward them.

"Do either of you think the man that died back there was the man you've been hunting?" she asked bluntly. She omitted the phrase *the man who busted me to my own boss and totally fucked up my life.*

She wanted it to be him. She wanted it to be finished. She wanted to be able to go in the next night to Redeemer One and face all the other addicts and say, *"It's over,"* and be able to reboot her life. She didn't believe this was possible.

She was unable to see that she had blended this anonymous killer together with moving forward, regaining her position at the state attorney's office, becoming again the hard-nosed prosecutor who used trying bad guys as a substitute narcotic. But, just as it was for the cops in Massachusetts they had left behind, everything was still in doubt. All of her training in criminal law told her there simply had to be a rock they could turn over that would expose something that might be formed into an answer—but she didn't know how to find it.

Andy Candy didn't immediately reply to Susan. Instead, she looked across Moth, out the window into the black sky. Its emptiness seemed a lie.

Moth looked over first at Andy, then at Susan. "I wish it was," he said. "If it was him that would make everything easier." He was silent, before adding, "I've never been that lucky."

"Lucky?" Susan asked.

"Yeah. You have to be lucky to get simple answers to complex questions."

This reply made Andy Candy smile. *That,* she thought, *is Moth in a nutshell.*

He continued, speaking past her to Susan. "What do we do? Wait until they've finished that autopsy and done some DNA tests—if they even can? Suppose we never know."

That was a possibility that terrified him. He did not know precisely why, but uncertainty seemed to him to be the sort of trigger that would pitch him back into drink.

"What will you have, young fella?"

"Scotch on the rocks and a heart filled with doubt, bartender."

He didn't speak this conversation out loud, but he guessed that both Susan and Andy Candy knew he was having it.

Instead, he said, "We need to find a concrete answer." This, he realized instantly, was much easier said than done. He turned away from the others, following Andy's gaze out into the black sky beyond the window. *Five hundred miles per hour and I'm wishing I could reach out and grab the right thing to do.*

Andy saw that he was struggling. She reached out, touched his hand. At this moment, she didn't exactly want it to be over. She did, but she didn't. *Over* meant safety. It also meant an end to her and Moth, she thought. *He will go his way. And I will go mine. That's the way the world works. That's the ending always been waiting for us. That was our first ending. It will be the same for our second.*

Susan leaned back. She glanced at her wristwatch. It had been ninety minutes since her last two painkillers, and they were wearing off. She signaled to a stewardess and asked for a bottle of water. She struggled to get the cap open, finally using her teeth to grip it, and took two more pills. She expected she was going to be fired in the morning, and knew there was no over-the-counter drug that would take away that particular pain.

When the trailer had exploded, Susan had lost her weapon, and it hadn't yet been returned to her by the forensic teams processing the waterlogged and charred mess. Moth's .357 was in her bag—she'd used her badge again to get it through luggage control—and she thought she had to return it to him. As for herself, she knew she could get another weapon in short order—obtaining firearms in South Florida wasn't a challenge.

So after landing and before splitting up to go to their separate destinations, she and Andy went into the concourse ladies' room to make an exchange. Neither was certain that Moth needed the weapon. He might. He might not. Andy Candy more or less made up her mind that she would keep the gun, at least until Moth was returning to Redeemer One with regularity.

The heft of the weapon seemed almost as frightening to her as what it could do. She thought it would require a special strength to lift it up, aim it at a human being, and pull the trigger—despite all the propaganda from gun enthusiasts to the contrary. She jammed it into her satchel, told herself to forget about it, realized that was impossible, and simply clamped her mouth shut.

The two of them emerged from the ladies' room and saw Moth standing in front of the ticket counter, staring at a line of people. His face was a little flushed and he seemed almost frozen in place, as if he'd seen a poisonous snake at his feet and was afraid that by moving he would spur a strike.

"Is something wrong?" Andy asked.

Moth shook his head slowly. He did not turn to face her, but he addressed Susan quietly: "We know he was here in Miami, right?"

Susan replied: "Yes."

"We know he went back to Massachusetts. Had to, right? Had to set up the explosion."

"Yes," she replied again, only this time she dragged the word out.

"Assume for a minute that wasn't him inside. It was some other body."

"Okay. That's what we think. But . . ."

"He's a dedicated killer. What would another corpse mean to him?"

"Nothing. Okay. Keep going."

"So, we know—loosely, but we know—when he had to fly back north to get there before we did."

Susan felt a little dizzy. It wasn't the pain or the Tylenol.

Andy Candy whispered, "We have a time line, don't we."

"Yes," Moth said. "And we know where lists of names on flight manifests are kept." He pointed at the ticket counter. "If Blair Munroe is on one of those that lists, well, dead end. Too bad. Move on. But if it's not . . ."

Susan looked a little confused. So did Andy Candy.

"What are you getting at?" Andy asked.

Moth tried to maintain an appearance of steadiness, but his voice was picking up momentum. "Everyone always looks for a clear-cut link. But in my field, sometimes it's the absence of something that is the telltale sign."

He pointed over at the ticket counter.

"A man we know was in Miami buys a ticket to fly home. That home belongs to a man named Blair Munroe. But did Munroe call Andy? Did he tip off the police about Susan's drug dealer? Did he threaten my aunt? Or was it someone else who boarded that plane north?" *Ironic,* he thought. *If he hid his identity, it can tell us who he is.*

I am a historian. Moth smiled inwardly. *An investigator of subtlety.*

42

Her appointment with her boss was not until nine the following morning, but she knew security would be on duty round the clock. It was close to midnight when she walked through the doors to the Miami-Dade State Attorney's Office.

The security guard behind bulletproof glass was reading a Carl Hiaasen comedy and laughing. But when he saw her, he instantly grimaced. "Jesus, Ms. Terry. What the hell happened to you?" He nodded toward her cast and sling.

"Car accident," she lied. "This is Miami. Uninsured driver, naturally. Ran a stoplight."

"Sounds like a mess."

"You better believe it. And you think this is bad . . . ," she pointed at her arm, ". . . you should see my damn car. Totaled." What she was hoping was, *Please don't look down and see a "SUSPENDED" notation by my name on your checklist.* She knew to keep up the distraction. "Hey, anyone else in here working overtime for no money?"

The security guard smiled. "Yeah, a few guys are still here. The team doing that big bank fraud case and a couple of the prosecutors involved in putting those home invasion badasses away are still here. Everyone else has gone home for the night."

"I won't be long," she said while continuing to smile and trying to act as if she hadn't a care in the world. "Just need to double-check some documents before a hearing tomorrow afternoon. You know how it is: You're sitting around at home, watching TV and chugging painkillers . . . ," she gestured with her bandaged arm, ". . . and going over all that courtroom stuff mentally, and suddenly you think you've forgotten something or left something out, or I don't know, screwed something up . . ."

As she said all this, she tossed her hair a bit and laughed and moved steadily toward the entranceway. *Come on,* she thought. *Don't check. Don't do your job. Just be tired and bored and not paying proper attention on a totally routine night.*

The guard reached down, made a notation on a clipboard that she'd entered the offices—she'd known he would do that and didn't see any way around it—and buzzed her into the warren of offices. The sound of the electronic lock was harsh but welcome. What she counted on was that her boss didn't check those overnight logs—or, at least, wouldn't check them until he had a bona fide reason to.

He would probably have that *reason* within the next few hours.

As soon as she slipped through the doors, she ducked to the side, into a shadow next to several tall filing cabinets. The overhead lights—ordinarily relentlessly bright—were dimmed. The office was quiet, ghostly. She craned her head and thought she could hear voices coming from one wing. This made her crouch down a little more, in a movement that made her arm ache brutally. The other prosecutors in the office would know she was suspended. And, like anyone involved in the world of crime and punishment, they would be curious if they spotted her. *Maybe suspicious. They will ask, "What are you doing here?" in a friendly kind of way, but this will conceal doubts. They won't believe whatever flimsy excuse I come up with. Someone will write an email that moves up the chain and that will be that. The boss will be furious.*

No. More than furious. He's already furious. He will be some entirely new red-faced, clenched-jaw angry.

She hesitated. She was struck with a sense of loss—the steel desks and closed offices surrounding her were spartan and colorless, but they were more her home than her own apartment was. It was the place where she'd felt both happiest and most stressed, a place of anxiety and accomplishment. All the contradictions that rippled through her were as painful as the throbbing in her arm.

Then—almost as rapidly as they'd flooded her—she dismissed every sensation, reenergized her focus, and, staying low, crept through the area toward her office. Carpet muffled any sound her running shoes might have made. She listened to her breathing, hoping it was even, although it seemed labored.

She was stealing something this night.

Her name was still on the door. This reassured her. She prayed that none of the locks had been changed. They would be after she was fired, she knew. But when her key opened the room, she breathed a sigh of relief.

She thought she was not exactly a break-in artist or a midnight robber. But what she was doing was certainly a violation of her agreement with her boss, and bordered on the criminal.

She wondered if some clear-eyed prosecutor would look at what she had done and see felonies. *Probably. Maybe. Possibly.* She did not know. She asked herself: *Would I?* She knew the answer to that was *yes.* But fear mixed with determination to create an odd concoction that could be summed up with an obscenity: *Fuck it.* All she knew was that she was swept up in something and that right at that hour in the middle of the night it was up to her to discover an answer.

Finding a killer—that might just possibly keep her job safe.

Everything she had done and was about to do would seem like a small price—if she was successful. She didn't want to imagine the alternative. *Disbarred. Arrested. Prosecuted.*

And worse: humiliated, knowing that she had been powerless to prevent a killer from walking away scot-free.

Susan closed the door to her office quietly behind her. She didn't turn on the overhead light, but in the small glow from the city that crept through her window, she could see around the barren space. *Everything is empty,* she thought. The only way to fill it back up was to do what she was doing. She moved behind her desk and booted up her computer. *Law enforcement access.* She said another small prayer that her log-on and password hadn't been compromised by her suspension. When the computer screen came to life, she was relieved—although a part of her was dismayed by what she considered genuinely sloppy security.

She hit a few keys. Each *click!* sound on the keyboard made her shift about nervously, hoping she wasn't heard.

A Transportation Security Administration site came up.

She knew there would be no hiding that it was Susan Terry seeking information. Each keystroke and password was uniquely hers, as solid a bit of evidence as a signature on a page, and eventually it would be traced to her. Any competent investigator would find out what and where and when she was looking for this information. She could run any "erase disk" program she liked and she knew it would be fruitless. When it came to computer technology, investigators were way ahead of any capability she possessed.

She didn't really care, but she knew this put a clock on everything she was doing. She could feel it ticking inexorably. *One second. Two seconds. Three seconds. A minute. An hour. A day. How much time did she have to find a killer?*

Susan bent toward the computer screen and whispered, "God damn it, Timothy Warner, I sure as hell hope you're right. It would be nice to lose my entire career doing the right thing for a change, even if it is totally illegal."

This was funny, she thought. Gingerly she removed her right arm from the sling.

For an instant she imagined herself to be a criminal seeking another criminal.

She typed rapidly, one-handed sometimes, sometimes overcoming the pain of forcing her right arm forward so she could move more quickly through the electronic police worlds.

Moth watched Andy Candy sleep.

He was slumped into his desk chair. His computer was open in front of him. Andy's bag was nearby, and he knew the .357 Magnum was inside, but for the time being he left it alone.

He knew she was exhausted. Once, years earlier, after some truly sweaty teenage coupling, she had abruptly fallen asleep beside him. They had been in the backseat of a car—a cliché, he knew, but it was where they'd found privacy that night. She was naked and he'd spent the minutes she dozed trying to memorize every curve and fold of her body. He'd watched her then just as he did now. He thought they had no chance to continue together, that the only thing linking them now was something dark and murderous, and that eventually there would be light shining on the two of them and they would split apart again. It made him sad, and anxious. He didn't know if he could bear losing her again—which didn't seem a very mature way to feel. But he felt crippled by all that being adult had brought into his life. Drink. Hopelessness. Near death. Salvation through his uncle. He wondered if avenging his uncle's murder—it seemed an almost Napoleonic notion—would cost him Andy's presence.

He guessed it would. This caused him to shift in his seat. He wished he could join her in the narrow bed, but he was waiting.

The email counter on the computer made its electronic sound.

That will be her, he thought. He wondered if he should awaken Andy. He knew he could use her way of seeing things. But he let her sleep. *Just a little longer.* He opened up the first email:

No Blair Munroe.

20 possible flights. Some connecting.

Sending all lists.

Meet you at 7 your place.

He hesitated, then started to open all the attachments and move them to his desktop.

Another email beeped.

He opened it immediately.

It read:

Dead?

I don't think so.

It was a Massachusetts Registry of Motor Vehicles driver's license picture of Blair Munroe, blown up to fill the page.

He printed the photo out and held it in his hands.

Moth stared, hoping he could see *killer* in the eyes, the shape of the jaw, perhaps the cut of the hair or the turn of the lips. But there was nothing that obvious or helpful. He shuddered, thought he should awaken Andy to show her, but then realized it could wait. If this was the man he had to kill, there was no sense in rushing her into the crime. She could have a few more minutes of innocent sleep, he thought.

43

Moth fell asleep a couple of hours before dawn. He lifted a pillow from his bed and lay down on the carpet beside Andy Candy. He had some odd thought about modesty and not disturbing her before stripping down to his underwear and shutting his eyes.

Andy, on the other hand, awakened just as the first rays of morning light crept into the apartment. She saw Moth on the floor beside her, rose, and stepped over him gingerly. She made some coffee as quietly as she could and splashed some water on her face in the kitchen sink, then went to the computer and read everything that Moth had been working on. She saw the information sent by Susan that he had printed out and then picked up the driver's license picture of Blair Munroe, going through many of the identical thoughts that Moth had processed just a few hours earlier. Then she took her coffee and sat down at the desk to examine flight passenger lists.

The first thing she did was rule out any women's names.

Then she cleared any obvious couples. *Goodbye Mister and Missus Last Names Alike.*

"You don't have a wife, do you?" she whispered to the photograph. "No common-law *Bonnie and Clyde* spouse cokiller at your side?" She paused, letting these questions hang in front of the computer screen, before mouthing her own answer: "No. I didn't think so. You started out a loner and you're going to end up one, too." She understood that she was speculating, and that she didn't really know much about murderers, although she no longer felt like a naïf in this particular school of understanding.

You've learned something about killing, haven't you? she said to herself.

The Transportation Security Administration lists on the desk in front of her included dates of birth. Anyone too young or too old was immediately removed from her consideration. She used a fifteen-year age window, thinking that the man they were hunting could be anywhere in that range. The photo on the driver's license had an indistinct quality to it; the man had a slippery look, and might be any of several ages. He was certainly older than her and Moth. Older than Susan Terry.

Ed's age, she realized. *Or damn close to it.*

The possibilities were narrowed.

Single men. Traveling alone. Aged forty-five to sixty.

She continued to quietly speak to herself: "Were you pretending to be a businessman finishing up some important deal? A tourist tired after catching a bit of illicit South Beach action? Or maybe a dutiful son returning home after visiting elderly relatives in one of the high-rises in North Miami? What did you want to show the world you were, because you weren't showing us even a little bit of the truth, were you?"

She drew lines through names she eliminated. By the time she was finished her own list was narrowed down to right around two dozen men traveling north alone who fit the modest profile she'd established.

One of those names, she realized, was either a charred body in a trailer in a forgotten little town in Massachusetts, or a killer luxuriating in newly found freedom.

Her money was on luxury.

We were close, but we weren't really close enough for you to kill yourself, were we? Questions resounded in her head. *You were clever enough to plan other people's deaths. Why couldn't you plan your own?* She imagined murders taking place on a stage in front of her. Like an actor, the killer they sought took a bow and exited to thunderous applause. Stage left.

Moth stirred. She looked up. He was moving stiffly. "Morning," Andy Candy said brightly. "There's coffee."

Moth grunted. He lifted himself to his feet and disappeared into the bathroom. A hot shower and vigorous toothbrushing cleared away some of the fogginess of too much tension, not enough sleep, and growing anxiety. When he emerged, Andy eyed his wet hair.

"I think I'll do that as well. Is there a dry towel?"

He nodded.

"Look at this while I shower," she said, pushing her list of names toward him.

Moth sat with his coffee cup, examining Andy's list but listening to the noise from the bathroom, working hard to not dwell on every memory of her naked form. It was a morning, he believed, like any old married couple might have, with only one small distinction: *A little conversation. Clean up. Some hot coffee. A modest pace to get the day going. Start to plan to murder someone.*

It had been some time since he'd felt the revenge energy that had dominated him when he'd pulled a semblance of his life together after his uncle's death. But staring down at the list, it stirred within him again.

"Where are you?" he asked each name on the list. This question was followed by, "Who are you?" and finally, "How do I find you?" Each question was whispered in a lower, rougher tone.

Susan Terry hesitated before knocking on Moth's door. She recalled that a few days earlier she had stood in the same spot, gun in hand, ready to shoot him because in a coked-up near frenzy of confused thoughts, she believed it was the history student–drunk who had called the police on her and thoroughly screwed up her carefully balanced life.

She shrugged and knocked.

As Moth opened the door, without a greeting she simply said, "I don't have much time. I have to be on the carpet in my boss's office at nine. We need to figure out the next step before then, because I think I'm going to be out on my ass at nine-zero-one."

Moth steered her toward the desk, where piles of papers—everything accumulated over the weeks since his uncle's death—were haphazardly strewn about. He saw Susan glance at the mess and frown. He pushed Andy's list to her just as Andy emerged from the shower, running a brush through damp hair.

"One of these, I think," he said. "It's what Andy came up with, going through all the stuff you sent. At least, maybe he's on this."

Susan eyed the two of them. There had been something utterly chaste about their connection up to that moment and she mentally sniffed the air to see if anything had changed. She couldn't detect anything, so she ignored it. But a part of her sounded a bell of concern.

Then, as quickly, she dismissed it. *Screw it,* she thought. *Deal with what you can deal with.* She looked at the list of names.

"Single men. Traveling alone. All within the right age framework."

Susan nodded. "You're thinking like a cop, Andy," she said.

Andy smiled. "Yeah. But that's as far as I got. How do we narrow it down further?"

The three fell silent.

Moth stared at the papers, letting his eyes sweep across documents over to Susan, then to Andy Candy, then back to the piles on his desk. *What does a historian do?* he demanded of himself. *How does a historian look at bits and pieces of information and determine how events are influenced?*

He breathed in sharply, a sound loud enough to make the two others turn in his direction.

"I know how," he said.

Shot in the dark, Susan thought as she hurried through the warren of desks toward the state attorney's corner office. *But as far as shots in the dark go, not a bad one at all.* Her boss's secretary usually guarded the entrance with Cerberus-like intensity and rarely smiled, but as Susan approached, she looked up from her computer and shook her head.

"Oh, Susan, that looks painful. Are you okay?"

Susan thought joking was the best approach. Make everything seem like no big deal. "Hey, you should see the other guy."

The secretary nodded and smiled wanly. She gestured toward the door to the inner office. "He's waiting to see you. Go right on in."

Susan nodded, took a step forward, then stopped. This was calculated, part of the performance. It had to be done *before* she got fired, if that was to be the outcome of the meeting.

"I wonder . . ." she started, then stopped. "Oh, probably won't help, but . . ."

"What is it?" the secretary asked.

Susan pounced.

"I have a list of names from the TSA. I need to pull state driver's licenses on each of them." She motioned toward her arm in the sling. "It's so hard for me to type into the damn computer right now . . ."

"Oh, I'll do it," said the secretary. "Shouldn't take more than a couple of minutes. Is this part of your investigation?"

"Of course," Susan said. *The boss's lie about an investigation seemed to be all over the office. Helpful.* She smiled. The secretary would have access to all the law enforcement databases around the nation. "Boy, would I ever appreciate it."

She handed the secretary the list Andy Candy had created. Now all she had to do was avoid being fired in the next few seconds.

She switched back and forth between concoctions and contradictions effectively, rapid-fire.

"I know what you told me, but it was a closed case where questions had cropped up, and with the sort of addiction problems I've experienced, lingering job-related issues can really trigger some of the behaviors I'm working my way through," she told her boss. She let words race through her lips, wanting to be persuasive, which required speed, but not wanting to sound manic, hopped up, or strung out. This required more performance on her part.

"The young people I was with, they were involved in the case and had raised some possibly legitimate doubts about our investigation." She looked over at the head of Major Crimes, searching his face for clues that what she was saying was having an impact. A frown. Raised eyebrows. A nod. A shake of the head. She barreled forward, hoping.

"I knew that you hate it when people have questions after some case has been officially closed, so, really it was intended to be therapeutic on my part. You know—quick trip up to speak with the potential witness. Get a statement. Rewrap the case up nice and tight, no holes anywhere. End of story . . ."

She noted a rueful smile. Her boss knew all about *no holes* and *end of story* and how unlikely that was. She persisted: ". . . Get back into the rehabilitation cycle. Back in time to make my meetings and see a counselor, just as you requested."

Now she shrugged.

"Look, I had no idea the guy I went to see was running some sort of backwoods, low-rent, small but dangerous meth manufacturing site in his old trailer, and when he saw us coming, thought that he was being busted and decided to go out in some sort of blaze of glory—like that guy on television did. Jesus, could have killed us all, but we were lucky and the local cop I was with was damn good—maybe ought to consider him for down here on our investigative staff . . ."

Every word she spoke was calculated to convert something murderous into something benign. She was particularly pleased with her suggestion that she was trying to make sure a mistake hadn't been made in a case. Like any top prosecutor, her boss was sensitive to anything in his domain that might devolve into a front-page news story that had the word *incompetent* implied somewhere in it close to *his* name.

"I know, boss, this all sounds like a major-league fuckup, and I'm not denying that it is, but my intentions were good . . ."

He believed that.

It surprised her.

He didn't change her status—other than to warn her that there could be no more incidents that got in the way of her rehabilitation program. She knew this was a sincere threat.

Thin ice that just got thinner.

But as long as she didn't move too quickly, she wouldn't plunge through into freezing waters.

As Susan was on her way out, back to what her boss assumed was the process of getting sober and straight, the secretary handed her a large envelope. She fingered the collected pages inside, almost as if they would burn a hole through the paper until they reached the killer.

44

Susan resisted the temptation to rip open the envelope instantly, waiting until she returned to Moth's apartment.

She was oddly formal as she dropped it on the desk. "Okay, Mister Warner. Here is the information you requested." She saw Andy Candy blanch slightly, not all of the blood draining from her face, but a good deal of it. The contents of the envelope, Susan realized, ranged from utterly irrelevant to extremely dangerous. Opening it had the potential to set them on a course that there might not be any walking away from. She realized—as the oldest person and the only real professional in the room when it came to crime and punishment—she needed to point this out.

"You sure you want to look at this?"

Moth hesitated. "That's what all this has been about, right?"

"Right. It's just that up to now no one has broken any laws—maybe stretched them a bit, I'll admit, but actually done something that I, or someone exactly like me, could successfully prosecute in a court of law? No. I don't think so. Not yet."

"There's a *but* coming, isn't there?"

"Yes. Open that envelope and then do what you've been saying you're going to do, well, that's a different thing altogether, isn't it? 'Conspiracy' is a word that comes to mind."

Susan used the same tone of voice that she'd employed when Moth first came to her office.

Moth didn't answer. He just stared at the envelope.

Susan softened her tone—which contradicted much of the harshness in what she was saying.

"Look, Timothy, I know what you've said you want to do, but have you really thought it through? I don't think you're a criminal—and I don't think you want to become one, either. But you're about to. Shouldn't we try to find some alternatives now?"

"*Alternatives* almost got us all killed," he replied.

"I just want you to consider—" Susan started, but Moth interrupted her.

"Isn't that all we ever do, Susan?" he asked quietly. "Every day. Is this the day we stay sober? Or is this the day we fail?"

Now it was Susan's moment to remain silent.

"I am tired of being who I am," Moth added. "I want to be someone different."

Moth's hand shook a little as he reached for the envelope, and it wasn't the sort of quiver that he was familiar with: the morning after a night-long bout with the bottle. He looked over at Andy Candy, who seemed frozen in position, because what had once been intellectual, a challenge, a puzzle spread out on a table in a thousand pieces waiting to be fitted together, was now something different. "Andy," Moth said quietly, "I see what Susan's driving at. This just might be that *totally crazy* moment we talked about. If you want to leave, right now would be a good time to walk out the door and not look back."

Saying this nearly nauseated him. A montage of grim futures flooded him. *She walks, I'm alone. She stays, and what are we doing?*

Thoughts pummeled Andy Candy.

Go, go, go, go, she thought. Then: *No way.*

She disagreed with herself: *You're being stupid. So? What's new? Been stupid from the start. Why stop now?*

When Andy shook her head, Moth felt an immense relief. Without explanation, she took the envelope from Moth's hands. "Let's see what we can see," she said, not really trusting her voice much. "Maybe he won't be here. Maybe yes. Maybe no. Maybe we won't be sure. Then we can make some decisions."

Coming to a decision seemed to renew her confidence. She reached over and grabbed the driver's license photo of Blair Munroe. Whether he was the dead man or not was something being determined miles away, by forensic analysts in Massachusetts. The *maybe* dead man seemed very distant. The man who had called her on the phone and pushed her into a near panic seemed much closer. She set the *maybe* dead man's picture on the table, then opened the manila envelope. Acting a little like a television game show host, she removed one sheet of paper.

The three of them craned over the pictures as Andy Candy set them side by side.

A man from a suburb outside Hartford, Connecticut.

"No," Susan said. "Timothy?"

"Agree. Not him."

Another picture.

A man from Northampton, Massachusetts.

"Nope," Moth said. "Wrong hair. Wrong eyes. Wrong height."

"Correct," Susan said.

A third picture.

A man from Charlotte, North Carolina.

This picture made each of them lean forward. There were some similarities, obscured by eyeglasses. For a moment, Andy Candy held her breath; then she exhaled slowly as she realized it wasn't the man they were seeking.

"Go on," Moth said. "Another."

Andy thought it was a little like playing the children's memory game Concentration, where the idea was to place all fifty-two cards in the deck

359

facedown, then turn them over two at a time, trying to remember where the previously exposed cards were to make pairs. She reached into the envelope and withdrew another picture.

A man from Key West, Florida.

Andy Candy gasped.

She wanted to shout. Raise her voice, let loose, keep going until she was exhausted. Instead, she simply put the remaining twenty-odd pages in the envelope aside, walked over to the sink, and drew herself a glass of water. She gulped it down, unable to tell whether it was hot or cold.

Moth was unsure how long the three of them were quiet. Might have been seconds. Could have been longer. It was as if he'd begun to slip through time. When he did speak, it seemed like his voice echoed, or else came from some distant location or some different person—a stranger.

"So, Susan," he asked quietly, "exactly how do I get away with murder?"

Andy Candy recalled a reading from a literature class, her third year at college. *An unraped year,* she thought. Lots of seminar discussions about existential writing. *The only real choice in life is whether to kill yourself. Or not.* She tried to remember: *Was it Sartre? Camus?* It was one of those French writers, she was certain. She glanced over at Susan Terry. *Well, she's caught between the proverbial rock and a hard place, isn't she?* This was almost a joke, and Andy stifled a smile. She didn't dare to look over at Moth. She tried to imagine what it was like for him to look down and see the man that killed his uncle pictured on something as ordinary as a driver's license. She felt an odd sense of things coming together, as if instead of confusion, things were slipping into place, joining up, linking into a chain. She stole a look at the killer's photo, but in her mind's eye it was replaced by the grinning face of the frat boy who'd fucked her, impregnated her, and abandoned her. *Kill them all,* she thought.

A small silence.

"Timothy, I cannot tell you that," Susan Terry said.

"Can't or won't?" Moth asked.

Susan ignored this question. "What we should do is call my boss. Hand over everything to investigators. Let them put together a prosecutable case. Make an arrest. Complicated, sure, but possible. Come on, Timothy, don't be dumb. Let's let someone with expertise handle this."

Moth paused.

"When you prosecuted murder cases," he said slowly, "it had to occur to you as you put everything together before going into court : This factor, this piece, this bit of evidence—take any one little thing away, and the whole case would crumble. The person best able to see how to avoid arrest and going to prison isn't the criminal, because he's wrapped up in what he's doing—it's the cop or maybe a prosecutor like you, who view it all in hindsight."

Susan Terry nodded. "Yes," she said. "That's a reasonably accurate statement." She sounded like a law school lecturer.

"So it stands to reason that an experienced member of law enforcement, like you, would—intellectually speaking, of course—know where the pitfalls and fuckups really lie."

Susan nodded. She felt a little as if she had awakened on some strange planet, where blood and death were treated like subjects for a term paper.

"All right," Moth continued, picking up a little momentum. "Let's speak hypothetically, then."

It was easy for Susan to see where he was going. She didn't stop him, although a part of her deep within was screaming for her to do precisely that.

"Hypothetically, and all together generally," Moth continued. His voice was cold with barely restrained fury. "What are the specific areas where people screw up and get arrested for murder?"

Susan took a deep breath. *Ah, well,* she thought. *Guess I can't hold back the tide.* "In my experience, and speaking hypothetically, naturally it's in connections. Relationships. What links the killer to the victim? Usually, they know each other, or they have business together. What the police look for is how they intersect."

Moth was leaning forward, almost predatory. "So the most difficult kind of killing to solve . . ."

". . . is when the connection isn't immediately apparent. Or remains hidden. Random. Witness-less. Obscured by something—shit, Timothy, pick whatever word you like. It's where the motivation for the murder isn't clear and how person A got into the same place as person B. With a gun."

Moth was thinking fast. Susan could see things turning over in his head.

Andy Candy interjected: "You mean like some guy who stalks and kills members of a medical school study group years after whatever the hell they did was done and everyone had moved on to something else, except the killer?"

There was much cynicism in her voice. Andy could hear it, and she actually rather liked it. It was like opening the door to a refrigerated room.

Susan tried to ignore her. She talked to Moth. "Look, there are also forensic links. Don't underestimate what police labs can do. I mean, it's not like how it's portrayed on television—you know, instant this and instant that and bingo, we know who a killer is. But they can match fingerprints, hair samples, DNA—you name it. They take their time, and they are reliable as all get-out. And ballistics. That science is pretty advanced."

Moth looked over at the desk and the two pictures. He picked up the photo of Blair Munroe on the Massachusetts license. "I know what connects me to this man," he said quietly.

He replaced the picture on the desk surface.

Taking the other picture in his hand, he looked at it for a moment. *Stephen Lewis. Angela Street, Key West.* "But what connects me to this person?" he asked.

Susan hesitated. "Just me, and what I've done," she said in a low voice.

Moth held up both pictures. "And exactly what do you suppose connects this man to this man?"

Susan inhaled sharply. It was as if in that second, she could see a murder. She didn't know whether Moth saw it as well. "Probably nothing, if he's as smart as we think he is."

Moth smiled.

"Goodbye, Susan," he said. "I think you should go to Redeemer One tonight. Yes. Absolutely. You should make one hundred percent certain you are at Redeemer One tonight. Make sure you testify. Talk about every one of your troubles in detail and make everything you say memorable. You wouldn't want anyone at that meeting to forget that you were there—in case anyone should ever ask them."

45

A one-sided conversation:

"Don't be rash."

"You can fuck up your entire future."

"You will get caught."

"You think I can protect you? Think again. I won't."

"Murder isn't a game, Timothy. It isn't some sort of academic exercise. It's real, it's nasty, and it takes a whole lot more toughness than you have."

"You think you can look that man in the eye and kill him? Ask yourself that question first. It might be easy for Hollywood movie stars in fake dramas, but in real life it's not so damn simple."

"You think you can pull a trigger?"

Pause. No reply. Continuing:

"Cops aren't stupid, Timothy. And they have time on their side. No statute of limitations on homicide. And they have resources you wouldn't imagine."

More silence. Words that exploded in the still of the apartment seemed to have no impact.

"What makes you think that when I pick up the paper tomorrow and read about a murder in Key West I won't go walking into the Major Crimes Division of the city police and say, 'I know who did this . . .' And even if it takes them a helluva time to piece it together, they will. Count on it. And if I decide to help them, it won't take all that long. So, kill that man and enjoy your final forty-eight hours of freedom, Timothy. Spend that time picturing what you might have done with your life.

"They will be the fastest forty-eight hours you will ever experience, waiting for that knock on your door. And don't try to run; it won't do you any good. And I don't care if you use all your uncle's money to hire the best damn criminal defense attorney in Miami—you will go to prison. You know what happens to nice white boys doing time for murder? Use your imagination, Timothy, and after you figure the worst that can happen to you up at the state prison, multiply that by about a factor of ten, because that's the reality."

Another wait for a response that didn't come.

"Please, Timothy. Don't be stupid. You're smart and well educated. You have a world of potential. Don't toss it because of some silly notion of revenge."

A smile. A shake of the head. His silence built up insistently, like a siren's wail growing in the room. Susan allowed frustrated anger to slide into her voice, and finally she came up with the best possible argument:

"And you will take down Andy, and maybe me, too, even if I cooperate and testify against you. I'll lose my job for sure this time, and probably my entire career. I might even be looking at jail time. But that isn't anything compared to what will happen to Andy. Do you want to see her go to prison?"

Deep breath. Moth's answer, simple, impossible: "No."

More silence. Susan's last, helpless question: "Well then?"

A lie: "I won't let that happen. Goodbye, Susan. I will see you tomorrow at Redeemer One."

One last effort, pivoting in a different direction: "Andy, please. Don't let him do this."

365

And Andy Candy's immediate response: "I've never been any good at making Moth do anything. Good or bad. Once he makes up his mind, he's as stubborn as a mule."

A cliché, to be certain—but accurate.

Susan eyed the two of them. They suddenly seemed very young. "Well then, fuck it," she said. She turned to leave, but at the door tried one last time: "Don't say I didn't warn you." Selfishly, she began to calculate her own exposure. It was significant. *Conspiracy. Accessory before the fact—that was certain. Accessory after the fact—that was equally possible.* A variety of criminal charges—ones she was accustomed to filing against the guilty— flooded her. She could see the entries in the criminal statutes, probably could even quote some of them verbatim if she were pressed. The lawyer within her wondered if she should quickly write up a warning and have the two of them sign it—some sort of statement that absolved her of any criminal responsibility. This was unfeasible, she thought, especially when Moth repeated, "Goodbye, Susan," and held the door open for her.

She wanted to strike out, slap sense into him. Grab him by the shirt and give him a jolt of reality. She did not do this. Instead she exited, and as the door closed behind her, she felt more alone than she ever had before.

Moth took the driver's license picture for Stephen Lewis of Angela Street in Key West and went to his computer. Whatever information he could unearth about this man was a few clicks away. His fingers hovered above the keyboard, but what he said was, "She's right, you know."

"Right about what?" Andy Candy responded, although she knew.

"All of it," Moth said. "The risks. The dilemma. The reality. I shouldn't go around fooling myself." This was said without conviction.

He paused before adding, "And us. She was right about that. Andy, I can't ask you for anything else. You need to leave now. Whatever happens, it has to be me, alone. Susan talked about potential . . . the future . . . not throwing it all away—pretty much every argument you would expect her to make. And every argument made much more sense than what I have in mind. Christ, I don't even know if I *can* do it. She was right about that, too." He shook his head. "I just have to try."

Andy Candy realized that good sense should absolutely dictate what she did next. She also realized it would not.

"Moth," she said in a low voice, "I'm not leaving you now." This, she knew, was both the best and worst thing she could have decided to do. *There are all sorts of rights that are wrong and wrongs that are right*, she thought, *and this is obviously one of them*. She did not know which category she meant.

"If I had a future," Moth said slowly, "it was because Uncle Ed provided it for me. And we turn all this over to the cops—and the killer will just disappear again. Maybe he has another identity somewhere. Maybe he has ten. And sure enough, no matter how much pressure Susan brings, and how many FBI flyers go out, they won't find him. People disappear in the USA all the time. It's a big headline when some guy who's been gone for ten, twenty, thirty years accidentally gets caught. Sixties radicals disappeared for years. How about that guy, the Boston mobster? His face was on every post office wall and FBI 'Most Wanted' list and it was still decades before anyone found him. And that was pretty much blind luck. This guy—our guy—doesn't seem like the sort that allows for either luck or accidents in his life."

Andy Candy wanted to be practical.

"He will kill us, Moth. I know it. Maybe not today or tomorrow—but someday. When he feels like it." This, she knew, was a truism. Saying it out loud added a layer of panic onto her fear. "Jesus," she said, but this wasn't a prayer.

Moth nodded in agreement.

"So, is there a plan?" she asked. She thought for a moment, *Maybe we'll be lucky and he won't be in Key West*. Then she contradicted herself: *Maybe that would be un*lucky.

"Yes," he replied, as he turned to the computer to do some research. Then a qualification in drawled-out slang: "Kinda."

46

Islamorada to Tavernier, then on to Long Key, Grassy Key, touching the Everglades, all the way down to Key West, the Overseas Highway meanders through close to seventeen hundred different islands. The view is spectacular: the Gulf of Mexico on one side and the Atlantic Ocean on the other—all glistening in sunlight, a hundred separate shades of blue waters. What Moth liked was the famous Seven Mile Bridge—which actually wasn't 7 miles long, but just shy at 6.79. It carried a name that was deceptive, that seemed both true and false at the same time. It was *nearly* seven miles, so why not call it that?

Andy Candy drove. It was late in the afternoon, but the traffic wasn't bad. She was cautious, not only because the highway that shifted from four lanes to two and cut through shopping malls and marinas is dangerous, but because if a Monroe County sheriff's officer were to pull them over in a routine traffic stop, it could ruin everything.

In a backpack in the backseat they had some clothes that Moth had carefully selected, along with the fully loaded .357 Magnum. They had a battered baseball hat, some sunglasses, and a wide-brimmed straw hat favored by old ladies afraid of the sun.

It wasn't much of a kit for murder.

They might have appeared to be a young couple heading for a snorkeling trip, maybe parasailing, or a sunset cruise. They weren't. What they didn't look like was a pair of killers.

They stopped near Marathon Key. While Moth went into a liquor store, Andy Candy found a damp, muddy spot in a corner of the parking lot. She took out some of the clothes Moth had packed and proceeded to rub them in dust and dirt, beating them up as much as she could. She glanced around, making sure that no one saw what she was doing. She looked a little like some ancient impoverished crone doing the wash by hand—only in reverse. She wished there were some stink—dried sweat, urine, fecal matter, maybe skunk scent—that she could add to the mix.

When she looked up, she saw Moth approaching. He had a plain brown sack, and she heard two bottles clank together.

"Never thought I'd do that again," he said. He tried to install confidence in his voice, but Andy thought it seemed shaky. She was unsure whether this was because of the liquor Moth held in his hands and everything it promised it might do to him—or because of the plan, which seemed to promise to do something else.

It hadn't quite worked out the way he thought it would.

Student #5 poured himself a cold beer and squeezed a freshly sliced lime into it, trying to postpone the sensation that had crept over him that morning and persisted through the day: He was suddenly bored.

Sunshine. Tourists. The laid-back, island lifestyle. He wasn't sure at all whether he fit. "Damn it," he said to no one.

He took his beer, a half-eaten bag of chips, and sat in his well-appointed living room. It was dark inside—Key West, which honors the sun religiously, is designed so that there are deep shadows; it keeps things cooler in the oppressive summer months. Combined with the constant soft hum of the central air-conditioning and the cool maroon Spanish tiles, it created a subtle quiet within his home.

For the first time in years, Student #5 actually felt alone. For so long, he had lived with the people lined up to be his victims. Now they were gone. It was like losing friends and companions. He felt the urge to open a window to the heat and street noise—although any sounds would be distant. Student #5 lived directly across from the Key West cemetery. The real estate agents' standard joke: *Quiet neighbors.* One hundred thousand people buried yards from his front door—or so the estimates went; no one was certain how many actually rested there.

He stretched out on a Haitian cotton couch and pressed the beer glass to his forehead. He felt a twinge of anger. *Should have seen this coming. What sort of psychologist are you?*

He frowned. Shifted in his seat. Tried to find a comfortable position, but was unable. Berated himself. "Where were you on the first day of basic shrink training?" he said out loud. "Absent without leave? Not paying attention? Did you think there was nothing left for you to learn?"

It was the simplest of emotional equations, he thought, and one he should have anticipated. The fantasies about what he would do with his life had merely been tinder to help obsessive fire take light. The real business of his life had been revenge—years of dedication, devotion to a single ideal, perfecting his craft. And now all of that was gone, along with all the intellectual stimulation and intensity of planning that had accompanied it.

He felt a little like the old white-haired geezer on the first day of a forced retirement, after decades of going in to the same office every day, sitting at the same desk, drinking the same cup of coffee, eating the same brown-bagged lunch, same time, same job, hour after hour, year after year.

"God damn it," he said out loud.

For him, no *Thank You* plaque, no framed picture signed by everyone, no nice but cheap retirement watch. No clap on the back from his boss, no firm handshake from the young guy who would replace him at half the cost. No tears from the more emotional of his coworkers.

"Damn," he repeated. The geezer in his mind's eye would shoot himself. Pronto. This he knew. "Son of a bitch," he said. He prided himself on being a cold-eyed realist about both himself and murder, but he was depressed. And lost.

The last few weeks had been filled with energy—first as he tormented The Nephew, The Girlfriend, and The Prosecutor. That had been flat-out fun. Challenging and amusing.

Then creating his exit from one of his lives—that too had been artistry. Not only had it set him free, but it had been an exercise in imagination. And it had worked—each piece fitting together like the shuffling of a deck of cards by a professional card shark.

He had arrived in Key West invigorated, ready to embrace his new life. And almost instantly had slid into a void. From the moment he'd seen the back of Jeremy Hogan's head explode to this one, nothing had been what he'd imagined.

Student #5 didn't want to read trashy novels or watch soap operas on television. He didn't want to fish or sail or swim or do any of the touristy sorts of things that brought folks to the Keys. He suddenly hated the crowds of cruise ship visitors with loud voices in different languages jamming the streets, and the high-priced huckstering that went along with catering to the money that arrived daily. Everything he'd expected to embrace had soured.

"So, what is it you want to do, now that you're footloose and fancy-free?" he asked himself sharply. "Now that you've entered—*retirement?*" He made this last word sound like an obscenity. He paused. He whispered his answer:

"Kill."

Then in a louder voice: "All right. Makes total sense. But who?" A smile. This question was a bit of a joke. "You know who."

An entirely new set of challenges. *After all,* he thought, *who poses a threat? Who can steal your life from you?* He knew the real answer to this question was *No one* because of the way he'd established his different identities. But the mere notion that someone might be dangerous to him after all he'd accomplished felt intoxicating. He began to calculate in his head.

The Girlfriend—*that won't be too hard. Young women are always doing stupid things that make them vulnerable. The key question will be when to strike. One year? Two? How long before her natural sense of safety and stupid overconfidence truly kick in and make her ripe?*

This was intriguing. Student #5 instantly moved on to Timothy Warner in his head.

The Nephew—*he's a drunk, but he won't slide so quickly into a false sense of safety. Still, he's young, and he's weak, and that will obscure whatever precautions he might take when he's sober.*

The Prosecutor . . .

He smiled. "Now, there's a challenge," he said out loud. "A real challenge. She's complicated—but when all is said and done, addiction or not, she's still a member of law enforcement, and they guard their own carefully. Planning her death will take effort. Bigger risks, no?"

He answered his own question: "Correct." Scheming the right death for Susan Terry would be intriguing. *Accident? Suicide? Overdose? Imagine all the enemies she's made putting people in prison.* This was a welcome puzzle.

He took a long swig of his beer and went to his computer. He had a small work area set up in a sparsely furnished guest room where he'd plugged in his laptop. There was a printer in a corner on the floor. He felt a surge of energy and a calming sense of purpose. *Might as well get started,* he told himself. Within a few seconds, he had typed in *Miami-Dade State Attorney's Office.* He went to the public information section on its website called "Who We Are." Then he printed out Susan's picture, her resume, a brief biography, and a list of some of her major cases.

Something to study. Just enough to get his juices flowing and his mind working. The simple act of clicking a few keys, then listening to pages drop into the receptacle on his printer gave him the sensation that he was *doing* something. The full-color head shot from the state attorney's website was the last item to emerge. *Nice long, sweeping black hair. A warm and welcoming smile. Firm jaw, wide lips, and green eyes. Really quite beautiful,* he thought.

"Hello-o-o, Susan," he said with a lilt. *There's going to come a day when you will wish that you'd been blown up in my trailer.*

He started to hum to himself—music that was rock-and-roll lively; he didn't pause to wonder why this particular song had leapt into his head. It was ostensibly a love song, in truth more a sex song, but he changed the words to the chorus as he began to sing along, crudely imitating the dead Jim Morrison's gravelly voice, as if it came from a grave only a few yards away instead of thousands of miles distant in Père Lachaise in Paris. He could hear the Doors singer: *"Love me two times, I'm going away . . ."*

In Student #5's mind, it became: *Kill me two times, I'm going away . . .*

47

The last few miles, from the National Key Deer Refuge, past Stock Island's marina and the entrance to the community college, Moth went through details in his mind. It helped him to focus on what he thought they might need—as opposed to examining what they intended to do. He thought it was almost laughable—a couple of college-age kids driving to Key West to become murderers.

The only truly good thing about their murder vacation was that he was with the only girl he'd ever actually loved and, oddly, for the first time in what seemed like years he hadn't thought about taking a drink, even if purchasing the two bottles—Scotch and vodka—had shaken him.

Beside him, Andy Candy drove steadily, cautiously, although the closer they got to Key West, the more she believed she should swerve her small car drunkenly across the road. Anything that might draw attention to them and prevent them from doing what they intended to do. That was her rational side. The irrational—which she knew was probably the *right* side— forced her to remain quiet, stay in her lane, and obey every traffic signal.

They found a parking spot on a quiet street just off Truman Avenue only two short blocks from the cemetery. Her car slid into a line of typical Keys vehicles: some shiny, brand-new, and expensive—Porsches and Jaguars—the others rusted-out, battered, dented, paint-peeling, ten-year-old Toyotas covered with bumper stickers proclaiming "Free the Conch Republic" and "Recycle Now!"

Moth shouldered his small backpack, with its clothes engineered filthy by Andy, the bottles of liquor, and the gun. Together, they walked to a nearby bicycle rental store—one of the dozens that dot Key West. Reggae music was blasting away over outdoor speakers, Bob Marley singing *"Every little thing's gonna be all right."* The dreadlocked salesman happily rented them two slightly run-down but utilitarian bicycles. He also showed them where to leave the bikes, locked up, if they decided to return them later that evening. Moth had told him they were unsure whether they would be staying one day or two. Andy Candy hung in the back, trying to make herself seem small and unnoticeable. Moth paid cash.

They biked across town and went into West Marine. Moth purchased a small foghorn—the sort that is a staple on every sailboat that heads to the Caribbean out of Key West. At the Angling Company he bought a pair of the neck buffs favored by fishermen—they can be pulled up to cover head and face, or else simply keep the sun off the back of the neck. Andy Candy got a pink one and he would wear a blue one.

He couldn't think of anything else. He was acutely aware of how much planning the man who'd killed his uncle had put into murder, and thought his own efforts were piecemeal and flimsy. He hoped they were adequate. He felt a little like a novice cook attempting some truly complex French recipe prior to an extremely important dinner for epicures, career and future in the balance of each small taste.

The two of them rode over to Fort Zachary Taylor beach, where they sat on a weather-beaten wooden bench beneath some palm trees twenty yards from pristine clear water. For a few minutes they watched a family finishing up a play day, mother and father trying to corral sandy and sunburned kids, pack up coolers and umbrellas, and leave. It was an incredibly benign sight. Andy was nearly overwhelmed by the contrast between this family on vacation and the two of them. She thought she should say something, but kept quiet as Moth rose abruptly, hustled over to a street vendor who seemed ready to leave as well, and purchased them each a bottle of water.

Andy gulped at the cold liquid feverishly.

"Andy, I don't think we can simply walk up to him and shoot him. Too many people might see us. Too much noise. We have to corner him some-place private," Moth said quietly. He'd taken a film history class once, and that was more or less exactly what Al Pacino did in *The Godfather*. But that was a different era. "It's as much confrontation as it is killing," he added. These words seemed oddly hollow.

"No shit," Andy replied stiffly.

"There's only one place I can think of," Moth continued.

"His house," Andy answered. She surprised herself with the sudden cool-ness in her voice. She was both terrified and organized. This made little sense to her.

"What I'm worried about is some sort of security system. We want to avoid cameras and alarms."

"No shit," Andy repeated.

"We can't break in. We can't just knock on the door and ask him to invite us in."

"No shit," Andy continued.

"So there's only one way in."

Andy thought her breathing was getting shallow. Asthmatic.

Moth hesitated. "Look, if everything goes wrong, leave me. Go back to the car, drive north, get the hell out of here, and then do exactly what Susan said to do. She'll help you."

"And what about you?" Andy asked.

"At that point, it probably won't make a difference," he said. He didn't say, *"I'll be dead,"* although he knew that phrase had crept into both their minds. Moth wondered in that second whether he'd been on some sort of bizarre suicide trip since the very moment he'd seen his uncle's body and realized that the sole tether keeping him sober, sane, and safe was dead.

"Well, I'm not going to do that," Andy said. "No running away for me. I was never one for retreat or surrender."

Moth smiled. "I know that. But this is different."

"I won't leave you alone, Moth. Not after everything."

"Of course you will."

Andy Candy nodded. She was suddenly unsure whether she was lying or telling the truth. "Okay, I will. But only if . . ."

She stopped. A sudden fierceness nearly overcame her. "If he kills you, Moth, I will kill him. If he kills me, then make sure you kill him."

"And what if he kills both of us?"

Logic. Cold and direct.

"Then we have nothing to worry about any longer and maybe Susan will put him in prison."

Moth thought all this sounded so absurd and crazy that it should have been funny. He shook his head, smiled, and shrugged.

"Okay. I promise. You?"

"I promise, too."

These promises sounded distinctly like those of a pair of fourteen-year-olds pledging eternal fealty—totally unlikely.

"Andy," Moth started. "There's a lot I want to say."

"And a lot I'd probably say back," Andy said. She reached over and squeezed Moth's hand. Then she laughed, nervously. "I don't suppose there's ever been a pair of lovers—nonlovers, ex-lovers, friends, former high school buddies; I don't know what are we, Moth—exactly like us," she said.

Moth grinned, but it faded swiftly. "No. I don't suppose so. Perhaps we fit into some different category. *Homicidal high school sweethearts*—that's got a bit of a ring to it. It would make for a really great story on one of the gossip websites, like TMZ."

He took a deep breath, glanced down at his watch. "Okay," he said. "Time to go. We can't let him see us. I don't think he would recognize you or me or even expect us here, but don't take any chances. And, no matter what happens, don't use your cell phone. It would register any call on the Key West tower."

He paused. He handed her the neck buff, which she pulled up for a moment like an eighteenth-century highwayman's mask. Then he passed her the floppy, wide-brimmed, old-lady hat and the foghorn. She stuffed the foghorn into her satchel, stuck the hat on her head. She realized it looked ridiculous.

"We are not here now. We aren't here later. We were never here. Remember that."

Andy Candy nodded.

"Let's go look at graves," Moth said.

Moth and Andy Candy parked their bicycles on the street and slipped into the cemetery as light faded around them. Angels with flowing robes, spread wings, and trumpets lifted to their cold-stone lips, smiling naked cherubs, wilted flowers, and faded headstones. It was a haphazard spot—many of the crypts were raised, creating a maze of rectangles. There was a memorial to the men who died on the battleship *Maine*, a section devoted to Cuban freedom fighters, and gravesites belonging to men of the Confederate Navy. Some of the headstones featured black humor—"I'm just resting my eyes" and "I told you I was sick"—while others simply proclaimed: "God was good to me."

How good could He have been, Moth thought, *if this was where you ended up?*

The cemetery was slightly off the beaten tourist path, but a spot where the occasional homeless drunk passed out in the shade beside a white marble crypt or a former mental patient off his medications stared with fascination at the endless array of names of the departed. Angela Street—where their target lived—was a single narrow and untraveled lane on the west side of the cemetery.

Moth and Andy Candy ducked down near a crypt belonging to a former charter boat skipper and let night shadows flow over them. They expected either the Key West police or some sort of cemetery security guard—Moth imagined there had to be some mood-lightening joke in that job description. He didn't try one.

They stiffened when they saw a light go on in the house. Andy's breathing was shallow, and in her crouch she could feel her legs tightening up and was suddenly afraid that they wouldn't respond when she asked them to. This seemed like the stupidest thing to her. She could feel herself sliding into a type of catatonic uncertainty, where every doubt that lingered in her life threatened to roll her into a ball and kick her into a shapeless mass. She wished, in that second, that there was just one, simple, solid thing in her life. Something that wasn't complicated, confused, or elusive. She would have traded everything for one small taste of normalcy.

She stole a sideways glance at Moth and realized *no she wouldn't*. She thought curiously that he would have the oddest of lives—he would become a professor, teach history to undergraduates, attend faculty meetings, write biographies that just might make it onto best-seller lists, raise a family, and find all sorts of different levels of accomplishment and fame, and all the time he would remain silent about the night he killed a man. With justification, she hoped. That was assuming they could get away with it.

And assuming he wouldn't return to alcoholism and drunkenly spill his story to a bartender somewhere.

This was a question she couldn't answer. Nor could she any longer picture her own life to come. All she imagined was an ending, and that was this night. Dying scared her, but not nearly as much as killing did.

Moth, for his part, didn't dare look over at Andy. He wanted her to run away. He wanted her to stay at his side. He could no longer tell what was right and what was wrong. All he could do was wait for slabs of dark night to grow a bit more thick and black and humid around them. To busy himself, because the waiting part made him want to scream like a banshee, he started to remove his filthy change of clothes from his backpack.

He heard Andy inhale sharply.

"There," she whispered. "Oh my God."

Moth saw the shape of a man—*their man?*—framed in the light that poured through the front door to the small bungalow. He was going out, locking the door behind him.

This was what Moth had hoped for. "It's him," Moth said coldly.

Moth felt his tongue instantly dry. Inwardly he screamed orders to himself: *Act! Think! This is the opportunity!* He croaked, "Stick to the plan. Follow him. Don't let him see you. When he comes back, signal when he's a block or two away."

Moth was unsure whether watching a killer or waiting for a killer was more dangerous. He realized he didn't have a choice.

Andy rose stealthily, and with a ballet dancer's grace she moved through the graves, paralleling the man walking down Angela Street. Moth could just catch a glimpse of the target, unconcerned as he turned toward town. A few seconds later, Moth saw the floppy hat, following a safe distance behind, moving from shadow to shadow, staying behind the wide banyan trees whose twisted bodies guarded each sidewalk. Then he started to strip off his clothes.

48

Student #5 ate a nice piece of yellow snapper filet and washed it down with a glass of cold Chardonnay. As he ended his meal with a sweet and tangy slice of Key Lime pie and a small cup of decaf espresso, he sat at his outdoor table and watched couples walk by. It was warm and humid and the night air seemed slippery. He tried to catch bits of conversation—arguments, pleasantries, even the punch lines of jokes. There was some laughter, and more than once a *"Hurry up,"* although one of the virtues of Key West was that there was precious little to ever hurry for. From time to time young people on rented motor scooters buzzed by, and he could hear carefree voices raised above the angry-bee sounds of the bikes. It was, he thought, a typical resort-town night: loose and easy.

He paid the waitress and stepped out onto the sidewalk, half-wishing he had a cigar to celebrate with, unsure whether celebration was actually in order quite yet. Leisurely walking the half-dozen blocks home, he whistled, thinking he probably should save his tune for when he arrived at the cemetery. Salamanders scuttled away from his feet. He was inordinately pleased with his decision. He had, he thought, once again assigned purpose to his life.

Preoccupied with killing plans, Student #5 hardly registered the sound of the foghorn coming from some distance behind him. Three sharp blasts faded up into the starry night sky.

Andy Candy had her back against a banyan tree, hiding in its dark folds. She listened to the foghorn blasts dissipate around her. She did not know if the noise would carry far enough to warn Moth or not. They were *supposed* to, but she was uncertain. She patiently counted to thirty, to give the target a little more time to add distance and just in case he'd heard the warning blasts, been curious, and turned around to look. Then she stuffed the foghorn into a waste container next to a house, tossing it in with bags of trash and empty beer bottles. She did not feel like an assassin completely, but she realized she was getting closer.

She picked up her pace, a quick march, hoping to silently and anonymously close the space between her and death.

The three peals were like triggers. They seemed odd, faraway noises from some other world, but he knew what they signaled. *He's on his way and nearly home.* Moth tried to blank everything from his head except actions. *Don't think about what you're doing. Just do it.* He gave himself shrill orders, like a drill sergeant frustrated with a raw recruit:

Put the clean clothes in the backpack. Shove it next to the grave. Remember the name on the headstone, the numbered row of graves, the distance to the entry gate so you can find it again. Hurry.

Empty the bottle of vodka on the ground. Pour some of the Scotch on your chest. Drain the rest out so you have two empty bottles. Don't let the smell of the liquor intoxicate you.

Check the .357 Magnum. Fully loaded. Safety off. Hold it tight.
Run.

He sprinted amidst the gravestones, reminded of football practice in high school when cruel coaches added laps as punishment for perceived errors. He could hear his shoes slapping against the pathways and he nearly stumbled once. In one hand he had the weapon, in the other the two now-empty bottles of booze. He raced toward the house.

The killer's home had a small porch with four steps. In front of it was a little garden area, enclosed by a white thigh-height picket fence. The fence was merely decorative, not really designed to keep people out. But it created a small, concealed space. Moth vaulted the fence. A small cone of weak light marked the porch, but stopped at the top step. Ferns and large fronds filled the tiny garden. Moth dropped to his knees and shoved himself into the bushes, curling into the fetal position. He tugged his beaten baseball cap down over his head and pulled up his neck buff so his face was obscured. He held the gun in his right hand, hidden beneath his body. In his left, outstretched haphazardly, was the bottle of Scotch. The bottle of vodka he tossed a few feet away, onto the small brick walkway leading to the stairs.

Moth thought: *Well, not many people have done more auditions for appearing to be a passed-out drunk than I have.*

Then he waited. Heart racing in his chest, a pounding in his temples, his breathing shallow, sweat gathering on his forehead, the night heat weighing down upon him like a huge white-hot stone. He closed his eyes; he imagined he'd soon be blinded by anxiety anyway. His hearing, however, was sharpened, more acute than it had ever been before.

Footsteps. Closing.

He inhaled sharply. Held it.

Heard: "God damn it. Fucking drunks."

Knew—through experience: *First he will kick me.*

The gathering that night at Redeemer One seemed distracted, impatient. Susan Terry shifted in her seat as one after the other regular attendees rose, proclaimed their days of sobriety, spoke about their latest struggles. She heard the usual successes and failures, hopes mingled with sadness. It was a typical night, she thought, except for the undercurrent of unease. More than once she caught the others staring quizzically in her direction, anticipating the moment when it would be her turn to share.

Sandy, the corporate lawyer, was finishing up. She was telling a variation on her usual theme: whether her teenage children could learn to trust her again. *Trust* was a euphemism, Susan understood, for *love*.

The woman's story seemed to fade away, losing color and heft, and finally she stalled. Susan saw her glance first at the philosophy professor, then at Fred the engineer, meeting eyes with just about everyone in the room before landing on her.

"Enough of my usual bullshit," Sandy said briskly. "I think we need to hear from Susan." There was a brief murmur of assent.

"Susan?" said the assistant priest running the gathering.

Susan rose up, a little unsteadily. She had prepared all sorts of explanations and excuses, even considered mingling some fiction into her latest story—all designed to follow Moth's admonition to be memorable this night. She had not formed the word *alibi* in her head—although as an expert in criminal law, she knew that was precisely what she was hoping to create. But as she looked out, she suddenly realized how silly everything she had planned to say would sound.

Still, she was obligated to begin. "Hello, my name is Susan and I'm an addict. I have a couple of days sober now, but I don't know if this time counts, because of the painkillers the doctors prescribed for me . . ." She gestured toward her broken arm.

"You shouldn't take anything. If it hurts, suck it up and tough it out," Fred the engineer said, cutting in with an unfamiliar harshness.

Susan was unsure how to continue. As she started to stumble for words, the philosophy professor stifled her with a furious swipe of his hand, as he might have in restoring order to an unruly classroom.

"Where," he asked sharply, "is Moth?"

Andy Candy broke into a sprint.

Whatever was happening in front of the house on darkened Angela

Street, she knew she had to be there. Her imagination filled to overflow—the killer they hunted was probably armed, the killer they hunted was far more clever than they, the killer they hunted was practiced, astute, experienced, unlikely to be taken by surprise by a couple of amateurs at the game of murder. She pictured Moth bloody, shot—no, stabbed—no, ripped somehow limb from limb, breathing his last. He was a *history student,* for Christ's sake—what did Moth know about killing? She—at the least—had watched her father the vet put dozens of animals *to sleep*—the nice way of saying *to death.* And she had been at his side when all the life support hoses, wires, and attachments had been shut down.

That wasn't all: She had, just a short time ago, lain beneath a bright clinic light, head back, eyes half-closed, barely hearing the nurses and the physician as life was taken out of her. It suddenly dawned on Andy Candy that she was the one who knew what to do. She nearly panicked, thinking: *I should have been in charge. I should have planned this.* She knew she had to get there, as fast as possible, to help guide Moth before he got killed.

"Moth is . . ." Susan Terry hesitated. She looked around the room. She swallowed hard, and said, "Moth is on his own. He wants to confront the man he believes killed his uncle."

She remained standing. But the people in the room exploded around her. She was inundated with cries, some as indistinct as the simple "What the hell!" or as scathing as "You let him do *what?*"

When the initial flurry of responses seemed to slow, Susan tried to respond: "He didn't give me much choice. I wanted him to go to the authorities, help create a prosecutable case against the man. But he was headstrong and determined, and he cut me out of the decision . . ."

This last bit seemed decidedly weak.

" 'Determined'?" Fred the engineer asked. His voice was cold and unforgiving.

"Haven't you learned anything about addiction by coming to these meetings?" This from Sandy.

Susan looked confused.

"We all depend on honesty and each other. It's not the only way to defeat addiction, but it's an important way. And you abandoned Moth? Let him go off on his own? Why didn't you just hand him a bottle or maybe pour out a couple of lines? It would kill him just the same," Sandy said in a voice filled with contempt.

"The whole point of coming here is for all of us to help each other *avoid* risks," Fred said sharply. "And you've let Moth—one of us, for crying out loud!—go off all alone? What were you thinking?"

Susan was about to say something about Andy Candy. But she believed that Moth's need to avenge his uncle's death was solely his. Her voice wavered as she spoke. "Timothy is right. Successfully prosecuting this man—this killer—would be well-nigh impossible. There. That's my professional opinion. And pursuing this man . . . well, it's kept Timothy sober. It's . . ."

She stopped there. What she was saying was either incredibly true or incredibly false. She no longer knew.

The philosophy professor jumped in.

"What do you think is happening with Moth right now?" he demanded.

"Right now?" She was suddenly aware that she was sweating. She felt like a high-intensity light was shining in her eyes and blinding her. She whispered her reply:

"He's facing a killer."

The room exploded again.

The first was a little toe nudge.

Don't move. Just groan a bit. Wait for it.

The second was a sharper kick.

"Get up, damn it. Get the hell off my property."

Another fake groan. Finger on the trigger. Two choices: He will kick a third time or else he will bend down and shake you. Either way, be ready.

"Come on, let's go . . ."

Hand on my shoulder. A hard tug.

Moth rocked over suddenly, changing from crumpled sidewalk drunk to determined assassin. His left hand dropped the empty bottle of Scotch and shot up to grab the front of the killer's shirt, pulling him off-balance and dragging him down to one knee. The man grunted in surprise, but Moth's right hand shot out, with the pistol extended, thrusting it up under the killer's chin. "Don't move," he said quietly. Despite his calm voice, his tongue was thickening and fear was racing through his core.

The killer tried to lurch back, but Moth held him steady. "I said don't move," he repeated. He continued to sound far more in control than he really was.

Out of the corner of his eye, he saw Andy Candy running up to them. Holding the pistol to the man's throat, Moth maneuvered first to his knees, then to his feet. The two of them stood up together, like a loving couple moving onto a dance floor as slow music starts to play.

"Inside," Moth said. For the first time, he looked directly at the killer. The man had a slightly bemused look on his face. "Do you recognize me?" Moth asked.

"Oh yes," Student #5 replied. His voice was low, even, and utterly without fear or panic despite the barrel pressed up beneath his chin. "You're the young man I should already have killed but now is going to die tonight."

49

Think like a killer. Easy to imagine. Hard to actually do. *"The young man who will die tonight?"* *I guess that's me. Well, here goes,* Moth thought, responding with significantly more bravado than he truly felt: "Well, maybe yes. Maybe no. We'll see, won't we."

The two stayed locked together, the gun barrel pressing hard into Student #5's throat. *A smart killer would just pull the trigger and run,* Moth told himself, then decided that was wrong. *Maybe that's exactly what a stupid killer would do.* He didn't know. His academic mind was struck with the notion that every action presented multiple possibilities with dozens of potential outcomes. Fascination and fear mingled within him—electric and ice. Still, he stuck to the design he'd come up with, having little to no idea whether it actually made sense from an assassin's perspective. He knew he would find out soon enough.

"Inside," he demanded again.

Student #5 smiled wryly. "You want me to invite you into my home? You think I'm that polite? Why would I do that?"

"You don't have a choice," Moth said, mustering toughness.

"Really?" Student #5 replied. Mocking. "There are always choices. I would think more than most people, a history student would know that."

Student #5 grinned a little. This hid the quick churning in his head. It had taken him half a dozen deep breaths to overcome his initial surprise at the gun's being pressed into his throat, then his realizing who wielded it. But yoga and Zen training had managed to stifle shock and replace it with calm. He knew he had to unsettle The Nephew quickly and change the dynamics of death. Then he would see how to seize the upper hand.

Student #5 started to envision scenarios, opportunities, and ideas— seeing things as if he were watching a drama being played out on a movie screen with an unruly and frantic horror film audience shouting directions impotently at characters who could not hear them. He knew one thing for certain: Every second that The Nephew delayed pulling the trigger, he grew stronger and the man with the gun grew weaker. Oddly, confidence surged through Student #5.

"Where's the house key?" Moth insisted.

"Okay. If you think that's the right thing to do, who am I to stand in your way?" Student #5 said with a small snort. "Right front pocket."

Moth nodded at Andy Candy, who stepped to the side and reached into the pocket, feeling around for the key.

"Careful there, young lady," Student #5 said with a dry laugh. "We haven't been properly introduced, and this seems a bit intimate."

Andy Candy listened to each tone in the killer's voice as she seized the house key. It was a little like hearing a distant song being sung, and she tried to recall every note from their prior conversation. "Yes we have," she replied. Her voice seemed hurried and high-pitched, a band being stretched tightly. "You introduced yourself on the phone."

She stepped past him, the key in hand.

"There just might be an alarm on that door," Student #5 pointed out as Andy opened it up. "Fail to hit the right code and maybe the cops will be here in a minute or two. That would make a mess of whatever you have planned for tonight, wouldn't it?"

Andy turned to him. She shook her head. "No," she said with fake confidence. "Calling the police for help? That wouldn't be you, would it?"

Student #5 didn't reply. Moth shifted position, moving the gun barrel around the killer's neck, and then giving him a small shove in the back. "Inside," Moth repeated.

"An interesting approach," Student #5 replied. "But you don't know what might be waiting in there, do you?" This was a thinly veiled reference to the booby-trapped exploding fake meth lab in Charlemont, but immediately he shifted the anxiety to other fears: "Maybe I have a big, loyal dog just waiting to rip your throat out."

"No," Andy repeated firmly, "that's also not who you are." She put the key into the lock. "You like doing things alone, don't you?" She turned the key and opened the door, not waiting for an answer. She did not see the shadow of anger pass over Student #5's face, nor the sudden clenching of his right hand into a fist. Student #5 did not like being categorized, and even more, he hated being categorized accurately.

"Move," Moth said, pushing Student #5 in the small of the back. Still linked by the pressure of the gun barrel, they entered the house, passing through the weak porch light. Moth wondered for an instant whether anyone might see them. He hadn't considered *accident* in his approach. A passerby noticing the gun. Calling the police. Disaster. The old rhyme came to him: *For want of a nail, the shoe was lost . . .*

Like a maître d' at a fine restaurant, Andy Candy held the door for the two of them, ushering them inside. Then she pushed ahead, as Moth jabbed the gun barrel into Student #5's neck at the same time that he steadied him with a hand on his shoulder.

"The living room is to the right," Student #5 said. "We'll be comfortable in there . . ."

For a man with a handgun being held to the back of his head, his voice was surprisingly even and collected. It might have been Moth's first indication of whom he truly was up against. Fantasy—*I can handle confronting a serial killer.* Versus reality—*Who do I think I am?* Outside of the weapon in his hand, he had little else that might be considered an advantage.

". . . until someone dies," Student #5 completed his sentence.

Andy Candy flicked on lights, then went to the windows and closed the wooden shutter shades. *Privacy,* she thought. *What else does murder need?*

The furor inside Redeemer One had increased in tempo. Angry addicts, infuriated alcoholics, raised voices, and relentless questions pummeled Susan Terry. She remained rooted in front of the gathering, like a bad comic being booed by a nightclub crowd. Inwardly she reeled.

"I simply don't understand how you could let Timothy try to face down a killer. You're the goddamn professional here. You know the danger he's putting himself in!"

This came from a quiet architect with a predilection for morphine-based drugs. He hadn't opened his mouth once in all the time that she'd been attending meetings, but now he suddenly seemed genuinely incensed.

"Right. Jesus," said a dentist. "Does Timothy really know anything about what he's up against? I can't believe—"

Susan interrupted. "He's more capable than you're giving him credit for."

"Well, that's just great. *Sure* he is," Fred the engineer said sarcastically. He followed this with, "Fine. Dandy. *Kee-rist!* What a lousy, flimsy excuse." He turned in his seat, looking toward the others, away from Susan, as he raised a hand and pointed directly at her and said, "If *she* had gone to confront this guy, she would have taken an entire fucking SWAT team with her."

A flurry of *"That's right!"* and *"No shit!"* replies flooded the room. The priest who ran the meetings tried to interject some calm. "Folks, listen . . . Susan isn't to blame . . ."

"Bullshit," Sandy the lawyer blurted, slicing off the mealy-mouthed priest instantly.

"What," the philosophy professor demanded, "do you—in your *professional* opinion . . . ,*"* this word spoken at Susan with utter contempt, ". . . think Timothy's chances of surviving this night are?"

This question, which went directly to the core of the matter, quieted the group. Coming from a man so attuned to oblique interpretations of obscurity, it carried even more weight.

Susan hesitated before replying: "Not good."

She could hear several regulars gasp. "Define *not good* please," the professor cautiously continued.

Around the room, addicts bent forward. She could feel electricity around her, as if each word she spoke was plugged into a socket. She looked at eyes that burrowed into her, and she realized that Timothy Warner meant much more to each of them than she'd ever imagined. The power of looking at Timothy Warner and seeing their younger selves in the mirror was profound. He was little more than a child, and he'd been lost—just as they once had been. His recovery was a part of their recovery. His life—*one day at a time*—gave each of their lives an added meaning and gave each of them an added incentive. This went beyond loyalty, into some realm of devotion. Timothy straightening out his life meant they could continue to keep their lives straightened out. Timothy finding love, a career, and satisfaction beyond the bottle meant they had found it too, or had reconstituted something they'd once had. Timothy surviving meant *they* might survive. His struggles mirrored their struggles. His youth gave them hope.

And all that was in jeopardy this night.

"By *not good* I mean exactly that. *Not good.* He's up against a smart, skilled, professional, and completely remorseless sociopath who has killed perhaps a half-dozen people, although that number is open to debate. An expert in killing."

The room erupted again.

"Should I sit there?" Student #5 asked lightly. "That's my favorite chair."

"Yes," Moth replied.

"Wait a second," Andy Candy interrupted.

She went over to a thickly upholstered armchair. She removed the seat, checking beneath it. Then she got down on her knees and inspected the back. *No hidden gun or knife.* There was a small side table with a lamp and a vase with dried flowers on it. She moved this several feet away, so that even with a lunge Student #5 wouldn't be able to reach anything. *Can a glass vase be a weapon?* She imagined the answer was *yes*.

Student #5 held his hands up and waited, watching what Andy Candy was doing. "The young lady is being wise," he said. "Thinking ahead. Tell me, Timothy, have you really thought this through?"

Moth did not reply, other than to grunt, "Okay. Sit down."

"Moth, are you sure he's not armed?" Andy asked.

Jesus, Moth swore to himself. It hadn't occurred to him to check.

"Frisk him carefully," he said, keeping the gun at the man's neck.

Andy moved behind Student #5 and ran her hands over his pockets. She removed his wallet, felt beneath his arms, checked out his shoes and socks, and even patted down his crotch area.

"Now we're definitely getting to know one another better," he said, laughing, as if she was tickling him. She wished she had some clever rejoinder that would put him in his place, but none leapt to her lips.

"Too bad," Student #5 continued, "that you decided to be here tonight. You know, now that I think about it, there's still time for you to leave. You can get away. Be safe. Not sorry."

A cliché from a killer, Moth thought. *Remarkable.* He didn't dare look at Andy Candy for fear that what the killer suggested just might make sense to her.

"I'm not—" Andy started.

"Think carefully about what you're doing," Student #5 interrupted. "Decisions you make in the next few minutes will last a lifetime." He gestured toward the chair, and Moth gave him a small shove in that direction.

Student #5 sat down, ignoring the pistol being pointed at him, fixing his glance on Andy. "You don't seem like the type to ignore good advice, Andrea, regardless of what the source is," he continued. His using her first name familiarly felt chilling to her. "You might keep that in mind. There's still time for you. Not much, but a little."

Student #5 thought, *Even a little wedge between the two of them is good. Play upon uncertainty. Tonight I know what I'm doing even without a weapon. But they don't, even if they do. So, who's really armed here?* This formulation made him grin.

Moth kept his gun trained on the killer. Andy Candy realized Moth was still standing, looking uncomfortable and out of place, so she took a chair from a corner of the room and placed it across from the killer for Moth to sit in, a few feet away.

Like a couple on a first date that wasn't going well, Moth and the killer eyed each other. Moth thought: *Duct tape. I should have purchased duct tape, so I could bind his hands and feet. What else did I forget to bring?*

"Actually . . ." the philosophy professor said deliberately, classroom style, "the pressing issue before us is simple: What can we do right at this precise moment to help Timothy?"

Silence filled the room.

"Wherever he is, whatever he's doing," the professor added.

The Redeemer One room remained quiet.

"Ideas?" the professor asked.

"Yes, God damn it, we need to send help," insisted Fred the engineer. "Right fucking away."

"It isn't that simple," Susan said. She didn't elaborate. She continued to stand in front of the group, but they were no longer encircling her with their gaze, turning instead to one another, before blurting out possibilities.

Sandy the lawyer snorted. "Let's call the police right now. No delays. Presumably Susan knows where to send them."

She dug her cell phone out of a large Gucci purse, and held it up.

"The wrong person will get arrested," Susan said quietly. "You don't get it."

The woman hesitated, finger poised over the dialing screen. "Get what? What do you mean?"

"It's Timothy who is the killer tonight."

Again the room burst into objections. *"No way"* and *"Don't be crazy"* and *"That's stupid"* filled the area, a torrential downpour of disagreement.

"It's Timothy who has the weapon and the motive and is breaking the law tonight. *Premeditated.* You all know that word. We're not talking about the bad guy—right now, he's innocent. So who do you think the cops will take into custody when they show up? The person who owns the house, or the person who broke in, armed and dangerous? That's assuming Timothy surrenders promptly. I wouldn't want to make that assumption."

"Well, perhaps," Sandy countered. "But a call from you would direct them to the right guy . . ."

"Without evidence? With only wild and crazy suppositions? I tell them, 'Hey, don't arrest the guy bent on murder and revenge. Arrest the other guy.' They won't do that. And even if they did—how could they hold him? And if they can't hold him, I know one thing for certain."

"What's that?"

"He will disappear."

"Ridiculous. He can be tracked, the same way that Timothy tracked him."

"No, not necessarily. That was dogged persistence and more than a little damn fool luck. And this guy won't make the same mistake a second time. He will vanish. It can be done; I would wager he's prepared to do just that. Actually, it's not that hard. So, count on one thing: Whatever happens to Timothy tonight, if the man who killed his uncle is still alive in the next few hours, he will be long gone."

The room silenced again. Susan could hear breathing. She added softly, "And that's assuming whoever we try to send gets there in time."

"We need to call someone," the dentist said.

Another pause. It was like the Redeemer One regulars' sudden silences were weighted, heavy, iron. People were sorting through possibilities.

"What," said Fred the engineer, "if you go?"

"He had the opportunity to include me." Susan shook her head. "Didn't take it. In fact, kicked me out of whatever he was planning." She thought that was *mostly* honest. But the word forming in her head at the same time was *coward*. She suspected that would be an accurate description of her behavior by the end of the night. Irony encapsulated her. The best outcome for her depended on her doing nothing. It would give her excuses, *deniability*, which were crucial if she was going to rescue her own career and her own future. There were felonies littering her world—and starting to avoid them was her priority. Of course, she understood, that *might* mean someone was dying that night.

"So what? We should protect him—even if we're protecting him from himself. That's what we try to do here, right?"

There was a murmur of assent.

"What if we all go?"

"Too late for that," Susan said.

Another silence. Then the philosophy professor said, in a cold, very hard voice:

"What is it that it is *not* too late to do?"

Susan hesitated. "I think," Susan spoke out slowly, "we should trust Timothy to do what is right."

She did not offer a definition of *what is right* for any of the people gathered at Redeemer One. For a second, she thought she might be able to walk away at that moment, but before she could move, another wave of furious obscenities and outrage surged through the room.

Moth sat across from the killer. An ironic thought pressed through him: *This is like sitting across from Uncle Ed. Same age. Same stakes.* The gun in his hand seemed to be heavier than he recalled its being earlier in the evening. He knew he'd completed the first phase of murder—now he had to move quickly to the next step.

"Andy," he said, trying to maintain toughness and determination in his voice, "why don't you give this place a bit of a search, see what you can find."

"Okay," she said.

Student #5 smiled at her. Teacher and struggling student. "Don't touch anything," he said with a helpful tone.

She stopped, looked hard at him, as if she didn't understand what he'd said.

"Fingerprints," he continued. "Are you sweating? That would leave a little DNA behind. Should be wearing latex gloves. I notice you are wearing that most attractive floppy stay-out-of-the-sun hat. No, no, don't take it off. It might pull out a stray hair. You don't want to leave a hair anywhere, because that can be traced to you . . ."

He turned back to Moth. "Those bottles . . . made you seem like just another Key West drunk sleeping it off in the bushes—I liked that touch. Clever. Showed enterprise. But fingerprints? Did you think of that? And what about the moist ground of the plant area—did you leave a shoe print in there? Whoa, that would be bad, too. Cops can identify the tread styles of almost any pair of shoes, and I bet yours are pretty common. And did you know that the dirt here in Key West has a different composition than other places? So a forensic scientist examining the soles of your shoes might be able to link you to that exact spot."

This last bit, Student #5 knew, was a stretch. Probably a lie, but it sure sounded good, and he was pleased with it. He assumed that most of what The Nephew and The Girlfriend knew about murder and subsequent investigations had been gleaned from television shows not known for their accuracy.

Andy Candy stole a glance down at her hands. She felt like a soldier walking through a minefield. She wondered if she would betray herself and Moth simply by allowing a droplet of sweat to fall to the floor. She didn't know what part of her body, or Moth's, might ruin their lives. No fear is worse than the fear associated with sudden recognition that one is treading in dangerous black waters far over one's head. Fear can create exhaustion, confusion, and doubt. All of these things flooded Andy at that moment, and she wanted to scream.

Moth didn't know why he said it right at that moment, but he did, very calmly: "Andy, don't worry. It'll be okay. He's just talking and it doesn't mean anything. Just take a look around."

Moth's voice helped her. She wasn't sure whether he was actually *in charge,* but it sounded like he was. "Okay," she said, stifling the desire to scream. "Give me a minute or two."

"So, we're just going to sit here and wait?" Student #5 asked sardonically. He shrugged his shoulders.

"Why not?" Moth answered. "Are you in a rush to die?"

50

Student #5 understood completely that he was in the midst of a deadly game, but it was one he was well trained for. Murder is psychology at its most elemental, as complex as chess, as simple as checkers. It has undercurrents of emotion at every stage, right up through the actual act. It can be sudden, and it can be sophisticated. It can be rash and impulsive, or cautiously planned. It can be driven by psychosis or post-traumatic stress disorder. It has as many variations as there are people and angers. This was a lesson he'd learned both as a killer and as a student of psychiatry.

Student #5 knew that he had to outplay the budding historian seated across from him. *Sometimes people stare at a gun barrel and know it is inevitable—there is no dodging that bullet. Not this night.* He thought: *This night: One death. Probably two, when I kill The Girlfriend as well.*

In his mind's eye, he could see the struggle and see the gun flying free. He imagined the sudden feel of it in his hand and the explosive jerk upward as he pulled the trigger: a happy and familiar memory. Then he would take his time—two hands on the handle, shooter's stance—and finish the night. His belief, his instinct, and his desire would all have led to the scenario he absolutely knew would play out.

He was already formulating an exit.

Leave everything behind except death. Say goodbye to Stephen Lewis, just as you did to Blair Munroe. Fast drive north. Flight from Miami. Go someplace different and unexpected, Cleveland or Minneapolis, then take another flight. Phoenix? Seattle? Hang in a hotel for a day or two. See some sights and have more than one good meal before heading back east in a leisurely way to Manhattan. Get swallowed up in New York City. Immediately begin work on a new set of backup identities. Start anew. I think California might be nice. San Francisco, not LA.

Moth's imagination was ricocheting wildly, uncontrollably. It was as if his thoughts were quivering. He was afraid his body would twitch, so he placed his index finger against the trigger guard of the .357 Magnum. He didn't want to fire the gun accidentally. His finger seemed stiff anyway, like a broken piece of machinery, and he doubted that it would work. His muscles had turned rubbery and useless. For so many days, miles, and obsessions, all his focus had been on first identifying the man who killed his uncle, then finding him, then finding him again, then getting the drop on him, like in some Old West dry-gulch ambush.

Murder is almost always about the past—but this was also about the future. It had been easy to lie on his bed in the darkness, thinking. *Kill him kill him kill him.*

Now that he'd arrived at the *kill him* moment, Moth realized that everything he'd done had brought him to this spot—but not beyond. He remembered Susan Terry's warning: *Can you pull that trigger?*

I think so. I hope so.

Maybe.

And this was a problem that had now frozen his gun hand into an unmanageable, unmovable block. He took a deep breath and aimed down the sight on the barrel, squinting his eye a little, training the gun on the killer's chest. Then he asked: "Why did you kill my uncle?" *Get that answer,* he thought. *The answer will tell you what to do next.*

Moth slid directly into a maelstrom of uncertainty. The man across from him doubtlessly could have told him that this was a poor realm for killing.

Obscenities and fury finally started to dwindle in the air around Susan Terry, like the final spent drops of a hard rainstorm. She stayed quiet until the atmosphere in Redeemer One turned into a sullen silence. "Well," she finally said, "nothing to do except wait and see what happens."

Waiting, she knew, was bordering on a felony. The *right* thing to do would be to immediately notify authorities. It was also the *wrong* thing to do. Susan was maneuvering on a razor's edge of legal culpability. She didn't even want to think about moral culpability.

"So, you propose—based on your legal education, familiarity with Timothy and understanding of the situation he's in, and all other relevant factors—we all just sit around and see what happens?" asked the philosophy professor in his didactic fashion.

"I suppose you could put it that way," Susan replied.

The professor stood up just as he would have had he been starting his addiction testimony, except that this time he addressed the gathering differently. "That is simply unacceptable," he said. Then he added, "Does anyone disagree?"

A low murmur filled the room: indiscernible words that amounted to a single *no.*

"If we cannot help Timothy do whatever he is doing tonight," the professor continued, "then we must help him when he survives."

Sounds of assent filled the room.

"And I believe he will survive," the professor continued, his voice ringing with unfounded confidence. "Just like all of us will overcome all the demons and flaws that brought us here to this place tonight."

Susan looked around. No one disagreed with the professor. In fact, she thought, the room was filled with a certain revival-tent kind of *Praise Jesus!* passion.

"Timothy is our responsibility," the professor said. "Like it or not." He put these last words at Susan like daggers.

"Just as he has been there for us, we have to be there for him," the professor added firmly. "That is what coming to Redeemer One is all about. This is where we are safe with our problems, where we support each other. So, tonight, I think Redeemer One and what it means for all of us goes well beyond the walls of this room."

"Damn straight," said Sandy the corporate lawyer. "Well put." The professor took a deep breath, paused to adjust his eyeglasses, and licked his lips. "If he comes out of this alive, then we must figure out how to protect him."

This was greeted with nodding heads.

"We have some resources," the professor added.

"Resources?" Susan blurted.

"Yes," he replied, turning abruptly toward her and pointing directly at her. "You, for one."

Susan did not know how to answer. Sandy rose to her feet and interjected rapidly: "Either you are a part of this gathering or you are not. What happens here is recovery. What happens out there . . . ," she waved toward the door, ". . . is not. It seems to me that you need to make up your mind. Are you an addict or an ex-addict?"

Susan hesitated.

"Do you want to ever come back here again?" Sandy asked.

Susan's mind churned. She had not considered this question.

Fred the engineer rose to his feet, standing shoulder to shoulder with the professor, reaching over and taking Sandy by the hand. "For starters," he said, wry grin on his face, "I think we can all agree on one thing . . ." He slowed his delivery, staring hard at each member of the gathering before looking for a long time at Susan Terry. "If someone—like a policeman— were to ask, I think we'd all say that Timothy was here with us tonight."

No one said anything, but each member of the group at Redeemer One stood up, even the priest.

Andy Candy wanted to sit, or maybe lean up against a wall, perhaps even lower herself to the hardwood floor and close her eyes. At the same time, she wanted to run in place, do sit-ups and push-ups, leap into the air or find a piece of jump rope and use it while singing some childhood exercise rhyme: *"Blue bells, cockle shells, easy Ivy over"* . . . She was exhausted and energized, terrified, yet calm.

She moved stealthily through the kitchen and saw nothing but kitchen. Into the bathroom, seeing nothing but bathroom. It was a small house, barely larger than an apartment, with only two bedrooms down a windowless corridor. She opened closets; the only one that held anything was in the master bedroom, and it contained just a minimal amount of clothing on hangers. She took some tissue paper and used that to cover her fingers as she opened drawers and poked around. *A killer's underwear, T-shirts, and socks.* She didn't know whether the tissue would prevent her from leaving any traces of her presence behind. She doubted it, but amateur hour that it was, she could think of no other approach.

Andy didn't want to be scared, but every minute that passed, fear grew within her—not just because they were lingering in a killer's home, but because she could find *nothing* that said *anything* about who the man seated in his favorite chair in the living room actually was.

She hadn't exactly known what to expect. Perhaps a closet filled with weapons? A wall of paintings devoted to killers, from Caligula to Vlad the Impaler through John Dillinger and Ted Bundy? She had no idea what she was searching for, although she knew her search was somehow necessary. She ransacked her memory, going to movie images, popular novels, television and theater, but couldn't recall anything actually set in murderers' houses that displayed items that unequivocally stated who they were and what they did. *Please, there must be something.* It wasn't like expecting to see law books on a lawyer's desk, or medical texts lining the walls of a doctor's office. There was no architect's diploma and certificate on the wall. There wasn't even a restaurant menu hung up prominently.

The last room was set up as a guest room. *Did killers invite friends to stay over?* She stepped inside quietly. There was a futon with a bright multicolored print cover, a small desk, and a chair. It was sparse, almost monastic. She was about to turn away when she noticed the laptop computer.

There's something, she thought. She looked around and saw a wireless printer stuck in a corner on the floor. There were a few stray sheets of paper next to it.

She approached these objects as if they were sharp-edged and dangerous.

"Why did I kill your uncle? What makes you think I did?"

"Don't screw around. Just tell me the truth."

"You believe I'm capable of murder, but not capable of lying to you?"

"I don't think people staring at a loaded pistol tend to lie," Moth replied.

"Ah, you're wrong about that, Timothy. That's precisely when people do lie. Enthusiastically. Flagrantly. Pleading and begging. Lies and lies and lies. But, leaving that aside, why would you believe the truth would help you?" The killer continued to speak in a bemused voice. He pushed forward slightly, so he was perched on the edge of the chair. It unsettled Moth immensely, increased his anxiety. He could feel sweat gathering on the back of his neck. He tried to impose a chill into his replies, to hide his shakiness.

"I'm the one asking the questions," Moth said stiffly. He moved the pistol barrel slightly to underscore his point. He thought for a moment that he sounded like he was caught up in some John Ford Western from the '40s. *"Smile when you say that, pardner . . ."*

The two were seated a few feet apart. The only light in the room was from a single lamp on a table that left most of the room in shadows. Moth thought every word spoken increased the darkness. A paddle fan rotated lazily above them, stirring air that seemed preternaturally calm.

Student #5 stared hard at him. He kept his eyes lifted beyond the angle of the gun barrel, almost as if he could ignore it and make it disappear. "All right," he said. "I didn't kill your uncle."

"Stop the crap, I know—"

"What do you know, Timothy?" Student #5 said, turning abruptly harsh, emphasizing every syllable of Moth's name: *Tim-O-See.* "You don't know anything. But let me make this simple, maybe even simple enough for a history student to understand. Or simple enough for a drunk to understand: *I didn't kill your uncle.*"

Moth thought he might be dizzy. The room seemed to spin, but he said, "You might consider this: That explanation is the only thing between you and dying."

Once again, Moth surprised himself with the determination in his voice. He had no idea where it came from, and it seemed a little like it was someone else speaking. It was all entirely false.

"Your uncle killed himself," Student #5 said.

Susan Terry looked at the group of alcoholics and addicts surrounding her, standing shoulder to shoulder, some with linked hands, in what to any outside observer would have appeared to be a prayer. But she knew it had nothing to do with asking the Almighty for help. She understood that she was being asked to examine her route forward. She could join or she could walk away, but failing to make a decision was not an option. It was as if she could see two entirely different lives mapped out in front of her. Both were deeply flawed. Both were dangerous. Both were filled with compromise and pain. Indulge her weakness. Try to find her strength. As simple as that. As complex as that.

She inhaled sharply.

Choose now! she screamed to herself.

Moth sputtered his reply: "That's crazy."

"Do I act like a crazy person?" Student #5 asked.

"No. But I know you killed—"

Student #5 shrugged, a motion that interrupted Moth. "I was there. Perhaps I even pulled the trigger. But your uncle killed himself."

Student #5 hid a smile. Every bit of confusion and doubt he could sow was a point scored in the psychological game. He was reminded of a scene in a movie—an Oscar-winning film from long before Timothy Warner was born. In *The French Connection,* the actor Gene Hackman played a police detective named Popeye Doyle. He would demand of suspects, "Did you ever pick your feet in Poughkeepsie?" It was a wonderful, nonsensical, utterly incomprehensible question. It rendered the people being interrogated speechless with astonished doubt as they tried to sort through their confusion to an answer, never having been in Poughkeepsie, New York, and having no idea what was meant by picking one's feet.

Student #5 was using a variation on the same theme.

"You killed the others, too," Moth objected.

"No. They, too, killed themselves."

"That makes no sense."

"It depends on your perspective. You would agree that actions have consequences?"

"Yes."

Student #5 lifted his hands in a dismissive gesture. "What they did to me in the past defined their futures. They killed me. Or killed who I was and what I was meant to be. Same thing as outright murder. In doing that, they effectively wrote their own death warrants. Same thing as killing themselves, no?"

The logic of revenge and murder twisted in Moth's head. He could *see* that argument. He wanted to disagree, but could not.

"So, Timothy, your uncle Ed merely paid the price for an obligation he'd owed for years. No more, no less. As a psychiatrist, he understood that completely in his last moments."

Moth felt pummeled. The killer's rationale was spoken with such undebatable precision that he was at a loss for a reply. He felt weak and suddenly even more afraid, about not only what he'd done, but what he was going to do. He teetered on a familiar brink of doubt, one that usually resulted in a trip to a bar and enough alcohol to make him forget why he was doing what he was doing. He knew he had to change the direction of the conversation. *If you want to kill him,* he thought, *best to create something different.*

His mind was racing through possible replies just as Andy Candy walked into the back of the room. She had a single sheet of paper in her hand.

"Kill him," she said shakily. "Kill him now."

51

Don't think. Take aim. Pull the trigger.

He didn't act.

Whatever her sudden reasons were for saying what she had, he knew she was right. He should fire the gun, grab Andy Candy by the hand, and flee. Never look back.

Moth immediately regretted not instantly doing what Andy told him to. A part of him understood that he needed to act impulsively in order to kill. That moment had come and gone, and he was wildly unsure whether he could re-create it. *Am I a killer?* he demanded of himself. *Well, not too long ago I was doing a fine job of killing myself. Of course, that's not the same thing. Is it?* Wrapped in conflicted thoughts, Moth caught a quiver in the man's languid, easygoing facade. For a moment, the killer across from him had been scared. *That's something,* he told himself. But what that *something* was he didn't know.

Andy Candy stepped farther into the room. She moved slowly, as if reluctant to get too close. Her voice was stretched thin. "Kill him now," she repeated, but this time softly, as if she was fading beneath the man's stare.

Moth quietly asked, "Andy, what is it?"

She seemed to be staggering. She lurched next to Moth and thrust a single sheet of paper in front of him.

It was a printout of a page taken from the "Prosecutor's Directory" at the Miami-Dade State Attorney's Office. Major Crimes. Susan Terry, Chief Assistant. A nice, full-color photograph, not unlike a high school yearbook picture, accompanied by her bio and a list of some of her more prominent cases. It was the sort of page that exists on almost every such website. There was little special about it other than one obvious detail: It was in the possession of a killer.

"It's Susan," Andy said shakily. Then she added, accurately: "But it's also us."

Moth understood its implications. Something that was speculation had changed into a reality. He looked over at the killer. "Jesus," he said. "You've already started."

Before replying, Student #5 took a second to assess the situation. *The Nephew hesitates. The Girlfriend is disintegrating. He clings to doubt. She is scared. Stay calm. Your moment will arrive.* When he spoke, his voice had dropped some of the toying pretense. Now it was ice cold, and each word was as sharp as a weapon.

"I like to know who I'm up against," Student #5 said.

There was silence. Moth was aware that Andy was breathing heavily at his side.

"Do you even know who I am?" Student #5 asked.

Moth's head reeled. He thought he'd learned a great deal, but right at this moment, he believed he knew nothing.

Andy Candy stammered a reply: "Your name is Stephen Lewis. You've killed more than a half-dozen people . . ."

"No," Student #5 said evenly. "Stephen Lewis has killed no one."

She stepped forward slightly, waving her hand as if she could dismiss this reply. "We were there, when the trailer exploded and—"

"That man is dead. The man who lived there."

"We were there when you shot Doctor Hogan . . ."

"The man who performed that murder is dead."

"When Moth's uncle died . . ."

"All dead."

Andy's voice started to get frantic. She waved her arms. "These are bull-shit arguments that don't mean anything . . ."

"You are wrong, Miss Martine. You are completely mistaken. They mean everything."

She stopped mid-wave.

"The man you see before you has no connection to any of those deaths. Right now, I am Stephen Lewis, happy-go-lucky, never-hurt-a-fly drug dealer who made a single big score like more than one person down here, walked away, and is now an independently wealthy resident of Angela Street in Key West and coincidentally a completely law-abiding citizen of the state of Florida. I'm a member of Greenpeace and a reliable contributor to progressive causes. You have absolutely no right or reason to kill me."

"We know who you really are," Moth said. Some of the frantic tones he'd heard in Andy's voice had crept into his.

"And you imagine that will justify what you do?"

"Yes."

"Think twice, history student."

He couldn't even think once.

The room grew quiet, before Student #5 said: "I won before you even arrived here. I won every step of the way—because I was right about what I did, and you are wrong. You don't have any choices left, Timothy. The gun in your hand is useless, because if you pull that trigger and try to kill me, you will take your life just as effectively as you take mine. You are the criminals here tonight, not me. This state still has the death penalty. But maybe you will only go to prison for the remainder of your life. Poor choice, that."

Again silence. Moth realized that the killer was saying almost exactly what Susan the prosecutor had said. The same warning. Opposite sources.

"And even were you to get up in court and claim you killed me out of a sense of revenge—well, can't you just hear someone telling a jury: *'What right did he have to take the law into his own hands?'*"

409

Moth didn't reply, at first; he thought hard, then said: "You took the law into your hands."

"No I didn't. The people I pursued didn't break any law. They were guilty of something far greater. They made their choices and then they paid their debt. That's not your situation, is it, Timothy?"

Moth swallowed hard. He had imagined much about this evening— but a conversation about psychological truths versus legal truths had not been something he'd considered. *I am lost,* he said to himself. He wanted to hide.

"No, Timothy, the truth is, you are screwed either way. You were screwed the moment you arrived here."

"If we walk away . . ." Moth started. Weak.

Student #5 shook his head.

"We could take all we know to the police," Moth continued. Weaker.

"Has that worked out for you before?"

"No."

"But even if they did follow up on what you say, what will they find should they actually listen to your crazy story?" Moth didn't answer, so Student #5 filled in the silence. "They will find some signs of an innocent man who no longer exists. And that will be where their trail ends."

Again the room grew quiet. It was Andy who finally croaked out: "Are you going to kill us?"

Student #5 recognized the provocative nature of this question. It was the last, crucial question. He knew if he said *no* they would not believe him, no matter how much they might want to. If he said *yes* then they might pull the trigger, because they had nowhere else to turn, no move left on the chessboard of death. And so, he decided on uncertainty.

"Should I?" he asked, returning the nonchalant tone to his voice even as he tensed every muscle in his body.

Moth felt like he was swimming, exhausted, barely able to keep his head above a darkened sea of doubts. He tried to picture his uncle's dead body, hoping that this vision would give him the strength to do what he knew he needed to do, even if it was wrong and touched on the same evil that had fueled him all the way to this room.

Andy Candy felt like someone had punched her in the stomach. Nothing was right. Nothing was fair. Everything that she had once imagined for her life had evaporated. *Fog surrounds me,* she thought. *I am trapped in a burning building being overcome by great clouds of smoke.* The only future she had was staring across the room at her. "Kill him," she whispered, without conviction.

"You are not killers," said the killer in front of them. "You should not attempt to be what you are not."

"Kill him," Andy repeated, even softer. *Can Moth fire a bullet into the cancer that killed my father? Can he shoot the arrogant date-rapist who pitched me into despair? Can he kill both our pasts so we can start anew?*

"I think this evening, interesting as it has been, is finished. Timothy, take your friend Andrea and leave now. Best to hope we never see one another again."

"Can you promise that?"

"There's no promise I can make that you would believe. You might want to believe it. You will try to persuade yourself to believe it. But all that is delusion. Really you can only hope that is the case. And that hope—well, that hope is your best option."

Moth looked at the gun in his hand. In all his studies—of great men and great events—he knew about risks and uncertainty. Nothing was ever certain. Nothing was ever sure. Every choice had unseen outcomes. But the choice of not acting was the only one that was crippling.

He lifted his eyes. "Let me ask you a question, Mister Lewis—or whoever you decide to be tomorrow. If I kill you now—whose fault really is it?"

An existential question. A psychological question. The exact same question the killer had demanded of his uncle.

Student #5 knew the only true answer was, *Mine.*

And in that same instant, Student #5 knew the game he was playing had abruptly changed. If he answered correctly, it would give a murderous license to the historian in front of him. And there was no convenient lie that might shove the question into some safer spot.

"Whose fault is it?" Moth repeated.

He waited for the reply.

"Kill him," Andy repeated, for the last time. But this time she added, "Please . . ." She didn't think she had the strength to say those words again. The words came out of her mouth like kicked gravel. Her voice sounded weak, sickly, as if she was going to pass out.

And, in that same moment, Moth made his first and worst mistake. He heard all the built-up pain in Andy's voice and, distracted by the river of emotions, turned slightly to the girl he had loved, now loved, and imagined he would always love, taking his eyes off the killer before them.

Student #5 had always prided himself on the ability to act. Even with all his planning, scheming, and analysis, he recognized there were moments when the demands of the moment required action. Instantly, he saw his opportunity: *Eyes averted. Concentration lapsed. Finger resting beside the trigger, not on it.* He had trained himself physically and mentally for this moment, seen it in his head on more than one occasion, and didn't hesitate.

He exploded.

Thrusting himself out of the chair, Student #5 threw himself the few feet between his chest and the gun barrel.

Andy didn't scream—but she shouted in shock.

Moth, too, cried out, in sudden panic. He tried to tell himself, *Shoot!* But the moment was fumbled.

And then, he and Student #5 were locked together.

The chair Moth occupied smashed backward, as the two of them instantly tumbled to the floor. A stray shoulder and wildly flung forearm caught Andy across the bridge of her nose, and she slammed sideways, crunching against the wall in a heap. She was overcome by panic and the shock of pain and she clasped her hands over her ears, as if the sounds of the fight threatened to deafen her. In her vision, amidst the shadows, Moth and the killer had become one entity, a hydra-like murder beast rolling on the floor. She could see kicking, punching, blows flying—but she lost sight of the gun. It had disappeared, trapped between the two fighters.

Moth was beneath the killer, feeling Student #5's weight bearing down on him. He kicked up, trying to bring a knee to the groin, anything that might turn the fight in his favor. He knew one thing: He could not release his grip on the gun—although he could barely tell whether he was still attached to it or not. His thoughts were like electric currents, sparking wild arcs.

The gun is death.

No matter what happens, do not lose it.

His right hand was wrapped around the pistol handle, a death grip in more ways than one. He tried to get his left hand free, to ward off the cascade of blows slamming down upon him. At the same time, he felt the killer's hand encircling his own, around the gun's grip, twisting his index finger savagely, threatening to break it. He could feel the killer's thumb trying to force its way inside the trigger guard. He could feel the barrel moving—away from the killer, toward his own chest—and he realized he was millimeters from dying.

Moth tried to shout, but words were stifled as the killer's free hand punched at him, then found his throat and started to choke him.

Student #5 battled—all his expensive tae kwon do and yoga training had made him exceptionally strong and well educated in points of vulnerability—but Moth's wiry muscles rendered the struggle oddly even. Student #5 fought furiously, one hand grasping for the gun—*Get the gun! Kill them both!*—the other trying to encircle Moth's neck and choke him into unconsciousness.

Using all his weight and strength, Student #5 thrust down and felt the steel of the weapon, and knew he was seconds away from jamming it against Moth's abdomen and shooting. He expected he might wound himself as well—but he didn't fear injury. Small price. He felt no fear at all, just a cold-minded singleness of purpose. And he knew he was about to win.

Moth could sense blackness creeping over him. Oblivion seemed near. *I'm going to die here now.* He struggled, gathering whatever he had left inside him and trying to concentrate it on the gun in his hand. But he could feel it all slipping away. He had faced so many ends with bottle in hand; that was how he thought he would die. Those moments were all lies.

This was death.

He felt his eyes start to roll back and he tried to swallow a last breath, lungs screaming for air.

He wanted to shout, *No, no, no, I don't deserve this,* but he could not.

In that second, there was a sudden rogue wave that struck him with immense power.

It was Andy Candy, slamming into the killer from the side. She hit him first with her shoulder, the way she imagined a football linebacker would, crashing the three of them sideways into a tangled heap on the floor. She wrapped her arms around Student #5's neck, pulling back as hard as she could, thinking only that she had to separate the killer from Moth before the boy who had been her only love was murdered.

In that second, the dying equation changed. Student #5 let out a grunt that was almost a shout. He released his hand from Moth's throat and reached behind himself to claw at Andy Candy. But his nails only ripped her shirt.

Moth gasped for air. Red fury replaced black oblivion.

Andy kept one hand around the killer's neck and fiercely grabbed at his wrist, dragging his right arm back. She was strong—not as strong as him, but strong enough to compromise his grip on the gun.

The three of them, entwined, tugging, battling, lost any idea or plan. They were animals now. Prehistoric. It was simply a fight for survival.

For an instant, it seemed like they were all balanced precariously on a cliff edge. Two against one—two young, naïve, and confused; one singular, determined, experienced.

Moth felt the gun shift position, caught between the killer and himself. He was pushing it as hard as he could, desperately trying to envision where it was pointed. He did not know if this second would be his first opportunity, his only opportunity, or no opportunity at all. He did not know if firing a bullet—*right now!*—would kill a furious killer, kill a one-time lover, or kill a recovering drunk. But he jabbed back on the trigger regardless, fearing death, hoping for life.

The blast from the Magnum was like a huge *thump!* in the room. The tangled bodies helped to muffle most of the report.

Moth thought for a minute that he was dead.

Andy Candy imagined a sheet of pain, blood pouring from her body.

Student #5 managed a thought: *Impossible.*

The force of the bullet lifted him a few inches as it crashed through his core, ripping through stomach, intestines, and lungs before finally lodging next to his heart. It simply ravaged his midsection.

He felt like a puppet whose strings had been severed. It did not hurt. But he could sense the collapse within him. He took three shallow breaths. Blood instantly burbled to his lips. He rolled over, pitched sideways by a great thrust from Moth, who used what he believed was his last remaining ounce of energy. Like two spiders scuttling away, both he and Andy retreated from the quivering killer. Student #5 stared up, saw the paddle fan spinning above him, thought, *This isn't right—I have been killed by children.* Then he twitched and died.

Andy Candy wanted to scream or cry, but remained in a crippled silence. The violence in the room had been like a waterfall of noise and anger, mixed with fear and adrenaline.

Moth stared at the dead figure on the floor, and his only thought was, *I can never go back,* but *back to what* wasn't part of the mental computation.

Both knew that they had to do something. Respond. Perform. But for a moment they were frozen.

Moth told himself, *Think!* It took what might have been only seconds, but seemed to both of them to be much longer, before Moth finally croaked out, "Andy, we have to leave. Now. Someone might have heard . . ." He stopped there. It was like being caught up in a film, sucked suddenly into a cinematic world where they no longer knew the plot, they hadn't memorized their lines, but everything was happening with supersonic speed around them.

She looked away from the body on the floor, locking eyes with Moth. She knew the answer was *yes,* but she couldn't actually form even that simple word in her mouth.

He finally managed to get to his feet. The silence in the room surrounding the killer's dead body threatened to crush him; the air of death felt as heavy as a weight crushing down on his chest. He wanted to run, but knew he had to maintain what shreds of composure he still had. "Come on, Andy," he said softly. "Now."

He stepped across and took her by the hand, lifting her up. He could not tell if she was hot or cold.

Still without speaking, Andy Candy found the piece of paper with Susan Terry's photo and information on it. She also grabbed the laptop computer. She felt like she was about to slide into some robotic world.

"We have to go," Moth repeated. "Don't leave anything behind," he said.

Andy Candy nodded, then stopped. An idea—as if spoken deep within her by some truly evil force—pushed to the forefront of her head. "No," she said. "We have to." She hurried into the kitchen. On the counter was a jar with a couple of pens and pencils, next to a notepad and beneath a wall-mounted telephone. It was the sort of arrangement one might see in almost any kitchen.

She grabbed a large black marker, then returned to the living room, where Moth was standing, stiff, pale, gun still in his hand.

"He said 'lucky drug dealer,'" Andy whispered. "What the cops should find is an unlucky drug dealer." She approached an empty white wall in the room. Using the marker, she wrote in large block letters: *Cheat Us Pay the Price Scorpions.*

The last word was the only name of any drug dealing organization she could recall. They were from Mexico, and operated in California, and so might not be locally known, but she didn't know if that would make a difference.

She put the pen in her pocket. Moth looked at what she had written, nodded, and went over to the killer's body. He savagely ripped a piece of bloodstained shirt from the man's chest. He took the cloth and smeared a streak of red on the wall, underlining the word *Scorpions*. An artist's touch. Perhaps a signature. He turned to Andy and saw her reach out to him—the same extended arm a drowning person might offer up to a rescuer in a boat.

Hand in hand, they staggered out of the house, supporting each other.

One step. Two steps. Three.

The night seemed oppressively hot, asthmatic, thick. They expected to hear sirens in the distance, heading their way. There were none. They expected to hear strange voices, shouting at them, *"Hey, you two! Stop! Freeze! Raise your hands!"* They did not.

Four steps, five.

They wanted to run.

They did not.

Six. Seven. Eight.

Darkness enveloped them. Moth managed to croak out, "Don't look back." Weak light from downtown crept along in the sky above them, a yellow glow beneath the wide expanse of starry night. But the street was nothing but shadows. They turned into the cemetery, greeting the rows of the dead like old friends, grateful for the headstones and raised crypts that concealed them. Moth found his abandoned backpack and thrust the gun inside, next to the two empty bottles of Scotch and vodka that the killer had warned him about leaving behind. He took the paper with Susan's picture and the laptop and tossed them in as well. He looked at Andy only once, and wondered whether he was as pale as she looked in the thick black air.

The two of them mounted the rented bicycles they'd left beside the graves and rode them back to the rental store. Moth dutifully locked them up, just as the Rasta proprietor had asked them to.

Then they walked down side streets, passing a few homes that were lit up, hearing a few voices from dinner parties in full swing. They passed one old lady walking her two pugs, but she was far more interested in the dogs doing their nightly business than in Moth and Andy Candy.

Andy thought this was remarkable, believing as she did that she was covered in blood. She realized then that she probably was not, but it sure felt that way.

Wordlessly, they returned to her car. She slid into the driver's seat, unsure whether she could steer. Instinct took over. A momentary fumble with the keys, an inner admonition to stop shaking even though her hands were quivering and her body was nearly convulsing, a few deep breaths that seemed to help a little, and they took off.

Andy did not need Moth to remind her to drive slowly and carefully.

One mile. Two miles.

She couldn't bring herself to look in the rearview mirror, for fear that she would see the flashing lights of a patrol car.

Four miles. Five miles. Six.

She didn't even dare look sideways at Moth.

Twenty miles, she saw a spot by the side of the road, and pulled over. She opened her door, leaned out, and gave in to nausea, vomiting repeatedly.

Still, they said nothing. She wiped her mouth, put the car back in gear, and drove on.

They passed over the Seven Mile Bridge. *6.79 miles,* Moth thought. He saw moonlight reflecting off the light black chop of the waters.

One hour. Two.

A frustrated man in a BMW sports car zoomed past them, just dodging the headlights of an oncoming panel truck in one of the single-lane portions of the road.

South of Islamorada, they passed Whale Harbor and then Bud and Mary's Marina, where a huge plastic mock great white shark hangs just outside the entrance. Moth thought it was curiously appropriate: a fake fish unlikely to ever visit those waters acting as an invitation.

Three hours.

They continued silently over Card Sound Bridge and swooped past the edge of the Everglades, where the night blends seamlessly with the swamp, then the city of Homestead, and finally descended into the bright lights that mark South Dixie Highway into Miami.

Moth wanted to say: *"I couldn't have done it without you,"* but that seemed wrong. He wanted to say, *"It's all over now,"* but he was afraid it had just begun.

Andy Candy pulled her car into a parking place half a block from Moth's apartment. Still without speaking, the two of them climbed out and walked arm in arm unsteadily down the street. It was like they were each holding the other upright. They went inside, climbing the stairs together. Moth found his keys, opened up, and held the door for Andy Candy. He dropped the backpack to the floor. She immediately went to the bathroom and stared at herself in the mirror for perhaps three or four minutes, searching every inch of her face for some sign of what this night had done to her, or even some bizarre other change. *Dorian Gray looking at his portrait.*

She knew she was different now, and she watched herself, seeking some outward sign, until, finally, not completely persuaded that some stranger wouldn't be able to see what had happened to her face, she splashed water wildly onto her lips and eyes, cheeks and forehead. It did not make her feel clean.

At the same moment, Moth was bent over the kitchen sink, washing his hands. Once. Twice. A third time, trying to scrub murder off.

They collapsed together on Moth's bed, arms entwined. For a fleeting instant Andy Candy thought they were like a sculpture resembling the fight earlier that night. There are, she realized, some touches more intimate even than sex. She closed her eyes, exhausted. Sleep, she thought, would feel like death. Still, she welcomed it, right beside the absolute uncertainty of life.

For a few seconds, Moth smelled her sweat, listened to her even breathing, stroked the skin of her arm. His last thought, before he, too, fell asleep was simple: He could not see how they could stay together. Nor could he see how they could ever be apart.

EPILOGUE
The Next Day and Beyond

24 hours after death:

"Hello," Moth said. "My name is Timothy and I'm an alcoholic."

"Hi, Timothy," the gathering at Redeemer One replied. Usually this response was pro forma, a muttered reply that was merely a part of getting the evening rolling. This night, however, it enthusiastically burst from the lips of all the regulars, and Moth could feel a groundswell of energy amidst relief wrapped in the greeting.

"We're very glad to see you, Timothy," said the philosophy professor. He did not add the word *alive,* though that was what they were all thinking. This reply—far out of the normal—was seconded throughout the room.

"I'm glad to be here," Moth said.

He paused.

"I have . . ." He hesitated. "Actually, I'm not exactly sure now how many days of sobriety I've got. Things have been confusing. A bunch, I think. I can't tell any longer."

There was a momentary quiet in the room.

"Are you safe?" asked Sandy in a no-nonsense, corporate-attorney voice.

"I think so," Moth answered. "How can anyone tell?"

He could have meant anything, from a killer stalking him, to a legal system ready to pounce and prosecute, to the constant desire to drink. None of them could have actually answered this question. Moth remained standing in front of the group.

Sandy tried again. "Timothy. Are you safe?"

Heavy emphasis on the word *safe*—as if all the membership were speaking this single word in unison.

"Yes," he replied. He could have said: *"There's no one left that's trying to kill me, except maybe me."* He did not.

"Then I have an idea," said Fred the engineer. "Let's call this Day One."

Moth smiled. This made a great deal of sense to him. He hoped it was true. What he truly hoped for, and what he believed his uncle had tried to teach him, was to be a fighter.

"Hello," he repeated. "My name is Timothy and I have one day sober."

"Hi, Timothy," the entire group responded.

When she finally arrived home, her mother was at the piano, doing scales before her next student arrived. Often this repeated practice irritated Andy Candy, but this time the notes seemed light and melodic. Up and down, sharps and flats. The necessary routine of a music teacher. The same was true of the scrambling, scuffling, tail-wagging response she received from the dogs. Expected. Happy. Musical.

Her mother looked up—afraid to probe, afraid to not ask, completely unsure what to say or do, with absolutely no idea whatsoever what her daughter had been through. The mother wondered whether she would ever know. She doubted it.

"Are you okay?" A bland question.

"I'm okay," Andy Candy responded. She thought this might be the truth or it might be a lie. She'd find out soon enough.

"Is there something we should talk about?"

Everything? Nothing? Murder and death? Survival?

"Is Moth . . ."

Love? Loyalty?

"He's fine," she said. "We're fine."

But changed. She did not say this out loud.

"Back together?"

"Sort of," Andy said.

She headed toward the shower, hoping that her scraggly, almost weather-beaten appearance hadn't shocked her mother too much. Over her shoulder, she called out: "I think I'm going to go back to school." She knew this would make her mother happy.

Fuck the date-rapist, she thought. *Fuck him and his evil. It will catch up to him eventually. Maybe not this week or next year. But someday it will. It will all balance out. Karma is a bitch.* She was absolutely sure of this, but didn't consider who it was that had taught this lesson to her.

"I need to finish up that last semester," she added, tossing the words toward her mother, back over her shoulder. The piano. The dogs. Her home. Familiar stuffed animals on her bed, framed family pictures on the walls. Everything was so normal it almost overwhelmed her. "Get my degree. Got to move on," she said quietly, not sure whether her mother heard her or not.

And, she realized, she had much left to learn in subjects far different from what she had studied over the past days.

Four weeks after death:

Susan, happily back at her job, stared down at the computer printout of her picture and bio. There was a bloodstain in the corner. She had the killer's computer next to her own, on her desk at the state attorney's office, but she had yet to open it, boot it up, and even make an attempt to see what it contained. She didn't want to know; her picture told her everything she needed to. She picked up her telephone, dialed a number. It was the Monroe County Sheriff's Office. A couple of quick electronic transfers and she reached a supervisor in the Homicide Department.

"Hey," she said, after identifying herself—giving her name and title with unequivocal toughness. "Are you making any progress on that killing on Angela Street the other week?"

"Not much, Counselor." She could hear the resignation in the supervisor's voice. "I mean clearly there was a helluva fight. Things were knocked around pretty good. The guy didn't want to get shot, that's for sure. You know, usually these drug gang murders are, well, I guess you'd have to call them 'cleaner'—if you know what I mean. Usually find the dead dude trussed up with blowtorch marks on his genitals, that sort of thing. Or floating in the mangrove trees where he's been dumped. Not too often do they get a chance to get a few licks in. But until we get some suspect in mind . . . well, not too much to go on. And apparently the dead guy, well, there's just not too much on him anywhere. Sort of a cipher. He did a pretty good job of concealing who he was. Maybe you can help? You know something?"

Susan Terry knew a great deal. But what she answered was: "No, not really. The guy's name came up in another narcotics investigation—you know, peripherally. I was just checking to see if there's any connection."

"You think?" the cop asked.

"Maybe. Maybe not. Probably just another wild-goose chase. Don't waste time. If I hear anything else, I'll be sure to call."

"Thanks." The detective hung up.

He probably didn't recognize that lie, she thought. Susan went to the paper shredder in her office. She carefully fed the bloody computer printout into it.

Six months after death:

Susan had waited diligently. She'd known it was only a matter of time before the right case with the right evidence came up in the courtroom worlds adjacent to the prosecutor's office. It was a convenience store robbery that had gone terribly wrong. A clerk was dead. Two suspects arrested within minutes. Facing life in prison. Not a good trade for the $323 they tried to steal.

The guilty pleas were taken in open court. Susan sat two rows back. Family members—both the victim's and the robbers'—sobbed behind her. The judge accepted the plea, banged her gavel, and that was it.

Susan paused until the room was clear, with only the judge's clerk lingering behind. Susan approached her.

"Hi, Miss Terry," the clerk said. She was an older woman and she had seen just about everything in her courthouse years. "What brings you here? Nothing special about this case."

Susan shook her head. "No, you're right about that. It's just I wanted to check some of the evidence out. I have this feeling that these guys might have done another robbery or two, ones I've got on my desk. Think I can look at that?"

She pointed to an evidence box on the clerk's desk.

The clerk shrugged. "Have at it. It's all going to storage anyway."

While the clerk busied herself with paperwork, Susan began to paw through the box. What she wanted was on top, encased in a sealed bag, with the court case number on it in thick black ink. A .357 Magnum revolver—exactly like the one Moth had given her. The only difference was the serial number on each weapon. Susan had placed Moth's weapon in a similar plastic container, with the identical court case number. As soon as the clerk was distracted enough to turn aside, Susan performed a little sleight of hand, removing the convenience store murder weapon from the box and placing Moth's gun inside. She hid the other gun in her briefcase. Switch complete.

"Thanks," she said to the clerk. "I got what I need."

The gun, she knew, was the only real piece of hard evidence that could tie Moth to the killing on Angela Street. She never underestimated ballistics scientists.

She would keep the convenience store gun for six months, then swap it out with yet another, in another case. One more switch—that would effectively destroy any connections that even the most dogged investigator could follow.

Susan smiled. *Goodbye, last key bit of evidence.* She had already had the laptop hard drive wiped clean at a local Apple store, and then had dumped it, wrapped in smelly garbage, in the Dade County landfill. The only other elements that might put Moth in that room with the killer were his DNA and Andy Candy. She had warned Moth about the first—*"Don't ever get arrested and put in some data bank"*—and the second wasn't likely to ever say an incriminating word.

She guessed she would see Moth later that night at Redeemer One, but she wouldn't tell him anything about what she had done. Her sobriety was all he needed to know about. *One hundred eighty-three days and counting,* Susan proudly reminded herself.